Debbi[illegible] writing, lo[illegible] of children and animals, and not co[illegible]usework. Her previous novels have included best[illegible]ng e-books *Cold Feet At Christmas*, *Pippa's Cornish Dream*, *Never Kiss A Man In A Christmas Jumper* and *The Birthday That Changed Everything*. She also writes fantasy and crime fiction, to keep her out of trouble.

You can find out more at www.debbiejohnsonauthor.com, and follow her on twitter @debbiemjohnson.

Also by Debbie Johnson

Cold Feet at Christmas
Pippa's Cornish Dream
Never Kiss a Man in a Christmas Jumper
The Birthday That Changed Everything

Summer at the Comfort Food Café

DEBBIE JOHNSON

A division of HarperCollins*Publishers*
www.harpercollins.co.uk

Harper*Impulse* an imprint
of HarperCollins*Publishers* Ltd
The News Building
1 London Bridge Street
London SE1 9GF

www.harpercollins.co.uk

A paperback original 2016
1

A catalogue record for this book is available from the British Library

ISBN: 9780008150259

Set in Minion by Palimpsest Book Production Limited,
Falkirk, Stirlingshire

Chapter 1

COOK WANTED – MUST BE COMFORTING

We are looking for a summer-season cook for our busy seaside café. The job will also involve taking orders and waiting on tables. The successful applicant will be naturally friendly, be able to boil an egg, enjoy a chat and have a well-developed sense of empathy with other human beings. Good sense of humour absolutely vital. The only experience required is experience of life, along with decent cooking skills. Pay is pitiful, but the position comes with six weeks' free use of a luxury holiday cottage in a family-friendly setting near the Jurassic Coast, with use of a swimming pool, games room and playground. Children, dogs, cats, guinea pigs and stray maiden aunts all welcome. No application form needed – if you're interested, send us your heart and soul in letter form, telling us why you think you're right for the job. Post your essays to Cherie Moon, The Comfort Food Café, Willington Hill, near Budbury, Dorset.

Chapter 2

Dear Cherie,
I'm writing to you about the job you advertised for a cook at the Comfort Food Café in Dorset.

This is about my sixth attempt at composing this letter, and all the rest have ended up as soggy, crumpled balls lying on the floor around the bin – my aim seems to be as off as my writing skills. I've promised myself that this time, no matter how long it gets, or how many mistakes I might make, this will be the final version. From the heart, like you asked for, even if it takes me the rest of the day. If nothing else it's pretty good therapy.

This is probably not the most professional or brilliant way to make a first impression, and you're most likely thinking about filing this under 'N for nutter' – or possibly 'B for bin'. I can only apologise – my hand's a bit cramped now and I have a blister coming up on my ring finger. I haven't written this much since my A levels, so please forgive me if it gets a bit messy.

To be honest, everything in my life is a bit messy. It got that way just over two years ago, when my husband, David, died. He was the same age as me – I'm thirty-five now – and he was the love of my life. I can't give you a romantic story about how we met at a wedding or got set up on a blind date by friends, or how our eyes met across a crowded nightclub – mainly because our eyes actually met across a crowded playground when we were seven years old.

He'd joined our school a few years in and appeared like a space alien at the start of term one in September. He was really good at football, was impossible to catch in a game of tag and liked drawing cartoons about his dogs, Jimbo and Jambo. We sat next to each other on the Turquoise Table in Miss Hennessey's class, and that was that – my fate was sealed.

That story sounds completely crazy now, I know. I look at my own kids and think there's no way anyone they mix with at their age could turn out to be the love of their life. That's what my parents thought – and his. I lost track of the number of times we were told we were too young. I think they thought it was sweet when we were seven, saying we were boyfriend and girlfriend – innocent and cute. By the time we were sixteen and we'd stayed together all through high school, they didn't think it was quite so cute any more.

I get it, I really do. They wanted us to see a bit of the world. See other people. Although they were all too polite to say it, they wanted us to split up. My parents would always phrase it nicely, saying things like 'I've nothing against David – he's a lovely lad – but don't you want to travel? Go to university? Have a few adventures before you settle down? Follow your own dreams? And anyway, if it's meant to be, you'll come back to each other in a few years' time.'

He got the same speeches from his family, too. We used to laugh about it and compare notes on the different ways they all tried to express the same thing: You're Too Young and You're Making a Mistake. We weren't angry – we knew it was because they loved us, wanted the best for us. But what they didn't get – what they never really understood – was that we were already following our dreams. We were already having the biggest adventure of our lives. We loved each other beyond belief from the age of seven, and we never, ever stopped. What we had was rare and precious and so much more valuable than anything we could have done apart.

We got married when we were twenty, and no matter how happy I was, people still commented on it. I even found my mum crying in the loo at the reception – she thought I was wasting my life. I'd got decent enough grades in my exams – including a grade A in home economics, I should probably point out, as it's the first relevant thing I've said. So did David. He got a job as a trainee at the local bank, and I initially worked in what I'd like to claim was some fancy five-star restaurant, but was actually a McDonald's on a retail park on the outskirts of Manchester.

I know it sounds boring, but it wasn't. It was brilliant. We bought a little two-up two-down in a decent part of the city, and even at that stage we were thinking about schools – because we knew we wanted kids, and soon. Lizzie came along not too long after, and she's fourteen now. She has his blonde hair and my green eyes, and at the moment is equal parts smiley and surly. I can't blame her. It's been tough losing her dad. I've done my best to stay strong for her, but I suspect my best hasn't been up to much. She's fourteen. Do you remember being a fourteen-year-old girl? It wasn't ever easy, was it? Even without dead dads and zombified mums.

Nate is twelve and he's a heartbreaker. Quite literally, when I look at him, it feels like my heart is breaking. He got David's blonde hair too, and also his sparkly blue eyes. You know, those Paul Newman eyes? And David's smile. And that one dimple on the left-hand side of his mouth.

He looks so much like his dad that people used to call him David's 'mini me'! Sometimes I hug him so tight he complains that I'm breaking his ribs. I laugh and let him go, even though I want to carry on squeezing and keep this tiny, perfect little human being safe for the rest of his life. We all know that's not possible now and sometimes I think that's the biggest casualty of David dying – none of us feel safe any more, which really isn't fair when you're twelve, is it?

But I have to remind myself that we had so much. We loved so much, and laughed so much, and shared so much. All of it was perfect, even the arguments. Especially the arguments – or the aftermath at least. Sometimes I wonder if that was the problem – we had too much that was too good, too young. Even after thirteen years of marriage he could still give me that cheeky little grin of his that made my heart beat a bit faster, and I could never, ever stay angry with him. It was the uni-dimple. It just made it impossible.

One of David's favourite things was holidays. He worked hard at the bank, got promoted and enjoyed his job – but it was his family life that really mattered to him. We saved up and every year we'd have a brilliant holiday together. He loved researching them and planning them almost as much as going on them.

To start with, they were 'baby' holidays – the most important thing was finding somewhere we'd be safe with the little ones. So we stayed in the UK or did short flights to places like Majorca or Spain.

As the kids got older, we got more adventurous – or he did at least! We started by expanding our horizons and going on camping holidays on the continent. Tents in Tuscany, driving to the South of France with the car loaded up, a mobile home in Holland. The last two before he died were the most exciting ever – a yachting trip around Turkey, where the kids learned to sail and I learned to sunbathe, and three weeks in Florida doing the theme parks but then driving all the way down to the Keys and going native for a week.

Every holiday, for every year, was also given its own photo album when we got home.

It wasn't enough for him to keep the pictures online, he got them all printed out and each album had the year it related to and the place we'd visited written on the spine on a sticker.

They're all there now, on the bookshelf in the living room. Lined up in order – a photographic journey through time and space. Lizzie as a baby; Lizzie as a toddler and me pregnant; Nate joining the party. They grow up in those photo albums, right before our eyes – missing teeth and changing tastes and different haircuts, getting taller each year.

I suppose we age as well – I definitely put a bit of weight on as the years go by; David loses a bit of hair, gets more laughter lines. We never lose our smiles, though

– that's one thing that never changes.

The only year we didn't have a holiday was when the kids were too old to share a room any more, and we had to buy a bigger house. We were skint, so we stayed at home – and even then, David set up a massive tent in our new garden and bought a load of sand from a builder's yard to make our very own beach! Even that one has its own album, although on quite a few of the photos we're wearing our swimming costumes in the rain!

If I'm entirely honest, the main reason I'm applying for this job – and doing a very bad job of it, I know – is because of all those holidays, and the memories that David managed to build for our children. For me. The memories that are all we have left of him now.

The last holiday David planned was over two years ago. We were going to Australia, flying in to Sydney and touring up to Queensland. The kids were buzzing about seeing koalas and kangaroos, and I was slightly concerned about them getting eaten by sharks or bitten by a killer spider. David was in his element.

He never got to go on that holiday. It was the first properly sunny day after winter – February 12th, to be exact – and he decided to do some house maintenance, the way you do once the sun comes out again.

While he was clearing some leaves out of the guttering, he slipped off the ladder and banged his head on the concrete patio. He seemed all right at first – we laughed about it, joked about his hard head. We thought we'd been lucky.

We were wrong. We didn't know it at the time, but he had bleeding around his brain – his brain was swelling and bit by bit a disaster was going on inside his skull.

By the time he started to complain of a headache, he'd probably been feeling bad for hours. Taking Paracetamol for his 'bump' and trying to get on with his weekend. Eventually he collapsed in front of all three of us – fell right off his chair at the dinner table. At first the kids just laughed – he was a bit of a buffoon, David. He was always doing daft things to amuse them – it was like living with Norman Wisdom sometimes, the amount of slapstick that went on in our house!

But he wasn't joking. And even though the ambulance got there so fast and the hospital was so good, it was too late. He was gone. He was put on a life-support machine and his parents and my parents came and his brother came, all to say goodbye. The kids? That was a hard decision. Nate was just ten and Lizzie was only twelve – but I thought they deserved it, the chance to say their farewells. I still don't know if it was the right decision or not – it was impossible to weigh up whether the trauma of seeing him like that, hooked up to machines, would be worse than knowing they never got to see him off to heaven. Was it the right thing to do? I suppose I'll have to wait and see how messed up they are over the next few years before I get my answer.

I can't go into any detail about how I felt, Cherie, having to make those kinds of decisions. I just can't. I'll never, ever get this letter written if I do that – it's too big and too raw, and even now, after all this time, I still have moments where the pain paralyses me – where I struggle to even get out of bed and put one foot in front of the other. They are only moments, though, and they are becoming further and further apart – I suppose that means my own brain injury is healing, which makes me feel strangely guilty.

I hate the fact that he died doing such a mundane thing. Cleaning the gutters. He was funny and kind and quietly brave – he was the type of man who would have thrown himself under a bus to save a child, or would have jumped into a raging sea to rescue a Labrador. Losing him because of leaves in the gutters seems so… pointless. He was an organ donor, though, which is some small comfort – the thought of all the lives he saved or changed for the better through that does help. I take consolation from someone walking around with that big, beautiful heart of his beating inside them.

So… by now, you're either hooked and wondering how this story ends, or you're considering calling the police to get a restraining order in case this crazy woman turns up at your café and tries to comfort random people.

The answer is, of course, that the story hasn't ended – the story is still playing out, albeit at a very slow pace. We had a holiday the year after he died, and it was a disaster – a trip to Crete to stay in a hotel that turned out to be full of eighteen to thirty-year-olds, all on a mission to give themselves liver failure and complete their set of STD top trumps. It was loud, it was foul, and we all hated it – mainly, of course, because he wasn't there. It was awful.

Now, I'm looking ahead and I see that there needs to be a change. David left us with enough life insurance to pay off the mortgage and the car loans, and to live on for a little while. We have no debt at all, which I know puts us at a big advantage over lots of families who are struggling to make ends meet.

But there's nothing coming in – no income. Which means no holiday – not because of my lack of planning skills, but because we can't afford it. Not if we want to eat as well. Don't get me wrong, our heads are above water, but there isn't much spare after paying the bills and doing the shopping and coping with what feels like the mountain of expense a teenage girl piles up!

If we ration we'll be fine for another year. Rationing means no holiday – and I just can't face it. I think we need a holiday – one that we actually enjoy, this time. We've all started to feel just a little bit better now. Almost against our will, there is more laughter, more easy chat, more smiling.

The kids' lives have moved on, certainly a lot more than mine! They're both in high school now, both starting to grow into young adults, both changing. I'd like to add another photo album to that shelf before they're too cool to be bothered with their poor old mum.

I also know that I need to get my act together. I need to get a job – and not just for the money. I need to get out there, back into the world. Because the kids *are* that little bit older and more independent now. They don't need me as much. They're out a lot – or Lizzie is at least, and Nate is showing signs of following suit. That's only right – it's good. It's what I want for them, to have normal lives. But me sitting at home in a rocking chair, counting cobwebs and watching *The Good Wife* on repeat isn't going to do any of us any good.

Getting a job will help me to meet new people. Get away from my own problems. Make my world bigger. I have my sister, my parents and his family too – but sometimes, if I'm honest, that feels like more of a responsibility than a help. They're all so worried about me all the time, I feel like I'm under a microscope. I think they're waiting for me to crack.

I think they're scared that long term, I can't live without him. Maybe they're right, I don't know – but I have to try. I don't want to forget David – that would be impossible even if I did – but I do need to start living my life After David. AD, if you like.

I started looking at jobs a few months ago and came to the depressing conclusion that I'm officially useless. I have the aforementioned Home Economics A level, which is the pinnacle of my academic achievement (I also have a C in Health and Social Care and a B in General Studies, which are really of no use to anybody). I worked at McDonald's for a year before I had the kids and I got a food hygiene certificate when I did volunteer work at the school kitchen. Not hugely impressive, I know – it's not like Marco Pierre White is hammering on the door with a job offer.

But I do cook – I cook a lot. Family dinners, occasional forays into something more exotic like Thai or Japanese. I do a mean roast and can make my own meatballs. I can bake and I can whip up marinades, and I can do a full English fry-up with my eyes closed.

I wouldn't get very far on *Masterchef*, but I can cook – proper home-made stuff – the kind of food that isn't just good for your body but good for your soul as well. At least I like to think so. I'm amazed, in fact, that the kids aren't the size of that giant marshmallow man in *Ghostbusters* by now – one of the ways I've tried to console them (and if I'm honest, myself as well) over the last few years is through feeding them. It keeps me busy, it makes me feel like I'm doing something positive, and it's a way to show I love them now they're too old for public displays of affection.

They just scarf it down, of course, they're kids – but perhaps, at somewhere like the Comfort Food Café, I could actually be of some use. It would be really, really nice to feel useful again – and to spend the summer in Dorset, and fill up another one of those albums.

So. There we go. I think that's everything. Probably more than everything. I'm not sure this is what you meant when you said send your heart and soul in letter form, but that serves you right for being so vague! I bet you got some really strange replies – this one being possibly the strangest of all.

I won't hold it against you, Cherie, if I never hear from you. But if you want to talk to me, or find out anything more, then let me know. Whatever happens, good luck to you.

All the best,
Laura Walker

WEEK 1

In which I travel to Dorset, sing a lot of Meatloaf songs, accidentally inhale what might possibly be marijuana, wrap my bra around a strange man's head and become completely betwattled...

Chapter 3

'They filmed *The French Lieutenant's Woman* there,' I say, trying to meet my daughter's eyes in the rear-view mirror. She's not interested, of course. She's too busy staring at her phone, thumbs moving quick as lightning as she types. So quick they're just vague pink blurs, in fact. If Lizzie was going to be a superhero, she'd be called Thumb Girl: the Fastest Text in the West.

Sadly, Thumb Girl doesn't seem impressed with my cinematic reference, and really, what did I expect? Was that the best I could come up with? A sappy Meryl Streep movie from before she was even born? A historical romance featuring some award-winning moustaches and meaningful glances? It's enough to give mothers the world over a bad name, for God's sake.

'Never heard of it, Mum,' she replies, grudgingly. I'm actually surprised she even vocalises her response and suspect she's saying something much ruder on her screen. I make a mental note to check her Twitter account later. Or Tumblr. Or Facebook. I've kind of lost track of which one is her favourite form of communication at the moment. It certainly isn't good old-fashioned talking. Not with me at least.

I scrabble for something more contemporary – something cooler. Something that might make her hate me ever-so-slightly less than she does right now. Something along the lines of 'the lead singer from Green Day will be living next door to us', but more... *true.*

'Yeah. I suppose it is a bit old for you. Well, they filmed *Broadchurch* there,' I finally say.

'The one about the murdered kid?' asks Lizzie, finally looking up, one eyebrow raised in query just about visible beneath her straight blonde fringe. The fringe has been getting lower and lower for months now – eventually I fear it will cover her whole face and she'll look like Cousin It dressed by Primark.

'That's it, yes, the one with David Tennant in it,' I reply, encouraged to have finally found some common ground. Even if it is common ground built on infanticide and *Doctor Who.*

'Wow. What a great advert for the place,' comes the sarcastic reply. 'Remind me to get a rape alarm.'

Okay. Deep breaths. There are at least four hours left of this fun family road trip, I remind myself. In an ideal world, we'll at least save the shouting until we're past Birmingham. I consider starting a 'count the red cars' game and realise that they haven't played that since they were a lot younger. And I also realise – for about the millionth time – that I suck at this.

David had a way of making car journeys fun. I'd be the one making sure we all had bottles of water and muffins to eat and spare carrier bags in case Nate threw up, and he'd be the one making them laugh. I'd be studying the map – Sat nav's for Slackers, he'd always say – and he'd be driving and somehow managing to keep everybody's spirits up.

Well, they're older now – and way less easy to amuse. Plus, I'm still not sure how it is going to be possible to read the map, drive the car and keep everybody's spirits up at the same time. I'm struggling with my own spirits, never mind theirs as well. And, even though I'd never drink and drive (honest), every time I think of the word 'spirits', I start to yearn for a large, super frosty G&T. Or maybe a mojito. Later, I promise. Later.

I take the deep breath I'd recommended to myself and ask – silently – the question that plays across my mind at least a few times every day. Even more right now as we set off on this exciting adventure that nobody, including me, seems to find very exciting at all. What Would David Do, I think? WWDD, for short.

David, I know, would be untroubled. He'd smile and ignore the cheekiness, and find a way to deflate the whole situation with a lame joke. Or he'd start to talk in a series of fart noises. Or put on a French accent and sing 'Barbie Girl'. Something like that, anyway.

But David did have the very big advantage of Lizzie adoring everything about him. He could never do any wrong in her eyes – whereas her feelings towards me, right now, aren't quite so generous. At best, I suspect they go along the lines of 'will someone please tell me I'm adopted?', and at worst, she may be using her birthday money to hire a hitman. To say she's displeased at being separated from her friends for the summer is something of an understatement – a bit like saying Daniel Craig is passably attractive.

'It's on the Jurassic Coast,' I add, trying again. I can practically feel the black aura creeping over my shoulders from the back seat, but I have to try. Because that is definitely what DWD and I need to keep going. Sat nav's for Slackers, and Quiet's for Quitters. It's 6.30am and I've only had one mug of coffee.

If somebody doesn't talk to me soon, I might actually fall asleep at the wheel, which would be bad for all concerned as I'm in control of a very full Citroen Picasso, complete with equally full roof rack and a fat black Labrador snoring in the boot.

Nate perks up at my latest comment, looking up from his DS for a moment. Presumably Super Mario/Sonic the Hedgehog/Pokémon/delete as applicable is on pause. His hair's a bit too long as well, but not for style purposes – we just haven't found the time or the inclination to go to the barbers very much. That was one of his dad's jobs, too. I've been trimming it myself with the nail scissors, which I really must stop doing – he's twelve. He needs to stop looking like he lets his mum cut his hair, even if he does.

'So did they film *Jurassic World* there?' he asks, hopefully. I hate to disappoint, but feel that leading him to expect a first-hand encounter with a friendly bronchosaurus might ultimately result in him hating me when he realises I lied. He is, as I've said, twelve – so technically he knows that velociraptors don't roam the hills and vales of Dorset. But he's also a boy, so he lives in hope that he's about to be whisked off to a super-secret island filled with Scenes of Mild Peril.

'Erm… no,' I admit. 'But we can go fossil-hunting, if you like? Apparently there are loads washed up on the beach.'

He gives me the smile. That small, sweet smile that says 'I remain unimpressed, but love you anyway'. The uni-dimple makes a brief, heart-wrenching appearance, before he turns his face back to what really matters. The small device on his lap.

I have a fleeting moment of nostalgia for the days when kids weren't permanently attached to electronic gadgets, and then realise I am being both hypocritical and very, very old. When I was their age, I thought my Walkman was the absolute bees knees and used to pull very rude faces when my mum suggested I might get ear cancer if I didn't take the headphones off every now and then.

'That sounds cool, Mum,' Nate says, already lost in his alternative reality.

'Are you okay playing on that?' I ask. 'You don't feel sick?'

'No. It's okay Mum. I haven't been car sick since I was eight.'

'All right. But I've put some bags in the glove box you know, just in case…'

He nods and gives me another grin before playing again. Beautiful boy.

I bask in my thirty seconds of maternal glory and glance out at the approaching motorway sign.

Hmmm. Sandbach Service Station – I wonder if they do mojitos to go?

Chapter 4

We drive down the M6 without a single mojito incident and very little conversation. It's quiet on the roads – due to most normal people being asleep – and even quieter in the car.

I combat this by playing Meatloaf's Greatest Hits very loud and singing along to 'Bat Out Of Hell', including all the motorbike-revving noises near the end. I'd do air guitar to the solos, but that's probably against the Highway Code. I can just imagine the signs: cartoons of Meatloaf with a big red cross through his face.

Nate frowns a little at my performance and I hear an exasperated sigh emitted from the back seat. Even the dog lets out a half-hearted woof. Everyone's a critic.

I choose to ignore them, as that's what they've been doing to me for the last few hours. Obviously, once I decide on this particular path of action, Lizzie has something to say. Initially, I don't hear her because of my singing. I've had three more black coffees since we first set off, so I feel totally wired and perfectly capable of appearing before a sell-out crowd at Wembley.

'What?' I shout, pausing the track when I realise she's speaking.

'Do you know,' says Lizzie, who I see in the rear-view mirror is still staring at her screen, probably googling 'ways to divorce your parent', 'that this song is about dying in a terrible crash?

Don't you think that's tempting fate a bit as we're driving to the end of the world at 600 miles per hour?'

'We're not driving to the end of the world, we're driving to Dorset,' I reply. 'And I think you'll find that not only was Meatloaf on a motorbike, he was hitting the highway like a battering ram. We are in a ten-year-old Citroen Picasso and I barely ever leave the slow lane in case Jimbo suddenly needs a wee.'

Jimbo is the dog. He's the third black lab that David owned – his parents had Jimbo and Jambo when we were little; then a new puppy called Jambo the Second, who died just after we got married. After that, they didn't want any more – they were very busy with their cruise club – so we took over, with Jimbo the Second. Poor Jimbo is almost thirteen now, completely grey around the muzzle and round as a barrel. He mainly sleeps, snores and snuffles, occasionally punctuated by moments of vast and unexpected energy, where he chases imaginary rabbits and scares much younger dogs.

He's a lovely beast, with very eloquent eyebrows and a powerful tail that can sweep a table clean when he's feeling happy. He's already on tablets for his arthritis and his heart isn't brilliant, and he has all sorts of lumps and bumps that so far haven't been anything serious.

I know he's not going to be around forever and secretly fear that when he finally goes I'll have some kind of nervous breakdown. That all my carefully managed grief and sadness will come spilling forth and drown me in emotion. That I'll start crying in the vet's surgery and everyone will be washed out, down the street, like they're on some kind of weird water-park ride made of widow's tears. Which sounds like the kind of water park Tim Burton would design.

I have had way too much coffee, it seems.

Lizzie doesn't reply to my defence of Meatloaf as a valid driving-song choice. I see that she has put her ear buds back in and is now pretending to be asleep. So much for that brief detente. I glance to my side. Nate is gazing out of the window, head lolling, eyelids heavy. He looks about three years old and my heart constricts a little, remembering a time when he was. The very best of days.

I press play again, but turn the sound down, just in case Nate does want to drift off. It's not his fault his crazy mother got him up at stupid o'clock to drag him to the far reaches of the country for the whole summer. It's not Lizzie's fault, either, and I get why she's angry.

She didn't want to come. She's fourteen. Her friends are her world and I have the suspicion there's a boy on the scene as well. There usually is at that age. David died during her first year at high school, so she got off to a rocky start. She was the Girl With The Dead Dad for ages, subject to the same mix of pity and fear that being bereaved always seems to provoke in people.

It's taken us all a long time to get anything like equilibrium back, and hers seems to be wrapped up with her pals, with angsty rock music and with black eye liner. So, no, Lizzie really didn't want to come to a small village in the countryside, even if I did try and sell it as a very long holiday.

She even asked if she could stay at my sister's instead, which upset me so much I had to fake an urgent need for the toilet and lock myself in the loo while I wept. This is something I do quite a lot these days, as her tongue gets sharper and her hormones get louder and I fail to get any tougher.

She's seen enough of me crying to last a lifetime, I'm sure – and it's better she thinks I'm suffering from IBS than continues to see me soggy. Anyway, getting your feelings hurt by your teenage daughter seems to be par for the course from what I remember. I can still recall the door slamming and the eye rolling and the telling my mum she just didn't understand.

Now I'm getting payback from my own daughter. I suppose it's all part of the great circle of life, but not the kind they sing about in the *Lion King.*

The problem with crying about one thing is that it inevitably leads onto crying about another. This is one of the many pleasant side effects of grief – you have a bit of a blub about one thing (like an especially sappy John Lewis commercial or a stroppy daughter) and you end up weeping about Everything That Hurt You Ever. But once I'd got that out of my system and left the sanctuary of the downstairs lav, I did consider it.

I know Rebecca, my younger sis by two years, would have welcomed Lizzie into her life, and her flat in the city centre, and would probably have been a heck of a lot more fun than I am.

Becca, you see, doesn't have kids. Or a dead husband. Or even an elderly Labrador. She has no responsibilities at all, which is just the way she likes it. She got her teenybopper heart broken when she was seventeen, and since then has remained steadfastly single and carefree.

Lizzie would undoubtedly have had a ball staying there for the summer, but I had to say no. Apart from anything else, Becca knows as much about boundaries and discipline as I do about particle physics. I may well have come home to find Lizzie pregnant, in rehab or starting a new life as a tattoo artist. All three risk factors could equally have applied to Becca herself.

Funnily enough, after that idea was knocked back, Lizzie didn't ask to stay with my parents… mainly because she's not stupid and knows their idea of a wild night out is getting all four corners in bingo at the church hall.

My parents are very sensible – so obviously they hadn't wanted me to do this either. They thought I was nuts, though they phrased it more sensitively than that. They tread carefully around me these days, which is kind of heartbreaking in its own way. I yearn for the days when my dad can look me in the eye and be rude to me again.

Maybe, I think, surveying the now-thickening traffic as we join the M5 and follow the signs that faithfully promise we are heading towards The South West, they're all spot on. Maybe Lizzie and Nate and my mum and dad are one hundred per cent accurate with their assessment: maybe I am nuts. Plus, now I come to think about it, Becca didn't try and talk me out of it at all, which is probably a sure sign that I'm making a poor life choice.

But somehow… I know it's the right thing to do. I just know it is, with a certainty I've not felt for a very long time. I feel scared and anxious and I miss David like hell – but I also feel something odd. Something fluttery and strange. Something that vaguely resembles hope and optimism, and a sense of potential. Perhaps it's just the sheer shock of it all, I don't know – but even if Lizzie hates me for a while (possibly forever) and Nate is bored, and my parents consider getting me committed, I know I'm heading in the right direction. Even without the sat nav.

It's all as unexpected to me as it is to my family. I'd say I'm not an impulsive person, but I don't really know if that's true or not. I don't really know what kind of a person I am, not in this version of reality. I was with David for so long – most of my life – that my entire identity was wrapped up with him. I've never been on my own – I've always been with him. I've never been just Laura, I've always been one half of David and Laura. Daura or Lavid… nah, neither of those work. We'd never make it in Hollywood.

Something about this – upping sticks and dragging us all off to Dorset – feels like the first step to finding out who I'm going to be next. That sounds weird, a bit like I'm an international spy with a bundle of fake IDs and foreign passports and stacks of Euros hidden in a heating vent.

But I know it's important, this feeling. It's taken me a long time to accept that there will even be a 'next' – to accept that I have to try and make a life for myself without David. Basically because I didn't even want a life without David – in fact I still don't. But it's not just about me, it's about the kids. I can't just shrivel up and fade into the West without him, much as Lizzie might like that right now.

I have to keep moving. I have to push on, to find the courage to even believe that there will be a 'next'. It's been over two years since he left us and that tiny, fluttering feeling – that hope – is what's keeping me going on this insane drive. Or, possibly, that tiny fluttering feeling is just all the coffee on an empty stomach. Either way, we're going. It feels like the right thing to do – plus, well, I got the job. That in itself is a minor miracle, all things considered, and it would be downright rude to reject a miracle, wouldn't it? Even a minor one.

I sent off that ridiculous letter two days before the closing date and genuinely never expected to hear from them. I mean, who in their right minds would give a job to a woman like me? A woman who not only wrote, but actually posted, a tear-stained letter that was the very definition of over-sharing?

Apparently, Cherie Moon would. Perhaps I should take that as fair warning – Cherie, my new boss, the woman who holds our destiny in her hands for the next month and a half, is entirely probably not in her right mind. Also, as Becca had helpfully pointed out, she did have what sounded like a 'very cool but probably made-up name'.

The response to my letter had been short but very, very sweet. It landed four weeks ago, in one of those small brown padded jiffy bags that people use when you've bought something off eBay. As I hadn't actually bought anything off eBay, and as my post usually consists of bills and people trying to persuade me to reclaim my PPI, I was a bit confused. I stared at it for a few minutes, jiggled it about, and eventually – in a fit of amazing clarity – actually opened it.

Inside was a small pink card, folded in two, from none other than the legendary and possibly fictitious Cherie Moon.

'Congratulations!' it announced, in tiny, curling handwriting. 'I could tell from your letter that you are exactly the right person for the job, and I'm so excited about welcoming you all to the Comfort Food Café for your working holiday. Enclosed are directions to both us and to your cottage, along with your keys, a bit of information on boring things to do with the house, and phone numbers in case you need them. I'll expect you on July 23 – and I'll have something sweet and special waiting for you at the café!'

And that was, quite literally, it. Even I, with very limited experience in the world of work, knew that this was unorthodox. There was no request for references (thank God) and only a couple of forms to fill in. There was just that pretty little card, with its tiny handwriting, a few photocopied sheets with a map and pictures, and the keys.

The keys that were currently tucked away in my bag, which was somewhere under Nate's feet, crammed in with a multipack of juice cartons and mini boxes of raisins and dried apricots that nobody would eat. I just like to be prepared, in case a freak snowstorm or a zombie invasion means we get trapped at the side of the road, you know?

David used to take the mickey out of me something rotten for what he called my 'survivalist streak'. I even miss that. I even miss being mocked, which is kind of tragic. But he mocked me in a nice way, and now nobody even knows me well enough or cares enough to bother poking fun at me.

I give myself a mental whack around the head and start to sing along to 'I Would Do Anything For Love' instead of allowing myself to follow this familiar path to Wallow Town. I Will Not Wallow – my new mantra – I think, as I join Meatloaf on a sonic journey through affairs of the heart.

'I like this one,' mumbles Nate, almost-but-not-quite asleep now. His comatose tone makes me smile – it's the way he speaks just before he conks out.

'Me too,' I reply, smiling.

'I don't,' mutters Lizzie from the back seat.

Oh well, I think, glad to hear her voice, even if it does sound pissed off. Two out of three ain't bad.

Chapter 5

Our arrival in Budbury doesn't go quite as planned. In fact, it's about seven hours later than I'd hoped for, we're all very hot and bothered, and the dog has been whining for the last thirty minutes. I know exactly how he feels.

It's also practically nightfall, that strange twilight between-time when the sun could be setting or rising. In this case, it's definitely setting, sinking as low in the sky as my morale by this stage.

We had a few problems once we left the motorway. First there was the sat-nav fiasco. Or the lack-of-sat-nav fiasco, to be more precise. I decided, in my infinite insanity, that it would be a really good idea to stop off at Avebury. We could see the famous stone circles and walk the dog, and get some air and sunshine that wasn't filtered through petrol fumes in service-station car parks.

As you can perhaps imagine, if you've ever met twenty-first-century teenagers, that idea went down very well.

This idyllic little detour lost us a few of the hours we'd gained by setting off early, mainly because I was convinced that we could find it without using the sat nav. It was on the map. It was a tourist attraction. Surely there would be brown signs or queues of druids in flowing white robes trekking down the lay-by?

Poor Nate was trying to read the road map, with Lizzie hovering behind him, glaring over his shoulder, poking the pages with her finger and yelling comments like 'It's to the right, you retard!'

Nate eventually elbowed her in the face, which I didn't entirely blame him for. He managed to connect with her cheekbone and made her howl so loudly the dog joined in. All the way through these familial delights, I had a tractor in front of me and a Land Rover driving so far up my arse he should really have brought a wedding ring.

By the time we'd circled the same stretch of admittedly very pretty road for about the gazillionth time, we'd all had enough. Lizzie was yelling. Nate was yelling back. The dog was barking. I was trying to retain my zen, but fast losing the will to live.

Things started to really deteriorate when Lizzie shouted 'for God's sake, use the bloody sat nav!' Nate had come out with the traditional response – Sat Nav's for Slackers – which provoked her to new lows.

'That's what Dad used to say,' she hissed. 'But Dad's not here is he? And Mum just isn't up to the job!'

That hurt, almost physically. It felt a bit like she'd actually stabbed me in the back of the head with a fork and blood was dripping down my scalp.

The worst thing about it was that it was one hundred per cent true. I might be getting my equilibrium back; I might be trying to move on. I might be less of a nervous wreck than I was this time a year ago. But I still wasn't up to the job – assuming the job was being her dad. Because much as I tried, I would never be her dad – and an epic fail on the road-map front was only a tiny part of that.

In the end I took the very sensible option of pulling over into one of those beauty spots where you're supposed to take photos of the stunning scenery. As the only scenery in my car consisted of violent kids and a senile Labrador, I refrained from creating a magical Kodak moment and instead simply got out.

I put Jimbo on his lead and practically heard his old bones creak as he threw himself out of the boot. He immediately cocked his leg to pee on a fence post and then tries to eat a small pile of sheep droppings.

I gazed out at the hills and valleys and luscious greenery and completely understood why Ye Ancient People had decided to locate their mysterious and allegedly powerful stone circle here. I just wished they'd thought to leave some better directions.

After Jimbo had sniffed and snuffled a few more times and I'd allowed the gentle sensation of sunlight on my skin soothe me down from the cliff edge the kids had driven me up, I helped the dog climb back into the boot, and slid back in the car.

Both of the kids were very quiet, which is always a worrying sign. I quickly glanced at both, making sure they were still alive, before fastening my seatbelt and preparing to move off.

'I'm sorry, Mum,' came a small voice from the back seat. I felt her hand pat me on the shoulder, which made me grin immediately. It was such a hesitant pat, like she knew she had to do it, but didn't enjoy it either. Almost as though she might catch leprosy from me if she kept it going for more than a few seconds.

'For what?' I asked, not wanting to give in too easily.

'For what I said about Dad. For being the Mean Girl. You're doing great, and I'll read the map if you want.'

I briefly touched my fingers to hers – keeping it quick so I don't ruin the moment with too much affection – and nodded.

'Thank you, Lizzie. And it's fine – we all miss him, and we all get mean sometimes. But you know what? I think you're right about this one. I think I'm going to have to break Dad's rule and hope he doesn't mind. Nate, get that sat nav out of the glove compartment…'

Nate hurried to comply, and within about six minutes, we arrived at Avebury – it appeared that we'd somehow managed to drive past it over and over again without ever noticing.

The visit was fine, the kids had ice cream and we all took photos. Jimbo discovered lots of new things to smell, and all things considered, I'd have to put it in the 'win' column.

The rest of the day, though, wasn't such a winner. It consisted of – in no particular order – our car battery dying and having to flag down passing German tourists to help us; getting lost again (despite the sat nav); Nate getting very, very sick and having to vomit his way through various picturesque lay-bys; getting lost some more; an emergency pit-stop at McDonald's in Yeovil; getting lost some more and Lizzie having to wee in a field.

'I'm never, ever leaving the city again…' she'd muttered, throwing the toilet roll at the car windscreen so hard it bounced off and flew away into the road.

With the various delays, it took us way too long to make the journey. We arrived in Budbury frazzled and irritable and, in my case, squinty-eyed from all the driving.

We spot the turning for the cottage complex – The Rockery – at the very last minute, and I veer suddenly to the left to pass through the open gates, thankful that the one-lane road behind me was empty of traffic.

We drive slowly past the shadowed playground with its colourful swings and slide, and past the games room, lit up inside and filled with what look like old board games, books, DVDs, table football and one of those air-hockey things, and follow the signs through to the cottages.

By the time we park up on a crunchy gravel-topped driveway that circles a large green lawn, the light is greying and I can see both the moon and the sun hovering in the sky. It's very strange and a little bit like the beginning of some kind of fantasy film.

I climb out of the car, so relieved to finally be here, squinting in the fading daylight as I try and figure out which cottage is ours. Hyacinth House, our home for the summer. The name sounds vaguely familiar, but not familiar enough for me to be able to identify why. This is becoming a more and more common sensation as I get older, which my mother tells me cheerily is the beginning of the end for my brain cells.

From what I can see in front of me, there are about seven or eight cottages scattered around the green. There's a terraced row of three, a couple of semi-detached pairs and one slightly bigger house near the entrance. Solar lights planted around the edge of the lawn are glimmering, looking like glow-worms in the gloaming.

The windows of most of the cottages are lit up, some with curtains drawn, others still open. I watch families inside, brief glimpses of kids running around, flickering television sets, one window steamed up as someone works in the kitchen.

I'm not sure if our cottage is one of the ones I can see or if it is further afield. I can just about make out a path running down the side of the terrace and the shapes of a few more buildings beyond.

I decide we can explore later – but first I need to figure out how to unpack the roofbox. It occurred to me about an hour ago that I have possibly made something of a tactical error with the roofbox. When I was putting the stuff in it, I had to stand on a foot stool so I could manage.

Obviously, I didn't bring the foot stool with me, and as I haven't grown on the journey, I'm still about inches too small to reach. It's a tricky one – and I suppose I'll just have to hope they have foot stools in Dorset, or perhaps tall people. At least we are here.

I pull open the front and rear car doors, and the detritus of the journey tumbles out of every footwell – carrier bags full of tissues, muffin wrappers and apple cores, old drinks cups from

McDonald's, soft bananas with blackened skin, a torn leaflet about English Heritage, and finally, groggily, two grouchy children. I gather the litter up to put in the bin and pull open the boot so that poor Jimbo can clamber out and stretch his old legs.

Except Jimbo, of course, decides that after being cooped up in the car for far too long, he isn't old at all. In fact he's decided that he's basically a puppy and sprints off over the grass like a gazelle on cocaine, springing and leaping and arcing through the dim evening sky.

He gallops in circles around and around on the grass, the solar lights highlighting the black gleam of his coat and reflecting off his eyes so he looks slightly demonic. He woofs and growls with sheer delight as he pursues his own tail and claws at the ground with his paws.

The kids start to laugh and I have to join in. I may be exhausted and frazzled and burned out, but the sound of my children giggling is enough to revitalise me even more effectively than a spa break and a bucket of chilled prosecco.

They're both at such awkward ages – half-baked humans, not quite grown up, not quite babies – that giggling isn't something that often occurs in our house. Lizzie's out with her friends more and more and Nate spends a lot of time in his room playing X Box Live. They bounce between needing me and not needing me, and in Lizzie's case between liking me and despising me. Even without the whole dead dad thing, I suspect it would have been a difficult time for us all.

Our laughter and the dog's playful gnashing, are pretty much the only sounds I can hear. It's almost alarmingly quiet at the Rockery. The families are all inside, living their barely glimpsed lives. There's no traffic at all. No loud music coming from loud cars, distant sirens screeching, or trains or trams rattling past. None of the usual urban noises we're all used to. Just the delicate twittering of birds at dusk, singing their last hurrah before bed time.

Jimbo jumps to his feet and his ears go on alert. We might think it's quiet, and he might be about a thousand in dog years, but he can clearly hear something we can't. His head swivels around, grey muzzle pointing towards the cottages, and he is suddenly galvanised into the fastest run I've seen from him in months.

He gallops away towards the path by the terrace, his inky fur starting to fade into the darkening light, his red collar just about still visible. I run after him and feel my now-frizzy curly brown hair billowing out behind me.

I catch up just at the point where the path stretches off between the buildings. There are a few more solar lights peeking out of the bedding plants here, so I can see exactly what has attracted his attention, and exactly why he's stopped long enough for me to reach him.

Jimbo currently has his nose buried in the crotch of a man who appears to be only wearing a white towel, tied around his waist. There's a lot more of him on display than I've seen of a man in real life for quite a while, and I'm glad it's not light enough for him to properly see my bright-red face – a combination of being too hot, running when I'm about as naturally athletic as an asthmatic tortoise and being a bit embarrassed.

He's tall, with wide shoulders that look on the brawny side. Like I imagine a blacksmith would look if I'd ever met one. Not many of those knocking round Manchester, funnily enough. His hair looks like it's probably dark brown, a bit too long, and it's dripping water all over his shoulders. I conclude from this, and from the fact that I can now see the swimming pool complex behind him, that he's been for a dip.

It's pleasantly warm now, even as evening falls, and I can see how that would be an attractive proposition. I quite fancy jumping into a pool and washing off the cares of the day myself. But first I have to try and drag my perverted old Labrador's face out of a strange man's nether regions.

I'm not quite sure how to go about it and am fearful that if I make a grab for Jimbo, I might accidentally dislodge the towel as well – which would be very rude indeed.

'Oh, God, I'm so sorry,' I mumble, trying to get hold of Jimbo's collar so I can tug him back from his erotic encounter. 'Jimbo!'

Jimbo has not only found the speed of a much younger dog today, he's also found the disobedience levels of a puppy and he fights me every inch. He's way too interested in having a good sniff.

So I tug and mutter apologies, and try to ignore the dog's disturbing snuffling noises as he buries his nose even further into the white towel. I also become aware that the kids have followed and are now sniggering away behind me. I realise that this really must all look very, very funny to someone who isn't, you know, *me*.

The man is taking this canine sexual assault extremely well and eventually he simply leans down, takes Jimbo's muzzle in one large hand and pulls it firmly away. He keeps hold of it and then kneels down in front of him, so he's on eye level. He lets go of Jimbo's mouth and starts scratching behind his floppy black ears, making his furry head twist around in ecstasy.

All the time, the man murmurs 'good lad'-type noises, while also gazing into the pooch's eyes and exercising some kind of Jedi mind-control trick that keeps him relatively still. For a few moments at least.

Jimbo suddenly darts forward to give the man's face a very thorough tongue bath, then plops himself down at his feet. Within seconds, he's snoring, curled up in an exhausted ball.

The dog whisperer stands up, holding on to the towel at his waist, although I have thankfully noticed the band of a pair of swimming trunks peeking out.

'How old is he?' the man asks, looking down at Jimbo, who is, I see, not lying at his feet – he's actually lying *on* his feet.

'Almost thirteen,' I say, 'and I'm so sorry.'

I am feeling suddenly very tired and very sad. The absurdity of my situation flashes across my mind: I have uprooted my children, myself and my very elderly dog on some kind of wild-goose chase, pursuing God knows what. Happiness? Progress? A break from the underlying misery that seems to have been wrapped around my heart every day since David died?

Well, whatever it is, I'm not pursuing it fast enough – all I'm finding is exhaustion, grumpy kids, senile dogs and a caffeine overload. That and chronic embarrassment as I apologise to a mostly naked man, in the dark, in a place I've never even visited before – a place I've unilaterally decided to make our home for the summer.

I clench my eyes together very, very tightly, squeezing back any watery signs of self pity that might be tempted to overflow, and force myself to look at the man instead of the dog.

I can only see bits of his face reflected in the silvery lighting, but he looks about my age. Maybe a little older, I'm not sure. His hair is definitely a bit too long, and will probably dry a lighter shade of brown once it's not soggy. His eyes seem to be hazel or brown or green, I can't really tell, and he's not smiling.

He *was* smiling when he was playing with Jimbo. But now he's not. Now he's looking at me. I guess I just have that effect on tall, handsome strangers.

'Are you all right?' he asks, gruffly, frowning at me with such style and finesse that I instinctively know he frowns at least as much as he smiles. I suspect he's one of those people who vastly prefers animals to people, and communicates much better with dogs than humans.

'Oh, yes, thank you… just tired. We've been driving all day and now we've got to find our cottage and unload the roofbox, and I don't know how I'm going to do that because I didn't bring the foot stool and I'm too short, and the kids need some dinner and I need some coffee… well, probably wine, to be honest, and…'

I catch a glimpse of his expression as I ramble incoherently, and note that he looks slightly frightened. I realise I sound like a crazy person and as I have the kind of hair that expands in heat and I've been stuck in a hot car all day, I undoubtedly look like one too.

'And yes, I'm fine, thank you,' I say, firmly. 'Do you happen to know where the Hyacinth House is? I have the keys.'

'I can help you,' he says, looking away from my eyes and gazing off into the distance. He sounds a little bit grumpy, a touch reluctant – as though he knows he should help, but doesn't really want to engage.

'No, I'm all right…' I insist, wondering how I'm going to get Jimbo off his feet without appearing rude.

'Let me help. I don't have any wine, but I can help with the other thing.'

'What?' I ask, staring up at him in confusion. 'You can help me stop being too short?'

Quick as a flash, a grin breaks out on his face and he lets out a laugh. It doesn't last long and he seems to clamp down on it as soon as he can, like he's not used to hearing the sound in public.

'Sorry, no. I'm a vet, not a miracle worker. But I can unpack the roofbox for you. I'll get dressed and come round. Hyacinth is just back there – next to the swimming pool. This is the nearest you can get the car, but I'll help you unload. I assume you're Laura?'

I feel a jolt of surprise that he knows who I am and also a jolt of a stubborn desire to continue insisting that I don't need any help at all. I settle for just nodding and giving him a half-hearted smile as he extricates his bare feet from underneath the snoring dog's tummy.

'Thought so. In that case, if I know Cherie, she'll have left wine in the cottage – so all your problems will be solved.'

Ha, I think, watching him disappear off up the path and noticing Lizzie still tapping away on her phone, face scrunched up in that very deliberate expression of vexed boredom that teenagers specialise in.

If only.

Chapter 6

Hyacinth House is rustic and pretty, and filled with the aroma of home-baked bread and fresh, sugary confections. It smells so good, in fact, as I push open the heavy wooden door, that for a moment I think it's been spritzed with one of those artificial scents that people use when they're trying to sell their home. Not that I'm sure those artificial scents even exist, but if not, they should. Maybe I'll invent them and make my fortune.

I flick on the lights in the hallway and then the living room. Actually, I realise, as I take it all in, it's one big open-plan room, really, in an L-shape. The little leg of the L is the kitchen and the big leg of the L is long but cosy and has a dining table at one end, and squishy-looking sofas and a TV at the other end.

There's a lot of exposed brick and wooden beams peeking out of the low ceiling and a big stone fireplace that we're unlikely to use in this weather unless we decide to do some hot yoga.

The interior design runs very much to the chintzy end of the style spectrum, with swirling floral patterns on the sofas and the throws that are on the sofas, the curtains and the lamp shades, and pretty much every available soft-furnishing surface.

The dining table is vast and battered and made from what looks like oak; it's solid and scarred and seems like it's led an interesting life. It's also bearing a big tray of delicious-looking cupcakes, all iced in different rainbow colours, and a huge seed-topped loaf that has the slightly wonky look of something home-made.

There's also a big bunch of wildflowers in a glass vase, and yes – praise the Lord! – a bottle of wine. Looks like it has a home-made label, so it is probably intensely organic and will get me very drunk, very quickly. Excellent.

Propped against it is a little note, which I pick up and read as I hear the kids stomping their way through. Nate heads immediately for the cupcakes, drawn like a moth to a fattening flame.

'Who's that from?' asks Lizzie, also reaching out for a cake. She's become disgustingly figure-conscious over the last few months and I count a day of her eating McDonald's and cupcakes as a positive, weirdly enough.

'It's from Cherie,' I say, 'you know, the—'

'The woman who was bonkers enough to give you a job?' she finishes. That obviously wasn't what I was going to say, but she kind of has a point. I don't answer, choosing to remain dignified and aloof.

'Don't do your 'who's farted?' face, Mum, you know what I mean!'

Apparently my dignified and aloof needs a little work, so I shove a whole cupcake in my mouth instead.

'I mean,' Lizzie continues, 'that it's all a bit weird, isn't it? She's never even met you. I didn't mean it as an insult – you're, you know, pretty good. At cooking. I'm sure you'll be all right at working in a café. I just wish you'd found one a bit…'

'Closer to home,' supplies Nate, helpfully. 'I think it took Matt Damon less time to get off Mars than it took us to get here.'

He flops down onto the sofa and straight away starts trying to figure out how to use the TV remote. Jimbo leaps up onto the couch next to him, circles precisely three times, then falls asleep with his muzzle buried beneath his own tail.

'So what does she say, then, the mysterious Cherie?' asks Lizzie, snapping a few pictures on her phone as she prowls around the room. A close-up of the bread, the flowers. A snarl before she takes one of the floral curtains, which are presumably not to her sophisticated tastes. One of Jimbo. One of Nate, who is now repeatedly pressing the same button on the remote, as though it might work the ninety-ninth time he does it. Then one of me, as I quickly realise that I shouldn't have put that whole cupcake in my mouth all at once.

I wait a few moments, chewing frantically, before I am able to answer.

'She says she's sorry she didn't get to see us earlier, but she has to go to her salsa class tonight. She says she hopes we enjoy the cakes and the wine – that bit's aimed at me, obviously – and that she'll see us all tomorrow. That we should spend the morning getting settled in and come round to the café for lunch. Isn't that nice?'

'Yeah, I s'pose,' says Nate, giving up on the TV and instead shuffling down on the sofa so he can rest his head on the dog. Jimbo absently licks his face, then goes back to sleep.

'Adorable,' says Lizzie. 'I can't wait. Do you think that tall bloke is going to come round or not? I think my phone charger's in one of the bags in the roofbox.'

'And what would happen if your phone ran out of charge?' I ask, sarcastically.

'I'd die of boredom,' she replies, deadpan. 'And I have a signal at the moment. Didn't you say it was a bit dodgy here? I have some serious communicating to do, so I'm going to make the most of it before we plummet back into the Dark Ages.'

Right on cue, there's a knock at the door and the Tall Bloke walks through into the living room. I hastily swallow the last mouthful of cupcake and wipe the icing off my chin with a half-hearted swipe of my sleeve. I have the awful feeling that when I next look in a mirror, there'll still be some there – along with the long, frizzy hair, the rosy cheeks and the harassed expression. The only sensible response to the entire situation is to never look in a mirror again. I may get Lizzie to go round the whole building covering them up with towels.

As the man enters, Jimbo looks up and lets out a high-pitched yip, thumping his tail a few times in appreciation. It makes the man smile, which I'm starting to realise is probably so rare in the wild that David Attenborough should make a documentary about it.

'Cake?' I ask, gesturing at the tray on the table. 'Wine? Bread?'

Dear Lord. I'm starting to sound like Mrs Doyle off *Father Ted*, and probably look even worse.

'No. Thanks,' he says, not quite making eye contact. He's dressed in a pair of faded Levis and an equally faded black T-shirt that fits very snugly around all the muscular parts of him I probably shouldn't even be noticing. His hair's been roughly towel-dried and is an attractively shaggy mass of brown and chestnut. The eyes, I note, are definitely hazel.

'Shall we get you unloaded then?' he prompts, which makes me wonder if I've been staring at him for two seconds or two hours. Awky-mo, as Lizzie would say. Or would have said last year, it's probably not cool any more. Like LOLcats or wicked.

'Right!' I reply, wiping my hands down on my jeans and nodding. I look at the kids and give them my very best 'get off your lazy arses and come help' face. Nate immediately feigns sleep, letting out huge fake snores, and Lizzie runs away up the stairs, presumably to call dibs on a bedroom.

I suck in a breath and smile.

'It's all right,' I say. 'I can beat them later. They're overdue a whipping.'

He raises his eyebrows and I have the feeling he's not a hundred per cent sure if I'm joking or not. Neither am I.

'Okay,' I exclaim, walking towards the door. 'Let's get started.'

I turn back and hold one hand up in a gesture of 'wait a moment' to him as he follows.

'Just cover your ears for a bit,' I say. As soon as he does, I bellow at the top of my voice: 'Lizzie! Nate! Come and help or there will be a ban on ALL electronic devices for the next week!'

I exit the cottage, smiling in evil maternal satisfaction as I hear Lizzie thundering downstairs and Nate groaning as he drags himself off the squishy sofa.

We walk back to the car, along the path, and around the terrace, and across the crunchy gravel. Just like we're all going on a bear hunt. It's properly dark now, bright spots flickering among the plants from the solar lights. The bird song has quietened down and the only sound is that of our footsteps and the occasional trickle of laughter from one of the other cottages.

'Weird, isn't it?' asks Nate, looking around suspiciously, as though a mad axe murderer might leap out of the bushes at any moment.

'What?' I say.

'Not hearing the police helicopter?'

'That doesn't happen often!' I snap back, somehow offended on behalf of our actually very nice part of Manchester. In reality, I suppose we hear it hovering somewhere nearby maybe once or twice a week – but it's not as though we live in some crack-den infested ghetto. There's a Waitrose, for God's sake!

Lizzie is holding her phone in front of her with the torch app switched on, her eyes staring at the ground as she walks, carefully measuring each step, like she's never walked anywhere in the dark before.

There's a sudden and very strange noise from one of the distant fields. It sounds vaguely like someone moaning in pain, deep and low and a tiny bit sinister.

'What's that?' I say, gazing around us and wondering if I've walked into some bizarre *Wicker Man*-type scenario. I notice the kids both freeze solid as well, looking very young and very scared. I tense, coiled with protective instinct, ready to kill anything that threatens my young.

'It's a cow,' says the man, who turns back to give me a sympathetic look. A look that says 'you poor, sad city person'.

I nod, and stay quiet. I'm not a hundred per cent sure I believe him – that didn't sound like a moo to me. I proceed with slightly more caution, following him to the car, feeling a little bit more aware of the fact that countryside dark really is a lot more serious than city dark.

We get to the car, I pass him the key and he effortlessly unlocks and lifts the roofbox lid. The one that took a whole lot of huffing, puffing, effing and jeffing for me to sort out the night before. I look on, standing on tiptoes and still barely able to reach. I am starting to hate him, a little tiny bit.

In the end I give up on my ineffectual stretching. It'll be easier if I just let him get everything out and then the rest of us start to carry it back to Hyacinth. Of course, what I've temporarily expunged from my mind about the roofbox is the way I've packed it.

Actually, 'packed' might be too generous a word. What I'd actually done was put masses of the kids' clothes and shoes into bin bags, put breakables and electrics into a cardboard box, added a few essentials like coffee and bog roll in one of those big reusable shoppers and then shoved most of my stuff down the sides, squeezing it all in to whatever spaces were left.

It had seemed to make perfect sense at the time, but as the man tugs hard at one of the tightly packed black bin bags, I start to regret it. It's a mess, frankly. The kind of mess you only ever want to see yourself.

I start to regret it even more when he finally manages to pull the bin bag away, with a grunt of effort. As it pops free, it brings with it a big, squashed clump of my underwear, which promptly scatters around us like an explosion of over-washed cotton being shot from a knicker cannon.

One pair of briefs gets stuck on the car aerial and another is caught mid-air by Nate, who immediately makes an 'uggh' noise and throws them on the floor. Jimbo, who has ambled out to see what all the fuss is about, straight away makes a beeline for the pants that Nate has just discarded and gobbles them up into his mouth. He runs away as fast as he can, a disappearing black blur with a limp pair of white undies hanging out of his muzzle.

I screw my eyes up in embarrassment and clench my fists so hard my fingernails dig into my palms.

This, ladies and gentlemen, is the summary of my life since David died – incompetent, incomplete and incapable of being even a fraction as much fun as he was. If my knickers had come flying out of the roofbox with him around, he'd have made a game of it. He'd have organised the Underwear Olympics. He'd have had everyone laughing, even me.

Sometimes, at the most unlikely and inconvenient of moments, I miss him so much I could quite happily lie down on the floor and go to sleep for a thousand years. I could use all my old drawers as a blanket and just sleep.

I open my eyes again, as going to sleep for a thousand years simply doesn't seem to be a realistic option. I see Lizzie, bless her, running around the driveway snaffling spare scraps of underwear from their new homes hanging off bushes and splayed over solar lights, and I see Nate chasing after Jimbo the Knicker Snaffler.

'So,' says tall, dark and helpful. 'I'm Matt, by the way. As I appear to have one of your bras wrapped around my head, it seems as good a time as any to introduce myself.'

I look up at him and see that he is grinning. It's a nice grin, genuine and playful and from what I've seen of Matt so far, quite a find. The lesser spotted Dorset Matt Grin.

I have to grin back, I really do, no matter how dreadful I'm feeling. Because what woman could resist a smiling man with a pair of 36C M&S Per Una bra cups hanging around his ears?

Chapter 7

I wake up the next morning with a mild hangover and a slightly less mild desire to throttle my own daughter.

I take a deep breath, grab the bottle of water I have thoughtfully placed on the bedside cabinet and glug down a few mouthfuls.

I lie still for a handful of moments, gazing at the hyacinth-covered lampshade and the rose-patterned wallpaper and the flowers-I-don't-recognise curtains, while snuggling under my sunflower-riddled duvet. I let out a huge sneeze. I seem to have developed psychosomatic hayfever, which is odd as I don't even get the real kind.

I have managed to snag the biggest bedroom by conceding the one with the en-suite to Lizzie. I am more than happy with that arrangement and I like my new home a lot. Even the bedrooms have beams in the ceiling and enough light is creeping past the edges of the curtains for me to know that the rooms will be bright and sunny and glorious. I can hear the TV on downstairs, which means that Nate is up and has conquered the remote, and I can actually hear Jimbo snoring all the way up here.

Other than that, again, it's just the sound of birdsong coming from outside, beautiful trilling harmonies that instantly make me feel more joyful. I don't think I've ever been anywhere so still and natural and peaceful.

There is, though, one small thing spoiling my burgeoning sense of tranquillity. Stopping me from reaching a state of Buddah-like zen. In fact, making me bite my lip so hard I taste blood.

It all started with the phone calls the night before. I chose not to use my mobile and instead called my mother using the brilliantly so-old-it's-now-retro-cool Bakelite phone – the type with the massive handset and a big circular dial that takes forever to click all the way around.

The children have stared at it as though it's a museum exhibit, Lizzie poking it cautiously with her fingertips as though it might be some deviously disguised creature from *Doctor Who*. She once watched an episode where plastic came to life as pure evil and she's never quite forgotten it. She was scared of her SpongeBob lunchbox for weeks afterwards.

Anyway, museum exhibit or not, the phone worked perfectly. Now, for the sake of sanity and brevity – and in fact all of humanity – I will paraphrase my conversation with my mother. It went something like this:

Me: Hi, Mum! We've all arrived safely and it's gorgeous! Best place ever!

Mum: Are you sure? It's a long way off. How are you going to cope?

Me: It's an adventure, we're all going to have a marvellous, brilliant, wonderful, life-changingly positive experience!

Mum: Your dad will come and fetch you all if you need to come home, you know…

It's a wee bit depressing how little faith she has in me – but I know, because I'm a mum myself, that it's only because she loves me so much. She knows what I've gone through and it breaks her heart.

It's not just me and the kids that David's passing affected – it's taken a toll on all of us. His mum and dad have never been quite right since; my parents constantly worry about me and I know that even Becca – beneath the drunken binges and party-girl persona – both misses him and feels for me and her niece and nephew, both of whom she loves beyond belief.

My next phone call was, in fact, to Becca herself. I was surprised to find her in on a Saturday night, and was touched when I realised that she was waiting for my call.

'Wassup, girlfriend?' she said, in a fake American accent. She likes to experiment with accents, my sister. Well, with everything really – but the accents are one of the many reasons the kids like her so much. They're especially fond of her 'Nordic noir' voice, where she orders food in the McDonald's drive-through as though she's a Scandinavian detective making a blood-curdling discovery in a Stockholm suburb.

I filled her in on the day's events – the driving, the singing, the vomiting. The ups, the downs, the sideways crab-walks. The uber-floral cottage. The peace and quiet and disturbingly dark darkness. The dog, and the man, and the cupcakes, and the roofbox and the delicious home-made wine I was sipping as I chatted to her.

'Hang on,' she said when I'd finished, and I heard a bit of shuffling going on in the background.

'What are you doing?' I asked, wondering if that was a wise idea. With Becca, it's sometimes better not to know.

'Adjusting the zip on my gimp mask,' she replied, jauntily. 'Or, just refreshing my laptop screen, I need to check on something. So – tell me more about this man.'

'Oh, he's just… a man. Well, a man called Matt.'

'Matt? That's a foxy name. I think I read a survey once that said men called Matt have very large penises.'

'No you didn't,' I said, laughing despite myself. It's impossible to keep a straight face when you're talking to Becca.

'What does he look like?'

I thought about that question and realised I didn't want to be totally honest in regard to how much I remembered about Matt's appearance. Mainly because I remember way too much: him, bare-chested, water dripping down onto broad swimmers' shoulders, towel hanging low on angular hipbones, the shape of muscular thighs pressed against the fabric… if I tell her that I'll never hear the end of it. She'll call the local vicar and start getting the banns read.

'He looks a bit like Harrison Ford,' I said, eventually.

'Saggy Harrison or fit Harrison?'

'Fit Harrison.'

'Han Solo Harrison or Indiana Jones Harrison? Because I think the latter might be useful – your vagina is so well hidden it might as well be in that warehouse with the Ark of the Covenant…'

'Becca!' I snapped, torn between horror and amusement. So, it'd been a while. I think your husband dying is pretty good excuse for a lack of sex life, don't you?

'Okay, okay… just saying. You could always borrow my Princess Leia outfit.'

'What kind, or do I need to ask?'

'Slutty slave girl in Jabba's palace, obv. You need to get a bit more slutty slave girl, you know.'

'I do not!' I spluttered, half-heartedly. She sounded distracted and was paying no attention to my half-hearted outraged spluttering anyway. To be honest, I'd had a couple of glasses of wine by that stage, which was definitely helping me feel more mellow. It's hard to do full-hearted spluttering when you're a bit tipsy.

'Aaah…' she said.

'Aaah what?' I asked.

'Aaah, I see – yes, he'd definitely get it. Han Solo, though, with that hair, don't you think? If Han Solo wore Levis that showed off his arse like that, anyway… gosh, he's really tall, isn't he? Total man totty.'

I was silent for a few seconds, wondering if Becca had developed powers of clairvoyance since I'd left home. Or if she was possibly having some kind of filthy, illicit sexual relationship with the head of NASA and he'd redirected all European satellites to focus on a small village in Dorset.

'What… what do you mean? How do you know what he looks like?' I said, frowning. I looked suspiciously around the room just in case somebody had installed a spycam and I was broadcasting live to the nation like some especially boring episode of *Big Brother*. There was no spycam. And no kids – Nate had dragged himself to bed, exhausted, and Lizzie had gone upstairs to 'communicate'.

Becca didn't answer straight away. She was too busy laughing. Not a polite chuckle either – but a fully throated guffaw. The type that makes you cry and potentially suffocate.

'Oh God!' she finally said, clearing her throat, 'that one of you with the whole cupcake in your mouth is priceless! All that green icing over your face! You look like a Teletubby!'

By that stage I was starting to get a vague inkling of what was going on. I poured another glass of wine and decided that I probably needed a firmer inkling. Also, I wondered what an inkling was – it sounded like it could be a baby fountain pen.

'Becca,' I said, as firmly as I could: 'Tell. Me. What's. Going. On.'

She giggled, obviously intimidated by my powerful big-sister voice.

'It's all on Lizzie's Instagram account,' she said, 'the whole day.

You with your mouth wide open in the car – looks like you're singing… oh yeah, it's a little video! Ha ha, Meatloaf – seriously, sis? This is too funny…'

She paused and I could hear her clicking through the images.

I stared at my own mobile and considered going online myself. In the end I decided it was bad enough hearing about it, never mind seeing it.

'There's one of poor Nate chucking up, the little love,' Becca added. 'You're holding his shoulders and leaning down over him. You have about seventeen chins, you'll be glad to hear. One of the back of your head. One of Nate asleep, dribbling a bit… there's loads. Oh… here's a nice one, though. It's one of you standing in a very pretty lay-by, gazing out over the hills… your hair's all flowy and hippy-ish, you're all thoughtful and pensive, and you look gorgeous, honest! She's even captioned it "Mum looking less than hideous" – isn't that nice?'

Nice, I thought… *nice*? That wasn't the word I'd have used. 'Nice' applied to Cornish cream teas, or a Cath Kidston tote bag, or a cosy night in with a box set of *Midsomer Murders*. 'Nice' was a way of describing your mother's new perm, or a bath towel set you've seen in John Lewis, or a recipe book you buy in a National Trust gift shop.

'Nice' was most definitely not the right word for this scenario – the scenario where my teenage daughter and budding photo-journalist has been reporting live to the world at large for the last twenty-four hours without ever mentioning it to the stars of the show.

As Becca went on to describe yet more of the photos, my heart began to sink even further. It really didn't feel nice at all. I felt humiliated and hurt and ready to cry, none of which was helped by Becca's laughter, or the fact that I knew Lizzie was entirely possibly upstairs as we were speaking, adding even more pictures.

I closed my eyes and listened as Becca continued her commentary. She was especially amused by my Incredible Escaping Underwear, and by a shot of Matt wearing my bra on his head. Oh God… Matt. I'd have to either get Lizzie to take them offline, or tell him. Or, possibly, simply pack us all back in the car and just flee the scene of the crime…

'You're not upset, are you?' asked Becca, presumably when she'd noticed I'd been stonily silent for a few minutes.

'Yes,' I said simply, draining the glass of wine and giving in as the tears started to flow over my cheeks and pool at the base of my neck.

'But you shouldn't be! I know it's cheeky – I know some of the captions are a bit rude – but it's harmless, really. It's just her way of dealing with the change… you know she didn't want to come. You didn't give her any choice, though, you made her, so she has to let that frustration out some way.

'It's hard at that age – you have no power, do you? You're grown-up enough to think you know your own mind, but not grown up enough that anybody ever listens to you… you're completely controlled by your parents, by school, by teachers. It's horrible – especially for someone as bright and independent as Lizzie.'

I nodded, miserably, then realised she couldn't see me. I knew she was trying to make me feel better, and I could even hear the sense in some of what she was saying. Lizzie was much more like Becca than me at that age, more naturally prickly, more fierce. Stronger in some ways, more vulnerable in others. Becca 'got' her, which occasionally makes me jealous, petty as it sounds.

So while the rational part of me could accept the truth in Becca's arguments, the rest of me still felt like crap. Crap and out of touch, and useless – a million light years away from the precious baby girl who was lying only a few steps away from me. I felt old and tired and mainly – mainly – I just felt terribly, horribly alone.

The kids were upstairs. Becky was on the phone. Matt was nearby in his cottage. The dog was on the sofa. The other holiday homes were full. I was not technically alone. But none of that mattered – I could have been at Mardi Gras in New Orleans, or at Trafalgar Square at New Year, or surrounded by family and friends at a party. I would still have felt alone – no matter how big the crowd. I'd felt alone ever since he left me.

'I know,' I mumbled, trying to pull myself together. My family were finally starting to believe that I was moving on, finally starting to believe that I was feeling better. That I might be behaving a bit irrationally, but I was past the worst of my grieving.

Clearly, they actually knew sod all.

'I know,' I repeated, more firmly the second time. 'I'm just a bit knackered. And I feel bad for Matt – I mean, he probably doesn't want the world to see him with a bra on his head, does he?'

'I don't know,' replied Becca, 'he might love it. For all you know he's the chairman of the Dorset Bra-On-Head-Wearers Committee, Han Solo branch. And anyway, it's not really the world – it's only people who are her friends on Instagram. That's me and a handful of teenagers in Manchester. I'm sure she'll add you as well, if you ask.'

'I'm pretty sure she won't… and that's probably for the best. You're right. She needs some privacy. She needs a way to blow off steam. I just need to tell her to lay off the innocent bystanders.'

'Yeah, do that. And look, don't feel bad – I'm sorry I described it all like it was hilarious, and I know you're sitting there half cut and pretending not to cry even though you are. There are some lovely pictures on here as well, honest. I've been looking through while we've been talking and lots of it's really nice – views of the scenery, the stone circles, a fab one of you and Nate eating ice cream under a huge weeping willow tree… one of Jimbo peeing on someone else's car wheel at a service-station car park and you looking a bit shifty as you try and drag him away… one of you outside McDonald's, with the caption "Best. Mum. Ever".'

'And there's an absolutely beautiful one of the front of your cottage. It's quite darkly lit and very arty… Hyacinth House? Is that what it's called, where you're staying? That's very hip for Dorset!'

'What do you mean?' I asked. I'd been wondering why it sounded familiar all evening.

'The Hyacinth House. It's a Doors song. Remember, from my hippy rock phase?'

Now that she's said it, I did remember, a little bit. Dimly and distantly, a vision of Becca with her tie-dyed T-shirts and greasy hair and the stench of patchouli oil came back to me. It had been a deeply unfashionable phase, that, not to mention smelly. Sadly we'd shared a room, so her taste in music became mine by default.

'Just about,' I said, a ghost of a tune playing in my head. 'Weird. Look, I'm going to go, Becca. I need to get some rest. I just hope she doesn't creep into my room at night and take a picture of me drooling onto my pillow.'

'I'm sure she won't. And just remember – there are far, far worse ways for a teenage girl to rebel than this. And I know, I tried them all.'

By the time I finally hung up, I was too exhausted to even think about it any more. I decided that the best course of action would be to let Lizzie know I knew, lay down a few ground rules, but not try anything too heavy-handed like banning her, or forcing her to close her account, or confiscating her phone, or killing her.

Besides, a sneaky part of me thought, as I let Jimbo out for his last wee of the night and prepared to climb the stairs, it might be the best possible chance I had of understanding what was going on in her brain. Surely Becca would warn me if she started posting pics of naked teenage boys or open condom packets or crates full of alcopops?

Jimbo had wandered back in and did his usual circling around routine before he curled up in a ball on his bed. I scratched his ears goodnight and went upstairs to do the same. Not circle around three times before curling up in a ball, but my own bedtime routine.

I took the framed photo of me, David and the kids that I'd brought with me and placed it on the bedside cabinet, facing inwards so it was the last thing I'd see before I went to sleep, and the first thing I'd see in the morning. It was taken when we were all scuba diving on holiday, and we have big plastic masks propped up on our heads. Nate's missing his front teeth; Lizzie's still a little girl, and me and David... well, we look happy. One of those perfect moments, frozen in time.

I positioned it perfectly and because it had been a very tough day and I was feeling emotionally drained, I resorted to the Sniff and Cuddle technique to settle myself off.

After David had died, I couldn't bring myself to wash his clothes for ages. They just sat there, in the laundry basket, with everyone else's getting thrown on top of them. Nothing was ever added to David's pile and nothing was ever taken away from it.

I never had to wash another clean work shirt for him or sort a fresh pair of socks, or dry his favourite Superman T-shirt that had holes in the armpits. I never needed to use the special Fairy non-bio because of his sensitive skin, and I never had to iron another pair of trousers. Because he never needed anything else from me ever again.

Eventually, my mother took charge and simply bundled the whole lot home with her to do herself. She washed them and dried them and folded them, and together we decided what needed to go to the charity shop, and what should be binned. To be fair, it's not as callous as it sounds – those clothes of his had been in the basket for three months by that stage, and it wasn't fair on the kids, apart from anything else, constantly seeing them there. It makes me cringe when I look back, in all honesty. I was definitely a teeny bit insane, which must have been frightening for them.

So I let my mum bag them up and bin them, partly because it was the right thing to do, and also because I was going through a kind of zombie stage back then. I was very malleable and easy to move around, like a lump of play dough in human form. I wasn't good at making decisions and I wasn't good at resisting them either.

Luckily, my mum didn't expand her Empire of Common Sense to the bedroom, and I took comfort in the knowledge that I had a secret stash of David lurking on a hook on the back of the door.

I had his dressing gown, a big bulky burgundy fleece. He'd had it for years and he'd lost the belt in the garden when we used it for an impromptu tug of war with the kids. Jimbo had chewed one sleeve and the left-side pocket was falling off. He'd really needed a new one and I'd mentally added it to his Christmas list.

But its ragged state didn't matter at all to me. What mattered was the fact that it still smelled of him; of him, and his deodorant, and the Old Spice aftershave the kids had bought him as a joke birthday present and he claimed to love.

If you've ever lost anyone, you'll know how important your sense of smell is. Walking into a room that smelled like David could literally take my breath away. An impromptu waft of his aftershave could reduce me to rubble. I couldn't even sit in the car for weeks afterwards, the aroma was so very 'him'. I also kept automatically getting into the passenger side, because he did the bulk of the driving, and waiting for him to get in next to me.

After a while, those little things – the outward signs of a life being half-lived, of a life in flux – started to fade. I got used to the driving. I accepted that his clothes were gone. I stopped bursting into tears every time I smelled Old Spice. But I never, ever, let go of that dressing gown.

I suspect it's a sign of some kind of mental breakdown, so I keep it secret, tucked away in a Tesco carrier bag in my underwear drawer, only getting it out at night. It's rarely seen, but always nearby – usually under the pillow he slept on (and yes, it did take me a very long time to allow my mother to strip the bed linens as well), or on particularly difficult evenings, cuddled up in my arms like a big, fleecy cat. The smell is faint now, barely there – but it's comforting anyway.

That night had definitely been a full-on fleecy-cat-cuddling kind of night, and I finally fell asleep after half an hour of Very Deep Thinking. About Lizzie. About Nate. About me. About our future, and what it might hold. About starting a new job tomorrow. About meeting Cherie Moon. About Matt. About the fact that Jimbo was so very old. About that scene in *Casino Royale* where James Bond is in the shower comforting a trembling Vesper Lynd and manages to be really sexy even though he's fully clothed... at that point, I suspect I drifted off into a happier place.

I was still cuddling my fake David, but he wouldn't mind. He'd always respected my relationship with Daniel Craig.

I'd slept surprisingly well, which was perhaps a result of the wine intake, and now I'm awake. Groggy, but awake. I glance at my watch on the cabinet – 9.38am – and give David a quick 'good morning' smile.

I stretch out, swipe the sleep out of my eyes and get out of bed. I carefully wrap my precious dressing gown up in the carrier bag and tuck it under the pillow for later.

I go for a morning tinkle and then tiptoe to Lizzie's room. I push the door open, just a teeny, tiny bit, and see her there. She's splayed across the predictably flowered duvet, one pyjama-clad leg under and one leg hooked over, and her hair is a mass of tangles against the pillowcase. She's still fast asleep, her eyelids moving slightly as she dreams, her lips open. She looks about ten years old, and my heart melts. Still my precious baby girl. Especially when she's asleep.

Today, I promise myself as I head for the shower, is going to be a good day. It will be positive and exciting, and fulfilling. And I will do my very best not to end up in any ridiculous situations that give Lizzie the opportunity to document my downfall live and online.

Chapter 8

'Mum!' shouts Nate, as I am busily burning toast in the kitchen. 'There's a picture of a strange man in the downstairs loo!'

I frown, throw the irredeemably black slices into the bin, and go to see what all the fuss is about. I make a mental note to dash back in time to turn the new, improved toast over on the grill. Some cook I'm turning out to be – completely flummoxed by the lack of a toaster.

I knock politely on the toilet door, because despite the fact that I carried this small person in my own body for nine months, Nate has become quite private since his twelfth birthday. When I have time, I feel a little worried about it – he's at that age where there is probably a lot of stuff going on with him; a lot of *boy* stuff, which he obviously doesn't want to talk to me about. So I tread carefully, let him know I'm available and don't barge into the bathroom.

He pulls open the door and points in something akin to wonder at a framed black-and-white photo that's hanging on the wall over the cistern.

At that point, Lizzie also comes in, her hair doing the Macarena over her face, phone in hand as usual. Just to complete the set, Jimbo pokes his way through our legs, sniffing at the toilet rim and wagging his tail so hard he's whacking the sides of my thighs like a carpet beater. It's suddenly very crowded in the downstairs loo.

'Who is it, and why's he there? It feels weird having him watch me while I pee…' says Nate.

I stare at the picture: at the long hair, the leather trousers and the arrogantly handsome face.

'It's Jim Morrison,' I reply. 'He's from a band called the Doors, and they recorded a song called the "Hyacinth House". I'd thought perhaps Becca was over-stretching to assume the cottage was named after it, but it looks like I was wrong…'

Lizzie pushes to the front of the crowd and gazes up at Jim. Poor dead Jim, one of the brightest stars of his time, now performing in front of an audience of three (four if you count the dog) in a very small lavatory.

She closes the wooden lid and climbs up on it, so her face is right next to the photo.

'Nate!' she says, passing him her phone. 'Take a picture! This is so cool – Becca did me a playlist that had the Doors on it. That song about people being strange. Come on, Nate, I can't stand on the bog all day. Take the bloody picture!'

She does that strange fish-like pout that seems to be a legal requirement of teenagers' photos the world over these days, and Nate takes the picture.

'Is that for your Instagram account?' I say, as she clambers down from the toilet lid. There's a brief pause, where she looks twitchy and nervous and then tries to hide it. Caught between being a little girl who doesn't want to get into trouble with her mum and a rebellious teen who wants to stick two fingers up at me.

I remind myself of what Becca said and remind myself that she was right – Lizzie didn't want to come here and I did, in fact, force her to. If the only thing she has power over is taking crazed selfies and embarrassing pictures of me, I can live with it – it's a shedload better than an eating disorder, that's for sure.

I'm interested to see which way she'll go, and can almost hear the cogs turning in her brain. In the end, she just shrugs, face neutral – not apologising, but not being aggressive either. Clever girl.

'Yeah. Is that all right?' she asks. She obviously knows now that I've spoken to Becca, and may be feeling a little anxious about my next move. Carefully, I also maintain a neutral face. We're both trying very hard to be Switzerland, here, which is perhaps the best we can hope for.

'It's fine,' I say. 'Apart from taking photos of people who aren't in the family. Like Matt. If you do that, you ask their permission to share, okay? You can't invade people's privacy like that. It's not respectful.'

She nods, agreeing to my terms, and I feel jubilant inside. Like I have negotiated a peace treaty that has ended all conflict in the Middle East, and should now be made the chairman of The Entire World.

'Mum!' shouts Nate, sniffing the air, 'I think that toast is burning again…'

Aaagh, I think, dashing out of the toilet, tripping slightly over the dog's arse and running towards the kitchen. Perhaps being chairman of The Entire World can wait until I've mastered turning bread brown without starting a fire.

I give up on the toast and we all eat cereal. Cherie has kindly left us a little welcome pack of butter, milk, coffee, a few other bits and bobs. Plus a giant box of Sugar Puffs, which is strangely enough the kids' favourite – an excellent guess from the mysterious Mrs Moon. I scoff down a huge mug of black coffee, and Nate and Lizzie guzzle some orange juice before disappearing off upstairs to get dressed. We have a couple of hours before we need to be at the café and plan to go and explore.

Having failed to cover all the mirrors up the night before, I was forced to confront myself in the bathroom after my shower. That resulted in a hefty spray of Frizz-Ease before I dried my hair, and a very light application of some tinted moisturiser. As a result, I look almost presentable and am dressed in some khaki shorts and a green T-shirt, along with a pair of Birkenstock sandals that were probably in fashion several years ago.

I take the precaution of hooking Jimbo up on his lead as we head out, just in case he decides he's a puppy again and does a runner, and he ambles alongside us, at a plodding pace I use as an excuse to go slowly myself.

We start with a stroll through the woods at the back of the house, which is a pretty magical place. The canopy of the trees is so dense that only a few rays of sunlight manage to creep through and dapple the mossy ground beneath our feet, and the only sound is birdcall and the bubbling of a nearby stream. It feels very isolated and mystical, almost as though we're in our very own private rainforest, even though I know the cottages are only five minutes away.

We do a loop, following a circular footpath that's dotted at all the junctions and forks with garden gnomes. Each gnome seems to be doing something different – fishing, clapping, playing what looks like a ukulele – and each one has a wooden sign next to it on a stick, bearing a few words of gnomish wisdom in colourful speech bubbles. One says 'the path to the cottages'; another says 'the way to the falls'. One is holding little binoculars, and his sign says 'the trail to the distant coast'. An especially jaunty fellow wearing a red beret tells us to follow the 'road to San Jose', but I think that one might be a joke.

Nate and Lizzie are fascinated by it all. Honestly, it's as though they've never seen trees before. Everything seems to take on huge significance – a giant fern still dripping with morning dew; the hollowed-out trunk of an oak big enough to squeeze inside; faded pink bunting hanging from overhead branches, as though someone has been having a party; a patch of wild mushrooms that Lizzie swears is the spitting image of David Cameron's face.

Nate isn't quite old enough to have totally developed his sense of cool yet, so seeing him running around isn't as much of a surprise. He still plays football on the street and likes to go to the swings.

But seeing Lizzie let go of her teenage diva image for even a few moments is a complete and unexpected delight. She's running and jumping and exploring, and taking photos of everything, and I don't even care when she takes one of me as I lean down to scoop up one of Jimbo's giant poos in a plastic bag. At least it shows I'm a responsible dog owner.

Eventually, we follow the advice of the fishing gnome and follow the path back to the cottages. The sunlight as we emerge from the deep-green shelter of the woods is quite dazzling and I turn my face up to the sky. I like the sun. It makes me feel better. I remind myself to make sure the kids get coated in suncream before we come out again, it's that warm.

Our cottage is right next to the swimming pool. We peek through the windows of the pool and see that it is small but perfectly formed. There is already a family inside, the water is bobbing with inflatables, and the dad is pretending to be a shark, chasing screaming primary-age children around while the mum looks on and laughs.

They look really happy and I quickly walk away. I don't want to feel jealous. I don't want to feel like I'm missing out. Not today. Today, I want to feel thankful and hopeful and strong. I want to feel like Katy Perry in the *Roar* video, although I don't share that image with the kids – they might actually die laughing.

'Mum, look!' says Lizzie, bounding back towards me, returning from her advance scouting party beyond the path. The pool and our cottage are the only buildings at the back of the complex, which is actually really nice. We're not just here for a week on holiday, we're here for ages, and the location means we'll have more privacy. You know, for when we have all our wild parties.

I follow her down the path, and back through to the central lawn we saw when we arrived last night. It's much prettier in daylight, with a big circular bedding area in the middle that's full of luscious flowers; deep red dahlias, multi-coloured begonias, delicate sweet peas, the purple trumpets of petunias.

There's a water feature in the middle, some kind of mock-Victorian affair that looks like a shower for fairies and elves, and pretty lilac clematis is trailing all around it. It's the kind of effortless-looking gardening that actually takes a huge amount of effort.

I'm all right at gardening. Ours back home isn't huge, and I gave up on a decent lawn years ago due to Nate's incessant footballing and Jimbo's pee patrols, but we have lovely borders and beautiful hanging baskets and a few trees that produce more apples and pears than we need every year.

David was always my slave labour, doing the weeding and digging and turning over and hefting bags of fertiliser around, while I was the evil mastermind. One of my more realistic 'moving on with life' plans was to get an allotment. It's still a good idea – I'm just doing the 'insane relocating to Dorset' plan first.

'What?' I ask, failing to see what's got Lizzie so excited. It certainly isn't a nice clematis, I know that much. I glance around at the cottages circling the lawn. Some are much bigger than others, and the tiny ones look quite higgledy-piggledy, but they all have features in common. Each has a little path leading up to the door, each has a name plaque, and each has a beautiful hanging basket in a riot of colour.

'This!' she says, as she points frantically at one of the cottages. 'Look at what it's called!'

I squint slightly in the glare of the sun, and try and make out the writing on the slate plaque adorning the pale stone wall of the cottage.

'Lilac Wine?' I say, looking a question at her. It's a weird name, but I'm not sure why it's got her quite so bothered.

'It's a song, by Jeff Buckley!' she says, snapping a photo of it. 'We were listening to it in our music class. By lots of other people as well, but his is the best.'

She skips over to the adjoining cottage, bats away a few bees hovering around the hanging basket, and takes a photo of that one as well.

'And this one,' she says, 'is called the Cactus Tree…don't you think that's odd, too?'

I nod. Because it is. Hyacinths and lilacs I get as names for Dorset cottages – but cactus? Not so much.

We stroll along, Lizzie and Nate exclaiming at the weird names of the cottages, her taking photos of each and obviously planning a long session on google at some point or another to solve the mystery. We pass Poison Ivy and the Laughing Apple and Cherry Blossom Road and then Mad About Saffron, which immediately strikes a chord with me.

'I think I know that one!' I squeal, obviously more infected with the excitement than I realise. And yes, obviously, I need to get out more.

'What is it?' squeaks Lizzie, bounding back towards me. Her hair is loose and wild and untainted by product, and it makes her look about five years younger. It's only the eye liner that reminds me she's a teenager at all.

'Is it a band?' she says, practically pogo-ing on one leg.

'It's a song, by…by…'

She looks at me expectantly, and I feel the pressure mounting. This is my chance to prove I'm cool, and I'm about to blow it. I start to hum the song, fragments of the chorus coming back to me. It was on an advert, I'm sure.

'I'm just mad about Saffron…' I sing, badly. I can't remember the next line, so I go back to humming, and Lizzie is looking increasingly agitated as I fail to fulfil her quest for knowledge.

'It's…it's… oh, lord, I can't quite get it! It's there in my brain, just give me a minute! It's by…'

'Donovan,' says a voice from behind us. 'Mellow Yellow.'

I whirl around to see Matt, the man from last night. He's wearing a pair of faded denim shorts with big pockets on the side, and no top. Again. He clearly doesn't own many shirts.

He's a bit sweaty, as though he's been working, and I notice things about him I didn't notice the night before. Like the fact that his brawny shoulders and back are really bronzed, as though he spends a lot of time outside. Like the tiny crinkles at the corners of his hazel eyes, and his very long lashes. Like the way the sun glints on the chestnut shades in his hair. Like the fact that he has really, really big hands.

My pulse rate speeds up slightly as I notice all of these things, and it takes me a while to identify the feeling. It's called fancying someone, and it's not happened to me for a very long time. This, I decide, is even weirder than the cottage names, and far more disconcerting.

I don't know how to cope with fancying someone. I mean, I met David when I was in juniors. And of course I noticed attractive men after that – I was married, not comatose – but certainly not since David died.

It's as though that part of me shut down at the same time he did. I'd not mourned it, or sought it out, or listened at all when various members of my family started to make subtle references to the fact that I was 'still young'. I knew what that was code for, and it seemed like a completely absurd idea to me. As far as I was concerned, that aspect of my life was over.

I now feel more than a little freaked out, as I look at Matt, to realise that my libido at least isn't entirely convinced that's true. I also feel a twinge of guilt, for all sorts of complex and uncomfortable reasons, and dart my eyes away from him as quickly as possible.

'That's it!' I say, turning back to Lizzie. 'Donovan. Your granddad likes him. 60s stuff. So, we've got Donovan here, and we've got Jim Morrison and the Doors in our cottage. And Lilac Wine. So there's a theme?'

Lizzie makes a slightly 'duh' face, and nods.

'What's the name of your holiday cottage?' she asks Matt straight away.

'Well, the cottage is called the Black Rose,' he replies, wiping one hand across his forehead. He looks hot. And thirsty. I notice gardening gloves hanging out of one pocket, and use my laser-like detective skills to figure out that he's the effortless gardener who actually puts in all the effort.

'But it's not a holiday cottage,' he adds. 'I live there permanently. Well I have for almost a year now. I was only supposed to be here for two weeks while I found somewhere else, but Cherie and I came to an agreement.'

'Black Rose…' she says, frowning, and starting to tap into her phone.

'It's a Thin Lizzy song,' Matt replies, saving her the effort. She looks a little bewildered.

'Rock band, mainly big in the 70s. All the cottages are named after songs or bands, you're right. There's Sugar Magnolia over there, which is a Grateful Dead song. Poison Ivy is the Rolling Stones. Laughing Apple, Cat Stevens. Cherry Blossom Road is

Heart. Cactus Tree is Joni Mitchell. You might not have heard of them, but they were all well known. Cherie's idea of a joke. Nobody quite knows if it's true or not, but there are rumours that she was either in a band herself, or toured with one, or was Jimi Hendrix's girlfriend… I've never asked.'

'Why not?' says Lizzie, clearly fascinated.

'Because that's her business,' he replies.

That is clearly an alien concept to Lizzie. It also reminds me of another issue, and I'm about to raise the subject of the Instagram affair when she pre-empts me.

Lizzie often does this neat mind-reading trick that occasionally makes me think she's psychic. Or more likely that I'm very predictable.

'Matt,' she says, smiling sweetly. 'I was wondering if you're okay with me using a picture of you in a kind of school project? I'm keeping a record of what I do over the summer in an online photo journal. It's on Instagram, but hardly anybody will see it, honest. I have all the privacy settings on, so it's only for friends and family.'

Well, I think, some family at least. I'm momentarily taken aback by her description of it as a school project, and wonder if that's true, or if it's something she's fabricated to make it sound more respectable.

Matt is gazing at a spot about three feet to the left of my head. I resist the temptation to turn around and see what he's looking it, as I am starting to realise that it's simply something he does.

He has a very slight disconnect going on that I recognise as the sign of someone not wanting to get too involved in a conversation or a social situation. I deal with mine differently – I smile a lot and pretend I have to dash off to the school/shops/doctor/library – but I instinctively know we're coming from the same place. A place of entrenched solitude.

'I'm not sure what Instagram is,' he says eventually. 'But as long as it's not something likely to go viral, or embarrass me, or upset anyone, then that's fine. Are you going to the café today?'

He's changed the subject quite quickly, but Lizzie takes it as a win, and says her thank yous before disappearing off to take more pictures.

Nate spots another lad of about the same age emerging from Cactus Tree, kicking a bright orange football around, and starts to edge in his direction. The siren call of sport. I know that within minutes, they'll be setting up penalty shoot-outs and having keepy-up contests and firing each other headers to practice, without even knowing each other's names. Sure enough, even as Iook on, the boy raises his eyebrows at Nate, who nods, and they're off.

'Yes,' I reply, turning my attention back to Matt, but using his tactic of not quite making eye contact. I feel very slightly awkward now we're alone, mainly because I have caught myself out having naughty thoughts about him.

I am both shocked at my own behaviour, and also a bit humiliated, as though he can tell and already feels repulsed at the very concept.

'Yes, we're going to the café. For lunch.'

'Good,' he says, nodding firmly. 'Have a nice time, then.'

He turns, not exactly abruptly, but certainly without any preamble, and starts to walk away. I am caught unawares and find myself watching his backside as he strides off towards what I assume to be the Black Rose.

He stops, suddenly, and comes back towards me, as though he's remembered something. Turns out he had, and I could have lived without it.

'I found these,' he said, digging his hand into one of his pockets. 'While I was working on the lobelia in the borders. I think they're yours.'

He hands a small, scrunched bundle to me, before nodding

again and walking more briskly away, like he really means it this time. I open my clenched fist, already slightly sick about it.

If I was feeling humiliated before, nothing he could have found lurking in the lobelia could possibly be about to make it any better.

And most definitely not a pair of size-fourteen skin-tone tummy-control pants with an elasticated panel for holding in the wobbly bits.

Chapter 9

We hadn't seen much of the landscape when we arrived, due to the failing light and the fact that I was mainly concentrating on finding the cottages and not killing us in the process. So we set off early, even though the café is only a few miles away from our new home, to explore.

We soon see that the area immediately around the Rockery – which now makes a lot more sense, given the cottages' music-inspired names – is stunning. Breathtaking. Even Lizzie is forced to admit it's pretty.

We drive carefully along criss-crossing one-car tracks and through stretched-out road-side hamlets, and through woods so dense the trees meet overhead, arching across the paths and holding hands above us.

We drive through rolling hills and wooded glades and open fields that stretch and tumble as far as the eye can see, in more shades of green than I ever knew existed. The roads twist and turn through the countryside, edged by gnarled tree trunks and vibrant hedgerows and quaint cottages with thatched roofs, looking like a living postcard.

We see birds of all kinds, from frantically darting tits and sparrows to soaring kestrels floating on the air currents overhead; we see scurrying squirrels and oceans of listless, sunbathing cows, and on one confusing occasion a small herd of llama. We see horses and sheep and signs that warn us of crossing deer and migrating toads.

We see so many different wild flowers, twined in the hedges, twisting around the tree trunks, swaying in meadows – some I recognise, some I don't. We see farmhouses and small shops and just one garage that seems to sell nothing but petrol and spare tractor parts.

And eventually, as we flow downhill with the road, trickling towards the coast like a man-made stream, we see the sea.

Nate is captivated and screams with excitement. 'First person to see the sea' was always a travel game we played – when they were too little to know any better, we even used to play it when we were staying inland, which was cruel but had them glued to the windows in silence for hours at a time.

At first, this time, it doesn't even look like the sea. It looks like a shimmering, shining turquoise blanket that's fallen down from the hills, rippling in the gentle breeze. We see increasingly longer glimmers of it as we wind our way downhill, glimpsed between bends and buildings, a distant, sparkling mirage.

After an hour's random driving and a steep last-minute descent, we're here. We drive through the village – a long, thin strip of road edged with a combination of fancy and functional shops, a pharmacy, a post office and a Community Hall – and take the coastal road out of it again.

I see the car park Cherie has advised us to use and pull in, reminding myself that despite our long sightseeing cruise to get here, we're only about three miles from the Rockery.

I'm nervous as we park up at the bottom of the hill, edging into a spot between a Land Rover and a Fiat Panda and hoping I can get out again. The car park is packed, which doesn't surprise me at all. The weather is divine and the location is even better.

Spread in front of us is a beach, small but perfectly formed, that curves inwards in a kind of horse-shoe shape. There are lots of families and dogs and walkers down there, enjoying the sunshine, paddling and swimming and spreading out over picnic blankets.

A single ice-cream van has set up at the far end of the car park, and is doing a brisk trade. Overhead, seagulls are wheeling and screaming and occasionally swooping down to snatch up a discarded cone or a wandering sandwich crust. The only other sounds are children laughing and adults chatting and the constant whoosh-whoosh-whoosh of the waves creeping ever closer, splashing frothily onto the sand.

Nate gazes out longingly and I just know he's already considering chucking off his trainers and rolling his jeans up to knees and making a run for it. Lizzie is trying not to look like she feels the same – because she hates Dorset after all – but I can tell she does. That alone makes me smile, and for a moment I consider suggesting we all head down for a quick paddle. But, you know, new job and all – best not to arrive barefoot and covered in sand.

The cove is surrounded by towering cliff tops and boulders that run from the bottom of the cliffs about twenty feet out into the sand. People are using them to sit on or drape clothes on to dry in the sun, and a few people are investigating the rock pools hopefully, looking out for crabs and creatures. At high tide the waterline undoubtedly comes all the way over, and I can see the dark, mossy marks left on the cliffs.

A path leads up from the side of the car park to the top of the hill. It's steep and I fan myself with my fingers, which is totally useless against the midday heat. I'm not thrilled at the thought of climbing that path, but I have to. Because up the hill lies the Comfort Food Café, and Cherie Moon, and my new job, and, well, a free lunch. So I usher the kids in that direction, promising them a dip in the sea later, and we start the upwards trek.

The path actually has low steps cut into it and a wooden handrail, so it's not quite as arduous as it looks. I see that over on the far side of the hill, there's a more meandering path that's been paved over, presumably so people can also make the Comfort Food pilgrimage if they have a pram or a wheelchair.

Near the top, by what is obviously meant to be a little viewing station, we pause. Not just to catch our breath – which is definitely a factor for me – but to admire the vista. It is pretty amazing, and Lizzie is silently taking photos already.

It feels a bit like we may have reached the edge of the world – all we can see is that glorious stretch of glittering blue-green water colliding with red and brown cliffs; dots of colour as backpacked walkers amble along high-up footpaths, patches of yellow sand getting smaller and smaller as they become more distant, curving off around the coastline.

The sun is shining down on my skin, I can hear the birds and the laughter and the waves, and I feel a moment of complete and utter peace. A rare sense that everything will be all right in our family's fractured little world. I close my eyes and turn my face to the sky and smile.

'You all right, mum?' Nate asks, poking me curiously in the side. 'You're not having a stroke or anything, are you?'

I laugh and shake my head, and gesture that we should carry on to the top, where we can now very clearly see our destination.

Lizzie bounds ahead like a mountain goat in a Nirvana T-shirt, clicking away. She turns back to face us and takes a picture of me as I smile up at her. She even smiles back – a proper smile, big and warm and genuine – and I take a solid hold of the railing to stop myself falling down in shock.

And at the very top, I see it. An archway built over the path, of wrought iron decorated with beautifully forged metallic roses, a kind of man-made trellis, painted in shades of red and green. Amid the roses and the leaves and the stems are carefully crafted words, made up of curling letters, all painted white.

'Welcome to the Comfort Food Café.'

Chapter 10

The café itself is one storey apart from a few attic windows and really rather ramshackle. It has the look of a building that has been expanded to suit varying purposes over a number of years, growing organically further and further along its cliff-top location. The entrance is surrounded by open green space looking out over the sea. The land here isn't entirely flat and is dotted with slightly wonky wooden tables and benches.

Plenty of customers are using them, families, walkers and people who have the weather-beaten look of those who spend their whole lives outdoors. None of them seem to be put off by the slope, but I notice that quite a few are keeping a tight hold of their drinks.

There's an enclosed patch of land off to the right, fenced in, with a wooden structure that looks a bit like an old-fashioned bus stop and offers a long, shady patch of protection against the sun. I realise that it's some kind of doggie crèche, and although a few of the tables still have dogs sitting under them panting away, there are also about six or seven inside the little paddock. Some are running around, sniffing each other's bits and play-fighting, but most are snoozing away in the shade or drinking from the water bowls.

We've left Jimbo at home this afternoon, as he seemed perfectly comfortable curled up in his bed, merely raising one eyebrow when I offered him his lead before we left – but it's good to know that on the longer days he can come here with me.

There's a decked patio section running the whole length of the building, with a few more tables and chairs, and off to the other side is a massive, industrial-level gas-powered barbecue. It's the barbecue that's producing the mouth-watering aroma and I see Nate licking his lips in anticipation.

An older man wearing a stripey blue-and-white chef's apron seems to be at the helm, flipping burgers, turning steaks and prodding chicken breasts. He must be roasting-hot himself, with the heat and the smoke and the sun, but he seems perfectly happy.

Next to it is a large trestle table set out with salads, corn on the cob, jacket potatoes, sauces and condiments of every possible shade. A young woman with a dazzlingly bright shade of pink hair is laughing with customers as she helps them, serving up coleslaw and offering grated cheese and drizzling a huge bowl of rocket with olive oil.

The woman with the pink hair looks wild enough to have once been Jimi Hendrix's girlfriend, but definitely not old enough, so I rule her out as a potential Cherie Moon. And as the barbecue master is most definitely male, that's not her either, unless she's in disguise.

Lizzie has disappeared over to the doggie crèche and is taking photos of the sleepy hounds, and Nate is drifting towards the barbecue, nostrils flaring, one hand rubbing his stomach.

'I'm just popping inside,' I say to nobody at all, as both kids have forgotten I exist, and I walk through the open patio doors and into the main café building.

Inside, it's surprisingly cool, which means there must be some kind of air-conditioning. Predictably enough, though, on a day like this, it's completely empty, which gives me time to take it all in.

It's not actually huge – more long and thin than spacious – and probably only seats about forty people at most. There are tiny circular tables meant for two, square ones for four and longer ones with benches that could sit families or groups. All of them are made of the same battered-but-beautiful shade of light-hued pine, and all of them are decorated with fresh flowers in tiny pottery vases.

The serving counter stretches the length of one wall and has all the usual things like a cash register and chiller sections full of cakes and a huge fridge of cold drinks. I see a big coffee machine and a selection of herbal teas and piles of plates and cups.

There is an ice-cream freezer and I peer in to see tubs of creamy vanilla, double-chocolate chip, rum and raisin, honeycomb, blueberry and pretty much every pastel shade of fruit I've ever seen.

The decor is eclectic, to say the least. There are lots of wooden signs, painted in bright colours, with pictures of flowers and food and fruit. Some bear slogans, like 'Keep Calm and Eat a Cupcake' and 'Life's Too Short for Celery', and my personal favourite 'We will assume you want your hot chocolate with marshmallows and cream unless you appear to be dead.'

Pretty much every available bit of wall space is taken up with this kind of thing, along with the paintings and framed photos of the coast, which are absolutely gorgeous. None of the photos have price tags hanging off them, even though they're easily good enough to be sold, and they have a slightly dated look that speaks of a bygone era; one that involved dark rooms and developing fluid and nothing digital at all.

In amid all of this are extremely random items, some hanging from the ceiling, some on shelves, others draped from small chains. My first sweep of the room reveals a one-man kayak in a faded shade of red; a decorated wooden boomerang; two halves of a broken oar; an old-fashioned Singer sewing machine in black and gold; a set of bongo drums; a huge, circular fossil as big as a tumble dryer's door; a dangling mobile of what looks like papier mâché rainbows and unicorns, and another made from old seven-inch vinyl singles.

Only one wall is free of the clutter and that's because it's lined with two giant bookshelves crammed full of paperbacks, hardbacks, magazines, colouring books and crayons, and board games that look like they've been there since my own childhood. There are several chess sets, draughts, Chinese chequers, backgammon, playing cards and dominos – as well as the likes of Ker-Plunk, Buckaroo and Frustration.

At the far side of the room is another set of patio doors, which flood the whole place with natural light. Fingers of sunshine fall over the tables and the flowers and the strange collection of items in bright-yellow stripes, and I have to squint as I look out in that direction.

The doors open out onto the cliff top and it looks as though a few tables and chairs have been set up there too. I wander towards it, wanting to feel the sun on my skin again, and as I get closer it feels so near to the edge that I experience a sudden rush of vertigo.

I hold onto the doorframe and calm myself down with a few deep breaths. I realise that it was something of an optical illusion – there is easily enough space for a long bench and a few scattered tables out here – and an extremely sturdy fence is also standing between me and Certain Death. Still, I can see why nobody would bring their kids out.

As I take a few tentative steps outside, I realise I'm not entirely alone. I jump slightly as I hear a tiny cough – the sort of clearing of the throat that people give to warn of their presence – and look to my left. There, sitting on the bench with her flip-flopped feet propped up on one of the tables, is a majestic-looking creature, who I immediately and instinctively know is Cherie Moon.

She's larger than life in pretty much every way – obviously tall, even though she's sitting, with bare, brown legs that seem to stretch for miles in front of her. Her bottom spreads sumptuously over the bench and her ample bosom is exactly the kind that men dream of getting lost in. She's wearing a flowery sundress that shows off plenty of tanned cleavage and her hair is draped over her shoulder in a thick brown-and-grey plait.

I couldn't possibly guess how old she is – anywhere between fifty and seventy-five, to be honest – and as soon as she smiles her whole face creasing up, she reminds me wonderfully of Ma Larkin in the *Darling Buds of May*. If, I think, sniffing the air, Ma Larkin had been at Woodstock.

There's a slight lingering smell of tobacco wafting around, so I come to the conclusion that she's been out here for a smoke break. And as the slight lingering smell is also a tiny bit herbal, I'm not entirely sure what she's been smoking. It's probably not polite to ask at this stage.

'You must be Laura!' she says, standing up and towering over me exactly as I thought she would. I nod and smile back, feeling suddenly nervous and anxious and worried that she'll take one look at me in real life and give me the sack.

Instead, she envelops me in a huge hug that simply will not allow nerves or anxiety or tension to exist anywhere within its sphere of influence. After the initial English reaction of 'oh-my-god-a-strange-woman-is-embracing-me', I give in and hug her back.

She's such an imposing figure I struggle to make my arms meet around her waist and find my head clamped to her chest. It's very comfortable there, and I suddenly understand – in an entirely non-sexual way – why men would find it so appealing.

By the time she lets me go, I am feeling much better, not only about my potential employment prospects, but about life, the universe and everything. Possibly, I think, I have inhaled something my system is not quite used to, which seems to have imbued me with a sense of warmth and wellbeing.

'Well,' she says, standing back and looking me up and down, still holding my shoulders as though she might drag me back in for another cuddle at any moment. 'Aren't you the beauty?'

I'm not quite sure how to react to that. Saying 'no' seems rude. Saying 'yes' seems arrogant. I settle for a humming noise that neither confirms nor denies.

'Look at all that gorgeous curly hair! And those green eyes! Oh, my, you're quite the Pre-Raphaelite, aren't you?'

Again, I'm not so sure what to say to this. All I can think is that Pre-Raphaelite ladies usually had red hair and mine's dark brown. I am thankful, however, that if she is going to use art metaphors, she doesn't go in the direction of 'Reubenesque' (snob code for fat), or compare me to those chubby, jolly Beryl Cook ladies. I'm not really fat at all – I'm just short, so it can look that way from certain angles.

'Um… thank you?' I say, hoping the power of speech will revisit me soon.

'Where are the little ones?' she asks, gazing through the patio doors and searching for them outside.

'They're at the back and they're not so little,' I reply. 'At a guess, Nate's standing by the barbecue drooling and Lizzie's taking pictures.'

'Oh – she likes photography, does she? You might have noticed the framed pictures in the café? My husband did those, many years ago.'

I'm not entirely sure that posting pics of Jimbo licking his own arse online qualifies as 'photography', but I keep quiet on that one. Better if I unleash Lizzie bit by bit, rationing her out over the holiday period. By the time Cherie's decided she wants to throttle her, it'll be time to leave.

'Yes, I think so,' I say, crossing my fingers behind my back. 'Only recently, though. Perhaps she can talk to your husband about it sometime.'

Cherie snorts with laughter and gestures for me to walk back inside the building. I notice her using her bare foot to give a big, copper ashtray a nudge under the bench as we go – obviously its usual resting place.

'She'll need a spirit guide for that, I'm afraid, love,' she answers, her mighty shoulders shaking in amusement. I take it from that comment that Mr Moon is with us no more, and wonder if I will ever reach the stage where I can joke about David's death, or not cringe and die inside every time I have to explain myself to someone.

Inside, the cool air hits me and Cherie walks towards the serving counter. She ducks underneath it with surprising suppleness for such a large lady and reaches for a blue ring-bound file.

'Now,' she says, tapping the folder with one scarlet-red nail, 'this is your homework. I'll give you a tour of the kitchens and all that jazz later, once you've had something to eat and drink, and had a chance to catch your breath. Will you be all right to start at eight to begin with? We mix the shifts up a bit and for the first few you can do them with me so we can get to know each other better. Once you're up and running, I'll leave you to it.'

'Leave me to what?' I say, frowning in confusion.

'Leave you to opening up and running the café.'

I feel momentarily dumbstruck at the thought of being left in charge of the whole place and decide that Cherie's youthful days on tour with Janis Joplin, or whatever, must have left her a bit broken in the head.

'You can do it,' she says quietly, smiling at me. 'I know you can. You have to trust me – I'm never wrong about these things.'

There's something in her tone, in her smile, in the confident way she holds her tall, strong body, which actually does make me trust her. This crazy woman, who I've only just met and who is entirely possibly high on more than life, somehow makes me feel that I *can* do it. I decide not to analyse it all to death and just smile back and nod.

'Right. Good. Well, we're usually open from eight until three in the week, and until four at the weekends. Mondays we're closed, so that'll always be your day off. You don't have to be here all the time; we'll work it all out together bit by bit. We need to be flexible because of Willow... did you see a girl out there? The one with the pink hair?'

'Yes, she was hard to miss.'

'That's Willow. She's like the daughter I never had, which means she's a bloody handful! Her mum isn't too well, so we try and fit in around her, when she can get care, that kind of thing. Is that all right with you? Nate and Lizzie are welcome to come here with you, if you don't feel comfy leaving them at home. To be honest, they'll probably soon make friends anyway – the kids round here tend to roam in packs; there's not a huge amount of fleshly pleasures on offer in Budbury, so they have to make their own trouble.'

She grins at me and I'm not sure how serious she is. I never imagined the Dorset coast was full of rebels without a cause, but I could be wrong. And Lizzie would fit right in, if only she could persuade herself to stop pretending to be so cool.

'That's all fine by me,' I reply, gazing curiously at the blue file. 'Flexible is my middle name.'

'It's not, though, is it?' she asks, still grinning.

'No. It's Jane – how did you rumble me?'

'I have a nose for these things, sweetheart. I'm like a human lie detector. And a human bullshit detector. I used to be a human metal detector as well, but then I had plates put in my arm after a skiing accident and I kept making myself bleep...'

I realise that I am laughing out loud as she rambles on, which only seems to encourage her.

'I'm also a human love detector,' she continues, her warm-brown eyes now almost entirely swallowed up in the folds of her face as she laughs along.

'I warn you now, Laura Flexible Walker, I can sniff out a romance a mile away.'

'Well you won't be getting a sniff of anything like that where I'm concerned,' I answer. 'I'm an entirely romance-free zone.'

Cherie tips her head to one side as she inspects me, her fat plait tumbling down over one shoulder as her face tilts.

'I wouldn't be so sure about that, my love. A single woman is a rare find in these parts. The men tend to count their women folk back into the fold like sheep at the end of the day, there are so few of them – especially young, attractive ones like you. I think you'll be more popular than you expect.'

An image of Matt working – bare-chested, on his knees, down and dirty in the soil – flashes through my mind and I jump on it with both feet. Once both feet land, I stamp and stomp and squash until the thought is barely there at all. I'm slightly concerned that Cherie Moon may be a mind reader on top of everything else.

'I don't see myself as any of those things,' I say, once I've stopped my mental stomp. 'I don't see myself as young, or attractive, or popular. And I certainly don't see myself as single…'

The truth of these words hits me hard as they emerge from my own mouth, as though they're vocalising thoughts I've never dared acknowledge to myself before now. I'm married to the memory of a dead man, which is not how I planned to spend my thirties.

Cherie's smile is gentle and soft, and sympathetic. It feels strange to have shared so much, so soon, with someone I barely know.

Maybe it's the fact that I'm always trying to hold it together in front of my own family. Maybe the sea air has gone to my head.

Maybe Cherie Moon just has that effect on people – but she feels like a safe haven. Like someone I can really talk to. Someone I can be myself with.

'I know you don't,' she murmurs, her eyes shining. 'But this is the Comfort Food Café, you know. And miracles can happen here.'

Chapter 11

I spend the whole evening doing my homework. That sounds tedious, but is vastly improved by the fact that I'm doing it while also sipping wine in our tiny back garden. I'm on a padded lounger, looking out over the hills as the sun starts to set. Everything is a heavenly mix of gold and green, and skylarks are chirruping and chirping as they rise and fall in a flurry of wings from the grass in front of me.

It's still warm, but there have been dire warnings – from Cherie, and from a couple of the locals I met at the café earlier – that the weather is likely to turn at some point during the next few days. I choose not to believe them and instead anticipate spending every single one of my Dorset evenings in exactly this position.

My homework consists of the contents of the blue file I'd seen Cherie with earlier. There's a plastic wallet full of recipes, some of them straightforward, some of them not so much, as well as some helpful pointers on kitchen maintenance – for example, 'if the espresso machine starts to make a low-pitched hissing sound, bang the top very hard with a hammer. If it starts to make a high-pitched hissing sound, get out of the way.'

It also contains photos of customers, scribbled notes about their preferences, and lots of asterisks and scrawled arrows that say 'ask me for more info', or 'that's a long story', or 'remind me to fill you in on this one', in Cherie's tiny, cramped handwriting.

At the very front is an A4-sized print of some kind of fiesta, with names jotted beneath each smiling face. Now, I know my experience in the world of work is limited, but I'm fairly sure that a group shot of the clientele all wearing sombreros and brandishing glasses of tequila isn't part of a normal first-day induction package.

But I'm also starting to realise that 'normal' isn't a word you can use in connection with the Comfort Food Café – or indeed its menu.

There are staples on offer every day, all of which you'd expect to find in most cafés. A limited range of pasta salads, jacket spuds, soups, cakes and muffins, hot and cold drinks, ice creams, sandwiches, paninis, toasties. In other words, the usual suspects.

Most of these won't be a problem. I already know how to make scones and sponges, and I'm a dab hand with a blender. Either Cherie or Willow will be able to help out in the kitchen during really busy periods and during the slacker ones I'll do the waiting on as well as the cooking.

What is proving trickier is the fact that some of the dishes in the file are linked to specific people, with equally specific instructions about their preparation.

Cherie's put together a list of the 'VIP' customers – the ones who come in most days, or most weeks, who she clearly knows well and counts as friends. From what I saw today, high season on sunny days means lots of tourists in addition to the regulars – but the ones Cherie is most concerned with keeping happy are the ones who live nearby and who seem to go towards making up a complex patchwork quilt of a community.

'They're my family, you see, lovey,' she'd said, once we were settled down with glasses of freshly pressed juice and ice-cream sundaes, 'and I'm kind of like their mother hen. Some of these people come here every day. Some of them have nowhere else to go and nobody else to talk to – it's not just about filling their bellies, it's about giving them a bit of company. A cheery word or two. Listening when they want to talk, backing off when they don't.

'Sometimes they might only be here for a fresh cuppa and a slice of carrot cake – but other times… well, other times, they'll have the weight of the world on their shoulders and it's our job to take some of that weight away from them, even if it's only for a minute or two. When they walk back down that hill, I want them to feel better than when they walked up it. That goes for all my customers – but especially this little lot. You take tonight to get acquainted, then we can meet up tomorrow and go through it all a bit more. You'll probably have questions, I reckon.'

She was right, I think, laying the file down on my lap and taking another sip of chilled rosé. I definitely have questions. Like what have I got myself into? And how am I going to remember all of this? I'm not always up to even making myself feel better, and am slightly daunted at the prospect of now being responsible for the wellbeing of what seems like an entire village.

Jimbo is snoring at my feet and the kids are off roaming around smoking crack or playing air hockey or something. Nate's new little footballing friend is here for the whole week, which means he's sorted, and Lizzie met a group of other kids her age at the café earlier. A few of them – with Cherie's permission – have come round this evening, and the last time I saw them they were heading for the swimming pool. Both of my offspring have loyally promised not to leave the Rockery, so for now I have only myself to worry about.

That, I decide, getting up and realising I am slightly wobbly due to drinking half a bottle of wine on my own, is probably more than enough.

I walk back into the house and pull together a tray of sandwiches for me, the kids and anyone else who happens to pass by. Nobody needs a big dinner. We were all well and truly stuffed full of food at the café at lunchtime – barbecue, fresh salad, home-baked breads and lashings of ice cream. I was quite tempted to roll down the hill and back to the car park like a giant egg, but was scared in case I accidentally toppled off the cliff.

The kids had a really good time there. I could tell that Nate did, because he laughed a lot and said things like 'I'm having a really good time'. And I could tell that Lizzie did because she also laughed a lot, but only when she thought I wasn't looking. Seeing her sitting on one of the slanting wooden benches, sun glinting off her golden hair, tentatively chatting to a gang of other teenagers, was one of the better moments I'd had in the last twenty-four hours.

None of them looked like they had gang tattoos – at least nowhere visible – and only a couple had piercings, which is kind of par for the course these days, isn't it? From what I've seen, you're actually more alternative if you *don't* have a piercing or ink. Anyway, she looked happy and that was enough for now.

I'd met Willow, the girl with the pink hair, and been introduced to several other people whose names I didn't remember. I could only hope that eventually, after memorising the file and actually doing the job, I'd start to process things a bit better.

Just as we were about to leave, Matt had turned up. I felt incomprehensibly embarrassed when I saw him emerge at the top of the steps, spotting him way before he saw me.

He was still in the denim shorts, but had added a white T-shirt at least. He gave me a nod as he walked past and took himself off to sit alone in a quiet and shady corner of the open field. He wasn't far from the doggy crèche and several of the dogs clearly recognised him and were poking their muzzles through the fence, trying to get to him.

I noticed him grinning at their antics and also noticed how the grin fell away once he turned back to face people rather than pooches. I also noticed that his glance grazed over me and felt a sudden blush sweep over my cheeks.

I don't usually blush, but something about Matt – and, more specifically, the way I reacted to him – had me unnerved. I made a silent vow to either stop looking at him or at least buy a pair of tinted shades so he wouldn't be able to spot it when I was eyeball-stalking him.

Cherie noticed me blushing, of course. In exactly the same way that she'd noticed me and Matt doing our polite-yet-distant nodding routine. I suspected that Cherie was one of those people who noticed absolutely everything and filed it away in the cavernous corners of her brain.

'He's not in the file yet,' she said, tapping the blue folder on the table in front of us. 'I've not quite got to the bottom of Mr Hunter, the handsomest vet in the county.'

I'd simply nodded again and tried not to choke on my strawberries. Poor Matt. I had the feeling Cherie was intrigued by his mystery and I was glad that I'd already told her everything there was to know about me in my letter. No mystery there, ma'am. No need for the alien mind probe with me.

After lunch, I'd gone with the kids for the promised paddle in the sea, which was cooling and gorgeous and very, very welcome. I'd half expected Lizzie to try and stay out with her new pals, but instead we came to the compromise of them visiting us later on. Cherie, obviously, seemed to know them, or at the very least their parents. One of them, I vaguely recalled, was the son of Scrumpy Joe Jones, who was one of my Comfort Food File VIPs.

By the time we rolled up back to our cottage, we were all warm and mellow and well fed and relaxed. Exactly as I'd hoped we would be on holiday – and certainly the most comfortable with each other than we'd been for a while.

Now, as I've done as much homework as my brain can cope with, and made the butties, and I've finished off the wine, I feel at a bit of a loose end. This is not an uncommon sensation for me. It's one of the reasons I needed to get a job.

There are only so many books to read and TV box sets to watch before the alone-time starts to get to you. Having kids around the house – with all their noise and filth and mess and fun – helps, but it's not enough. And, more to the point, it's not fair for me to expect it to be enough – I want them to live their own lives, worry about their own problems and chase their own dreams. I don't want them feeling responsible for me in any way.

Times like this can be dangerous. Times when they're busy and I'm tipsy and the dog's sleepy. That's when it can creep up on you.

When you've lost your partner in life, it's not the big stuff you necessarily mourn. It's the little stuff. The goodnight cuddles rather than the spectacular sex. The quick chat over a rushed breakfast rather than the romantic three-course meals in a posh restaurant. The casual contact, the taken-for-granted communication, the fact that if you hear a noise in the night, there's someone else to send to investigate.

It's the small stuff that can break you – small stuff like listening to skylarks out in your new back garden and wanting to tell someone how beautiful they sound.

So to avoid any potential emotional hiccups, along with the physical ones, I get the lead and hook Jimbo up. He's so tired he pretends he hasn't noticed, and I have to physically drag him along the wooden floor for a few feet before he gives in and agrees to stand up.

I lock the door behind me – because you can take the girl out of Manchester, etc etc – and walk past the swimming pool. I squint my eyes to try and see through the steamed-up windows, but don't see or hear any teenagers. Which means they've escaped.

I walk down along the path and can't help but have a little nosy at the other cottages we pass. All of them seem to be inhabited by happy families getting ready for their dinner, although at least one contains a teenager leaning out of the bedroom window having a sneaky fag. That cheers me up, in a totally mean-spirited way.

We amble up to the car park and I see that the playground has been colonised by the Teens. Lizzie is on a swing, kicking up dust clouds with her feet every time she scuds downwards, and a boy who I vaguely remember is Scrumpy Joe's son is next to her, also swinging. Two more are hanging upside down from the climbing frame, all dressed in black, like human-sized bats.

I can hear low-level chatter and bursts of laughter and am lulled into a possibly false sense of security as I walk towards them. Lizzie spots me and her eyes narrow slightly as she meets my gaze. I narrow my eyes back at her and hope I've sent some kind of subliminal dominance message that will stop her saying anything rude to me.

They all go quiet as I approach and I'm reminded yet again of how every single generation of teenagers who ever existed was utterly convinced that their parents Don't Understand. That we were all born, fully grown and boring, obsessed with curfews and eating vegetables, our voice boxes pre-loaded with dire warnings about looking twice before you cross the road, not going out with wet hair and avoiding dark short cuts on the way home.

'Hi guys,' I say, keeping my voice neutral. I'm comfortable enough with Lizzie's friends back home and know them well enough to not worry about whether I'm going to mortify my daughter or not – but this is all new. These are potentially summer friends, who will both keep her sane and keep her off my back and I don't want to embarrass her without even knowing I'm doing it.

There are polite murmurs, mumbled greetings and a slight shuffling around as they wait for me to either say something else or leave.

'I've made a load of sandwiches,' I say, working on the basis that teenage boys, at least, always love food. 'And Cherie sent us home with a suitcase full of leftover cupcakes. Come back to the cottage in a while, if you like.'

More murmurs. A few thank yous. A couple of glances at phones – possibly to check the time. It's around seven now and I have no idea how long these kids are allowed to stay out or how they get home. These are countryside rules and they may well be different to the ones we're used to. I only hope none of them are expecting a lift back to the village as I am ever-so-mildly shitfaced. Not enough to fall over or vomit in a bin, but definitely enough to stop me from driving.

I move on towards the games room. It's actually a very pretty summer house and the door is propped open to let the warm evening air in. I poke my head around it and see Nate is in there playing air hockey with the boy whose name I can't quite remember but might be Jacob.

I let them finish their point before I speak – air hockey is a game that requires vast concentration – and then give them the same small, food-based speech as I gave the teenagers. I add to the friend-who-might-be-Jacob that he's welcome too, as long as he tells his mum and dad where he is.

Jimbo and I wander back round to the central lawn and my eyes are drawn to the bigger cottage at the corner. It stands by the main gates and looks out over both the grass and the rear part of the Rockery, where we live.

I walk towards it, planning to pass it on my way back round to Hyacinth, and try very hard not to look in the windows of this particular house. Because this is Black Rose, where Matt lives, and the last thing I need is another brush with the blush patrol.

Obviously, I look anyway. I simply can't help it. I tell myself that it's all right, I've stared in every other window, and there's no reason this one should be any different.

Unfortunately, it's that time of the evening when the light is fading and people decide to turn on their lights. Often, when they turn on their lights, they also decide to close their curtains – probably to stop total strangers gawping at them as they go about their business.

Just as I take my almost-against-my-will peek through the big Black Rose windows, Matt appears, his face framed by the floral curtains he's holding in each of his hands. He stares out at me and our eyes meet. He sees me standing there with the dog. He pauses, then pulls the curtains together with a determined tug, shutting me out.

I experience a sudden rush of humiliation so strong my hands fly to my face, holding my own cheeks as I feel them flame up. Jimbo looks up at me, confused at the jerky movement of the lead and I clench my eyelids tight to squeeze out the bitter tears that have started to sting.

I have no idea why this snub – this tiny snub from someone I've only just met and couldn't care less about – has made me feel so completely and totally awful. The only explanation is that I was already feeling pretty awful, just beneath the surface, and this one rude gesture has stripped away the veneer of 'okay' I was covering it up with.

I start to walk, briskly, past Black Rose, aiming for the safety of Hyacinth and the calm of my own solitude. Jimbo isn't too happy at the uncharacteristic pace and I have to restrain myself from pulling his head along too hard. It's not his fault, I remind myself, that I for some reason feel like a big fat loser from Planet Arsehole.

As we half-jog, half-amble along the path, crunching on the gravel and, in my case, keeping my eyes front and forward as I make my escape, I hear a voice from behind me.

'Laura!' he says. 'Wait up!'

I don't particularly want to 'wait up'. I want to curl up, and wise up, and entirely possibly blow up. But Jimbo hears something different in Matt's voice – he doesn't hear potential embarrassment, he hears the sound of someone who fondles his ears and gazes into his cataracts and lets him lick his face. He plants his paws in the gravel and then follows with the rest of his body. He's fat and solid and determined and impossible to budge.

Short of dropping the lead and making a run for it – which wouldn't be at all dignified – I have no option. I plaster a fake smile on my face, hope my blush has died down and turn around.

'Hi,' he says, as he leans down to scratch Jimbo's head. 'I saw you through the window.'

'Yes,' I reply, with scorching banter.

'And I wondered how you'd been today. And if you wanted to…'

He stands upright and tucks his hands in his pockets. His hair is flopping over his forehead in the gentle breeze and his hazel eyes are yet again fascinated with a spot just over my shoulder. I wouldn't have thought it was humanly possible, but he seems almost as awkward as me.

'… come in for a drink?'

Chapter 12

Black Rose has a different layout from Hyacinth inside. There's a separate kitchen and a dining room with open double doors that leads through to a lounge. The lounge is cosy and feels snug, even to me. Matt automatically bends his head when he walks under certain beams and I suspect he's learned the hard way when to duck and dive.

The windows take up most of one wall and the others are lined with bookshelves, all of them crammed with paperbacks and textbooks and files. There are papers scattered over a small work station, and a closed laptop. I wonder absently if he's been checking out pictures of himself with my bra on his head, but decide he probably hasn't.

There's also a guitar lying across the sofa, as though he was just playing it. I wonder idly if he's a 'Stairway to Heaven' kind of guy or a classical flamenco kind of guy.

Jimbo immediately curls up in a ball in the corner, tucking his head under his tail but leaving one eye poking out so he can watch what's going on, and be alert in case any bacon appears. I am standing up, feeling confused, and wondering why on earth I walked through the door at all.

Matt appears with two cans of Guinness. Not my first choice

of drink, but it's chilled, and if I drink it quickly I can leave. I can stop feeling like a teenager, because really, that's Lizzie's job.

This is, quite obviously, not the first time I've been alone with a man since David died. I was alone with the funeral director on several occasions. There were parent-teacher meetings about Lizzie's eyeliner, with me and Mr Jeffers saucily close in his broom-cupboard office. A whole five minutes with the bloke who came round to read the gas meter that time. And… well, my dad.

As I compile this mental list, I realise that none of those men had given me the nervy, tingly feeling in my tummy that Matt does. Which, in the case of my dad, is clearly fantastic news.

This is new, and therefore frightening, and I don't feel entirely in control of my mind or my body. Both of them, for example, wanted to say no when he asked me in – but somehow, here I am. Hoping I don't spill Guinness on his laptop and wondering how quickly I can drink it without being sick.

'Who's this?' I say, pointing to a framed photo of a dog. It's massive, possibly some kind of Great Dane/Grizzly Bear cross. Behind it is a woman, or at least her legs. Bare, slim, fashionably brown ones.

'That's Nico,' he replies, smiling at the picture in such a genuine way that I immediately know that Nico is the dog, not the girl.

There is no sign of a giant dog roaming anywhere around the cottage, which tells me it's either dead or elsewhere. Maybe with Legs.

'Did you lose him in a custody battle?' I say, before I have time to censor the words coming out of my mouth.

His shoulders stiffen slightly and he takes a good, long pull on his can of Guinness. The room is small, the beamed ceilings are low and I feel like I've hugely overstepped, in his own territory. I prepare to apologise for being such a nosy cow, but he starts to talk before I get the chance.

'Kind of,' he says. 'Although it wasn't quite that simple. Nico was her dog – that's how we met. She brought him to me for his injections when he was a puppy. I suppose our eyes met over a crowded waiting room and the ice was well and truly broken when Nico peed on my leg. We moved in together eventually, but... well.

'Let's just say it didn't work out. As ever with these things, it was complicated. It's one of the reasons I came here, though. I'm covering for the regular village vet. She's off working in South Africa on a sabbatical. It was only supposed to be for a year, so I should be leaving in September.'

'And how do you feel about leaving?' I ask, intrigued by his story and surprised he's told me even a part of it. Maybe I'll be able to give Cherie a run for her money after all.

'I don't know, to be honest. This place has been good for me. It's... special. The place, the people. Cherie and her gang of merry pranksters. They've welcomed me – sometimes a bit too much – and made me feel at home. They've constantly tried to set me up on dates and Cherie's fed me so much cake I must have put on a stone.'

He slaps his midriff and his T-shirt rides up. All I see is perfectly toned muscle, flat beneath bronzed skin. I suspect it's all I'll see for a while.

'Oh God, I'll have to be careful!' I say, meaning it in all kinds of way, but one hundred per cent about the cake. I can't afford to gain an extra stone. I'd have to leave Jeans Town and head for Leggings Land if that happened.

'So... how was your day? How are you finding things?' he asks, obviously keen to move the subject away from his failed relationship, his missing dog and his obesity problem. I can tell, from his carefully neutral tone, that he already knows at least part of my story.

I wonder if Cherie made some kind of announcement about the arrival of the poor old Widow Woman, or even if she photocopied my letter and handed them out to the regulars… I doubt it, but I don't know her well enough to be sure.

'Good!' I say, full of beans and positivity. I've had enough of people feeling sorry for me, and am desperate not to hear pity creeping into this man's voice. Pity makes me feel useless and pathetic and, well, pitiful.

'You caught us at our worst last night,' I add. 'I don't usually scream at the kids or have to chase my own underwear, honest. It had just taken too long to get here and everyone was exhausted. A good night's sleep and a day in the sun has sorted us all out. I'm looking forward to starting work on Tuesday, and getting to know everyone, and… do you mind me asking, Matt, if Cherie has told everyone about me? About my family situation, I mean?'

He shakes his head and gives me a small smile.

'She told me because she knew you'd be arriving here and she wanted you to be met by a friendly face… or me, at least. I'm not the world's best at friendly. I seem to fall into grumpy without even knowing it… and, to answer your question, she didn't hold a meeting in the village hall or anything, but she'll have told Willow about you, and some of the regulars. Does that bother you?'

I ponder that question and ultimately decide that it doesn't.

'No,' I reply, firmly. 'No, not at all. In some ways it's a bit of a relief. It saves me explaining myself to everyone over and over again. People always assume I'm married, and when they inevitably ask about it, it's a bit of a mood-killer telling the whole dead-husband story. They always feel embarrassed and don't know how to react, and usually can't get away fast enough. So no, this will be better.'

I see his gaze wander briefly down to my ring finger, which is, indeed, still graced with both my engagement and wedding rings. He doesn't say anything, though, which is good. He could, of course, have said something along the lines of: 'Maybe they wouldn't assume you were married if you stopped wearing those?'

My mother has actually uttered similar words to me, at around the time she started suggesting I sign up to match.com, and it did not go down well. Matt is obviously made of more sensitive stuff.

'And,' I continue, before the silence has a chance to stretch, 'you were perfectly friendly. I don't think people need to be grinning like idiots twenty-four hours a day to be friendly. I understand the need for the occasional grump, and not everyone can be a social butterfly. Some of us don't want to be, and some of us—'

'Are so out of practice, they've turned into moths,' he finishes for me.

I nod, because I know exactly what he means. If you become socially isolated for any period of time, it's hard to throw yourself back into it. It's easier to stay away from people, to avoid awkward situations, to cocoon yourself in the peace and quiet of your own company. I mean, I don't live in a dark wardrobe and eat holes in clothes, but I get his moth metaphor completely.

The problem with moths, though, is that every now and then they have this crazy urge to fly towards the bright light – even if it's going to sizzle their wings and send them spiralling down to the ground, where they will be eaten by predatory spiders or sucked into a vacuum cleaner.

I find myself staring at Matt, which doesn't surprise me at all, bearing in mind my recent hormonal imbalance, and find him staring back at me, which is more of a surprise. I can't think of a single thing to say and, more importantly perhaps, I don't feel like I need to. We're just two little old moths, chilling out and drinking hideous beer together…

Jimbo helpfully breaks the moment by letting out an almighty fart and then looking around, confused, as though he's wondering where on earth that noise came from. We both laugh – it is impossible not to – and I finally realise that I cannot possibly finish this beer. I decide that if I never drink another Guinness again, I will be happy.

'Would you like another?' he asks, gesturing at the can.

I am halfway considering saying yes, which is weird, when the delicate sound of screeching hell bunnies reaches us from outside. Matt frowns, unsure as to what creatures are emitting such strange other-worldly cries, but I am fairly confident I know.

I pull the curtain back and, sure enough, a gang of bored teenagers is running around out there playing tag. There's a lot of rough and tumble, some kicking and a lot of yelling. It's a bit like the Hunger Games, but hopefully without the weaponry and the big gongy noises announcing that someone is dead.

'Better not,' I say, passing the can back to him and dragging Jimbo back to his reluctant feet. 'In my experience, the only way to stop this kind of thing is with food.'

Chapter 13

The man sitting at a table for two in the window could easily be a hundred years old. His face is deeply tanned and the creases and crevices marking his skin look like the symbols on an ordnance survey map. Piercing blue eyes are looking up at me and he's offering me a walnut-shaded hand to shake.

'Alright, my luvver?' he says, laughter playing around those eyes. 'Feeling joppety-joppety, are 'ee?'

I resist the temptation to slap myself around the ears to clean out the wax and instead I say, 'I'm sorry? I didn't quite catch that.'

'Ignore him!' shouts Cherie from behind the serving counter, where she's sorting cutlery and keeping an amused eye on me.

'He's just trying to get you all betwattled!'

The two of them explode into laughter and I join in, because it's better than standing there looking like even more of an idiot.

'I think he's succeeding,' I reply, much to their amusement.

'Now, what can I get you, Frank?' I ask, praying to God that I've remembered correctly and this is actually Farmer Frank. The man who I've already seen photos of in Cherie's magic file. 'The usual?'

'I daresay that'll do,' Frank replies, his accent curvier than

Jessica Rabbit. 'I'll have a nice bowl of low-fat gluten-free granola and a pint of zider, please.'

He looks deadly serious, but I can hear Cherie sniggering away in the background, and know that this old dog is winding me up. There was no mention of gluten-free or 'zider' on his notes.

'Coming right up,' I say, giving him a quick smile and walking away. I flash Cherie a broad wink as I pass by, just to let her know I'm in on the game, and head for the kitchen.

The kitchen, unlike the rest of the café, is all sharp edges and shiny chrome and mod cons. It's a thing of beauty and I'm already looking forward to experimenting in here – Cherie's given me the go-ahead to try out a few ideas, and I'm planning a foray into the exciting world of ice-cream milk-shakes as my first try-out.

My kids love them flavoured with their favourite chocolate bars, and you can get them all over Manchester – made with Flakes or Dime or Bounty or Mars Bar. There's nothing like them on the menu and I think the tourists, at least, will love them. Especially if we go all right-on and use 'locally sourced' milk, which Cherie does anyway.

My current job, however, doesn't involve any experimentation at all. It involves sticking several lovely fat rashers of bacon on the griddle and letting it sizzle until the crispy bits are almost black. Then I carve two extra-thick slices of the white bread that Cherie's just pulled out of the oven and slather it with home-made chutney. The bacon goes on next, still juicy, and I can't help but inhale appreciatively as all the aromas blend together.

Before I started the bacon, I found Frank's mug on the shelf – it's the size of a bucket and bears the motto 'Farmers do it in tractors' – and poured hot tea over a bag, which I've left in now for so long that it looks more like treacle. This, I recall from the notes, is exactly how Frank likes his breakfast – the breakfast he comes in for every single morning.

I slice the sandwich in two, give the tea bag a final stir and I am ready. Ready to serve my first-ever customer at the Comfort Food Café. I feel a moment of sheer excitement and am secretly a little bit triumphant inside. It might just be a bacon buttie, but it means a lot to me.

I bear the plate and the mug back out, and put them down in front of Frank.

'One bowl of low-fat gluten-free granola and a mug of finest scrumpy for you, Frank,' I say, giving him a little mock curtsey.

He salutes me with one of his gnarled hands and gestures for me to sit down with him. I wonder if I should check with Cherie, but realise that's a daft thing to even consider. There are no other customers right now. Everything I need to prepare is under control and when the lunchtime rush comes these few minutes of peace will be a distant memory.

So I sit down and within seconds Cherie arrives, plonking a mug of coffee in front of me, giving Frank an affectionate pat on the shoulder before she takes herself off again.

'So,' he says, between bites, 'it's Manchester, is it?'

'It is,' I reply, sipping my drink and wondering what stories this man has to tell. He looks fit as a fiddle, his forearms still corded with lean muscle, his eyes still clear and sharp, his hair silver-white but still very much attached to his head.

'This is grand, lass,' he adds, in a more than passable Northern accent. I laugh and ask him if he's a secret Mancunian.

'Oh no, my love, Dorset born and bred is I. But I was stationed up in Cheshire for a while during my National Service. Had some proper good times, we did. This is before I met my wife, mind. I've had a soft spot for you Northern girls ever since…'

'I'll have to watch myself,' I say, imagining him young and handsome and charming, and not finding it all that difficult. 'I can see you're a bit of a Jack the Lad. Is that tea all right for you?

Cherie said strong, but I wasn't sure exactly how strong she meant.'

'This's perfect, don't be worrying. I've had the same breakfast for the last fifty years, you know – it's the key to a happy marriage.'

'What?' I say, suspicious that he's about to wind me up again. 'Bacon?'

'That, and knowing when to keep your mouth shut. When I first wed my Bessy she was a terrible cook. Burned the bacon every day. Made tea so thick the spoon stood up. But I loved her more than I loved my stomach, so I never complained. And because I never complained, I got the same thing, every single day. Even on the day she passed.

'And after she passed, year and a half ago now, I realised that I'd gotten so used to it, I felt hungry all day if I went without. I tried making it myself, but, well… I'm supposing it takes a special kind of person to burn bacon in exactly the right way. So I started coming here instead and Cherie looks after me.'

'She seems to look after a lot of people,' I reply, biting my lip to stop myself from getting too emotional about his story. Because it's exactly that – *his* story – not mine, and I need to stop letting my own feelings piggy-back on to everyone else's. I'll be exhausted by the end of the day if I do that. I have been known to cry at an especially cute Andrex puppy, never mind tales of lifelong love.

'That she does. Keeps her out of trouble, you know. Needs to stay active, that one, or she'll get into mischief. I know the kind. And I reckon I see another one heading right towards us…'

I look up, and see Lizzie heading in our direction. I'd expected a battle, but both her and Nate were happy to come in with me this morning. They've been down by the beach searching for fossils, trying to skim stones and generally larking around. I suspect that the detente has now come to an end and Nate is possibly buried up to his neck in sand as the tide comes in.

'Have you buried your brother up to his neck in sand so he'll drown when the tide comes in?' I ask, taking in her yellow-coated hands and the damp patches on the knees of her skinny jeans.

'What?' she asks, in mock horror. 'Of course not! And if I did, I'd have only packed the sand in loosely, so he could wriggle out like a little worm…'

I'm not a hundred per cent sure what all of that means and suspect the only way to know for sure is to go and peer down at the cove from the terrace at the front of the café, which always makes me feel a bit dizzy and a bit weird.

Lizzie sits down with us and switches on one of her huge, gorgeous smiles, purely for Farmer Frank's benefit. She holds out her hand for him to shake and properly introduces herself. The two of them chat for a moment and I notice the twinkle in Frank's blue eyes get even more twinkly as he lays on the thick Dorset 'I be jus' a simple country bumpkin, me' accent that he seems to slip in and out of as suits.

Lizzie is explaining her alleged school project to him and asking if it's okay to take his picture and use it in her online journal.

'It's kind of like a diary,' she says, obviously trying to translate it into Old Person, 'but using computers. Phones really, but these days phones are actually just teeny tiny computers that let us do everything those massive ancient ones used to let people do.'

'Oh, I see,' says Frank, eyes wide in apparent amazement at the state of technology in the twenty-first century. I've only known Frank for half an hour, but it's half an hour longer than Lizzie. I sit back and sip my coffee, trying not to smirk as I wait for the punch line.

'So, what do you think, Frank?' asks Lizzie, buzzing with enthusiasm now. And, to be honest, I can see why – Frank has the sort of brilliant character face that would photograph amazingly. Her energy is high and I start to think that perhaps she's genuinely getting into this, rather than just using it as a way to let off steam.

'Weeeeeeell,' replies Frank, drawling out the word until there are about ten syllables in it, and rubbing his chin in confusion. 'To be honest, young 'un, it depends on what photo-sharing system you're using. Are you going Instagram? Tumblr? Have you got a Pinterest board set up? And have you ever tried Flickr? Or are you going to be Snapchatting my devilishly handsome face to all your friends?'

I knew this – or something similar – was coming, but I still spit coffee out of my mouth at the expression on my daughter's face. Seriously, she couldn't have looked more taken aback if the table had started talking to her.

To give her credit, she recovers quickly. One annoyed sideways glance at me and she's back up and running.

'Instagram. Not completely public, so I can add you as a follower and you can see what I'm posting, if you like. To be honest, it started as a bit of a laugh and a way to stay in touch with my mates back home, but I'm taking it a bit more seriously now. Do you have grandkids, Frank?'

'How did you guess, my lovely? I do – and they live in Australia. I like to stay up with the trends an' all, or they'll be thinking I'm just some old duffer, won't they?'

Lizzie has the good grace to look vaguely apologetic before standing up and announcing that she has to leave now.

'Why?' I ask, feeling slightly suspicious.

'Because the tide really is coming in and I need to check that Nate's managed to get out of his sand prison before he dies…'

She jogs off and out of the door and I resist the urge to chase after her and check on my baby boy. I need to give him a little bit of independence. Plus I can see from the terrace without him even knowing.

'That should be a good picture, eh?' says Frank, leaning back in his chair. 'The little lad with his head poking up, maybe a crab on top?'

I'm suddenly not feeling quite so laid back and scrape my chair on the floor as I jump to my feet and dash towards the terrace. There's one of those mounted telescopes out there, which thankfully doesn't need coins, and I twist it around, scanning and scoping until I finally see Nate.

He's not buried in the sand. He's throwing sticks for Jimbo, who is ignoring them. There are no crabs slowly and agonisingly eating his nose and he looks perfectly happy. I see Lizzie join him and see her phone come out to take photos. Or at least I think that's what she's doing, until there is the ding of a text landing.

I pull mine out of my jeans pocket and open the message.

'U R A SUCKER!!!' it says, with a few hilariously amused emojis draped after the exclamation marks.

WEEK 2

In which I am desperate for a nice long nap, almost get killed by an espresso machine, discover I am crap at yoga and lose one of my shoes in a wheat field…

Chapter 14

By the end of my first week at the Comfort Food Café, I am several things. The main one, I decide, as I wearily finish stacking the dishwasher at Hyacinth, is exhausted.

I would never in a million years diss the role of a stay-at-home mum. I've done it and it's not easy. It's not as though most of us are living like the Real Housewives of Wherever, going to expensive lunches and organising charity events and scheduling our botox sessions around our kids' piano recitals.

Most of us are very, very busy, keeping the house running, making sure the kids are all right, ensuring that hubbie has everything he needs and anticipating everyone else's requirements before they've even thought of them.

It is, alone, a full-time job, and I'd always looked on in wonder at those women who had demanding careers as well. The ones I'd see occasionally at school events, who not only seemed to have perfectly well-adjusted children, but could also wear business suits and heels and clearly have Very Important Jobs.

Now, after my first week as a working mother, my feelings have moved away from wonder and more towards 'how-the-fuck-do-they-do-it-and-stay-sane?' Excuse my French, but I am genuinely amazed and awed.

It's not as if working flexible hours in a café is even a Very Important Job. I'm never going to be named in the New Year's Honours for my services to blueberry muffins, am I? Plus my kids are almost at the stage where they look after themselves; it's not as though I have a labour-intensive toddler or an inquisitive five-year-old. I have kids who, in other cultures, would be living in their own homes by now. In comparison to many working women, I have it easy.

So I feel like an absolute wusser for saying it, but I am *knackered.* I have worked every day – sometimes a full shift from eight until three, other times far less than that – and I am wiped out in every conceivable way.

My feet feel like they've been buried in concrete, my lower back needs a TENS machine and my eyes are closing almost against my will. I've kept going on adrenaline and sheer bloody-mindedness, but now I've finally stopped and made the mistake of sitting down, the fatigue is crippling me and I fear I may never leave the sofa. I may not even have the energy to drag myself up to bed.

It is 8.45pm on a Sunday. Tomorrow is my day off. I am planning to celebrate with a wild sleeping party, where I get my snooze on, ride the crazy snore train and generally have it large. The kids seem to feel the same as they have both gone to bed already. Nate, I suspect, will actually be asleep. Lizzie will be doing something that involves her phone. They're both wiped out as well.

I don't think they've had this much fresh air for a very long time. Cherie found them both bikes to borrow and they've been tootling around, enjoying the kind of freedom that they never get at home. Lizzie's hair is much less EMO-groomed, which is wonderful to see, and both of them have permanently rosy cheeks.

Not that we're suddenly living in some *Swallows and Amazons* idyll. The kids around here do the same stuff as kids anywhere. They hang around in small gangs, trying to give the impression that they're cool. The big difference here is that there is a lot less to do – the nearest cinema is in Lyme Regis; a bowling alley is likely to include grass and older people in white, the fleshpots of Weymouth and Poole are miles away and getting around is a lot less easy without Manchester's convenient tram stops.

In the city there's so much – water parks and giant shopping centres and laser quest and multiplexes and interactive museums and massive indoor ski slopes and dry bars and enormous hangars full of trampolines.

Here, there's none of that – and yet they seem less bored. Everything's less structured and less organised, and every day I've seen them doing things I know they (I mean Lizzie) would have sneered at not so long ago. Like scrambling around the rock pools. Cycling all the way up hills just so they can freewheel back down. Jumping over waves. Climbing the edges of the cliffs. Eating ice-cream in the sun. Trying to hand-feed seagulls, then leaping back in terror when one swoops down. Fossil-hunting. Just… being.

A few of Lizzie's new friends have younger siblings, so Nate has people to play with too, and even when they are just trying to look cool, they're generally doing it in the fresh air rather than in a deep, dark dungeon full of flashing video games and beeping noises.

I'm not making out it's as straightforward as City Bad and Countryside Good, because I'm not enough of an idiot to think life here, outside the glories of the summer season where the weather is fine and tourists are spending, is easy. But for the kids, it seems a lot simpler.

Now, after being convinced she was going to die of boredom, Lizzie is blossoming, and I can't describe how happy that makes me feel.

Happy, however, doesn't apply to the way my body feels as I ease myself down onto the sofa and reach for the phone. I've not properly spoken to Becca for days, despite the odd text, and have promised her that I'll ring tonight. I'm half looking forward to it, half wanting to pretend I forgot.

'Hello?' I say, as she picks up. There is loud music in the background and the sound of laughter. I'm hoping she's having an impromptu house party and I can get off lightly.

'Hey, sis!' she says, obviously walking away from the source of the noise as it gets quieter. I hear a door close and the background shenanigans fade to a manageable hum.

'Are you having a party?' I ask, needlessly.

'Kind of. Just a few of the guys – we thought we'd drop some acid and watch *Charlie and the Chocolate Factory*, see just how weird it actually gets.'

'Really?' I ask, hoping she's joking. Also wondering if she means the original, or the definitely-more-scary Johnny Depp version. I wouldn't fancy seeing that evil dentist while I was on hallucinogens.

'Nah,' she replies. 'Just having a pizza with the girls. We might watch *Spice World* later, though, which is pretty trippy. So, how's you? I like the look of that Cherie woman, and what's going on with you and the old farmer dude? Have you dumped Matt the Hot Vet for him? And those lemon drizzle loaves looked amazing, I could practically smell them from here...'

Ah. Instagram strikes again. I wonder why I even bother communicating with words when Lizzie seems perfectly capable of doing it in pictures.

'Farmer Frank is almost eighty,' I answer.

'And? Don't knock it 'til you've tried it.'

Frank is still a handsome man, fit as a whippet, but I shudder slightly at the thought of 'trying it'.

'Plus he's gay,' I add, in the vain hope that it will shut her up.

'What?? No way! Lizzie didn't put that on her captions!'

'Because I just made it up to stop you encouraging me to shag someone older than granddad. I have no idea if he's gay or not, but the fact that he was married for donkeys' years suggests otherwise.'

'It could have been a lavender marriage. He could be the only gay in the village, for all you know.'

'Well, it is a small village, Becca, so maybe. I've not done a sexual orientation survey yet so I can't say for sure.'

Becca is quiet for a moment and I realise she is looking through Lizzie's photo collection. I'm used to this now and don't freak out at all. Much.

'So, who else have you met? There's a photo here of you sitting with a middle-aged woman who has helmet hair – you know, like one of those Playmobil people? In fact, there are lots of pictures of you sitting down chatting to people. Are you sure you actually work there? Have you secretly been fired and now you're just hanging around in an embarrassingly needy way, scaring the locals?'

'Thanks for the vote of confidence, and no. It's difficult to explain… Cherie, well, she's unusual. I suspect she sneaks outside for a spliff every now and then, for a start.'

'I like her already.'

'I thought you would. Anyway, that's not the only way she's unusual. She seems to run the café as much for the people as for any profit. I don't know if she's even bothered about money – nobody is entirely sure about her past, but she seems to own both the café and the Rockery and she never does that usual small-business-owner thing of fretting when the place is quiet or moaning about the taxman.

'She welcomes the tourists, but she also has this little group of locals… her VIPs, she calls them. I don't know all their stories – that's a work in progress – but I do know what they like to eat. That's why it's called the Comfort Food Café.'

'I'm not sure I get it. It'll be the acid kicking in. Doesn't the name just mean they serve nice cake?' she asks.

'No. Well, we do serve nice cake. But each of these people has their own version of comfort food, and it's very often not even on the menu. She keeps it all in stock, though, so they can always have what they want. And each of their comfort meals seems to have a story that goes with it. Like Farmer Frank, the hot old bloke – almost-burnt bacon butty, white bread and tea so strong a builder would think twice. Every day, for his breakfast – the same breakfast he's had ever since he got married.

'His wife died a while back, after they'd been married for, like, forty-six years. So now he has it at the Comfort Food Café instead. And the lady with the Playmobil hair? That's Ivy Wellkettle.'

'She is NOT called Ivy Wellkettle!'

'She is, honest. Well, she runs the local pharmacy and she's so nice. Dead quiet, really reserved, obviously clever. But she's also a bit sad because she's been a single mum ever since her daughter Sophie was born and now Sophie's gone off to Durham to study medicine. It's the hols, but the daughter's off backpacking for a month with her new mates now. She never says it, but you can tell Ivy's lonely. She talks about Sophie all the time, her whole world literally revolves around her – and now she's gone, she still eats their favourite lunch, the one they used to eat together when Sophie was a kid.'

'She's a pharmacist, so I'm guessing something healthy?' asks Becca, sounding genuinely interested.

'No. Fishfinger butties. Cherie always has a few boxes of Captain Birdseye's finest in the freezer just for Ivy. And Pot Noodles for Surfer Sam.'

'Okay, now I think you're winding me up. Surfer Sam? That sounds like a kids' cartoon about a lovable slacker!'

'Yeah. I know. I only met him yesterday. You should see if he's on the pics, though I'm not sure Lizzie's aware of him yet. He's not actually a surfer – not a professional one anyway – but he kind of looks like one. You'd like him. He's a coastal ranger or something, really outdoorsy, dead funny.'

'What does he look like? Can't see any photos… I'll have to put a special request in…'

'He's a bit of a hunk, as our mother would say. Got that tall, lean thing going on that you always seem to go for. Anyway, his comfort food seems to be Pot Noodles. Chicken-and-mushroom flavour. He's from this massive family in Ireland – he has, like, seven siblings or something – and he misses them like mad. Couldn't wait to get away from them, but now he misses them. They used to have Pot Noodles for a treat every weekend, so now that's what he has here, every Saturday.'

'Okay,' replies Becca, sounding amused. 'I get it. Cherie's like some old rock-chick mother figure for everyone? Who else have you met?'

'Well I've met loads, but I don't know all their stories. That's why I'm sitting with people a lot on the photos. Cherie encourages me to, so I can get to know them as people, not just as orders. Like, I know that Scrumpy Joe Jones, despite his name, has a real yearning for home-made almond biscotti, which we make from scratch, but I don't know why.

'And I know that Edie May takes home an extra portion of everything she eats for her 'fiancé', although she's got to be knocking ninety.

'It's all… very mysterious. The way the whole place works. Cherie seems to be universally adored, and she's one of the most intuitive people I've ever met – even when complete strangers come in, she just seems to know what they want. Same with our kids – they came in for lunch the other day and she brought them both a jacket spud, Lizzie's with beans, Nate's with cheese. Which is weird, because—'

'That's what David used to make them,' she finishes for me, sounding sadder than I do. 'I know. That's what they always asked for, that time when I stayed with you.'

Ah. Now I understand her tone. 'That time I stayed with you' is code. It's code for a period of our lives so horrendous, so unspeakably awful, that we can't even properly talk about it. It was about four weeks after David's funeral and, to put it bluntly, I lost the plot.

Suddenly, just as everything was starting to get back to normal – ashes scattered, kids back at school, condolence cards taken down – I had a mini-breakdown. I woke up one day and simply couldn't get out of bed. All I could do was stare at the ceiling and sniff the pillowcase next to me, and lie very, very still. I couldn't even cry.

My poor children – bless them so much – didn't know what else to do, so they called their Auntie Becca. She came round and for a week she was their mum. She was kind of my mum as well, sitting on the edge of the bed and chatting to me even when I didn't answer; putting the TV on even though I didn't seem to be watching; putting up with me even when I hadn't showered for four days. Doing the school run. Cooking the tea. Having video nights with the kids to make it more fun for them. Walking Jimbo. She did it all and I will be forever grateful.

David, God love him, had many skills – but cooking was not one of them. On the occasions when I wasn't around to make the tea, or on special events like Mother's Day, when I was given the day 'off', he would always make jacket spuds. Because even he couldn't go wrong with that. As a result, it became his signature dish – and one the kids always associated with their dad.

'Yes,' I reply simply. I can't apologise to Becca for that week, not again. I had no control over it, it wasn't a matter of choice – and I know from experience that she'll come down on me like a ton of bricks if I even try to say thank you.

'So. Moving on and not-so-subtly changing the subject,' she says, 'what about the vet? There's a picture of you with him here. What is that? Some kind of soup? Is that his comfort food? Because that's boring.'

'He doesn't seem to have a particular comfort food. He just likes things that are healthy and home-cooked. The weather's been a bit cooler the last few days, so I've been experimenting with soup.'

'You crazy bitch, you,' she interjects. I ignore her.

'So that one is probably Matt eating red pepper and lentil soup. Which is about as intimate as it gets, sorry to disappoint you. I did go into his cottage for a drink, though.'

'When you say "a drink", is that a euphemism for wild monkey sex?'

'No. It's a euphemism for a can of Guinness.'

'Oh. Well. Don't worry. In my experience, enough cans of Guinness can lead on to the wild monkey sex eventually. What's his story, anyway? He's gorgeous. He's a vet. If he was on *Take Me Out*, everyone would leave their lights on. Why's he single? What's wrong with him?'

'There's nothing wrong with him!' I say, and notice a certain snappish quality to my voice. I immediately regret it, as I know that Becca will notice too.

I expect her to start making some quip about me feeling protective towards him, or mocking me for caring, but instead there is just a moment's silence.

'Well,' she says eventually. 'Good. And I really don't need to ask how the kids are doing – I can see for myself. They both look so happy. I know Lizzie was mooning over that Callum boy from her class before she left, but that all seems to have been forgotten. Who is this Josh kid anyway?'

It's my turn for silence as I wrack my brains to remember if Lizzie has ever mentioned a 'Callum boy' to me before now. Nope,

I decide, she definitely hasn't. I bite back a small surge of bitterness at the fact that she's confided in Becca and not me, and remind myself that as long as she's telling someone, that's all that matters.

Besides, I don't blame her – I'm fairly sure Becca has a better understanding of normal teenage crushes than I do. I only had the one and it lasted the whole of my life.

'Erm, he's nice enough,' I reply, recalling a dark-eyed, lanky sixteen-year-old who seems to wear a beanie cap twenty-four hours a day, no matter how hot it is. 'Very polite. Eats a lot of sandwiches, doesn't like cheese. The son of Scrumpy Joe, actually, the almond biscotti man.'

Becca laughs out loud at my descriptions, which is always worrying.

'Have you just come across a photo of me with my face covered in raspberry jam?' I ask, quickly, assuming the worst.

'What? No! Why? Have you been covering your face in raspberry jam? Is it some kind of rural beauty ritual?'

'No,' I respond, relieved. 'I was working on some Victoria sponges for the cake trays and I couldn't get the jar open. We had a bit of a tussle for a while and I did that thing Dad always used to where he kind of squeezed the lid in the doorframe? Except the whole thing just exploded and… well, I'm glad it wasn't caught on film for posterity. I never know where she's lurking these days. It was easier when she was locked in her room reading that Morrissey autobiography you bought her.'

Becca laughs some more and I let her. Fair game.

'No,' she says, once she's stopped giggling. 'I wasn't laughing at that – I am now, though. What I was laughing at was the fact that you seem to have started to think about everybody you meet in terms of food. Joe likes biscotti. Josh hates cheese. It's like they're all just taste buds on legs.'

She's right, I think. I have started to do that – or maybe I always did. Most mums keep an extensive mental list of food likes and dislikes. There'll always be one child who won't eat tomatoes, or another who hates mayonnaise; and they'll have a friend who's allergic to nuts, and another who can't tolerate eggs, and a husband who only likes his spuds mashed not boiled… we carry it all around with us, logged and filed for future culinary use.

Maybe Cherie's notes are just an extension of that kind of mum logic. Which, when I think of it like that, means that my family suddenly got a whole lot bigger.

For some reason, this random leap in logic makes me happy. I chat to Becca for a few more minutes and I go to bed feeling lighthearted and optimistic and warm. My feet might ache and my back might be breaking, but for once, as I say goodnight to photographic David, I have a smile on my face.

Chapter 15

Cherie has now decided that I am more than capable of running the café by myself during its quieter periods. This means, generally speaking, early morning and later in the afternoon.

It will give her more time, she says, for 'having lovely lie-ins', and for planning the big annual summer party that she throws every year for Frank's birthday – this was the origin of the Mexican tequila photos in my file, and as it's Frank's eightieth, it's going to be a special one this year. I, she assures me, am completely up to the job.

That she has come to this conclusion after only ten days seems to me to be a very foolhardy and reckless way to run a business. It especially seems that way when I've only been in for half an hour, and already seem on the verge of blowing the whole place up.

I arrived at half-seven, reluctantly leaving Nate and Lizzie at home in bed. I feel slightly guilty about this, even though they begged me to, and promised to be really sensible and not use the cooker or have fistfights or push each other down the stairs. Lizzie, I remind myself, is fifteen soon, and Nate's thirteenth won't be far behind. Plus, they're in a complex of family holiday cottages packed with responsible grown-ups, Matt is on the corner if they need urgent help, and they have a killer Labrador for protection.

There are also, I'm told sarcastically by Lizzie, these fantastic new inventions called mobile phones.

Still, I feel guilty. Also, nervous. In case one of them hurts themselves. Or someone tries to break in. Or there's some kind of natural disaster – an earthquake maybe? And they've been left Home Alone by their evil, selfish mum.

Perhaps this vague, nagging anxiety is part of why I don't notice at first when the espresso machine starts to make a low-pitched humming sound. As my own brain is already making a low-pitched humming sound, casting my beloved children in a variety of disturbing imaginary scenarios, I simply block the real-life one out of my consciousness.

By the time I do notice, I've sliced tomatoes and washed lettuce, put the fresh milk away in the fridge, made pancake batter and put the spudders in the old-fashioned jacket-potato oven ready for later. I'm zesting lemons to make a dressing for the couscous and cucumber salad when I start to wonder if I've got tinnitus.

I drop the lemons and dash towards the coffee machine, grabbing the hammer that is kept hanging from a little chain next to it for just such occasions. I've seen Cherie do this a few times, so know what to expect. I whack the top of the casing and a big jet of steam shoots out. I anticipate it and do a swift sideways tilt to avoid getting it in the face. My eyes water a little, though, so I wipe them clear, realising, too late, that my fingers are essentially covered in citric acid from the fruit.

I wait for the machine to calm down and feel even more angsty when it doesn't. I squint at it from between my, by now, sore and streaming eyelids and whack it once more with the hammer.

More steam and then an even higher-pitched sound. I recall very clearly my instructions for just this kind of event – 'get out of the way'. So I nip around to the other side of the serving counter, far out of reach, and duck beneath a table.

I'm not quite sure why I duck beneath a table. Perhaps because I was thinking about earthquakes just a few minutes ago.

It does, however, allow me to have a much better view of Farmer Frank's legs when he walks in at about ten past eight. He always wears heavy-gauge cords, no matter what the weather, and a checked shirt. He pauses and makes an impressed-sounding whistling noise when he sees the steaming espresso machine rattling away.

'Hey Frank!' I shout, making myself heard over the racket. He leans down and pops his head under the table to give me a confused look.

'What are you doing under there?' he asks. I feel that is a silly question, as there is clearly something very dangerous going on on the other side of the counter.

'Hiding in case I blow the place up,' I reply, crawling out so I'm on knee-level with him. 'It said in the instructions Cherie gave me to get out of the way if it makes that noise, so that's what I'm doing. I'm too young to die in a freak coffee-maker accident.'

It sounds silly when I say it out loud, but my belief in freak accidents has increased massively over the last couple of years. I don't walk around paranoid expecting planes to fall on my head, but when the opportunity for random harm presents itself, I assume the worst.

'Right. Well, our Cherie sometimes misses the obvious,' he says, walking calmly over to the counter, scooting under it and pulling out the plug. Immediately, the sound starts to fade, and the steam visibly thins.

Ah. It all seems so simple now.

I use the table to help myself back to my feet and grab a napkin to wipe the lemon-induced tears from my eyes. It's obviously going to be one of those days.

As soon as I think it, I start to worry about Lizzie and Nate even more. I bite my lip so hard it bleeds and wonder if Cherie would hate me if I went and woke her up. She lives in a little apartment above the café, in an attic with sloping eaves and the most amazing views out over the coast. I've only been up there once and was too busy looking out of the dormer windows to notice much else.

Frank is now steadily dismantling the espresso machine and wiping various unidentified metal parts down with a gingham tea towel. I am guessing that he's done this before, as he seems to know exactly what he's doing.

'She'll be all right and proper again soon, she will,' he says, and I notice the drawl of his accent is thicker as he concentrates on his task. I wonder why he's decided the machine is a 'she', but fear the answer I'll get if I ask.

I nod and smile, but don't reply. I am feeling superstitious now and genuinely considering driving back to the Rockery to check on the kids.

'You all right, my love?' asks Frank, pausing in his job. 'You're looking a bit peaky there. Plus you've not made my tea yet and I'm fair parched, here.'

He's right. I'm being rude, as well as daft. I go and switch the hot-water boiler on and start his bacon.

'Sorry Frank,' I say. 'I've left Lizzie and Nate at the cottage and I suddenly got a bit worried about them. Just being silly, I know.'

'Well,' he replies, his blue eyes shining with sympathy, 'that's a mother's job, ain't it? Worrying about her little ones? You can't fight human nature. Should've seen my Bessy when our Peter was emigrating to Perth. You've never seen a woman fuss so. It was almost as though he was moving to the other side of the world…'

I smile and carry on with the butty-making and reflect on how nice it is to have this kind of gentle humour in my life. I know there won't be another customer for a good twenty minutes or so, so I make myself a coffee – instant, just in case – and join Frank again once I've burned his bacon for him. He finishes with his chore and we sit down together.

Before he tucks in, he fishes his flashy looking iPhone from his trouser pocket and scoots through a few screens. He does this a lot more than you'd expect for an almost octogenarian. During one of our regular morning chats he explained it away by convincing me that he'd installed hidden CCTV cameras around the fields of his farm and had a few on collars around his cows' necks as well, just to check up on his staff. I believed him for about thirty seconds as well.

I knew he was proud of his son, who worked as a surgeon in the land of Oz, but I also suspected that he missed having family to help around the farm, the way he and his late brother had with his father and grandfather. He constantly mocked the 'whipper-snappers' who laboured for him, calling them all manner of work-shy names, even though he seemed genuinely fond of them.

'Checking up on the loplollies?' I say, using a bit of Dorset slang Willow taught me over the weekend.

'Oh, very good!' replies Frank, his eyes disappearing into his wrinkles as he grins. 'We'll make a Dorset lass of you, yet… but no, I'll be seeing those good-for-nothings soon enough. I'm just looking at your Lizzie's Instagram account, if you must know. Thought it might put your mind at rest. This was fifteen minutes ago.'

He turns the screen towards me and I lean closer to get a clearer look.

Nate is sitting at the dining table holding a spoon and eating a huge, sloppy bowl of Sugar Puffs. Somehow, they've also managed to get Jimbo to sit on a chair at the dining table as well, as though he's a human being, and his wide black head is almost buried in an even bigger bowl of Sugar Puffs.

I sigh and roll my eyes. Sugar Puffs are not on the recommended food list for dogs and there is going to be an almighty mess when I get home. But… well, they all look fine. I was, naturally enough, worrying over nothing.

Frank, I can see, is struggling not to laugh. I throw a packet of sugar at his head just to make myself feel better.

'While your phone's out, show me some pictures of your son and grandchildren,' I say, hoping he agrees this time. He's always found an excuse before, but this morning we have bonded over my incompetence, so it's different.

He raises his eyebrows in concentration, fiddles with the screen and turns it to face me. I see a photo of the man I presume to be Peter, his son, at some kind of graduation ceremony, his arms around the shoulders of a boy and girl, smiles on all their faces. Peter looks to be in mid-forties, and the kids are maybe sixteen.

'This one's a bit out of date,' he says, gazing at it and grinning. 'Erin and Luke are eighteen now.'

'Twins?' I ask.

'How did you guess?' he replies, giving me a cheeky wink.

'They're gorgeous,' I answer, because they are. His son looks exactly like I imagine Frank did when he was younger – blonde, fit, handsome and suntanned. The twins are equally blonde and both look like Olympic athletes. 'When did you last see them?'

'Oh, now, not for a while. I went there with Bessy when the twins were ten, I think, and they came here for the funeral and stayed for a few weeks. Great kids, they are. Loved having them around. Brought the old farmhouse back to life, it did. Truth be told, Laura, I was as sad about them going back as I was about Bessy. Fair broke my heart waving them off at the airport, pretending I was fine and dandy.'

I lay my hand on his and give it a little squeeze. His blue eyes are shining with what looks suspiciously like tears and there's a catch in his voice I've never heard before. Loneliness I think, for possibly the millionth time, is one of the worst human conditions of all.

It can eat you up from the inside out before anybody even notices there's a problem, killing you softly with no outward symptoms. I wonder how many people are suffering, hiding it all beneath their brave faces?

Well, I can't do anything for most people. But I can do something for Frank. I can give him bacon butties and builders' tea, and as much company as he needs.

'Why don't you invite them over?' I say. 'Or fly out to them? I know you're busy with the farm, but there must be ways around it.'

'I reckon so,' he answers, squeezing my fingers in return. 'But I don't want to be a burden to him, you see. I was a hundred per cent behind him when he left – I knew it might mean the end of having the farm in our family, but it's a hard way to make a living, especially these days. No life for a bright young lad like him. And being a surgeon? Well, that takes some beating, doesn't it? I suppose I thought he'd… come home. Work in a hospital here. I know Bessy always did. She wanted more babbies, we both did, but we were never blessed.

'No, he's made a life for himself, and it's a good one. So when we talk, or we Skype, me and him and the kids, I make like everything is fine. I talk about how well the farm is doing and how good the lads are, and how busy I am. I make him think I'm as happy as that there Larry, whoever he may be. And most of the time, I am. You've just caught me at a low point. I always feel vulnerable after I've dismantled the espresso machine. It brings out my feminine side.'

And with that, I know the period of sharing has passed and

Frank is back to his usual jovial, mocking self. I shake my head in resignation and finish up my coffee. We usually get our first tourists in at around nine – normally walkers doing one of the coastal trails – and I need to check everything's ready. I usually make the most of the lull to start preparing the sandwich plates for lunch, and today I'm doing a fruit-salad meringue with fresh cream to add to the usual desserts.

As I stand up, planning to leave Frank to finish his breakfast in peace, the door opens and a woman I've never seen before walks in. This in itself wouldn't be unusual, apart from the fact that she is barefoot and wearing a pair of pale-blue pyjamas. Her grey hair is almost as curly as mine, but wild and windswept, as though she's been out on the cliffs. I glance at her feet and see that they are grubby enough for that to be true.

She looks nice and calm, though, and gives me and Frank a small bow as she walks towards us. I'm about to ask her if I can help when she starts moving tables and chairs around to clear a space on the floor. Frank meets my eyes, giving me a gentle shake of the head as I move towards her. I follow his lead and let her carry on.

'Mornin', Lynnie,' he says, standing up and walking in her direction. He helps her clear even more space, which seems to relax her completely. She turns to face us both and announces: 'The class will begin in five minutes. Please spend that time trying to clear your minds of everyday concerns and preparing to unite your body, soul and energy.'

She sits down on the floor, in full lotus position, and closes her eyes. I make the most of the pause to pull a full-on WTF face at Frank, who gestures for me to go with him through to the kitchen. I silently follow him and hope nobody else turns up looking for a bacon toastie while Lady Buddah is at work.

'It's Willow's mum,' he whispers, as soon as we are out of

earshot. 'It happens occasionally. She… I want to say escapes, but that makes the poor love sound like she's in jail… she slips away, out of the house.'

Jesus, I think, recalling what I know about Willow's mum – mainly that she has early-onset Alzheimer's – and realising that she has indeed probably been wandering around the cliffs barefoot. Willow lives on the edge of the village and walks ten minutes along the footpaths to get here. I actually shudder a little bit as I consider what could have happened to her along the way.

'I'm going to go upstairs and get Cherie,' says Frank, 'and she'll call Willow. You need to stay down here and go to her yoga class, all right? It's what she used to do for a living, amongst other things. Sometimes she just thinks she still does. It's best to go along with it if it's doing no harm.'

I sneak a glance at the incredibly lithe woman twisted around herself with complete ease and suspect that perhaps trying to keep up with her might cause me more harm than her.

I nod and walk back into the main room. Her eyes snap open wide as I arrive and she raises her eyebrows at me.

'Frank has had to… erm… go to the toilet!' I say, silently apologising to my farming friend for the undignified excuse.

Lynnie simply nods and stands up on her feet in one supple movement. Whatever is going on in her brain, her body is still in perfect condition.

'We will begin with the sun salutation…'

I try and follow her moves, I really do. But I'm just not that bendy, truth be told, and my boobs seem to get in the way of everything. She's very patient, coming round and prodding my pigeon, working on my warrior and tweaking my tree.

It's when I'm in plank position and thinking I'd quite like to die, that the troops finally arrive in the form of Cherie and Frank. They've taken ages and I'm half tempted to ask them what the hell they've been doing, but I don't think zen master Lynnie would approve.

Cherie looks a bit ruffled and her hair is loose, flying all over her broad shoulders and flowing down her back. Her eyes are red and puffy and I realise that Frank has had to wake her up from what looks like an extremely sound sleep.

After I've taken in that much, my head collapses down onto the floor and I lie there panting for a few moments. I hate the plank more than I've ever hated anything in my entire life.

Cherie and Frank join in with our impromptu class and I silently resent them for the fact that they have arrived in time for child pose and missed all the hard stuff. While I'm lying there, arms stretched out and forehead on the floor, I hear the door opening and the sound of footsteps. I know, without needing to turn around, that I now have an audience. I am hoping it's just Willow.

Lynnie's hypnotically calm voice has us all lying on our backs like corpses and she tries to take us on a mental walk down a rose-tree-lined path to a thatched cottage on a sunlit day. Sadly, I am prevented from enjoying this particular meander through my happy place by the fact that both my children and Matt the Vet are standing watching me, with varying levels of amusement.

The kids are wide-eyed and barely holding it together, and I have the sinking sensation that they've been there a little while. Lizzie, let's face it, will have taken photos of my arse wobbling around in the air and will post them online with some suitably sarcastic comment.

Matt, who probably knows who Lynnie is and has some idea of what is going on, isn't actually laughing out loud, but there is a crinkle around his eyes that seems to suggest that internally he's wetting himself.

I am wondering whether I can take all three of them out with a single karate chop when Willow finally arrives, looking as flustered as you'd imagine.

Willow is about six foot tall and built like a supermodel. She's extremely pretty, but offsets being too attractive by dying her shaggy shoulder-length hair a neon shade of pink, having a nose ring and sporting some mysterious-looking Celtic tattoos on her arms. It's probably the only way she avoids getting stopped by talent scouts in the supermarket.

Right now, she looks terrible. Her eyes are practically superglued together, her hair looks like a matted carpet and there is a look on her face that is both frantic and exhausted. I can only imagine how caring for her mother drains her energies and am reminded yet again that absolutely everybody has their problems. Not that you'd ever guess from Willow's personality – always upbeat, always positive, always laughing and joking.

Lizzie kind of hero-worships her, which I can understand, and Cherie adores her. Her mum, however, is currently looking at her with nothing more than polite interest.

Willow plasters a smile on her face and walks over towards the older lady. Lynnie smiles back, but shows no sign at all that she recognises her daughter. Willow pauses and I see the pain flicker across her face. She quickly masks it and joins her mother.

'Hi Mum,' she says, reaching out and gently stroking her arm. Lynnie looks confused, but not distressed. 'It's me, Willow.'

'I have a daughter called Willow,' she replies, 'what a coincidence!'

This is obviously something that has played out before and Willow has come prepared. She pulls a small envelope out of her bag and I see it is filled with photos.

'Can I show you these?' she asks, quietly, calmly. 'It won't take long, I promise.'

Lynnie looks to check her watch and frowns when she realises she isn't wearing one. She looks back up at Willow and touches a tangled strand of bright-pink hair with one finger.

'I like your hair,' she says, finally. 'But I can't stay long. I've left my children at home, and I need to get back to check on them.'

The two of them sit down at the table and I watch as Willow pulls out the pictures and arranges them in front of her. When she's finished, there is a timeline of photos – her as a baby, cradled in her mother's arms; as a toddler; as a gap-toothed girl with pigtails holding her mum's hand outside the school gates. As a wild-looking teenager, both of them with a Border terrier on their lap. And finally, one of her as she is now – standing with her mum outside their house.

I see the memories start to seep back into Lynnie's mind, and the way that Willow chews her lip as the light dawns, and the way their fingers creep together across the tabletop to intertwine. And then I have to turn away.

It is one of the most heartbreaking things that I have ever seen, and I suddenly feel like I am intruding on something so tragic and so private, like an emotional voyeur. I love my kids so much I sometimes think I might explode and even the thought of them going through what Willow is going through now is enough to bring sudden, stinging tears to my eyes.

I turn away and blink the tears back, and look at the people in front of me. Cherie, still sleepy, ample bottom perched on one of the tabletops. Frank, next to her, shaking his head in sympathy. Lizzie and Nate, who even at their age realise that this has stopped being funny and turned into something serious. And finally Matt, who is the only one looking back at me and not at Willow and Lynnie.

He sees that I'm upset and he gives me the sweetest smile, such a gentle curve of his lips, that it's barely there. Our eyes stay locked for a second and I feel like burrowing my head in his chest and having a big, soggy cry.

Instead, I say: 'Right. I have pancakes. And I have Nutella. Who thinks that's a good idea?'

Every single hand in the room goes up, including Willow and Lynnie's.

Looks like it's the perfect time for comfort food.

Chapter 16

I pack the last slice of white-chocolate and pistachio cheesecake into a tin-foil box and carefully seal the cardboard lid around it.

The cake took me a lot of time, and even more willpower, to make and I'm not entirely sure where that final piece is going.

Edie May is one of my favourite customers and she is pretty much a complete mystery to me as yet. It's been a busy day and we've sold out of everything other than a few chicken avocado sandwiches and the leftovers from the barbecue.

The weather, after a brief and gloomy hiccup, is back to being glorious and Willow has been running the grill all afternoon.

The scene outside the café is very similar to the first time we visited, but to me it all feels very different. I don't feel like a visitor any more, for a start. Despite only having been here for a fortnight, I already know a lot of people, by face if not by name.

I know where everything is; I have mastered the cash register, and even have my very own chalkboard for my ice-cream milk-shake specials. I also have a reasonably good grip on Cherie's VIPs.

I know that Scrumpy Joe Jones, for example, had an Italian grandmother and spent several childhood summers in Pisa. Hence the biscotti.

I know that Surfer Sam doesn't just eat Pot Noodles, he also likes an Irish potato dish called colcannon that I've learned how to cook for him.

Bit by bit, the mysteries of the comfort food have been revealing themselves to me in all their tasty and emotional glory.

But one of the things that I still don't know is why Edie May always takes an extra portion of food home with her, and how she can possibly have a fiancé.

Edie comes in two or three times a week and has a tiny suntanned face that looks like a raisin. Her hair is white and closely cropped to her head and she's approximately the height of an Oompah Loompah.

She's talked openly about the party she had for her ninetieth birthday, but she still seems to live independently with the support of nothing more than a crook-handled walking stick. Every time she comes in, she chats about the weather and what she watched on television the night before, and about the goings-on in the village. She loves fruit loaf and gingerbread and reading large-print romances from the library and Anton du Beke off *Strictly Come Dancing* ('such a gentleman!').

Edie has the more pronounced West Country accent that a few of the older folk have, but she says 'fiancé' with a great deal of care and style, enunciating every syllable until it sounds like a foreign word. Which I suppose it is, now I come to think about it.

Today, after the barbecue crowds have cleared and Willow and Cherie are cleaning up, she's still here, perched on a stool next to the counter, walking stick propped up next to her, entertaining me with a big long speech about farm animal behaviour and what it tells us to expect in the weather.

'An' that,' she says, triumphantly, 'is why you should always take your brolly when they're all packed together, like – because sheep in a huddle, tomorrow a puddle!'

She waves one bony finger at me as she announces this piece

of wisdom, as though warning me against disagreeing with her. As if I'd dare. I hand over the boxed cake and ask her if she wants anything else. She eats like a bird when she's here, pecking away at tiny amounts of food, so I always secretly hope the extra portions she takes back for her 'fiancé' are actually for her.

'No, my love, that'll do me just grand, it will. My fiancé will be right happy with that!'

She carefully stands on her feet and tucks the box away in the backpack she always wears. The rest of her looks like pure old lady – sensible walking shoes, tights even when it's hot, a beige cardigan – but the backpack is fluorescent orange and has a VANS logo on it. She's very proud of it and told me Cherie bought it for her for Christmas – I suspect as much to provide her with a bit of hi-vis protection as anything else.

I wave goodbye and watch as she takes small but steady steps towards the door, neon backpack over her frail shoulders.

Cherie passes by, a bin bag full of rubbish in her hands, and pauses in front of me. Her hair is in a giant wispy bun, so big you'd assume there was a donut beneath it if you hadn't seen it all loose. Her skin is glowing from the heat and from the effort and her cheeks are rosy on top of the tan.

'You all right, Laura?' she asks. 'You look a bit… what's the word? Wistful?'

'It's Edie,' I reply, reaching out and taking the bag from her so I can take it through to the bins at the back. 'She always has that effect on me. What is her story, Cherie? With the others, I've kind of found out myself, bit by bit, just from getting to know them over the last couple of weeks. But with Edie, I never want to ask.'

Cherie grabs a bottle of cloudy lemonade from the fridge and plonks herself down on the stool that Edie has just vacated.

'You're right not to, darling. She's a robust woman, but only in certain ways. Edie got engaged when she was twenty, to a local lad called Bert. Or Bernard – there's not really anybody left who remembers it that clearly, even that old codger Frank was too young to have paid much attention. Anyway, the story has it they were deep in love and he asked her to marry him while he was on leave from the navy.

'This was around 1944, something like that. Well, again, I'm not sure of the details, but he never came home from the war. His ship was sunk by a U-boat somewhere in the Atlantic. We lost a lot of local lads, like everywhere else back then – my parents told some terrible stories of those 'regret to inform you' telegrams getting delivered in the village, everyone looking through their windows praying the knock didn't land on their front door. Awful.

'Anyway, the love of Edie's life never came home, and neither did a body – and by all accounts, it broke her heart. She never accepted he was dead and, over time, became more and more convinced he did come home after all.

'She carried on through her life, working at the library for most of it, looking after her parents when they got old, but she never let go of the idea that Bert was still with her. Most of the time she's completely normal, but occasionally, if you catch her at home on a quiet night, you'll hear her talking to him. And as you know, she takes home food for him too. To her, he's as real as day and has been for as long as I've known her.'

I am a bit stunned by this story and stay quiet for a moment or two while I try to process it. Essentially, Cherie is telling me that Edie became unhinged by grief as a young woman, which I completely understand, and has lived for decades with the delusion that her dead fiancé is waiting for her at home. And that he likes pistachio and white-chocolate cheesecake.

'Shouldn't she have had… I don't know, some help?' I ask, frowning. 'Been taken to see a doctor? Had some therapy or bereavement counselling?'

'Bereavement counselling! No such thing during a war, I suspect, Laura. Everyone's just expected to keep calm and carry on, aren't they? And as for therapy, my love... well, you're young. You don't understand the times we're talking about here. This was the dark ages in comparison to now. She might have been shipped off to an asylum and the therapy may well have involved electrodes getting attached to her forehead!

'No, that's not the way it was handled at all and I can completely see why. We all talk about mental health problems now, or at least more than we used to back then. There's not the same shame or stigma attached to it, people are generally less ignorant. But back then? They would have said she was tapped in the head, and she'd have probably spent her whole life in an asylum, at least until everyone was kicked out of them and expected to fend for themselves.

'Instead, she stayed here. Everyone looked after her – not that she really needed it, mind. You've met her – she's wonderful. If I'm anywhere near that active when I'm her age, I'll be tickled pink. She worked her whole life, she cared for her family, she still helps out on the village committees. She organised summer fayres at the school and drove the mobile library van round to the farms. After she retired she carried on working as a volunteer. She doesn't just function, she contributes.'

'But she's...' I struggle to find a word that I feel comfortable using, one that doesn't sound too awful, but Cherie doesn't give me the chance.

'Mad as a hatter? Well, aren't we all, in our own way? I know I've had my moments and I'm betting you have as well, my sweet.'

I stay silent and reluctantly recall all the times I've lain in a snivelling heap sniffing a dead man's dressing gown, or talked to a photo and imagined it replied, or sat in the passenger seat of a car holding an imaginary hand, or called David's now-defunct mobile phone, still somehow hoping he might answer, or send me a text from heaven. Yep. I've definitely had my moments – but they haven't lasted a lifetime. Not yet, at least.

Still, it's enough to make me realise I'm in no position to judge. So what if Edie May takes cake home for her long-dead fiancé? It's not as though she's doing anybody any harm. And, in fact, she's led a full and useful life, is fit as a fiddle, and still walking up this hill at ninety.

So I stop disagreeing and simply nod. Things are done differently here and that's not necessarily a bad thing. I get it.

'I hope she eats the spare cake herself,' I eventually say, signifying my getting of it, and start to wipe down the counters. There's nothing much left in the chiller cabinet, so I decide that today would be a good time to clean out the shelves. I start to pull the salad containers free and head towards the kitchen.

'Don't get too carried away with all that housekeeping, my love!' shouts Cherie as I retreat. 'And don't you forget we're going out tonight!'

Hah, I think, as I scrape the leftovers into the food recycling bin – Frank collects it 'for his porkers' – as if I'm going to be allowed to.

Because while a whole village has quite happily allowed Edie May to indulge her delusional solitude for an entire lifetime, I have been here for just two weeks and am already being dragged out from under my rock.

Tonight, I am going out for dinner. A proper, grown-up dinner, at a restaurant, wearing a dress and everything. It is the first time I've done this for quite some time, unless you count those family-friendly pubs where you get a free colouring sheet and some blunt pencils with your burger and chips.

Willow is babysitting – or 'coming round to hang out', as we have phrased it to Lizzie – and I will be joining Cherie, Frank and Matt at an Italian place in Lyme Regis.

It is only the presence of the first two names that is stopping me from freaking out completely.

Chapter 17

'I like that dress,' says Lizzie, as I walk downstairs and into the living room. I automatically turn around to see who she's talking to and realise that it's me.

'Um... thanks?' I reply. 'I've had it for ages. Wait... were you being sarcastic and I didn't notice?'

'Mum! You don't have to always be so suspicious!' she replies, pulling out her phone and raising her eyebrows at me. I strike a somewhat awkward pose and she takes the shot.

'Come on, ballbag,' she says to her brother, who is staring at the TV as though he's never seen *Top Gear* before. I am about to reprimand her for swearing when she holds up one hand and adds, 'It's an old Dorset word, Mum. It's a term of endearment.'

I remain completely unconvinced of the truth of this statement, but am amused enough by her antics that I let it slide. Nate is dragged to his bare feet and he comes and squeezes in for a Lizzie-directed selfie. Her direction mainly consists of telling me my hair's too big to fit in, but eventually it's done. She even shows me the end product and it is lovely.

'You look really pretty, Mum,' says Nate, before he slouches back down on the sofa. He spent the afternoon at Frank's farm helping out – in return for a tenner – and is exhausted. And smelly.

I'm pretty sure Frank didn't really need the help, but Nate was keen to go and see the place, and it kept them both out of trouble. Plus that tenner means five less ice-creams for Mum to buy, let's face it.

Lizzie has also been demonstrating an enterprising streak, working with Scrumpy Joe's son Josh at the family 'cider cave'. I'm a little worried about my teenage daughter working in a cider cave, but have been reassured by both Joe and everyone who knows him that there is no way he will allow Lizzie to get high on her own supply. According to him it's because he's a responsible adult and according to everyone else it's because he's too mean to give anything away for free.

She's been handing out his marketing leaflets to tourists and helping them sort stock. She's also been murmuring about his 'lack of online presence' for a couple of days now, so I wouldn't be surprised if poor Joe gets dragged kicking and screaming out of his cave and into the twenty-first century sometime soon, whether he likes it or not.

'Yes, you do look pretty,' adds Lizzie, reaching out to tuck my hair behind my ear. My hair is crazy and there is no controlling it. 'Where are you going again? And who are you going with? And when will you be home? And how will you be getting home? And are you sure you have some credit on your phone?'

I open my mouth to answer her before realising that she actually knows all of this already, she's just messing with my head by giving me the same speech I usually give her.

'Ha ha,' I say, checking my bag for essentials – cashcard, lipstick, phone, packet of Rennies. Always best to be prepared for an antacid emergency.

There is a knock on the door and Lizzie opens it to find Willow on the doorstep. I feel guilty having her here babysitting, knowing as I do that she rarely gets a night away from her duties at home.

She works at the café and cleans the cottages for Cherie, and seems to spend the rest of her time with her mum. When she has a night away from all that, she should really be spending it out with friends or having a rave, or even just down the Horse and Rider in the village.

'Yo!' she says jauntily, giving me a salute as she walks through, pink hair bouncing on slender shoulders. She is dressed like some kind of space punk from the future and I realise she reminds me of Milla Jovovich in *The Fifth Element*. Her elderly Border terrier, Bella Swan, scoots past us and into the living room.

Bella Swan is something of a canine femme fatale and Jimbo immediately gets up on creaky legs and comes over to lick her ears. She endures it, then wanders off to curl up on the dog bed that was previously his.

'I have both *Zoolander* and *Dodgeball* on DVD,' says Willow, as she passes me. 'Ben and Jerry's ice cream in my bag and I will call you if there are any problems at all. No, I don't mind doing this, no, you don't need to thank me yet again, and naturally I will feel free to help myself to anything in your fridge.'

As I have yet to utter a word or ask a single question, that's a pretty comprehensive reply. I wrack my brains to come up with something to add, but fail.

'All right. Thanks. Again.'

She gives me a hug and heads through to the living room. She knocks Nate's feet off the sofa and plonks herself down, scratching Jimbo's head with her foot. Lizzie appears from the kitchen with three dishes and spoons and, without even asking, puts the first movie into the DVD player.

I stand there looking at them, dogs and humans all splayed in various positions around the room and wonder if it would be all right for me to stay there as well. The curtains are closed, the lights are off and it all looks very… cosy. Very safe. Very comfortable. I'd much rather lurk in the background here or have an early night than go out for dinner. In fact, I'd probably rather sit on a pissed-off porcupine than go out for dinner, truth be told.

I'm very much enjoying my time in Dorset. I'm making new friends, I'm learning new skills and I'm gaining experience that will make my CV look much better when I get back to the real world and go job-hunting in Manchester. The kids are having all kinds of fun, haven't uttered the words 'I'm bored' once since they got here and look glowing and healthy from all their time outdoors. Even Jimbo's having a good time, or he is when he's awake, anyway.

Crazy as this plan sounded when I first came up with it, it's working. It's working for all of us, in its own way. David, I know, would give me a huge thumbs-up and be super-proud of what I'd done. And he'd be pleased, I hope, at the way we're all changing and growing – not forgetting him, but learning how to live better without him.

I still think about him every day. Probably every hour. But it is less with quiet desperation and more with affection and gratitude. Gratitude that we ever had him in our lives at all – I've said it before, and as I'm quite a predictable person I'll probably say it again, but I do feel lucky to have had that kind of love. To have known that kind of closeness to another human being, to have shared that kind of connection for so long.

It was precious and it will always be cherished, and he will always be part of me. But bit by bit, day by busy day, I am feeling stronger. More able to treasure the past, more able to deal with the present, more able to imagine a future. The David-substitute dressing gown has stayed under the pillow most nights and I've found myself asking WWDD much less often. Instead, I'm trying to plough my own path and find my own way of doing things. To focus more on WW 'I' D instead.

All of that is good. Better than good – it's excellent. I definitely feel more confident and a lot less isolated, and a lot less sorry for myself. Sharing the lives and stories of Cherie's VIPs has really helped on that front – technically, of course, I always knew I wasn't the only person in the world to have suffered a personal tragedy.

I know it's a big, sometimes ugly, world out there. But in my world – the world of me and David and our friends and family – I was always the centre of attention, the star of the misery show. The poor little widow, struggling to adapt to life as a single parent.

Here, without that pressure, I feel more free to be just one more person in a crowd. One more person with a story to tell and pain to cope with, and challenges ahead – but not the *only* person.

Here, I feel accepted for who I am now – messy and uncertain, as that may be – rather than seen as a fragile creature to be watched over and worried for. I feel like more of a grown-up. Nobody here really knew the 'old' me, or ever saw me at my lowest – they don't judge, or prod, they just accept. It's unbelievably refreshing and, after two weeks of it, I feel so much more relaxed.

Or at least I did, until now. Because now, I am wearing a nice strappy green sundress that shows a bit of cleavage, and I have applied make-up, and I have product on my hair and I have sprayed my neck and shoulders with perfume. I am going out with what, on the surface, is simply a group of my new friends, but is now starting to feel worryingly like some kind of double date.

Perhaps, if I was going out with Frank and Cherie and one of the other men we know, it wouldn't feel like that.

But we are going out with Matt, and Matt makes me feel confused. We have become friendly, over the last two weeks, in a wary and cautious way. Viewing it from the outside, I suspect we look like two slightly wounded animals circling each other, trying to find safe footing.

He may be big and brawny on the outside, but he treats me with a kind of gentle, reserved kindness that makes me feel appreciated and respected and also a bit befuddled. I am new to having close male friends – close friends at all, if I'm honest – and I'm not at all sure what the rules are.

I have helped him with the gardening, simply because I enjoy the feel of being outside in the sun, working in nature. He has helped me by keeping an eye on the kids and giving them a lift into the village in the mornings. Nate is learning to play the guitar with him and has mastered the opening chords to 'Yellow Submarine'.

We have shared some pleasant and completely non-committal chats. He's given Jimbo a new lease of life and he's displayed some pretty awesome footballing skills in impromptu kickabouts with Nate and the other kids down at the beach. I've found myself making an extra portion of dinner and sending it over to him on a foil-covered plate, and he's always returned the said plate, washed and dried.

We have made small steps into each other's lives, and though I spend more time with Cherie, and have more lengthy conversations with Frank, Matt has still somehow become a big part of my Dorset life.

Becca, when I talk to her, is now careful to not push too hard – I think she suspects there is something there, something delicate that is trying to grow and bud, and that her usual heavy-handed approach might destroy it before it has a chance to blossom.

I have no idea if she is right. Or if I even want her to be right. I do know that when I am with Matt, I feel both comfortable and nervous – but nervous in a thrilling, tingling, kind of delicious way.

When I catch a glimpse of him – at the café, around the Rockery, in the village – my breath stutters and I blush a little, and I find that I automatically hold my tummy in a bit. And if I happen to see him walking past the window on his way to or from the swimming pool, I lie down on the floor and hide – because I would simply find it very embarrassing to talk to him with so few clothes on.

I suspect I am acting like a sixteen-year-old virgin and don't know quite what to do about it. I suppose, though, that I don't actually need to do anything about it. In a few more weeks, we will be packing up and driving away from this place, back to Manchester and back to our real lives. I'll probably have to get him to help me with the roofbox, and after that it'll all be over.

I feel a slump in my mood coming on at that thought, so I snap out of it and do a final face-check in the hallway mirror. I try and smooth my hair down, but that is impossible. I add a slick of lipgloss, touch up my mascara and blow myself a kiss in an attempt to lighten my spirits.

'Bye! Love you, kids!' I shout as I leave. I am completely ignored, which is probably a good sign. Willow is the only one who responds. She waves one blue-fingernailed hand at me and replies, 'Love you too!'

I smile as I close the door behind me and crunch my way along the gravel path to meet Matt. I feel a little like a child who is going to call for a friend, but a child who is pretending to be an adult, dressing up in her mum's wedge-heeled sandals.

By the time I arrive at Black Rose, I have several chunks of gravel stuck under my sole of my feet, and have to lean on his wall and shake them out before I knock on the door.

He pre-empts me and the door opens just as I am balancing on one leg waving my sandal around in the air. He looks at me, looks at the sandal and grins.

'Gravel foot?' he asks, closing the door behind him.

'Yes,' I reply, elegantly hopping around before I manage to get it back on again. 'I imagine that's a common Dorset condition.'

'Indeed,' he replies, 'closely related to pebble toe, which you can catch down at the beach. Are you ready?'

'Why, don't I look ready?'

He meets my eyes and I feel the dreaded blush beginning. I realise, as the words leave my mouth, that it sounds like I'm fishing for compliments. And maybe, I ponder, I am. It's been a long time.

Matt himself is wearing dark jeans and a pale-blue shirt that is moulded to his shoulders and biceps, a few buttons undone at the collar and golden skin peeking out. His chestnut hair is still very slightly damp from the shower, and his eyes… well, his eyes are carrying out exactly the same kind of assessment of me that I've just made of him.

His gaze flickers up from my high heels, past my bare legs, pausing slightly as he journeys past the not-usually-on-display cleavage, and to my now-surely-beetroot face. It's the first time a man has looked at me like that in years and I feel like I am actually having sex, or at least some pretty good foreplay.

'You look beautiful,' he says simply. 'I hope Lizzie took a photo.'

'Of course she did,' I answer, grateful to talk about something else. 'She takes a photo of everything. Should we wait out on the road for Frank or will he drive into the car park?'

'Ah,' Matt replies, a small frown developing.

"Ah' what? What does 'ah' mean?' I ask, frowning back.

'Frank's not coming. He texted me earlier to say he had a migraine. And Cherie called ten minutes after that to say her stomach was off. I thought they'd let you know as well…'

I feel my eyes widen and my mouth open in shock. The absolute bastards. I know exactly what they're doing and I don't appreciate it. Cherie's made a few comments about Matt before now and I've always deflected them – I have no idea what I even think about Matt and my non-existent love life myself and I certainly don't want anybody else interfering.

'You know what's going on, don't you?' I say, hands on hips, feeling a bit belligerent at being manipulated.

'Well,' Matt replies, doing the looking-over-my-shoulder thing again. 'I think I'd have to be brain dead not to. And honestly? I don't mind. Let them have their fun. They're probably down the Horse and Rider having a pint together and congratulating themselves on being such good matchmakers. Cherie's tried getting me out on dates with pretty much every single woman within a fifty mile radius before now, and the only thing that surprises me about this scenario is how long it's taken.'

I feel slightly deflated at the thought of being the latest in a long line of ladies that Cherie has essentially pimped out to Matt. I don't know why – seconds ago I was angry about being pimped out at all. Now I'm upset I'm not special. FFS, as Becca might say. It's all very confusing. I'm thinking that if I go home now, there might still be some Ben and Jerry's left.

'The difference is,' Matt adds, bringing his gaze back to mine and looking at me very directly, 'that I didn't actually go on any of those dates.'

'Oh,' I say, lamely. It's hard to think straight with him looking like he does, and with his hazel eyes meeting mine, and with the smell of some very luscious aftershave reaching my nostrils, and with the fact that every time he moves, the cotton of his shirt clings a little tighter to his torso. It's like being in some kind of sensory fun house.

'None of them?' I add.

'None of them. I always preferred staying at home, playing my guitar and being mysterious and moody. But I'd quite like to go on this one. Assuming you're not about to run back to Hyacinth as fast as those heels will take you.'

There's a little half-smile on his face now, a slight sideways tilt of his lips, as though he knows exactly what I'm thinking. If he's as nervous as I am, he's not showing it, which in its own way helps to calm me down as well.

I mean, what am I getting all breathless about anyway? I can say no. Or I could go and have a meal with a friend. It's no big deal, I tell myself, unless I turn it into one – no need for drama at all.

I turn my face up to his, and smile back.

'All right,' I say. 'I'll come, even if it's just to avoid another brush with gravel foot.'

Chapter 18

I was going to say that it's hard to explain exactly how I found myself in this position, but it's actually not. It can all be explained with one little word: alcohol.

I am lying on my back in a field of wheat. Stalks of the stuff are gently swaying around me and I am staring up at the most incredible night sky I've ever seen. There are no streetlights around here and the stars are crisp and clear and crystalline, glittering jewels embedded in a purple blanket.

I hear the occasional hoot of an owl, the distant moo of a cow and every now and then a rustling sound in the undergrowth. I don't feel jumpy, though, not like I did that first night we arrived. I'm much more experienced these days – practically a country bumpkin myself. Plus, I'm really very drunk and would most likely laugh in the face of a zombie scarecrow apocalypse right now.

The fact that Matt is lying beside me, and that our fingers are loosely twined together between us, is probably also helping.

'I feel completely emasculated,' he says, sounding horrified. 'That was one of the most humiliating experiences of my entire life.'

'Don't worry about it,' I reply, reassuringly. 'These things happen. I'm impressed you lasted as long as you did.'

'But I'm supposed to be a man! And nothing like that has ever happened to me before!'

'Look,' I reply, between giggles, 'it's no big deal. I told you you wouldn't be able to give me a piggy back all the way home. I think you managed about half a mile, though, which is bloody good. I'm not exactly a featherweight. And it's my fault for wearing the stupid sandals anyway.'

'That's true. They did look nice, though. Shame we've lost one.'

'I know. I may bring the kids here tomorrow and send out a search party.'

'Hmmm,' he replies, thinking it over. 'But then you'd have to explain why you were lying in a wheat field with no shoes on. I'm no expert, but I'm thinking that's not a normal mum-thing to do.'

Damn him, I think. He may have a point. I mean, it's not as though I've done anything wrong. But I know how I'd react if Lizzie came home plastered, covered in grass and minus one shoe. I'm fairly sure that will occur at some time in the not-so-distant future and I can only hope that I'm kind to her when it does and remember how easy it is for these things to happen.

Matt and I had decided not to go to dinner in Lyme Regis after all. We didn't see the point in trekking all that way when neither of us was even that hungry. And in my case, I suppose I was wanting to stay closer to home.

So we cancelled the reservation – which, funnily enough, we discovered had only been made for two anyway – and did the sensible thing. We went to the pub.

We drove to a village about three miles inland, called Battercombe, and found a cosy corner in the beer garden. To start with, we were going to just have a couple, get some bar food and leave. I had it in my slightly panicked brain that I could still be tucked up in bed by 10pm.

But somehow, it just didn't work out like that. Matt came back from the bar with a pint of the dreaded Guinness for him and a lager for me, with two bags of crisps clenched between his teeth.

'They stopped serving food half an hour ago,' he said, after he'd dropped the packets down on the table. 'This is the best I could do.'

To be fair, they were posh crisps – the kind that has sea salt on them instead of the normal salt – but I don't suppose they did much of a job of lining our stomachs. I, for sure, was a bit nervous, and probably drank quicker than I normally would. In fact, I'd finished my pint before Matt, who raised his eyebrows at me and asked if I wanted another.

'Just the one,' I'd replied, convinced that I would stop there, that Matt was driving and I wouldn't become the embarrassing drunk person who repeats their stories over and over again to the bored and resentful sober person.

When I finished the second one, also in record time, Matt asked, again, if I'd like another.

'No thanks,' I said, 'you're driving.'

'Umm... yes. But you're not. Being drunk isn't a contagious disease. I'll be okay.'

'Thank you, but no. I don't want to carry on drinking if you're not.'

'Scared of what you might let slip?' he said, giving me that little half-smile that always made me feel a bit funny inside.

'Exactly,' I replied. 'I wouldn't want you to find out about my secret life as an undercover inspector for the British Vets' Association.'

He threw his head back and laughed and his face was half in shade, half in the dying sunlight, and all I wanted to do was reach out and touch his hair and see if it felt as soft as it looked.

'Listen,' he said, draining his Guinness with one more gulp. 'I know this isn't what you planned for tonight. I know you probably feel as resistant to Cherie's evil plots as I do. But I'm enjoying myself and I think you are.

'Neither of us is exactly the type to be at the centre of the social whirl, and I'm sure we both have good reason for that. Still, this is… nice. If you like, I could join you for another drink. I'll leave the car here and we could try and get a taxi back. Though I warn you that might not be easy – there only seems to be one cab driver in the whole area. So we could end up walking home.'

'I don't think I could in these heels,' I said, 'especially if I have much more to drink.'

Part of me wanted to go home now and settle in for the night. The other part of me – the part that had drunk two pints and put make-up on and felt a bit feisty – wanted to stay out to play. I was willing to use the heels as an excuse if Matt was.

'Don't worry,' he replied, grinning, 'I can always give you a piggy back.'

From that point on, we drank and talked and drank and talked and drank some more. We ate several bags of posh crisps and mixed it up with some dry roasted peanuts, but it probably wasn't enough.

We were both careful to avoid any subjects that could fall under the heading of Big, Serious or Important, and instead focused on things we were comfortable with. Cherie and Frank and whether we should pay them back by fixing *them* up on a date; the best places to take the kids fossil-hunting; what Budbury was like in the winter; his home town in Shropshire; my sister in Manchester; his time at uni in Liverpool; my time on hen nights in Liverpool; dogs, dogs and dogs.

Eventually – I'd say about five pints in – I realised that a, I was sloshed and b, I was well and truly relaxed in Matt's company. I'm usually more of a listener than a talker and I suspect he is too, but somehow we made it work. There was never a gap in the conversation, never an awkward silence, and never a point where I found myself wishing I was back at the cottage.

In fact, for the first time in what felt like forever, I was enjoying myself as a grown-up woman in the company of an attractive grown-up man. Willow had texted me earlier to say everything was fine and that Hansel was so hot right now, so I wasn't even stressing about the kids for once.

Sadly, all good things come to an end – and all good pubs ring their bells for last orders. Truth be told, it was probably an excellent thing that they did. Matt wasn't quite as hammered as me – I'm guessing he's used to drinking pints more than I am, plus is at least a foot taller – but neither of us was up to spelling Mississippi or walking in an especially straight line.

We had no luck getting a taxi and the one person left in the pub who offered us a lift seemed even more drunk than us, so we politely refused. That left a long walk home, luckily most of it downhill.

I started well and made good initial progress following a tip that Becca had once given me – when inebriated and facing a long walk, sing 'The Grand Old Duke of York' in your head and it makes you march faster.

It completely works and I eventually shared my secret by singing it out loud instead. Matt joined in and we positively flew for the first part of the journey.

'The Grand Old Duke of York', though – and probably his ten thousand men as well – never attempted to march while wearing four-inch wedges, I'm guessing. I don't think they'd have been winning many battles that way, because marching in heels bloody well hurts.

After a while, I took the sandals off and walked barefoot, carrying them instead. That kind of thing always seems like a good idea when you've had a few, doesn't it? The roads were quiet and if there was a car heading towards us, you could see its lights ages in advance, so there was no danger there.

The roads were, however, not the smooth, even pavements of the city. They were rough and bumpy and strewn with all kinds of natural litter – seeds and berries and twigs and even some piles of horse poo, which I luckily spotted before the evening took a very dark turn.

After that near miss, Matt decided that it would be a good plan if he had his go at walking barefoot, while I wore his shoes. That was a bit of a non-starter, though, as I'm a five and his Timberlands were a size twelve. I just stood in them, unable to actually move as I was laughing so much.

The piggy-back came next and it's a testament to how tipsy I'd become that I ever agreed to such a thing. Like most women of my age who've popped out a couple of sproglets, I'm a bit conscious of my weight. The scales tell me I'm still within normal limits for my height – just about – but I am far from toned.

The concept of climbing onto a man's back, wrapping my legs around his waist and allowing him to carry me down a dark country lane is not one I would entertain under normal circumstances.

These, however, were not normal circumstances – and that is how we made the next part of our journey back to the Rockery. Eventually, after staggering down a particularly steep section of hill, it became apparent that Matt was struggling to cope with both the woman on his back and the fits of laughter we couldn't seem to shake off. Everything was hilariously funny in Drunk Town.

'I need a break,' he'd said, lurching towards a gap between the hedgerows and a metal fence and squeezing us both through. I half-fell off his back and landed on my own, with him collapsing next to me. The sandals had gone flying during my stylish dismount and only one remains visible a few feet away. The other has disappeared off to its own patch of wheat.

Somehow, amid the falling and the collapsing and the flying sandals, we've ended up holding hands. And somehow, I don't seem to mind.

'So,' I say, after a few minutes' silence. 'Was this actually a date?'

'I don't know,' he replies, his fingers softly stroking my palm. 'I suppose it depends on your definitions. There were two of us. We socialised. There was alcohol. Too much of it, probably, for those of us who have to get intimate with farm animals tomorrow. We talked. We laughed, a lot. And now we're lying in a field, looking up at the stars. I'd say it was a date… unless you don't want it to be. In which case, we can write it all off and forget about it.'

I turn my head to look at him and he's pretty gorgeous. His hair is bathed in moonlight, his cheekbones are catching the shadows and he's very, very long and very, very nicely put together. I smile at him and let my hand rest against his thigh. I can feel denim and muscle and heat.

'I think it was a date too,' I say, smiling. 'My first ever.'

'What do you mean?' he asks, rolling onto his side and propping his head up on one arm to look down at me. 'You were married.'

'I know. But we met when we were seven, me and David. Our first date was to Chester Zoo on a school trip. To be fair, we did hold hands and there might even have been a piggy-back, but there was definitely no alcohol involved. We stayed together all through school and got married when we were twenty.'

I see the look on his face and it is one I'm familiar with. It's one we got used to seeing; one that David called the 'you must have been a child bride' face. We realised that it was very old-fashioned, and possibly downright weird, to be settling down so early in our lives – but we didn't care. We were happy and happiness has a way of making other people's disapproval seem completely irrelevant.

'You're thinking we were daft to get married so young, aren't you?' I say to Matt, feeling slightly disappointed in him.

'No, not at all,' he answers, his tone gentle and sad and a little bit emotional. 'I was thinking how wonderful it must have been to find the person you wanted to share your life with so early on. To miss out on all the game-playing and hurt and wasted effort that most people go through. And I was thinking about how terrible it must have been to lose him.'

I feel tears well up immediately, and can do nothing to prevent them rolling in big, fat blobs down the side of my face. It wasn't what I was expecting to hear and his sympathy almost breaks me. It's not so much the thought of David that provokes me, but Matt's consistent kindness.

He gently wipes the tears away and tucks wayward curls behind my ears. I reach up and twine my fingers into his hair, which is something I've been wanting to do all night. It is exactly as soft as I thought it would be.

I want him to kiss me, I realise. I want it very much, to the point where it almost feels like need. I suspect he is too gentlemanly to make a move on a crying woman. I mean, I am lying here touching his hair and letting him touch mine, and our faces are inches apart. But I am also shedding tears after talking about my dead husband. Poor Matt. I am the living embodiment of 'mixed messages'.

'Please,' I say, quietly. 'Ignore the tears. I can't help them. Just… see the rest of me.'

Matt nods. And he smiles.

'I do see the rest of you,' he murmurs. 'And it takes my breath away.'

He strokes my skin, fingers skimming over my cheekbone, my jaw, my throat, coming to rest on my bare shoulder blade. He slips the strap of my dress down, just a little, and leans forward. He doesn't kiss my lips, not straight away. He kisses my shoulders, so soft, so warm, his touch meandering in a sensual trail along bone and flesh, nuzzling the sensitive spot beneath my ears before finally, finally, reaching my mouth.

My heart is beating so fast I'm sure he must be able to hear it and both my hands are now in his hair, holding him closer to me. I feel the subtle touch of his tongue on mine and a strong hand caressing the side of my body, and the hard outline of his thigh and torso pressed against me.

His hand drifts down, sure and maddeningly slow, until it connects with the bare skin of my leg. I gasp and writhe and want nothing more than for him to push that skirt up further, and to pull those straps down completely, and to feel his hands on all the parts of my body that haven't been touched for so long.

I take my hands away from his hair, sliding them between us, trying to unbutton his shirt. I fumble, trembling, too excited to manage. I tug the shirt instead, so hard I hear buttons pop, and immediately spread my hands over his chest, his sides, his back. Hard body, smooth skin, so much strength and power.

He pulls his mouth away from mine and I feel the muscles of his back bunch up and tense as he moves, lifting his head up so we can see each other's eyes. He is almost completely on top of me now, and I have one leg hooked over him, my arms wrapped around his back. If he stood up, I could probably hold on.

His gaze is intense and his breath is coming in rapid bursts. He is as aroused as I am, in ways that no man could hide and the feel of him pressed up against me is almost enough to bring me to orgasm. I want to rub up against him and ride the crest of the wave I can feel building, and lose my mind beneath the beautiful night sky, over and over again.

Except… he's stopped kissing me. And he's stopped stroking me. And he's taken his hand away from its gradual exploration of my flesh. He's looking at me and he's smiling, and he's shaking his head.

'This,' he says, leaning down to give me one last kiss on the lips, 'isn't right.'

He rolls onto his back and his sudden absence leaves me cold in all kinds of ways. As if to compensate, he scoops me up into his arms and pulls me onto his chest. My cheek rests against his warm, bare skin and I slip my arm around him.

'I disagree,' I reply, letting my fingers drift around his torso, following the trail of silky hair that runs down to the waistband of his jeans. 'I'd say it felt very right.'

He places his hand over mine and holds it still. Spoil sport.

'That's because you're very drunk. And because you've never been on a date before. And because we're both… a little bit lost at the moment. I just don't want you to rush into anything, or do something you'll regret.'

I stay silent for a moment and ponder what he's said. I try to concentrate on the words and not the way it feels to be held in a man's arms again, to feel small and safe and secure there. I've slept alone every night for over two years now and I've missed this. Not just sex, but contact. Comfort. A physical connection with another human being.

Lying here, like this, wrapped up in Matt's embrace, his beating heart beneath me, feels both hauntingly familiar and excitingly new. I am sure he is right – and that tomorrow I may feel entirely differently. But in this exact moment, I regret nothing.

'All right,' I finally say, gently kissing the golden skin of his shoulder. 'I understand. And thank you.'

'For what?' he asks, running his hands over the crazy landscape of my hair.

'For taking me on a date. For giving me a piggy-back. For kissing me. And for stopping me from ravishing you in a wheat field.'

'Believe me,' he says, squeezing me closer. 'That last one was the toughest of all.'

WEEK 3

In which I become a one-woman emergency-rescue service, get rumbled by my own daughter, develop a crush on Bruce Banner and see one too many people stark naked…

Chapter 19

'I tell you what,' I say to Jean, my new best friend. 'Why don't you just stay here for a bit? Have your lunch. Have a chat. Rest up a while. I finish at two and I can drive you to your next stop.'

'That would be cheating,' she replies, though I can tell she's tempted.

'I won't tell if you won't,' I add, topping up her coffee without her even asking.

Jean has been in the café all day now and I'm really hoping she'll hang around for a little while longer.

I knew there was something different about her the minute she walked through the doors this morning.

For a start it had only just gone eight and my only other customer was Frank. She was kitted up in what I now recognise as full walker's gear, with sturdy, well-used boots, a packed rucksack and a pair of hiking poles.

She wasn't young, but wasn't old either – maybe early sixties, I'd say, with the trim body and weather-lined face of a lifelong rambler. Her hair was a little wild, a little greasy and she had the vaguely unkempt look of someone who has been neglecting themselves. It's a look I recognised.

She'd paused in the doorway, seeing me and Frank sitting there alone staring at her, and was clearly considering walking straight back out again. I'd jumped to my feet and ushered her in, leading her over to the table next to ours.

It was a bright day, but still cool this early. Her lips were tinged slightly blue and her hands were trembling. She was obviously very chilled, despite her clobber, and looked completely exhausted.

Frank gave her a cheery good morning and I bustled around getting her toast, jam and coffee. I'd offered a cooked breakfast, but she insisted that toast was fine. She spoke quietly, hesitantly, as though she didn't want to be too much trouble.

We gave her her space while she ate, but I kept returning and giving her more to drink and a couple of magazines to read. After Frank left she was the only person in the café until Surfer Sam turned up to collect some cupcakes for a kids' event he was holding on the beach later. I'd iced the tops in the design of fossils, simplifying the pictures I'd seen of the kinds you might find on the Dorset coast.

'Nice ammonites,' said Sam, raising one eyebrow at me and somehow making it sound dirty. His Irish accent was pretty sexy, so perhaps it was just me imagining the dirt. It wouldn't be the first time.

'Why thank you, kind sir,' I replied, packing them up into a box and thinking yet again that Sam and Becca absolutely had to meet. They'd spend the whole time trying to out-double entendre each other.

Well, I thought, looking at his outdoorsy physique and bright-blue eyes, maybe not *all* their time.

He glanced over at the lady and then back at me. She was reading an OS map and had it spread out across the table, a marker in her hand.

'Walker?' he asked. 'She's in early.'

'I know,' I replied, whispering. 'And it looked to me like she'd been walking for ages when she got here. Possibly through the night, if I'm honest.'

'Are you worried about her?'

'A bit, maybe. Yes. I don't want to be rude, but I do want to make sure she's all right.'

'Don't worry,' replied Sam, reassuringly. 'This place has been welcoming waifs and strays for a long time. Try and keep her here and find out what's going on and if she needs help. You'll find that if she stays long enough everyone will chip in. She'll leave in a better state than she arrived in.'

Sam strode off towards the lady's table and pulled out a chair. She looked up, slightly taken aback, but instantly disarmed by his broad and open smile. He was wearing his ranger uniform and, of course, he had the voice as well, so within minutes they were chatting away as Sam pointed out spots on the map for her.

After a few minutes, he came back to collect his box of cupcakes.

'She's called Jean,' he said, hefting the box up off the counter. 'And she's on a mammoth trek around the whole of the coastline. She started in East Anglia and has been on the road for over a month. Plus, you're right, I think she did walk through the night, which is just dangerous around here.

'I showed her some safe paths, gave her a bit of advice about places that aren't even on the map and told her I'd be back later if she was still around. I hope she is. She seems a bit fragile. Like I said, try and persuade her to stay for a while. Everyone else will help. I'll let them know.'

I had no idea what he meant by that, but as the morning wore on, it became clear. Cherie emerged from her slumber at about ten to find the place busy with both tourists and locals, and immediately asked me what the story was with Jean. There was something about her – a sense of vulnerability, perhaps – that we'd both picked up on.

'I don't know what the story is,' I said. 'It's been non stop down here. You'll be able to retire to Spain on this morning's takings.'

'Excellent news. Gracias. Now go and see what you can winkle out of her and see how we can help. Poor love looks wiped out.'

I'd just pulled a fresh batch of scones out of the oven, so I plated two up with some butter, jam and clotted cream, and took them over. Jean had folded up her maps and was staring out across the bay, her eyes glassy and unfocused.

'Mind if I join you?' I asked, sitting down without waiting for a reply. Fortune favours the nosy.

'I've just made these and thought we might test them out before lunch.'

I push the scone over to her and she looks at it slightly suspiciously. Perhaps my reputation as a super-chef has spread wider than I thought.

'My name's Laura,' I said, smoothing butter on my scone. It was still deliciously warm and the butter started to melt as soon as it made contact.

'I'm working here for the summer,' I continued, when she didn't respond. 'My husband died two years ago and I couldn't face another summer at home without him. I packed my two kids and my dog into the car and drove here without ever having met the woman who owns the place, visited Dorset or had a job for donkey's years. My family back in Manchester think I've gone mad.'

Jean looked at me, weighing up my words and possibly admiring my efficient scone-eating technique. She gave me a small smile and I'm glad I trusted my instincts. I thought that if I over-shared, she might open up – either that or file a restraining order.

'Well, grief makes you do funny things, doesn't it?' she said, finally taking a small nibble at one tiny piece of the scone.

'It definitely did with me,' I replied. 'But so far, so good. I'm enjoying it here. It's been… new. And I've not felt anywhere near as scared of the future since I came here. I used to be so scared – all the time. Worried I was raising the kids wrong, worried I was going mad. Worried I was going to die too and leave them all alone. Worried about money, about the house, about everything really. I don't think I realised how anxious I was until now.'

I had, of course, come over here to get Jean talking – but everything I was saying was one hundred per cent true. Three weeks away from everyday life in Manchester and my stress levels were nowhere near the same. Maybe Jean's walk around the coast would do the same for her, even if she did look like she needed a whole wheelbarrow full of TLC.

'I'm doing this walk,' she added, still staring out of the windows at the admittedly gorgeous view, 'because me and my husband, Ted, were supposed to do it. He'd retired and we'd planned it all. He used to watch that programme, you know, on the telly? *Coast.* He loved it and he always used to say 'Jean, when I've finished with work, that's what we'll do – we'll walk round Britain'. It was a real hobby for him, looking up the routes and plotting out where we'd go and what we'd see.'

She paused, ate another mouthful and drank some more coffee. I had a very bad feeling that this story wasn't going to end with Ted changing his mind, or Ted meeting up with her at the next hotel.

'What happened?' I asked, softly.

'Stomach cancer,' she replied, her voice barely a whisper. 'He'd had a few problems and ignored them, as men tend to do. He was gone in a matter of weeks. This was all booked, all paid for. I thought… I don't know, I thought it would be good for me. We never had any kids and neither of us have much family left. There was nothing for me to stay at home for and I thought he'd want me to do this. I thought it would help.'

'And has it?' I say, biting my lip hard to stop myself from crying.

'Maybe. I've seen some beautiful things. But I've seen them all alone. All the cliffs and the sunsets and the sunrises and the storms. It's not the same, somehow, is it, with nobody seeing it with you? And I've got it all mixed up, done it wrong. Missed part of Sussex, lost a few days in Hampshire.

'Last night, I arrived at the place he'd booked a day late. Luckily they still had a room, but I just couldn't get to sleep. I was exhausted, but I couldn't switch off. Just lay there, in that big bed, wishing he was there with me and worrying that I was falling behind with his schedule. So I got up, got dressed and left… it was about three in the morning and I've been walking ever since. Until I called here, anyway.'

Her story was all too believable to me and I was thankful all over again for having the children. Pains in the backside as they sometimes were, they gave me a reason to carry on when I lost David. They gave me – and continue to give me – a reason to keep trying. Poor Jean is trying to drag herself out of the pit all on her own.

We chatted for a few more minutes and she ate most of the scone. I know I can't actually adopt Jean and take her home to live with me, but I kind of wanted to. I settled for making her so warm and content in the Comfort Food Café that she wouldn't leave just yet.

It's now the middle of the lunchtime rush and we are frantic. Peak season in the school holidays and it feels like the whole world has come to visit Dorset. We serve endless sandwiches and wraps and toasties and bowls of soup and pasta salads. My peach and apricot tarts sell out within half an hour and the banana and toffee muffins not long after. The scones are gone as soon as they're laid on the counter.

Jean is looking self-conscious, as though she doesn't want to be taking up a table when the place is busy. It's nice and sunny outside, but there is a strong breeze blowing in from the coast, so the inside tables are also full.

Cherie has managed to get Jean to admit that she's 'partial to a slice of cheese on toast', and has presented her with a delicious pile of melting Cheddar on thick-sliced home-made granary. She seems to be pondering my offer to drive her to the next stop on her tour and I'm glad. I'll have to do a bit of logistics juggling with the kids, but I want to do it. I want to help her, to show her the tiny bit of kindness and understanding it's in my power to share.

And, I realise, as the day wears on, I'm not the only one. Word has spread about our special customer and the café regulars respond in a way that warms my heart.

Sam does indeed come back and sits with her while he drinks his milkshake (Bounty-flavoured) and eats his Pot Noodle (chicken and mushroom, as usual). How he stays so slim I have no idea.

Ivy Wellkettle calls in, not for her usual fishfinger butty, but to drop off some Bach rescue remedy and a packet of chewable multivitamins. She sits with Jean for a few moments drinking a cup of tea and discussing the route she's planning to take through Devon, before handing them over and insisting there's no charge.

Scrumpy Joe arrives just as Ivy leaves, ready for a slice of pork pie and a glass of apple juice. I pop a couple of 'his' biscotti on the plate as well, as I know he'll want them. He gives me a nod, tells me Lizzie is 'making him famous' and takes his lunch outside. Before he goes, he passes me a plastic bag that contains two bottles of his home-pressed cider smothered in bubble wrap.

'For the walking woman,' he says, nodding in Jean's direction. 'Heard she'd had a rough day. Wrapped it up well so it can go in her rucksack, like.'

Joe – who is legendarily mean – even refrains from asking for payment in return. I'm not sure Jean is a cider kind of girl, but who knows?

'I'll make sure she gets it, Joe,' I say, patting him on the arm. He gives me a little salute and heads out to the garden.

Edie May is in, and as usual is perched on a stool by the counter. She knows when we're busy that we don't have much time to chat, but she sits it out, pecking away at the tart I saved for her. The extra slice I know she'll want is tucked away in a box already, waiting to be taken home.

As the worst of the rush calms down and Willow and Cherie are able to take up most of the slack, I tell her about Jean and her epic trek around the coast.

Edie – who has seen her fair share of hardship in her ninety years – makes a sympathetic 'tsssk' noise, halfway between a tut and a hiss, and shakes her white-haired head.

'Ooh, the poor love. She's so young as well. Tell you what, my dear, give her this delicious cake from me. I know my fiancé would love it, but he won't mind it going to someone in need. Maybe she can take it with her as a treat for when she's on the road, eh?'

I smile and give Edie's papery hand a little squeeze.

I glance at my watch, and see that it is now 2pm. My shift is over and I have managed to keep Jean here all day. I would normally go home and collapse soon, but instead I am going to drive this complete stranger over the county border into Devon and hope that she takes away a little bit of comfort as well as the various random items that have been donated to her cause.

Nate has already asked if he can go to Frank's for the night, so he can help him with his jobs around the farm and listen to his horror stories about deformed animals being born with two heads.

This, I have discovered, is quite a common topic of conversation among rural types – the intriguing horrors that Mother Nature occasionally throws out into the world. It's like a competition to see who has the goriest story and Matt is just as bad, throwing in his vet-school legends as well.

Frank seems quite happy with the arrangement, though, and I think he is secretly happy to have Nate there for the company.

Lizzie is back from her adventures with Josh and her friends, is rosy-faced and mellow and has agreed to come with me when I drive Jean to her hotel later. I am surprised but pleased by this, then wonder if she is somehow trying to butter me up before telling me she is pregnant or asking my permission to go to a cage fight.

I start my final clear-up back in the kitchen, washing out the milkshake blender, as Cherie comes in to check on me.

'You did a good job there, my love,' she says. 'At least she's rested and well fed and watered. She'll be leaving here feeling a bit better.'

'She'll also be leaving here with a bag full of swag,' I reply. 'People have been popping in all day bearing gifts. I'm just going to run her to… well, Devon.'

Cherie laughs and gives me a huge hug. One of those specials of hers, where my head disappears into her bosom and I struggle to breathe. Best. Hugs. Ever.

'Good girl. I'd give her a few minutes, though. She's having a final cuppa with Matt. I think he's talking to her about dogs…'

That, I think, as I turn away from her and carry on washing the various dismantled parts of the blender, is entirely probable. Cherie is quiet and seems to be trying to dislocate her neck to get a proper look at my face.

Since our date-night set-up, Cherie, Frank and Willow have been beside themselves with curiosity about exactly what happened between me and Matt. There have been subtle inquiries ('nice night, was it, then?' – Cherie) and there have been less-subtle inquiries ('so, did you snog him?' – Willow).

Then there have been Frank inquiries, which revolve around asking where we went – I have the sneaking suspicion that he knows every single person in the county of Dorset and will be asking his spies if they saw us together.

I did get home in a slightly dishevelled state, so Willow has an idea that something may have occurred – but so far I've stuck to my story that we just got tipsy and had a long walk home. Which is, of course, true.

The rest? Well, that's none of their business.

For the last two years, I've lived under a microscope. Every move I've made has been discussed and dissected by my family, bless them. And with very good reason.

Now, I'm very much enjoying having some privacy and so far I've resisted all probing. I've fought down every blush. I've avoided every clever trap. And I've not even talked to Becca about it.

It's our little secret – which has somehow, in a way I don't quite understand, made it even more special.

I wipe my hands down on a clean tea towel and refrain from touching up my hair or looking in a mirror. Anything like that will tip Cherie off that I care what I look like in front of Matt, and where would be the fun in that?

I gather my bag and my jacket and the tart and the cider, and walk through into the café, which is now only about a quarter full.

I stroll over to where Jean has been sitting all day and pull up a chair to join her and Matt. He gives me a small nod that is absolutely nothing more than polite, but beneath the table, his thigh nudges up against mine and his hand rests on my bare knee.

I feel as excitable as a schoolgirl on a first date and hope it doesn't show on my face.

'I was just telling Jean here about a friend of mine who runs a dog-rescue centre in the Midlands, not too far from where she lives. They're always desperate for good homes and she'd be doing them a huge favour if she considered adoption.'

'That's a great idea,' I say, looking encouragingly at Jean. 'A bit of company on your walks – what do you think?'

'I'm not sure,' she replies, sounding totally convincible. 'We used to have a dog. Lovely little Jack Russell called Patch. But… well, we both decided against another one, later in life. Thought we'd be busy with all our holidays once Ted retired. I don't know… maybe it would be nice.'

It would be more than nice, I decide. It would be exactly what she needs – a friend to love, who loves her in return and who licks her face in bed at night. Isn't that what we all want? Though admittedly, the face-licking should probably be optional.

'Why don't you leave me your number?' Matt says, pulling out his phone, 'and I can give you a call once you're back home. So if you have any questions or you want me to talk to Ian about keeping an eye out for the right dog for you, we can stay in touch.'

It's practically a speech, by Matt's standards, certainly to a stranger. But it seems Jean has tugged on everyone's heartstrings, including his, and he is offering what he can. His views on pets. It is very sweet and I slip my hand under the table to hold his.

He blinks rapidly and I think: actually, *we* are sweet. The two of us. We are sweet and innocent and new. We are at the very beginning of something I don't understand, and don't even try to.

Because if I think too hard, I might notice how absolutely terrifying it all is.

Chapter 20

Driving to Devon sounds like a big deal, but it is actually not. In fact it only takes about forty minutes to get to Sidmouth, where we deposit Jean at her cosy B&B.

She looks much better than when I first met her and has been positively chatty on the journey. Lizzie has been very polite in the back seat, for which I am grateful, and I feel a spark of pride when Jean compliments me on my beautiful family.

I take a quick glance back at Lizzie, who promptly sticks her tongue out without Jean seeing, and think: yes, they are indeed beautiful. And I love every last cheeky inch of them.

I give Jean a big hug before she leaves and she disappears off with a wave. She has promised to stay in touch and says she will send us postcards from her journey at every stop. She also says that she now plans to have a long bath before she eats her cake, drinks her cider and chews up her vitamins. I only hope she doesn't overdose on the rescue remedy.

Nate is with Frank for his tea and Lizzie doesn't seem to have plans for the evening, so I suggest that we go out for an early dinner. There are lots of nice-looking pubs and cafés scattered along the picturesque esplanade and Sidmouth feels a little like Las Vegas after living in Budbury.

'What?' she says. 'Dinner? Just us?'

'Yes,' I reply, heading towards an especially pretty pub with whitewashed walls and splendid hanging baskets. 'Is that a problem?'

I don't wait for an answer, I simply head straight for a table. It's quite dark inside and there's a huge stone fireplace that looks like it could be used to roast a rhino. There are a few scattered families and some elderly couples, and a menu that includes everything you could want in a pub lunch.

Lizzie follows – she really has very little choice as she can't drive – and slumps into a seat opposite me. Her phone is on the table and I see the screensaver is a selfie of her and Josh with the bay shimmering blue behind them. It looks like it was taken from the café's clifftop garden and they both look very young and very happy.

Becca had told me the night before that Lizzie had changed her Facebook relationship status to It's Complicated. I couldn't help wondering exactly how complicated a fourteen-year-old's relationships could be, but what did I know?

'Scampi and chips?' I say, knowing the answer, because it's what she always has in pubs. She nods and glances at her watch as though she has somewhere better to be.

I order the food and sit back down. I point at the phone and the photo, and I say: 'That's really nice. Are you and Josh… you know, seeing each other?'

I try not to gulp audibly as I force the words out, reminding myself that she is in fact almost fifteen and it's perfectly natural for her to be interested in boys, and that even though Josh is sixteen and therefore a much older man, he seems a nice-enough kid. Plus, I know where he lives and will disembowel him if he hurts her.

Lizzie looks at me with an expression that is half horror, half hope. I suspect my expression is very similar. I want to be able to talk to her about this stuff in a way I couldn't with my mum, but I'm also grappling with sheer embarrassment and hoping it doesn't show. If I seem to feel comfortable and relaxed, there's more chance that she will.

'Umm,' she starts, sipping her Coke. 'Not really. We're just friends, mostly.'

'Oh. Right. What do you mean 'mostly'?'

'I mean just friends. He's just come out of a long-term relationship and he's not looking for anything serious.'

I have to stifle back a laugh at that one – the thought of the lanky, beanie-hatted wonder having a 'serious relationship' makes me want to giggle. Obviously, she notices.

'I don't think you're in any position to comment, Mum, as you and Dad were planning your wedding by his age.'

She has a fair point and I try to wipe the smirk off my face. Teenagers, I sometimes forget, can be very serious. Life seems to get sillier as you get older and you realise how little point there is in trying to control anything – but at her age, with the future rolling in mystery and her every feeling magnified by wayward hormones, it all feels Very Very Big.

'True enough,' I reply. 'But, as you always tell me, that was weird, wasn't it? I'm not saying that people you meet at your age can't be important, or really special – but they're not usually the person you end up marrying.'

'I do realise that,' she snipes, and I suspect I have touched a nerve. That she likes Josh a little more than she is letting on, and she is in that horrible wilderness of I-like-him-but-I-don't-know-if-he-likes-me. The one I pretty much skipped, but saw Becca and all my friends tortured by.

'All right, then. Well, we're here for a few more weeks – are you having a good holiday, at least?'

Our food arrives and she spears a chip straight away. Her appetite has increased since we've been here, because of all the time she's spending outdoors, I think. Plus, perhaps, no longer being surrounded by a group of borderline catty friends who are all obsessed with clothes, make-up, looking ten years older than they actually are and hanging round Affleck's Palace pretending they're in a band.

She munches away and looks thoughtful.

'I am having a good holiday,' she eventually replies. 'I didn't think I would, Mum, but I'm really enjoying it. I like taking my photos and I like helping out at the cider cave, and I like helping Josh and Joe with their social media. I know I'm still in school, but I think it might be something I could do as a job when I'm older. And I just… like it here. It's dead pretty and the other kids are cool, and there's definitely a lower shithead per capita ratio.'

I grimace at her choice of words, but am grateful to hear her sounding so positive. A small part of me would like to say 'told you so', but I am mature enough to squash it down.

She narrows her eyes at me, staring from beneath her long blonde fringe, and adds, 'You really want to say 'I told you so', don't you?'

'As if!' I exclaim, laughing, and holding my hands up in protest. 'I wouldn't dream of actually *saying* it. I'm just *thinking* it… and, anyway, I'm really glad. I know you didn't want to come and I know you hated me for a while, but I'm enjoying it too.'

'I know you are,' she replies, looking a bit smug. 'And I think I know why. I should be the one asking you about boys, not the other way round.'

'What do you mean?' I ask, suddenly feeling my eyes widen and an adrenaline rush slam through my veins.

She doesn't answer and instead picks up her phone. She swipes it on and flicks through a few screens. I'm desperate to nose at her photos, but purposely don't. One day, I like to think, she'll show them all to me anyway. I'll receive an invite to join her precious Instagram account and all will be good in the world.

'Well,' she eventually says, 'I was down at the beach the other day. Josh and his dad were doing some heavy lifting and I couldn't be arsed, I'm too much of a delicate flower for manual labour. So I got the book that Edie May let me borrow – Thomas Hardy, don't you know – and I just went and had a lie-down.

'It was when you were on a late shift and I think Nate was in the park or playing footie or doing whatever he does all day. It was pretty quiet down there and I was tucked between two rocks at the end of the bay. *Far from the Madding Crowd* and all that.'

I nod and poke my chips and drink my orange juice, and play with my hair, and find the fake oil paintings of haywains and shire horses very, very interesting. I know exactly the spot she's talking about – it's the most remote part of the bay and I've only walked along there once recently.

'And lo and behold,' she says, clearly enjoying my squirming, 'who should appear from nowhere but you and Matt the Vet? Which wouldn't be weird, really, as Jimbo was with you. What was a bit more weird was the fact that as soon as you got round the corner and presumably thought nobody could see you, the two of you started holding hands. You and Matt, I mean. Not you and Jimbo.'

She turns the phone towards me and I see a picture that I would normally think was pretty gorgeous. The sun is setting over the glimmering turquoise waves and Matt and I are both barefoot, and Jimbo is ambling along behind us carrying a stick in his mouth. We're both laughing and yes, indeed, we are holding hands.

I am well and truly rumbled. And also a bit confused.

'Have you posted this online?' I ask, wondering why it is that Becca and Cherie and Frank and the rest of the world who watch my life via my daughter's photo-sharing accounts haven't commented on this development.

'Of course not,' she replies, frowning at me as though I've accused her of kicking kittens. 'This is private.'

I bite down on the sarcastic retort I want to give – that that's never stopped her before – because I am both grateful for her unexpected sensitivity and aware that I am now the one who has some explaining to do.

'Thank you,' I say simply. 'I appreciate that. I'm guessing you have questions?'

'Erm… I don't know if I do. I mean, it all looked pretty lame. There wasn't even any snogging, just all that laughing and looking into each other's eyes. And the hand-holding. It was a bit Fifty Shades of Tame if you ask me.'

I can't help myself, I laugh out loud. Almost against her will, she joins in and we both end up with tears in our eyes. But good tears, for a change, not the angry/morose/desperate ones we've both shed so much of in the recent past.

'Well, that's me well and truly put in my place,' I say, wiping my face. 'And, in all honesty, there isn't much more to tell. Not much has happened. I'm glad I didn't embarrass you with any old-lady snogging and don't worry, I'm not about to start. I… like Matt. He's kind and sweet, and when you get to know him he's really funny. Plus, you know, he's got that whole Han Solo thing going on… and the guitar, and the singing… and…'

I drift a little at this point and Lizzie makes a retching sound to demonstrate how she feels about it.

'Anyway,' I say, snapping back to the here and now, 'the thing is, it's not even a thing. It may never be a proper thing. It might just stay at being a tiny fraction of a thing, a hand-holding thing. And even if it was more of a thing, if you were unhappy with the thing, I wouldn't take it any further. Does that make sense?'

'All I heard was the word "thing" on repeat, Mum,' she replies, grinning at my discomfort. It must be nice for her, this role reversal.

'Right. I'm bad at this. What I'm trying to say is that whatever happens with Matt, or doesn't happen with Matt, some things will stay the same. I will always love you and Nate, and your Dad. Nothing will change that. Ever.'

Lizzie ponders this for a moment. Either she is thinking some deep thoughts or just has an especially chewy bit of scampi.

'I know that, Mum. I know you'll always love me and Nate, and Dad. We'll all always love Dad. But Dad's dead, Mum. It's not like he's coming back, is he? And I really don't think he'd mind the fact that you're holding someone else's hand.

'Maybe I'd have felt funny about it nearer the time, or if it had been some bloke you met at home, but… well, it feels different here, doesn't it? Everything here just feels different.'

She's right, I think. She's completely right. Everything here does feel different. And I'm not sure that any of us will be going home as the same people we were when we arrived.

Chapter 21

I have specifically asked Lizzie to take some pictures of Surfer Sam so my sister can check him out.

'Why?' she asked, contrarily, considering she'd been taking pictures of pretty much every bloody body else in Budbury, including the postman and guy who works in the village chippie. Actually, now I come to think of it, that might be the same person. Anyway.

'Because I think Becca might fancy him, and it'll be funny,' I said.

'So you want me to take slutty-looking photos of Sam, so my auntie can lech over him?'

I'd thought it over, looking for ways I could argue with that statement, and nodded.

'That about sums it up, yes.'

To be fair, she'd done a lovely job and actually showed me the pictures before she posted them. Sticking to our agreement, she'd got Sam's permission and I suspect had blagged him into thinking she was writing something about surfing. Although Sam is nothing if not a flirt – if we'd simply told him we wanted some stud-muffin shots to send to a family member, he'd probably have been fine with it.

Now, it is quite late in the evening – by which I mean 8.30pm – and I am on the phone to Becca in Manchester, waiting for her to log on and look.

'So, what do you think?' I ask, realising I sound pathetically eager. I am not at all sure why I want Becca to fancy Sam. She is hundreds of miles away and that is unlikely to change. I think I just want her to be as enthusiastic about this place, about these people, as I am.

She is my family and, truth be told, the people of Budbury are starting to feel a little bit like my family as well. Even though I have only been here for just under a month, they have welcomed me so completely, involved me so totally, accepted me without analysis or judgement or too much probing, that I feel like a whole new me has been allowed to emerge.

Maybe it's that holiday thing. That thing where you get to know people so much faster and life feels so much more intense. Part of me knows it's not real, but it still feels so good to be here and to be part of their lives, even if it is only temporarily.

'Wow,' says Becca, as she flicks through the pictures. 'He's a hottie, all right. Totally ripped. And I love his tattoos. I would hundred per cent definitely do him.'

I laugh and feel like fist-punching the air in victory.

'I knew it!' I say. 'Isn't he? And I like the tattoos too... didn't even know they were there until I saw those photos...'

'Hang on,' says Becca, interrupting me. 'Back off my man, girlfriend! I thought Sam was mine? What are you doing panting over him?'

'I'm not panting! I'm just... appreciating, that's all. And now I feel a bit sleazy, because he's actually a lovely bloke as well and we're just objectifying him because of his magnificent abs...'

There is a moment of silence, where we both appreciate their magnificence a little bit more, before Becca replies, 'Don't be daft.

A man who looks like that isn't going to complain at being objectified. I bet he'd be chuffed.'

'He would, actually,' I say, grinning. 'He likes ladies. And I don't mean that to sound like he's a player... though he might be, I don't really know... I mean he likes women. He comes from a huge family on the coast in the south of Ireland and he has *seven* older sisters. He misses them like mad and he hasn't been home since February. I get the feeling he was desperate to get away from so much mothering, but now he's escaped, he wishes they were here... anyway. Because of that, he just kind of *gets* women.'

'He sounds like a dreamboat. I may name my new vibrator after him.'

I pull a face and don't respond to that one. It's best not to encourage her.

'So, the kids still look great,' she says. 'I'm liking Lizzie's new unpaid job as a drug-pusher.'

'She's not a drug-pusher, she's managing the Twitter account for Joe's cider cave. And I think he might occasionally give her the odd fiver as well.'

'Wow. Big spender, eh?'

'Not really. But I think she does it as much to spend time with Josh as anything. Apparently, they're just friends.'

'Yeah. Well, we'll see. Maybe there's a holiday romance brewing for one of you at least, eh?'

I bite my lip, realising I look a bit cagey even though she can't see me. If there was ever a time to tell Becca about Matt, this is it. I don't like keeping things from her, but I also don't want the pressure of being quizzed by her. Anyway, as I remind myself again, there isn't much to tell. One roll in the hay – or wheat – and a bit of flirting and hand-holding since. By Becca's standards, it is virginal.

'There's a lovely picture here,' she says, when I remain quiet, 'of Nate. He's playing football on the beach, with Matt the Hot Vet – who is topless, I might add, very nice – and the sexy old farmer.'

'Do you fancy everyone?' I ask, laughing.

'Not Nate, I assure you. But the rest are fair game… anyway. It's just nice. You know, for him to have blokes in his life again, even if it's just for a few more weeks.'

I know what she means and yet I still feel a prickle of annoyance. I recognise the prickle for what it is – being overly defensive – and ignore it.

Nate and David used to spend hours kicking a ball around in the garden. Pretty much every day when it wasn't raining, they'd be out there. The lawn was a streaked and scuffed mass of sliding tackle mud, with bare patches where they stood in goals, and I was forever hearing the sound of plant pots smashing and windows getting whacked. It was the soundtrack to my life when I was in the kitchen.

After his death, Nate would sit in the conservatory, looking outside, the football abandoned and the garden neglected. All of us neglected, truth be told. My dad did his best and I tried very hard to master some silky skills, but it wasn't ever quite the same.

Here, with the kids who've been staying at the Rockery, with his friends from the village, and with the likes of Matt and Frank and Sam, he's been blossoming. Turning into a proper boy again – in other words, constantly starving hungry, always filthy, smelling awful and able to fall asleep the second his arse hits the couch. It's a joy to see.

'I know,' I say to Becca, 'he's loving it. So's Lizzie. So am I…'

'You don't have to come back, you know,' Becca says, quietly. She sounds serious, which is so unlike her that I am worried I should be calling the paramedics.

'What do you mean?'

'I mean what I said. You don't have to come back. You're all happy there. Maybe this is what you need – a fresh start.'

'Are you trying to get rid of me?' I ask, in an attempt to lighten the tone.

'Yeah,' she says, sarcastically, 'I am desperate to get all of Mum and Dad's attention to myself. Not. I just... well, I miss you. And I really miss the kids. But all three of you seem so much more carefree than you have for... well, *since*. All I'm saying is that if it works for you, perhaps you should consider sticking with it. It's been over two years, Laura – and this is the first time I've heard you sounding even remotely like your old self.'

Although I have been sad at the thought of leaving, I have never seriously considered making Budbury my permanent home. We have the house in Manchester, which isn't just a roof over our heads, it's the place we lived with David.

It's full of memories and I would struggle to part with it. Plus the kids are settled in their school and my parents are there, and David's parents are there when they're not on a cruise, and... no. It's insane. I couldn't afford to live down here without a job anyway, and I'm guessing café work is much harder to come by in the winter when all the tourists have left.

Plus, I silently acknowledge, if I stay here, then this thing with me and Matt – this small, precious, thing that is growing between us and helping me heal – will be exposed to the trauma of too much time and the frostbite of familiarity. I would rather enjoy it briefly blooming than watch it wither and die.

'I don't think so, sis,' I reply. 'This isn't real life. It's just... a very special holiday.'

'If you say so,' she answers, sounding unconvinced. 'When are you coming home, then?'

'Well, apparently the highlight of the social whirl down here is Frank's birthday party. They have it on the last night in August, which pretty much marks the end of tourist season as well. They have a big bash every year, stay open at night and everyone who's anyone comes and joins in. It's his eightieth this time, so it's going to be a biggie. Lizzie's trying to persuade Cherie to let her new band play.'

'She's in a band now?'

'No, she's not. But she heard Matt and Nate on the guitar and reckons she could sing. Josh has a bass, though he's not played it for three years. So far she's thought of a name – the Dead Tulips – but nobody else is interested. But who knows? They may change their minds and make their rock and roll debut at the party… hey… maybe you should come!'

'I honestly don't think I could take the excitement,' Becca replies, and I can picture her smirking as she says it. 'Especially if your stoner boss lady is arranging it.'

'Cherie is not a stoner,' I reply 'She's a successful business woman and property-owner.'

'Who likes a spliff every now and then.'

'Yes, so it seems. But it really is every now and then – a bit like other people would have a glass of wine at the end of the day, maybe. I don't ask and she doesn't tell.'

'Maybe you should ask,' says Becca, and I can hear the laughter in her voice. 'Maybe you should loosen up and join in.'

'I don't think so, Becca. It's not my style.'

'Hey, don't—'

'Yeah, I know. Don't knock it till you've tried it – your motto in life. I'm happy with the glass of wine, thank you.'

What neither of us says – because, why would we? – is that another reason it's not my style is because of her. Becca was a precocious teenager on the narcotics front and we had more than one scare with her. Her life seems relatively even now, in comparison, but it was enough to put me off for life.

'Anyway,' she continues, happy to move on. 'I have to warn you about something. You'll be getting a phone call sometime soon. Mum and Dad are talking about coming to visit. I'm clearly not keeping them busy enough.'

Oh good, I think, slightly shaken by this news. Now I really have something to look forward to. You know, in the same way you might look forward to a smear test or getting a filling done.

It's not that I don't love my parents, I really do. But I am conscious of how far I've stretched them – admittedly not through choice – over the last few years. I realise, because I have kids of my own, that we never, ever stop feeling for our children; they can break our hearts just as easily when they're grown as when they're tiny. In fact, it's somehow even worse when they're older – because you can't protect them.

When they're tiny, you can scoop them up and hold them tight and fight off all the wolves. When they're taller than you, you still feel just as protective, but the reality is that they will go out into the world on their own and the world will very likely hurt them.

To my mum and dad, I'm still a little girl, and I always will be. I get that. I understand it and I'm devastated that they've gone through so much on my behalf.

I know they've felt my pain as their own and have been unable to scoop me up and hold me tight, as I'm sure they wanted to. They had to watch me grieve and watch me fall apart, and watch me suffer, over and over again. That's unbearable for a parent and I really want it to stop – for them to get on with their own lives and stop keeping an eye on mine.

Being here, in Budbury, has allowed me to outrun that sense of guilt, at least for a little while. It's allowed me to break the never-ending cycle of them worrying about me and me worrying about them worrying about me and us all generally worrying about each other.

Now, it seems, they're chasing me down. And I feel the worry popping right back up again.

'Any idea when? Or why? Or if there's any way to stop them? Can't you pretend you're having a baby with one of the United players or something?'

'Ha! That would definitely give Dad a heart attack… I don't think he'd mind if it was City… but no, I'm not sure. I think they're bored, truth be told, and fancy seeing the kids. They said something about taking them off for a night in a caravan. I think Lizzie will be absolutely thrilled at the prospect, don't you?'

'Beyond belief,' I reply. 'Especially if they bring their 1980s edition of Trivial Pursuit. Look, I've got to go. I can hear a lot of yelling from upstairs and I need to check if she's drowning Nate in the toilet.'

'Roger that. Over and out,' says Becca as I end the call.

There is a lot of yelling upstairs and Lizzie may well be trying to drown Nate in the toilet. But he's almost as big as her now, so I'm fairly confident that mama's little soldier can take care of himself. There's a sudden Lizzie-shaped squeal that confirms I'm right and I decide to leave 'em to it.

Mum and Dad are coming. And they're taking the kids away for the night.

There are several downsides to that, which I'm sure I'll have plenty of time to ponder when I'm lying awake at night thinking about it.

But, it suddenly occurs to me, there is also an upside. I will have a whole night to myself. Or, if I manage to find enough courage to see this one through, not by myself.

Chapter 22

The night starts off normally enough.

All three of us are in Hyacinth, watching *Avengers Assemble*, which Lizzie and Nate found on DVD in the games room.

It's been my afternoon off and the three of us have spent it at Charmouth beach with Jimbo. We took a picnic and hired fossil-hunting kits that involved huge plastic goggles that made us look like spacemen, and used hammers to whack rocks very hard.

It was all very cathartic and everyone is quite tired and happy, in that languid way you feel when you've been outside in the sun all day and it seems to leave its warm fingerprints on your skin.

I am quite happy sitting there with them, sipping wine and trying to decide if I fancy Thor or Iron Man or Captain America more, and finally choosing non-Hulk Bruce Banner as my super-hero date. With Hawkeye as a close second.

Lizzie, predictably enough for a girl of her age and eyeliner inclination, is firmly in Camp Loki. Nate is simply disgusted with the whole conversation, before grudgingly admitting that Black Widow is 'not a minger.' I'm sure Scarlett Johansson would be thrilled.

My phone beeps and I see a text from Matt has landed. I am immediately distracted from the movie and spend the next few minutes tapping away in a conversation that goes something like this:

Matt: 'How was your day?'

Me: 'Good. Yours?'

Matt: 'Fine. Be better if you called round.'

Me: 'Can't. Having movie night with kids. Sometime soon?'

As I hit send on that last one, I become aware of the fact that both my children are staring at me with annoyance.

'What??' I say, annoyed at their annoyance. 'It's not like you guys don't spend half your lives texting! And we've seen this film, like, three times already! You *know* Agent Coulson dies!'

'Yes, but you're an old lady. You're not supposed to spend your nights texting,' replies Lizzie, shaking her head in disgust.

'Yeah, Mum,' chips in Nate. 'And you always tell us it's rude to use our phone while we're watching films or eating tea, or whatever. What happened to the "no phones during family time" rule?'

I screw up my face and want to slay them with a sharp retort. Sadly, Nate has made a fair point – I do always tell them it's rude and all I can come up with is blowing a huge raspberry in their general direction. Being in Budbury has clearly done wonders for my maturity levels.

'Why don't you go and take Jimbo out for a walk?' says Lizzie, raising one eyebrow at me. I suspect she knows who I have been texting and is facilitating my flirtation. There is something very wrong with this whole scenario.

'No, no, I don't want to leave you guys,' I say as convincingly as I can. Truth be told, I have spent all day with my kids, and lovely as it has been, I wouldn't actually mind half an hour in adult company instead. This probably makes me a very bad mother.

'Whatever,' says Nate, turning his blonde head back to the TV.

'Just go,' adds Lizzie. 'I know where you'll be, and it's thirty seconds away. We'll be fine.'

She turns away too and I am pretty much dismissed. I glance at my watch. It is 7.15. It is probably, all things considered, perfectly safe to leave them for a bit, as it's still broad daylight, I'll be round the corner, and they don't need me that much anyway. I'm just a kind of bouncer to them, really, once they've been fed.

I murmur something along the lines of 'okay then, I do feel like stretching my legs…', and hook Jimbo up to his lead. He doesn't want to come at all – he is getting more and more stiff, despite the various supplements Matt now has him on. His cataracts are worse and the only time he really displays his old alpha-dog self is when Bella Swan comes to visit. He doesn't seem to be in any pain beyond his joints, but he's a very old chap.

I tickle him behind his velvety ears and he licks my hand. I explain to him in that strange baby-talk voice that many of us use with dogs, as I pull him towards the front door, that we are going to see Matt, and I think he half understands. Certainly he stops dragging his feet and even has a spring in his step as he heads towards his traditional first pee point – the bushes on the corner of the path that leads through to the front half of the Rockery.

We amble past Poison Ivy and the Laughing Apple and Lilac Wine and Mad About Saffron, which reminds me of our second day here, when none of this made any sense. As usual, I can't stop myself looking in the windows of the cottages as we pass, taking a peek at the snapshots of other people's lives.

Some are still empty, as it is relatively early and a beautiful evening. But I see a dad collapsed on the sofa in Lilac Wine, with a beer in one hand and the remote in the other. He's trying to point and shoot with the remote above the head of the curly-haired toddler who is slumped across his chest, totally floppy and sleeping deeply in that way they have at their age, like someone has taken the batteries out.

Mum is sitting next to him with a baby on her lap. They all

look exhausted but happy. It's exactly the kind of scene that would have made me itch with jealousy a few weeks ago. Well, not jealousy exactly… just yearning, for something I once had and will never have again.

Now, I realise, I feel better about what I see. It makes me smile and remember those times with two kids in nappies. How tired we were. How little sleep we got. And yes, how happy we were too. I am thankful for ever having had those days at all.

I pass by and on to Black Rose, and I knock on the door. I wait patiently, although Jimbo starts to whine and tug at his lead once we get there.

It takes a few minutes for Matt to answer, but when he does the wait feels worth it. He is wearing a white towel wrapped around his waist and Jimbo makes a predictable lunge for his crotch.

Wise to him now, Matt steps quickly back and ushers us in before Jimbo can lodge his muzzle where no dog has the right to go.

'I thought you couldn't get out,' he says, leaning down to pat Jimbo, but keeping his hazel eyes on me. 'I was just about to have a shower.'

'Um. Yes. I see that,' I reply, feeling slightly hot under the collar. I've seen Matt without his top on many times since I arrived in Dorset, but it never fails to make an impression.

'The kids are watching the movie without me. I can't stay long, though.'

'In case they kill each other?'

'Something like that,' I say, letting Jimbo loose.

'Well, I'm glad you came. I think I've… missed you?'

He frowns as he says it and I understand why. It is strange, this missing of someone you hardly know and who wasn't even in your life a month ago, but I know exactly what he means.

Part of it, I think, is because we have been unable to spend much time together. Things between us have been left unsaid, and undone, and therefore untainted by anything going wrong. Since we went to the pub with each other, we have been alone precisely twice. Between his work and my work and Cherie and Frank and my children there is not a lot of solitude.

We have kissed once and held hands on the beach, and shared secretive glances and found excuses to be in the same place at the same time. We have texted and spoken on the phone and continued to do all the other things we did together before – like garden and meet at the café, and sit on the beach, and watch Nate play his guitar, and chat to our mutual friends.

But we've done those things with the shared knowledge that there could be more if we want there to be. Perhaps it's the potential for more that makes it so thrilling.

We still haven't had conversations that I would file under the category Deep and Meaningful; I've not poured my heart out about David and he's not filled me in on what happened with the woman with the Legs. Matt is far more relaxed around me than I see him around anyone else, and that feeling is mutual. We are both happy in each other's company and content not to push it further than that.

We both have pasts and we both have our emotional burdens – but right now, we are simply enjoying each other for who and what we are now, rather than dwelling on how we got there.

The small steps we had already taken into each other's lives now feel more important and every moment we spend together feels more enjoyable. Or maybe, I think, casting my eyes over his golden torso, I am just horny. I have not had sex for over two years and never thought I would want to ever again. I now realise that I was very, very wrong about that.

Jimbo jumps up onto one of Matt's armchairs and curls up in a ball. He is asleep within seconds.

I see Matt walking towards me and there is a purposefulness in his stride that I find both frightening and knee-knockingly exciting. I take a step back and hit the wall. I am trapped and I think I like it.

'You can't have missed me,' I say. 'You saw me yesterday when you came into the café for some pea-and-ham soup.'

Damn, I'm sexy. With dirty talk like that, what man could resist?

Luckily Matt doesn't seem to be focused too much on talking.

He closes the distance between us and slips his arms around my waist, palms sliding down over my bottom. He leans into me so our hips are touching and nuzzles his face into my hair. I can feel his breath against my neck and his strong thighs against mine, and his warm, bare skin beneath my fingers. My hands have wandered up to his shoulders, without me even noticing, and are very happy there, tracing the muscular ridges and curves of his body.

He lightly kisses the skin beneath my ear and works his way around my jawline until he reaches my mouth. My lips open to welcome him and I'm clinging to his arms, and his towel is doing little to contain his excitement. One of his hands is stroking the bare skin of my side, slowly smoothing its way further beneath my T-shirt, and I feel my nipples tighten and bud at the thought of him reaching them.

If I was capable of thinking straight, I'd probably be thinking I should slow things right down. That I'd just nipped out to walk the dog. That my children could come looking for me at any moment. That I was behaving like a terrible slapper, and if this was a slasher flick we'd definitely be the first to get murdered by the monster in the Scream mask.

But I'm not really thinking at all. I'm just enjoying. I'm enjoying touching and being touched. I'm enjoying kissing and being kissed. I'm enjoying desiring and feeling desired. I'm enjoying feeling alive and like a woman who can still make a man want her, and want him in return.

Matt pulls away from me slightly and his eyes meet mine. We have reached a point here where things could take a very intimate turn. I hope he's not going to try and talk to me about it, or ask me if it's okay. Because if he asks, I'll have to think and if I have to think I'll probably say no.

Instead, though, he frowns and points at the pocket of my shorts.

'You're vibrating,' he says. 'And I don't think it's all down to me.'

It takes my mind a few seconds to disengage from the things my body is still feeling and to register the fact that, yes, there is indeed a buzzing of a different kind going on down below.

'It's my phone,' I say, with lightning wit.

'I thought it might be,' he replies, smiling at me in a way that makes me want to throw the phone out of the window. His hair is all mussed up and his pupils are dilated and he's just so wonderfully… big.

I shake my head to clear away the lustful thoughts and scoop my phone out. I'd had it on silent during the movie and there's no way I can ignore it. I defy any mum to concentrate on what they're doing – even the pre-amble to possibly terrific sex – if their kids are alone and the phone starts ringing.

I frown as I open it and see that this is the second missed call. It's not either of their mobile numbers, or the cottage landline, or my parents, or Becca, or David's family. Once I've ruled out those possibilities, I'm down to thinking it might be a cold-caller wanting to talk to me about a cheaper tariff.

Except it's a local number and it looks familiar. Not one I have in my contacts, but one I've seen before. As I try and figure out it rings again and I answer straight away.

'Laura? Is that you?'

It's Cherie. I recognise her voice immediately, but she sounds… strange. Not quite her usual self.

'Yes. Are you all right?' I ask, watching as Matt walks out of the room to give me some privacy. He has no idea who I'm talking to, I realise, and as we still know relatively little about each other's lives, he's making an exit in case I need to talk alone. This is a lovely and respectful thing to do and I just as respectfully watch his backside jiggle about in that towel as he leaves.

'No! I'm bloody not! I've had a fall, love… can you come round? I need a bit of help. I can't seem to stand up, you see.'

'Have you called an ambulance?' I ask, all thoughts of Matt wiped from my mind. She sounds awful and I guess she is in a lot of pain.

'I have, my love, but it'll be a while. I'm not about to pop my clogs, so I'll have to wait, plus the doors are locked up so they'll have to break in if you can't make it. I've managed to pull myself over to the counter to get the phone, but I can't do much else. I'm in a bit of a state… I wouldn't ask if I didn't need it, but do you think you can get here?'

'Of course,' I say, without hesitating. Good job I've only had the one glass of wine. 'I'll be there as soon as I can. Hold tight and try to stay calm.'

I hear her suck in a jagged breath and am horrified to realise she is actually crying.

'Matt!' I shout, in case he's upstairs. 'I need your help!'

Chapter 23

Matt agrees to keep an eye on the kids and I drive to the café as fast as I safely can.

I let myself into the place, which is eerily quiet and cast in flickering shadow as the sun sets over the bay.

I find Cherie lying on the floor, completely naked. She has tugged the phone from the counter and has managed to snag a tea towel from the shelf, but it isn't really a match for her physique.

She is a large lady and one scrap of red-and-white gingham isn't doing much to protect her modesty. I immediately see why she called me and not Frank. Her face is screwed up in pain and her skin is coated with a clammy sheen of sweat.

I crouch down next to her and touch her forehead. There is a lot of Cherie on show and her forehead seems like the least embarrassing bet. She is absolutely freezing, I discover.

I run through to the storeroom in the back, where I know there is a pile of fleecy blankets. She keeps them there for colder days out of season, so customers can still sit out in the garden and admire the view from the cliffs, wrapped up as they sip a hot chocolate.

I bring back a bundle and start to drape them over her. She lets out a loud yelp as I tuck one beneath her leg and I suspect she may have broken her hip. My gran did the same years ago and this looks very similar. I squash another fleece up into a ball and tuck it under her head like a pillow.

Once she is settled, I squat down beside her and hold her hand. I stroke the damp hair away from her face and we wait.

'What happened?' I ask, when she is as comfortable as I can possibly make her.

'Oh, it's so bloody stupid, Laura,' she says, sounding frustrated with herself. 'I ran out of milk upstairs, so I was coming down here to get some. I've no idea why, but I went and slipped down the last few steps and ended up in a right pickle.

'The pain is terrible, I tell you. I thought I'd have to spend the night like this, I did, until I managed to get to the phone. I was so relieved when you answered, my sweet… I know Willow's at home with her mum tonight, so I didn't want to bother her, and Frank… well, you can see the state I'm in. Plus he's getting on in years, I didn't want him rushing over and putting his back out trying to lub me around…'

'I suspect Frank could lub both of us around without it bothering him,' I reply. 'But I wouldn't want him seeing me starkers either. Why are you, by the way? Naked?'

'I always walk round the house naked – don't you?'

When my expression clearly tells her that no, I do not, she carries on.

'Well, I was at home, wasn't I? Work done for the day. Settling in for a nice quiet night, bit of telly, bit of party planning for Frank's do. Saved myself a bowl of that risotto you did yesterday. Always makes sense to me to take my clothes off once the day is finished. Maybe it's a throwback to my younger years. Anyway, I was all set, I was, until I wanted a cuppa and decided to nip down to the kitchen, and… oh, I'm such daft old bat!'

'You're not daft and you're not old,' I say, soothingly, trying to get my head around a world where your default setting is to walk round naked. 'But you are a bit batty.'

She manages a weak smile at that, but the pain is clearly taking its toll. Her tanned face is pale and drawn and every line and wrinkle on her skin seems so much more pronounced. For the first time since I've met her, she actually does look old and it breaks my heart.

There are a few tears building up in her eyes and they leak down the side of her cheeks. She swipes them away, angry with herself, and instead starts to swear, loudly and creatively, about how long the '****ing ambulance' is taking.

This seems a healthier course than self-chastisement, so I join in. We are still swearing when a paramedic in a dark-green uniform eventually bobs his head around the corner.

'Hello?' he shouts, as he steps into the now-darkened café. 'Anyone home?'

Cherie pulls a face at me, her eyes rolling up into her head in a gesture of annoyance.

'I'm over ****ing here, aren't I?' she yells.

WEEK 4

In which I hear a sad story, take a step up the career ladder, join a girl band from outer space and come to a very un-sensible decision…

Chapter 24

I am visiting Cherie in the hospital the next day when I get an attack of the collywobbles so strong that I have to lock myself in the disabled toilet.

I realise this is wrong and that someone with a real disability might need it, but at that precise moment I feel incapable of taking one more step or saying one more word, or doing anything more than hyper-ventilate and panic.

My heart is banging so hard it is like someone is punching my chest cavity from the inside out and my hearing has gone all fuzzy. The sound of life outside the toilet door is riddled with crackling static as it filters through my freaked-out brain.

My breath is coming in short, sharp, inadequate bursts, my vision is blurred around the edges and my hands are trembling. I am both cold and sweating at the same time and feel a little like my throat is closing up and choking me.

This is not my first anxiety attack, so I recognise it for what it is and don't worry that I am about to drop dead. The first time it ever happened, I was at Becca's, and she called an ambulance. Now, I know and understand what is occurring and that makes it easier to deal with. Easier to deal with – but still crippling.

I lean against the wall of the cubicle and slide slowly down until I am on my bottom. I tip my head forward so it is between my knees and try to slow my breathing. I suck in long, deep breaths through my nose, counting in my head as I do it. Then I gradually let it all out again through my mouth, still counting, and aiming to take double the time exhaling as inhaling.

It sounds quite complicated, but I've found it the most effective way of dealing with these attacks. If I'm concentrating on breathing and counting, it seems to calm the rest of my body down.

Slowly, bit by bit, it starts to work. The more oxygen I manage to suck in, the more controlled I manage to make my breathing and the better I feel. I am able to hold my hands still on my knees and blink some of the unreality from my eyes, and feel my heart pounding at a less terrifying speed.

After a few more minutes, once my hearing has cleared, I risk standing up and walk to the hand basin to splash my face with water. I look in the mirror and see that I am pale and clammy and that I have curls of hair stuck to the side of my face. My eyes still look a little wild, as though I am coming down from an especially powerful trip.

I use a paper towel to pat myself dry and sit on the loo and take a few more calming breaths before I am ready to face the world again.

By the time I walk into Cherie's room I am feeling, and hopefully looking, a lot better.

'You look terrible,' she says straight away, which completely blows that theory. 'Worse than me. What's happened?'

Cherie is propped up on a pile of pillows, looking uncomfortable but not in agony any more. She is going in for surgery on her hip later today.

'I'm fine,' I lie. 'I just don't have as many good drugs in my system as you obviously do.'

I pull up a chair and sit next to her. She is looking at me with concern, which isn't the way it should be at all.

'No, seriously, Laura, what's wrong? I can tell you're not right and I'll only fret that some disaster has occurred if you don't tell me!'

'It's nothing to worry about,' I say, smiling at her in what I hope is a reassuring manner. 'It's just… hospitals. And me. We don't mix well. I know nobody likes them, but since David… well, they seem to set me off even worse. I get these little… episodes. But it's all under control and it's nothing at all for you to worry about. You need to concentrate on getting better.'

Cherie reaches out and takes my hand in hers and, despite her own problems, gives my fingers a sympathetic squeeze. I blink my eyes very quickly, getting rid of the stray moisture that suddenly springs up.

'Now,' I say, keeping my tone of voice brisk, 'is there anybody you want me to contact for you? Any friends or family? I know you're going to be absolutely fine, but this is a big operation. Is there anyone you need?'

'No,' she says, shaking her head so her loose hair shimmies in a silver-grey sheen over her shoulders. 'My family is Frank and Joe and Edie and you and everyone else at the café. Frank's down as my emergency contact and I'm happy with that.'

'Okay… but what about real family? The kind you're related to by blood or marriage?'

I have never pushed Cherie about her background before, but feel like I need to now. It's all well and good saying her friends are her family and I completely understand what she means. But I also know from very bitter personal experience that sometimes – though hopefully not this time – someone has to make difficult decisions about medical care.

Nobody lives forever and we all need to face a little bit of reality sometimes. She obviously wants to keep her secrets – but as the old song goes, we can't always get what we want.

She stares at me, as though she is deeply offended, and crosses her arms across her breasts defiantly. It would perhaps look more intimidating if not for the fact that she is wearing one of those washed-out sickly green hospital gowns.

'Cherie, listen to me,' I say, meeting her eyes. 'I am not asking because I'm nosy. I'm asking because you're in hospital. You're about to have major surgery. Even if you don't need support from your family, you need to think about involving them, or at least think about the consequences of not involving them. Now, is there anybody you want me to call for you?'

She turns her head away from me and looks at the window instead. I suspect she is fighting back tears and I feel like a horrible bully.

'There's nobody left to call, my love,' she says quietly. 'Not any more. My hubbie's long gone, God rest his soul, and there never were any kiddies. I had a sister… well, I probably do still have a sister. She's a few years older than me, so she'll be in her mid seventies now. We lost touch a good many years ago.'

'Why?' I ask softly – because she is visibly still very upset. 'What happened?'

'Silliness, that's what happened,' she says, viciously swiping tears from her eyes, angry with her own weakness.

'It was all so long ago. I was a kiddie myself, really. Took me a long time to grow up, it did. Our mum died when we were younger and my dad brought us up. When he passed away, I was just turned twenty, and wild. Oh, lord, was I wild!'

'I've heard the rumours,' I reply. 'And we did wonder about the cottage names.'

She laughs at that, which is a blessed sound.

'Oh, I know, everyone thinks I was married to someone rich

and famous, don't they? Jimi Hendrix's secret lover? I let 'em think it! It's good for a laugh. And I was wild. I followed bands around, bit of a groupie… it was the sixties, mind, so it was all allowed. My whole life was one big gig, truth be told. I was Cheryl Whitcomb to start off with – and I ended up as a Cherie Moon. The Moon came from my husband and was very gratefully received, but the Cherie was all my own work… never thought anything was good enough, see?'

'And your sister?' I ask. 'Was she like you, back then?'

'Lordy no! Brenda was much more sensible than me, which wouldn't have taken much, really. She stayed at home with our dad while I went to festivals. She nursed him through the end stages of his emphysema, while I hitched rides on tour buses and drank mushroom tea. And when he died, and I finally came back, I told her I wanted to sell the house.'

Cherie's face clouds over as she reaches this part of the story, and I can see that she is still deeply ashamed of her behaviour. I understand why she doesn't share this part of her life with anyone – it still has the power to hurt her, in the way that only guilt and regret can.

'Ah. And I take it she didn't?' I ask.

'No, she didn't. I had this crazy idea that she'd want to. That she'd feel the same as me – that she'd want to take the money and run. But I forgot, see, that she was basically a lot more content than I ever was. She loved that house and I made her sell it. It was left to both of us in the will and she didn't have the money to buy my half, so it got sold. All so's I could have a few more bob in my pocket, travel the world, see more bands in more places…'

'You were only young,' I say, trying to soothe her.

'I know that,' she replies. 'I was young enough to be an idiot. It's only when I met my Wally and calmed down a bit that I realised how selfish I'd been, making her leave the house she grew up in. The only place she'd ever known our mother.

'I'd like to blame the booze and the drugs, but I think it was just my personality. I was lucky Wally saw through it and found something better in me, to be honest.'

'And how did you two meet?' I ask, wanting to keep her talking but worried that the sister angle is upsetting her too much. She's probably on morphine, and exhausted, and anxious, and it might be better if we explore what seem to be happier memories.

'He gave me a lift from the Isle of Wight Festival in 1970. That was the big one – Hendrix, The Doors, Joni Mitchell, The Who – the British Woodstock. In reality, I don't remember much about it. I got separated from the people I was there with and ended up trying to hitch back to the mainland. Wally stopped, in his shiny new Mini, and the rest is history…'

'Was he in a band?' I say, 'or just a music fan?'

'In truth, neither. He was an accountant for quite a few of the big record labels, as well as some of the bands. He lived in their world, but he was the money man. They accepted him because he had the long hair and wore the right clothes, but underneath all of that, he was very sensible. That's why I ended up so comfortable, because of his investments. I think the only wild thing Wally ever did in his life was marry me, and I'm sure I made him regret it on many an occasion! He's the one who made me try and find Brenda again, but… well, she'd gone.

'I think, with a bit of clear hindsight, that I felt so bad about making her sell the house that I kept moving forward and never looked back. Couldn't handle the guilt, you see. Years went by and she must have moved on too. I've never spoken to her since.'

It would seem odd to a child of Lizzie and Nate's generation, this tale of disappearing sisters. They live in an era where the whole world is on Facebook, and existence is mapped out online and publically shared.

I'm old enough to remember a time before – a time of letters and phone calls and visits – and Cherie, of course, is older still. From the era where you could so much more easily disappear and lose touch with people. I think of Becca and how devastated I would be if she wasn't in my life.

'Would you want to see her again?' I ask. 'Have you tried to find her recently?'

'I heard via someone who knew us – back in the day – that she'd got married and moved to Scotland. I suppose I could have tracked her down, or hired someone to do it, but… well, the years seemed to pass so quickly. And she never got in touch with me, either, so I had to assume she didn't want me in her life.'

'But you can't assume that! She could have tried – and it was all so long ago! I'm sure she'll have forgiven you…'

'That's as may be,' replies Cherie, firmly. 'But let's leave it alone now. All this traipsing down memory lane is quite tiring me out. Let's talk about something else. I'm going to be out of commission for a while with this bloody hip of mine and I'm not quite sure what we're going to do about the café. It'd break my heart to see it close, but I'm not sure what else we can do.'

I sit back in my chair and realise that it would break my heart to see it close as well. I opened up this morning, as usual, and managed to cope on my own until Willow arrived at eleven. Lunch was a bit of a nightmare and in some ways we were lucky that a rainy spell kept a lot of tourists away.

It took us both ages to do all the clearing, sort the till, do the banking and get as much as we could ready for tomorrow. I hadn't quite appreciated how many extra jobs Cherie did until she wasn't there.

We'd coped for one day, but it hadn't felt right without her. It would also be completely exhausting trying to maintain the whole place on our own, especially bearing in mind the fact that I had the kids and Willow had her mum. Cherie had been the backbone, the one who kept everything running smoothly – and I wasn't at all convinced that Willow and I were up to the job of replacing her.

I didn't want to tell Cherie any of this, though – I wanted her to go into the operating theatre thinking all was well, and that everything was going to be fine. And I owed it to her, and the other customers at the Comfort Food Café, to at least try and make that true.

'Don't you worry about it,' I say, patting her hand. 'Just get better. Me and Willow were fine without you today. To be honest, it was easier without you wafting around, bossing us all about…'

She slaps my hand and cracks a wide smile at my joke. That, I think, is definitely better than tears or bittersweet nostalgia.

'Seriously, Cherie, it'll be fine. You can leave it to us. We'll make it work somehow.'

She is looking at me quite intently and I get the feeling she is somehow trying to read my mind, probing for lies and other signs of duplicity. I school my face into the very picture of confidence and hope it fools her.

'You think you'll be able to manage? I mean, the cottages are let out by an agency and Willow usually deals with changeover day for me anyway… but the café, that's a lot of work…'

'"Manage" is my middle name,' I reply, sounding as confident as I can.

'I thought your middle name was "flexible"?'

'I had it changed by deed poll. I'm flexible like that. Look, don't worry, please. The café will be fine. It'll still be standing when you get out and I promise not to poison anyone or run it so badly you get slated on Trip Advisor… it'll be great. I'll even carry on with the arrangements for Frank's party. Hopefully you'll be up and about by then, or at least well enough to boss us around from a wheelchair. Honestly, it's the least I can do.'

'There is money,' she says, gazing off into space, obviously letting her mind race ahead now.

'I'm glad to hear it,' I reply. 'That always helps.'

'No, I mean, there's plenty of money… like I said, my Wally didn't leave me short. The cottages are more of a hobby than anything, and the café… well, that's a way of life, not a way of making a living. So there's money – if you need to hire someone else, or if you want to pay for Willow's carer to do extra shifts or—'

'I get it,' I say, interrupting her with a smile. 'And I don't want you to worry. The Comfort Food Café is in safe hands.'

Chapter 25

By the following day, I am starting to regret that statement.

The weather has picked up and the bay is back to its busy, beautiful self. The coastal path is lined with walkers looking like hungry little ants as they crawl along the track towards us, and our first tourists start to arrive just after 9am. The garden is soon busy and I can hear the screeching of gulls swooping overhead looking for freebies.

Willow can't get in until later, but I have persuaded Lizzie and Nate to help out. When I say 'persuaded', I obviously mean 'bribed'. I am not in favour of child labour on the whole, but I am not currently in a position to make decisions based on ethical niceties.

Anyway, they've been worried about Cherie too, and this is their way of showing it. That and their way of ensuring they do, in fact, get the cash I've promised them.

Lizzie is surprisingly excellent at customer service and charms everyone so much that they don't even object when she gets things wrong or drops their bacon butties, or forgets to put their order through at all. She is so smiley and young and pleasant that they simply let her off the hook and often, I notice, leave her a tip as well.

Nate is a general dogsbody for the day, which he doesn't seem to mind. I have him collecting plates and clearing tables, and have taught him how to load the dishwasher.

As the day wears on, he also gets one of my least-favourite jobs – heading out to the doggie daycare field with a shovel and a bin bag. It's a dirty job, but someone has to do it. As our own dog is out there contributing his additional deposits, he can't complain. He does it with a clothes peg on his nose for comedic effect, which seems to cheer him up no end.

By the time Willow arrives at eleven, the place is absolutely packed, inside and out. I have forgotten to put the jacket spuds in, we have already sold out of scones and muffins and the world and his wife seem to want a chocolate-bar ice-cream milkshake. The damn things take forever to make when you don't have a spare pair of hands.

On top of all this, we're running out of pound coins, the card machine is playing up and someone has broken the baby-changing unit in the ladies' loo. Willow is running backwards and forwards with orders and trays, Lizzie is trying to keep up with the till and Nate is scurrying around trying not to spritz customers in the eye with cleaning fluid when he wipes the tables down.

I am intermittently doing all of the above, while also keeping on top of hot-food orders, making up more rolls and paninis, and wishing I could throw the bloody blender down the cliff.

All things considered, it is turning into a shit of a day, and I feel on the edge of a nervous breakdown for much of it. I am quite tempted to take all of the cans of Coke and lemonade and orange fizz out of the giant fridge and stand myself in it instead. That'd give people a fright when they opened the door.

Frank calls in at about half-one, just before heading to the hospital to see Cherie. He takes in my frazzled halo of hair and bright-red face and looks around the crowded room.

'What can I do to help?' he asks straight away. I fight the urge to climb right over the counter and into his arms and instead blow out a sigh of relief.

'You can keep an eye on the counter for literally thirty seconds,' I say, draping a tea towel around his neck and giving him a quick peck on the cheek.

I don't give him time to ask any more and instead dash off to the loo, which I have been fantasising about for what feels like hours now.

When I get back, in a much better state of mind now I'm not in imminent danger of peeing myself, Frank has rebooted the card machine, sliced and plated up a whole chilled lemon meringue and cleared up the mess I made when I forgot to put the raspberry ice-cream back in the freezer after making a sundae.

Either I have been gone for more than thirty seconds or Frank is some kind of superhero who can slow down time.

Willow dashes through from the garden, order pad in hand, and slaps a torn-out sheet down in front of me.

'Aaaaaagh!' she says, before going straight back out again. I look at the paper. Two bowls of pea-and-mint soup and, predictably enough, two ice-cream milkshakes. One Kit Kat, one Maltesers. I pull a face and Frank peers over my shoulder.

'You do the milkshakes,' he says. 'And I'll do the soup. Even an undomesticated old goat like me can't get that one wrong.'

I smile, too grateful for words, and start to smash up a Kit Kat with far more force than is really necessary.

Bit by bit, minute by minute, order by order, we get through it all. We feed the hungry masses, we provide shelter to the weary and we rehydrate the thirsty mob. We may all collapse from heat exhaustion as a result, but we've done it.

We finally turn our open sign to 'closed' and there is what seems like a mass exhalation of relief as we all gather in the now extremely untidy café. There are dirty plates and empty mugs and screwed-up napkins and half-eaten jars of baby food on the tables, and blobs of lemon meringue on the floor, and stray cutlery pretty much everywhere.

We often get knocks on the door, even when we're closed, from people desperate for a cold drink. Usually we can oblige, but not today.

Instead, Lizzie has sold us on the idea of leaving an 'honesty box' outside, and she and Nate have lugged out a cooler full of cans of pop and bottles of water. She's made a sign with prices, adding that any extra will be donated to charity, and found a little metal lockbox that people can leave their cash in.

I remain cynical, but am willing to let her try – at most we will lose some stock and at best Lizzie feels like there is hope for the human race, and for her future as a business woman.

Once the kids are back in, I serve up drinks for everyone and also experiment with a simple recipe I've been meaning to try for a while.

I don't have a name for it, but it's made of honey and natural yoghurt and frozen berries, blitzed together to make a kind of chilled, fruity pudding. I grate some of the Galaxy chocolate I have in for the milkshakes over the top and give everyone a bowl.

Nobody talks for a good five minutes, so I assume it is a success. Nate gives it a thumbs-up and declares it to be called 'Super Fruity Fro-Yo'.

'Crikey,' says Willow, stretching her feet out and kicking off her sandals. 'I think that's the busiest day we've ever had.'

'Or maybe it just feels that way because Cherie's not here,' I reply.

'I'd say it's both,' adds Frank, the voice of reason. 'And we need a plan to help you ladies keep this place going until she's back. I spoke to her this morning and she was good as gold. Still in pain, but already itching to get up. She'd seen some physio lad and the poor thing had dared to suggest she might need to lose a bit of weight to avoid putting too much stress on the new hip.'

There is a collective hiss of horror as we hear this and imagine Cherie's response.

'Is he dead?' asks Lizzie, which is what most of us are thinking.

'No, but he has recommended she's put some kind of enhanced recovery plan, which means she'll be out of there quicker than usual… I think he wants rid of her.'

We all laugh, perhaps louder than it merits, because we are all so tired and wired and slightly hysterical.

'If all goes well,' he continues, 'she'll be out of the hospital in three or four days. She should be able to hobble around with crutches, but she won't be back to normal for a few months.'

'Where's she going to go when she gets out?' I ask, frowning as I think it through. Her flat is up a steep flight of stairs and no matter how determined she is, that's not going to work. As far as I know, all the holiday cottages are let for the summer. I could sort out the lounge of Hyacinth as a make-shift bedroom for her, but it won't be ideal.

'She doesn't know it yet, but she'll be coming to stay with me at the farm,' replies Frank, a steely glint in his blue eyes. 'There's plenty of room downstairs and there's a little shower room we had set up so I don't track mud into the house. She won't like it, Little Miss Independent, but she'll just have to lump it.'

'Good luck with that one, Frank,' says Willow, pulling a better-you-than-me face.

'It'll be fine – her bark's worse than her bite. Now, then, what are we going to do about the café? Another few days like this and you lot will explode.'

'I know,' I answer, because it's true. I was on the verge of it today. 'There are so many jobs Cherie did that we took for granted.'

'Well,' says Nate, face still splattered with Fruity Fro-Yo from licking the bowl, 'make a list of the stuff you've noticed went wrong today because she normally does it. Like getting the change from the bank for the till. And getting the stock in – there's only about five bottles of water left and hardly any cans. That was probably her job as well, wasn't it? There'll be others. Make a list and we can sort out who does what so nothing gets missed.'

It's a good idea and I smile fondly at him. What a clever little lad. He gives me the uni-dimple back and I fight the urge to crush him in a great big embarrassing mum-hug.

'Good thinking, Batman,' I say. 'I'll do that. But we need an extra pair of hands, basically – maybe even two. Cherie's given me her online bank details, so I can either embezzle the lot and retire to Barbados or use some of it for staff. She also mentioned she'd be happy to pay for extra shifts for your mum's carer, Willow, if you were able to cover more hours here.'

'I'll talk to her about it, see what I can do,' says Willow. 'But we still need a bit more help, I'd say.'

'What about Scrumpy Joe's wife?' suggests Frank, who is leaning back in his chair and chewing on a toothpick. 'Didn't she used to work in a restaurant in Lyme?'

'Joanne?' says Willow. 'She's pretty busy these days, what with the online dating and all. But we could ask – she might do it, for Cherie. I'll go see her on the way home.'

'Hang on,' I say, holding up my hand to bring a temporary halt to the proceedings.

'Are you saying that Scrumpy Joe is married? I never knew that – how come I've never met her? Plus she's called Joanne and he's called Joe? Do people call her Scrumpy Joanne?'

'Not if they want to live,' answers Willow. 'She's ferocious.'

'And what's that about online dating?'

'Rural Romance,' replies Lizzie. 'It's an introduction service for countryside types all over the UK. It's really taken off. She's found wives for shedloads of farmers who never managed to get out on dates before.'

I shake my head and wonder if I am hallucinating this whole conversation. Still, if she's happy to help, I will welcome Scrumpy Joanne with open arms.

'Me and Nate can carry on helping out if you need us to,' says Lizzie.

'Thanks, sweetheart,' I reply. 'That's very kind. But this is supposed to be a holiday for you guys, so hopefully we won't have you in here slaving away all day.'

'That's okay,' she says, patting her jeans pocket. 'I made £18 in tips. I can live with it.'

Nate snorts at the unfairness of this and I have to assume that nobody gave him a tip for clearing out the dog poo. I will correct that injustice later.

'Ivy Wellkettle's daughter's home,' says Frank, which does explain why I've not been grilling up Ivy's fish-finger butties for a few days. 'She might help out too, the days her mum's working. I'll have a chat to them later.'

It sounds like there is some kind of plan being percolated at least, which helps to calm my rising sense of panic. I was starting to think that I'd bitten off more than I could chew with this and was worried I was going to let Cherie down after all. I should have guessed, really, that the Comfort Food Café was a lot bigger than just one person.

The door opens and I hear footsteps. I turn around to explain that we are closed and see both Matt and Surfer Sam walking towards us. I suppress a giggle as I look at them. They are both tall and nicely built and good-looking in a slightly ungroomed, outdoorsy way, and for some reason seeing them stride towards us together, as though they're in some kind of impromptu fashion show for cargo trousers and walking boots, makes me want to laugh. I'm probably still hysterical.

Matt gives me his usual polite-but-distant nod – the one we use in public – and I return it. We are perfectly calm, perfectly respectful, perfectly friendly neighbours. He gives me a little wink as he pulls up a chair, when nobody else is looking, and I feel my heart do a tiny bounce in response.

'This place looks like a bomb's hit it,' says Sam, looking around at the tornado of litter, plates and discarded food. 'You need some help? I've got to lead a twilight nature walk later, but I can be yours for the next hour or so. Do with me what you will – I'm your slave.'

As ever, his tone is flirtatious and the grin he gives me and Willow is extremely saucy. I remain immune to it, as I am already engaged in flirtation and sauciness elsewhere, no matter how privately. Willow, who is clearly used to this kind of behaviour, just laughs and throws a tea towel at his blonde head. Poor Sam – his gift of the gab is getting him nowhere today.

'I think I need to go and get some stock,' I reply, thinking it all through. 'Sam, can you stay here with Nate and Lizzie for an hour and do some clearing? Willow needs to get home to her mum and Frank's on his way to fight with Cherie.'

'Is it all right if Josh comes round?' Lizzie quickly adds and of course I say yes – she's worked hard today, and not just for the money.

'What can I do to help?' asks Matt, and I struggle to keep my face straight as I meet his eyes. I have a few ideas, but none of them are suitable for public consumption.

'Take me to the wholesalers in your big truck,' I say, somehow imagining that even that is some kind of double entendre, and wondering if the others will notice.

Apparently not as nobody bats an eyelid. Everyone stands up and starts to move on to the next stage of their day.

I feel far more positive about life than I did an hour ago. We have a plan to get more staff and keep the café open without killing me and Willow. Sam and the kids are going to handle the cleaning. Frank will be able to tell Cherie that everything here is fine.

And I am going for a ride in a big truck with a big man. It's a win all round.

Chapter 26

Unfortunately, our ride in the big truck is the last time we are alone for quite a while. A cash and carry isn't the most romantic place on earth, but we do get to have a nice chat, and I do get to enjoy watching Matt lugging giant crates of soft drinks around for me. I realise this is very sexist but remain unrepentant.

Lizzie texts me to say that the cleaning is done and she has gone round to Josh's for her tea. Nate has gone with Sam on his nature walk and taken Jimbo with him. The café, she assures me, is totally spotless. I will believe this when I see it, as Lizzie and I often have very different definitions of the word 'spotless'.

Matt and I have to get the stock back and unloaded, using the little trolley Cherie keeps out back to wheel things up and down the hill, but we do make the most of our journey by visiting the coast around Lulworth on the way back. He parks the truck at the top of the cliff and we make our way down to the beach at Durdle Door.

I have seen pictures of it before, but never been here. It is beautiful – a stunning limestone arch rising from the water, almost mystical, as though mermaids should be splashing around out there. It is nearing the end of full daylight and the curved beach is quiet. It is quite a trek to get to, down steep steps carved into the rock and I imagine it gets packed earlier in the day.

Now, there are only a few of us down there, some throwing sticks for dogs, some paddling, some playing with their kids. Some, like us, simply sitting still on the gravelly sand and enjoying the tranquil sounds of the waves, the birds and pretty much nothing else.

I lean into Matt's side and he puts his arm around my shoulders and snuggles me towards him. I rest one hand on his thigh and neither of us speaks for a good few minutes. Partly it's because neither of us is an especially chatty person. Partly it's because it's just so peaceful and pretty, and perfect. It seems a shame to spoil such a pleasurable silence and I think we both feel that.

We're happy being quiet together and I wonder if it is because we don't want to spoil the sense of comfort that has sprung up between us. Yes, I most definitely fancy Matt – a lot – and I know that he feels the same. But equally, being together like this is just… nice. That sounds like such a bland word, but I don't underestimate the power of 'nice'. I have had a lot of drama in my life and this respite from it feels wonderful.

Even the day before, I was having a panic attack at even setting foot in a hospital – so the serenity of sitting here, in this beautiful place, being held by this beautiful man, is more than enough for me right now. Physically, I know I am ready for more. Emotionally, I am not so sure – so the fact that Matt seems as content as I am to simply go with the flow and enjoy the moment means a lot. It makes me feel safe and secure, and unpressured.

Eventually, of course, being female, I have to go and spoil it.

'My parents are coming down next week,' I say, purposefully keeping my voice bland and non-committal. I don't want him worrying about having to declare his intentions to my father or anything.

'Oh,' he replies, sounding equally bland and non-committal.

'They're planning on taking Lizzie and Nate away for a night…'

'*Oh...*' he says, this one more laden with significance.

Yes, I think. Oh.

'Perhaps we could... go out?' he says, nuzzling my hair as he talks. 'Or stay in. Whatever you want to do. No pressure.'

I feel both excited and scared at the prospect of actually being able to spend a night with Matt. On the one hand, it's about time I got 'back in the saddle', as Becca so tastefully puts it. But on the other... I've only known him for a month. That qualifies as a lifetime commitment to her, but I'm built differently. I've never had sex with anybody but David. Plus, obviously, there is no future for me and Matt – I'll be leaving again very soon.

Perhaps it is actually this – the knowledge that I will be leaving – that makes it easier in some ways. I can make some mistakes here without them haunting me. Without my family knowing everything. Without having to look those mistakes in the face every day for the rest of my life.

I am away from reality, and away from home, and away from the need to behave a certain way.

I am, after all, kind of on holiday, where different rules apply.

Matt has made me realise that my libido is far from dead and he has also made me realise how very lonely I have been. How much I have missed both the touch of a man's hand on my body, and the sense of companionship that used to be the bedrock of my life.

He has made me realise that perhaps – just perhaps – everything is not over for me. If I can feel this for Matt, with Matt, then I can feel it with someone else. Maybe I am using him, in the nicest possible way – and maybe the same is true for him. I know he bears his own scars, that he was deeply hurt by the breakdown of his relationship with Legs, and that I am helping him to recover as well.

'I think,' I say, turning my face up to kiss him softly, 'that I would very much like to stay in with you. Although you have to understand that I haven't, erm, stayed in with anybody for quite some time.'

'Neither have I,' he replies, treating me to a sexy sideways grin that somehow makes me feel like it will all be okay. 'Don't worry. We can be gentle with each other.'

Chapter 27

The next few days pass in something of a blur.

Scrumpy Joanne turns out to be an absolute battleaxe and I am terrified of her. She has perfectly coiffed eighties hair and looks a little bit like Dynasty-era Joan Collins only more ruthless. She is, however, a heck of a worker, and comes to help out every morning between nine and twelve.

I have learned that a mere nod from Joanne is the equivalent of an intimate girly chat for most women, and I now understand why she is not more involved in village life, or a regular at the café – she seems to basically hate people and despise all social interaction.

Sophie Wellkettle does the eleven to three shift and she is extra-adorable to make up for Joanne's Bride of Frankenstein demeanour. She looks like a younger, perkier version of her mum, Ivy, and is glad to not only help Cherie but earn an extra few bob before she goes back to uni.

Willow has arranged extra hours for her mum's carer so she can stay later with me and do the clean-up and prep for the next day, which is a huge relief. Lizzie and Nate intermittently buzz in and out, and the biggest favour they do me is staying out of trouble and making sure Jimbo is all right.

I am absolutely exhausted, between one thing and another, and spend most evenings curled up in a foetal ball on the sofa, too tired to even engage with re-runs of *Pointless*.

My job at the Comfort Food Café is now much more demanding – mainly because I have taken on Cherie's responsibilities as well. She was let out of hospital only three days after her operation, which I suspect was down to sheer determination on her part. That and perhaps the strong survival instinct of the staff.

To everyone's surprise, she agreed to move in with Frank, as long as he 'didn't mollycoddle her', and is visited by a nurse every day as well. Frank still calls in for his bacon butties and his mood seems high – in fact having Cherie around seems to have actually perked him up. I have had a growing suspicion that there could potentially be more to those two than just friendship, but so far I think both of them are too stubborn to see it.

Cherie is being forced to take it easy, which isn't sitting too well with her, but she's not daft enough to rush it. She's been told that if she does anything to jeopardise her recovery now, it will ultimately take much longer to get completely better.

As a result, she is grumpily staying in the back seat, letting me get on with running the café, and reluctantly allowing me to carry on planning Frank's party. Most of it was booked anyway – the food, the drink, a local electrical firm who are going to set up fairy lights and arrange a sound system. The theme this year is the Wild West, as opposed to last year's Mexican, and she has already ordered in a boxload of cowboy hats and toy guns from eBay.

As I said, most of it is done. I'm just planning some… extras. I don't know why I am choosing to make this more difficult for myself, but for some reason I feel I have to.

Cherie, Frank, Sam, Matt – everyone here in Budbury – has made me feel so welcome, made me feel so much stronger. They have given me a new lease of life and given me the hope and determination I need to go back home and carry on living – not just surviving, but living. The way David would want me to and the way I deserve to. They've embraced my whole family, made my teenage daughter less surly, played football with my son and even tolerated my flatulent dog.

I want to do something to say thank you and the party seems like the perfect opportunity to do it. In fact, the last opportunity to do it, as I'll be going home the day after.

So, I came up with some ideas. They are works in progress and they involve a lot of phone calls and internet hours, and on one occasion a visit to a Records Office in Devon.

They will also involve using some of Cherie's money, but she really wasn't lying when she said she had plenty – I remain amazed at the number of zeros on the end of her business bank balance and feel certain she won't mind me using a little bit of it up. In fact she's told me so. She's also given me a raise and the official job title of Restaurant Manager, which will look grand on my real-life CV when I'm back home.

I have had an unexpected amount of help from Edie May, who knows everything and everybody, and have been just as busy juggling my almost-secret party plans as I am juggling work and the kids.

Edie seems to think it will all work out and who am I to argue with a ninety-year-old veteran of life? I only wish, with all my heart, that there was a way I could conjure up a happy ending for her – but she seems content enough to help and use the skills she developed as a librarian, and the gossip she's acquired throughout her time in Budbury.

My routine has settled into opening the café at eight, working a full day there, and when I need to, staying on until about six dealing with the party. I don't want the kids accidentally overhearing, and some of the conversations I am having are sensitive – the last thing I need is the sound of those two pummelling each other in the background, or turning the TV up loud enough to drown out my voice with the *EastEnders*' theme tune.

Matt knows that I am not only busy but wiped out as well, and calls in to see me at the end of each of his work days to cheer me up. He comes with small gifts – freshly picked flowers, coffee I haven't made myself, a bottle of wine for later.

Mainly, he comes with his smile and his humour and his calm, gentle, self-assured sexiness. He knows that if he touches me a certain way, or kisses me for long enough, or does that thing where he wraps my hair around his fingers and turns my face up to his, that I will quite literally melt into his arms.

This is as far as it goes and it works well for us both. His self-assured sexiness is giving me the chance to rebuild my own and I am incredibly stoked about the prospect of spending the night with him the week after.

He never stays long – just long enough to make me feel a bit giddy – and he never pushes for more, either physically or emotionally. He asks if there is anything he can do to help, and he checks on Jimbo, and every now and then he does a few jobs around the café. If only he could also turn into a hot chocolate fudge cake, he'd be perfect.

I learn, during the course of one of our casual chats, that the village vet he has been covering for has emailed him to ask if he would consider staying on for another year, as her contract in Africa has been extended.

'Oh,' I say, genuinely not knowing what his reaction will be, 'Is that good news? Do you want to stay here?'

He does the looking-over-my-shoulder thing that he hasn't done for ages and I realise that he is carefully considering his response.

'I think so,' he replies eventually. 'I mean, I only came here to escape problems in London, in all honesty. I needed to get away, to spend some time away from it all, get my sense of perspective back. Does that makes sense?'

'Perfectly,' I say, wondering exactly what went wrong between him and Legs, and how bad it could have been to make this seemingly strong man run away like a wounded animal. I wonder, but I remain strangely reluctant to ask. If it was anyone else, I probably would – I'd give in to my nosiness and try to find out the whole story.

But we seem to have an understanding, me and Matt, that we keep things on this level. We laugh and joke and fool around and occasionally act like hormonal teenagers who've just discovered snogging, but we don't push each other about the past. We have established a delicate balance that allows both of us to leave it alone, and that works as well for me as it does for him.

'Now I'm here, though,' he continues, 'I'm… happy, I suppose. Definitely happier, anyway. So maybe I'll agree to another year and then take it from there. I'm still technically a partner in the surgery in Clapham, but nobody there is expecting me back at all. I'm a free agent and this seems as good a place as any to spend a few more months. How about you? How are you feeling about going back to Manchester?'

I look around at the café, and all its strange posters and found objects and dangling mobiles, and know that I will miss this place. I look out of the French doors to the cliffside terrace and down at the bay, and know that I will miss that view too. Finally, I look at Matt, sitting there with his tousled hair and his brawny body and his kind eyes, and I know that I will miss him as well – possibly too much.

That, however, is a thought for another day.

'It'll take a bit of getting used to,' I reply, 'but it's where our real lives are. Our home, the kids' school, my family. This has been… *un*real. In a good way. I'm sure I'll look back on it all some day and wonder what the hell I was thinking, but, well, it's been what I needed. What we all needed. I'm sure we'll all take something away from our time here.'

He is gazing at me in a slightly more intense way than usual, and it looks as though he is going to say something more. Something significant. I feel a tremor of both anticipation and dread at what that might be.

Instead, he just grins, stands up and stretches tall, and announces, 'I'm going to go and look at that baby-changer again. It's still not quite right.'

Chapter 28

'So,' I say to Becca, 'I now have pink hair.'

'I have seen this,' she replies. 'And I am awestruck. Was there alcohol involved?'

'There was. Rather too much. It was Cherie's first night 'out' since she came home – although it wasn't really a night out, it was a night at Hyacinth with me and Willow. Frank drove her here, with her special tall chair to sit in, and he went round to Matt's to have a pint while we had a girls' night in. Cherie wasn't really drinking much – she's still on strong painkillers, plus obviously doesn't want to fall over paralytic while recovering from a hip replacement.'

'That would be bad,' replies Becca, sounding distracted, which tells me she is rooting out the photos that Lizzie has posted online. The ever-present, and for me unseen, companion to all our conversations.

'You look like you're in some kind of girl band from outer space,' she says, laughing. 'Willow with her totally pink hair, Cherie with the pink tips and you with the big pink streak down one side. Maybe you'll get a record deal or be chosen to represent England in the Eurovision Song Contest… or play the Pink Ladies in a stage version of *Grease*…'

I have actually seen these photos, for a change – Willow got Lizzie to take some shots on her phone as well – and I completely understand where she is coming from. Cherie is perched on her tall chair, pink tips flowing over her shoulders, and me and Willow are posing on either side of her, making *Saturday Night Fever*-style disco shapes with our arms.

'Well, what can I say? It seemed like a good idea at the time. It's basically all Willow's fault – it's not like I would've had a box of pink hair dye lying around, is it? She took advantage of us when we were under the influence!'

'That,' replies Becca, 'is the story of my life. So… hair escapades aside, how's tricks? How's the party-planning going? Have you blown up the café yet? Have you blown anything else?'

I roll my eyes at her long distance. She's so rude, my sister.

'Party planning is… good. I think. Everything seems to be coming together – I'm just not entirely sure whether I'm doing the right thing or not. I mean, what do I know, really? Maybe I'll just be causing problems for everyone.'

'You know enough,' she answers, firmly. 'You've always been the one with the good instincts, Laura, so don't start doubting yourself now. You know Mum and Dad were on the verge of getting you committed when you said you were moving to Dorset for the summer, but your instincts were right – it's done you all so much good. So carry on trusting those instincts and it'll be fine, I promise.'

That is a very nice pep talk and I am reminded that beneath the rudeness and the outrageous comments, and the various layers of screwed-up, Becca is always well and truly, one hundred per cent on my side. As allies go, she kicks derrière. She should be part of the pink-hair gang too.

'Thanks,' I say simply. 'And… well… Matt.'

It is about time I told her, really.

'What about Matt?' she asks, super-quickly.

'It's... complicated.'

'Have you shagged him?'

'No!'

'Are you going to shag him?'

'I don't know! Maybe... yes, I think I am...'

Becca is quiet, which is not the reaction I was expecting. I have even removed the phone from my ear by a few inches, in anticipation of her whooping and hollering and general revelry at the thought of me doing the dirty at long last.

'Okay,' she eventually says, her tone cautious and neutral and various other words that can never usually be associated with Becca. 'Just be careful.'

'What do you mean? Are you talking about contraception? I know it's been a long time, but I think I remember how it works...'

'No, silly arse, I'm not talking about condoms. I'm talking about feelings, which believe me, doesn't come naturally. It's just that... well, I've seen the photos. I've listened to the things you've said – the gardening, the chatting, the amount of time you've spent together...

'I've watched this last month unfold. And I've seen how close you two have got, even if you haven't noticed it yourself. I'm not talking about physical stuff – I mean the *other* stuff. In every picture I see of the two of you, you look so relaxed, sis. You're always laughing or smiling, or... I don't know. Kind of glowing.

'You might not realise this, but he means something to you – and to the kids. So... be careful, is all. If it was me, it'd be different – we all know I'll jump into bed with anyone.'

'That's not kind!' I interject – because while Becca definitely has more experience than me when it comes to men, I don't like her making out that she's some kind of thoughtless slut, because she's not.

'You know what I'm saying. I am more than capable of having great sex with someone I find attractive, without it meaning anything at all. I can bonk and say 'bye'. For me, it's physical – a fuck is just a fuck. To you, it's a little bit of forever.'

I feel a bit deflated by this reaction and also unnerved. Perhaps she is right. Perhaps I have been deliberately underplaying the way that Matt has snuck into my life – into all our lives. Perhaps I have been fooling myself into thinking that I, too, can be as cool and casual as Becca.

Perhaps I'm wrong and sleeping with Matt will result in me falling ridiculously, stupidly, head over heels in love with him. Perhaps I am simply not capable of separating the physical from the emotional. Perhaps she is right to sound so worried. I might be thirty-five, but when it comes to this kind of thing, I am basically a babe in the woods.

'Right,' I say, quietly. She has popped my balloon and I don't really know how to react. 'Okay. I see your point.'

'Aaah, come on, Laura – don't go all floppy on me! I'm not trying to bring you down! God, I wish I was there so I could explain myself better…'

'No, it's fine,' I say. 'I get it. You're worried about me. It's just… well, you've been winding me up about Matt, and about my lack of a sex life, and… I suppose I thought you'd be pleased. That we'd have a giggle. That it would be fun. Instead, it's all gone serious again – and I'm… well, I'm so bloody fed up of serious, you know?'

'Ignore me,' she replies, quickly. 'Forget everything I just said. I know I've been encouraging you, but I genuinely didn't think it would ever happen – that's what made it funny. Maybe I'm just shocked. I'm over-thinking it, which is rarely a good thing, especially when it comes to men. Rewind our whole conversation, and instead imagine it like this: good on you, sis! Please, please, please don't let me knock your confidence or make you question what you're doing, or make you feel bad. Like I said, you have good instincts.'

I am trying to rewind our conversation like she suggests, but it is quite difficult to un-hear something once it's out.

'I shouldn't have said anything,' she adds, sounding genuinely regretful. 'It was stupid of me. I of all people have no right to tell you to be careful – I've never had a careful moment in my entire life, and you're well overdue a little bit of care*less*. Ignore me. Go for it. Don't take it seriously, babe – you're right. You've had more than enough of serious. Bang his brains out – and I'll stick that Princess Leia costume in the post…'

WEEK 5

In which I mostly cry.

Chapter 29

I put the phone down and look across the counter at Edie May.

Edie has been here all day and has sat quietly and unobtrusively through a busy breakfast, the lunchtime rush and the post-closing clean-up. Willow has gone home and the place will be peaceful and quiet now until either Matt calls in or one of my children appear demanding food, cash or a ride in mum's big blue taxi. Lizzie is at the cider cave and Nate is out on a fossil walk with Sam. Jimbo is snoozing away in the doggie crèche and all is well with the world.

Or at least I hope it is. I am biting my lip, so sharp I taste blood. I feel a headache – one of those tense, nervous kinds – starting to intrude on my temples.

One of Edie's many grand-nieces has bought her one of those fancy mindfulness colouring books and she has been perfectly happy perched on her stool, using a pack of rainbow-shaded felt-tipped pens. Intermittently she proudly shows me her work and I have to admit it is lovely – an intricate design of many-shaped hats, scarves and coats, all hanging from an elaborate hat stand.

She pushes the book towards me, so I can join in on the facing page if I like. What the heck, I think, starting to shade in the feathers of a peacock. Why not? I could do with a bit mindfulness right now. I've run out of Rennies and I need a bucket load of Paracetamol. Maybe colouring in will have the same effect.

My party-planning has taken on a life of its own and I am now starting to feel more than a little consumed with anxiety. I am second-guessing all the decisions that seemed to make perfect sense just a few days ago and worrying that I'm going to accidentally organise the worst party that Budbury has ever seen.

My intentions have been pure, but I can't help wondering if I am paving a nice path to hell with them – a path my new friends may be quite keen to speed me towards after the big event.

'All sorted, is it?' asks Edie, peering up from over her specs to raise her fluffy white eyebrows at me.

'I think so,' I reply, 'could you pass me that pink, please?'

'I'm not sure peacocks have pink tail feathers,' she says, passing the pen anyway. 'But I don't suppose it matters, eh?'

I bite down on a sharp retort. Edie is ninety years old, she's right about the peacock, and it's not her fault I'm feeling stressed out.

'What did she say? Is she coming?' she continues, all the while colouring away. Edie has been the one person I've confided in about this aspect of my party plans and I am not entirely sure why. Initially, it was because she used to work in a library and had helped lots of people trace their family trees. I needed to chase somebody down and her advice was actually incredibly useful.

I'd visited her tiny house that faces directly onto the main street of the village and sat with her in her pretty front room drinking the kind of strong, sweet tea that only old ladies and bricklayers seem to like. She explained that her fiancé was still asleep upstairs, so we both had to whisper in case we woke him up.

After that initial blow to all things rational, I found myself quite settled, murmuring away and explaining my ideas, while

Edie nodded and stirred in more sugar and occasionally asked a question.

She'd made some suggestions and pulled a face at others, and clapped her hands in delight at the whole concept. After agreeing that it would all be 'our little secret', she's been brilliant – my sounding board and confidante and sometimes my counsellor.

I was right to tell somebody and I didn't want it to be anybody who was directly involved. Willow already has a full plate, Joe didn't seem right and I don't really know Ivy well enough. Matt, also, I'd kind of kept in the dark about this part – he knows I'm up to something and I've recruited his help on other aspects, but he seems happy to go along with an element of mystery. I was a bit worried that he might try and talk me out of it all, to be honest.

Plus, if it doesn't work out, I don't want half the village knowing – because this isn't my story to tell.

Edie, though… well, as we have already established, Edie is not one to shy away from a crazy idea or two. Maybe that's the other reason I chose to talk to her about it all.

'She's going to see what she can do. She's a long way off and she's not been in the best of health, but she's going to try. She was surprised, obviously, but… pleased, I think? Oh God, I'm not sure! What if it's all been a horrible mistake?'

I can feel my pulse rate speeding up and that headache is solidifying into a real humdinger.

'Calm down, my love,' says Edie, pausing in her work long enough to pat me on the hand reassuringly, 'you're going outside the lines and making a terrible mess, look.'

I know she's talking about the colouring book and my now-psychedelic peacock, but the description applies just as well to what I'm doing for the party. I'm going outside the lines and I can only hope that I don't end up making a terrible mess of that as well.

Just one aspect of my evil mission – but by far the most terrifying – has been tracking down Brenda, Cherie's long-lost sister. With Edie's help, some rooting through marriage certificates and a lot of luck, I've managed to find her.

It was fortunate that she'd started with an uncommon name – Brenda Whitcomb. Cherie had heard that she'd got married and moved to Scotland, but I started on the basis that the wedding took place in this part of the world and worked on from that.

I'd had to guess at time frames, but eventually found a record of her marriage in East Devon in 1969, to an Adrian Applegarth. I suppose I was lucky he wasn't called John Smith.

Adrian was listed on the marriage certificate as a shipbuilder and there was an address in Glasgow.

I got nowhere with that – the street didn't even seem to exist any more and none of the Applegarths I managed to contact in the city (there were more than I expected) could help me.

One of them, though, suggested I look in Clydeside and even the North East of England, as the family might have followed the work around. From that point, I just got lucky – a search on a local paper's website showed an archived photo of the final group of men leaving one of the shipyards that was closing down, and sure enough, one of the serious-faced men it featured was an Adrian Applegarth.

Once I'd got a better idea of place, I did it the old-fashioned way – I made phone calls. Eventually, I ended up talking to a Robbie Applegarth in Dumbarton – Brenda's son. Obviously, he was a bit nonplussed at first, when this strange woman called him out of the blue to ramble incoherently about the Auntie Cheryl he'd never met.

'I've heard about her, of course,' he said, once he was convinced I was genuine and not out to somehow scam his elderly mum, 'but it always seemed to upset her if we asked too many questions.

I'm one of five and she'd absolutely lather us if we fought too much. Which of course we did, all kids do – but we knew that if we went too far, it'd really upset her. She'd cry and tell us we were wee brats and we should all be taking care of each other instead of squabbling.

'We grew up knowing that something had happened, that our ma wasn't in touch with her sister any more, but never really understood why. When we were old enough to properly ask, she'd say 'och, it was just silliness, it was…' and change the subject.'

That struck such a chord with me – 'silliness' was exactly the word that Cherie had also used to describe what had happened.

Robbie agreed to talk to his mother for me and he was true to his word, leaving me her phone number and a bit of advice on when to call. She'd had a tough few years, losing her husband to a stroke, and being in and out of hospital herself with conditions that weren't life-threatening but enough to make her children all worried sick.

Neither of us said it, but I suspect we were both thinking it – Cherie and Brenda are in their seventies, and who knows how much time they have left? Who knows how much time any of us have? If there's one thing I've learned in recent years, it's to make the most of every moment you have – even if it means uprooting your whole family and moving them to Dorset on a whim.

Now, though, as I have to stop colouring my peacock because of my trembling hands and impending brain explosion, I am not feeling quite so sure that my latest whim is going to pay off. Not that it was a whim – it took a lot of effort to track down Brenda – but it was definitely a risk. What if one of them has a heart attack? What if Cherie never forgives me? What if they take one look at each other and start a geriatric catfight?

'It'll all be fine, you know,' says Edie, not even looking up. 'You're having a panic for nothing, you are. They're sisters. Family.

Once they see each other, they'll be so happy. They've been lost for so many years and you're going to bring them together. It's good. It's marvellous. Don't think about it too much, dear.'

I smile at her and try to regulate my breathing. She's right, of course. At least I hope she is. Brenda had sounded a little shaky and unsure of how to react. I told her a bit about Cherie's life and her recent operation, and the café and the world she'd built for herself, and hoped it was enough.

Because although it had taken effort to find Brenda, it hadn't been insurmountable – and I can't help thinking that either of them probably could have done it too, if they'd set their minds to it. Maybe I'm trying to scratch an itch that they're both content to ignore, who knows?

Only time will tell – either she'll turn up or she won't; and either Cherie will kill me or she won't. No use worrying about it now, I tell myself – especially when I have other plans to hatch. Plans that are less controversial, but logistically challenging.

Still, I decide, it won't do any harm to perhaps sound her out a bit more thoroughly.

'I think,' I say to Edie, 'that I'm going to take a couple of painkillers. Then I'll run you home. And then I might go and pay Cherie a little visit…'

Chapter 30

I have dropped Edie in the village and I have checked in on the kids. Sam is going to give Nate a lift back to Hyacinth later and collect Lizzie from Scrumpy Joe's on the way. I am not the only one party-planning, and I will be checking Lizzie's rucksack for any smuggled cider later. She's a good kid – but she is still a kid. Cider and teens seem to have a certain magnetism that has survived the ages.

She's excited because all of her collective Budbury friends, and the younger ones who hang with Nate, are coming round later on. The two of them will be going away with my mum and dad in a couple of days and I've said they can have a bit of a gathering – a maximum of ten, and no going in the swimming pool if there are actual paying guests in there who might not want to be swamped by harmless-but-loud teenagers.

Lizzie is preparing for this one night away with my parents as though she may never return. She is talking about her pals here with such affection and yearning that she occasionally has tears in her eyes at the thought of being parted from them, even for a night.

I remind myself that this is how she felt about her Manchester friends not so long ago and that she was miserable about leaving them as well.

Being a teenager these days seems like a lot more work than it did when I was one, that's for sure. So many ways to communicate, and not communicate, so many ways to judge and be judged. So many tribes to join and music to like and styles to rock. It all seems very complicated, but I suspect that every generation thinks that about their children.

Maybe it was all much simpler when we were on rations and had world wars and women couldn't vote and everybody died of diphtheria.

I have Jimbo in the boot of the car and on the backseat there are a couple of boxes of muffins and cupcakes – some for Cherie and some for the kids' bash.

I forgot they were there and am now driving along the country lanes towards Frank's farmhouse hoping that the dog doesn't catch a whiff. If he does, I'm fairly sure he'll find a sudden burst of agility and manage to leap over the seats and bury his nose in them. He'll emerge, muzzle covered in pink frosting, with an innocent look on his face – like 'What? Cakes? Me?'

I pull up on the gravel driveway that leads to Frank's place, next to his muddy Land Rover, and open the boot. Jimbo, far from stealing the cupcakes, seems to be so tired he doesn't even want to get out. He thuds his tail a couple of times in greeting, but refuses to budge. I shrug, give him a quick tickle behind the ears and leave the boot open. I can see the car from Frank's living-room window and will notice if there is any sudden canine movement.

Frank's farmhouse is low and solid and built of beautiful pale-yellow stone. It has mullioned windows and a big, red-painted door and various outbuildings that have been added to the main house over the decades. It is set amid rolling green fields as far as the eye can see, the twinkle of the sea a distant glimmer along the coast.

It's a warm day, not too hot, but mellow and lazy. The kind

that is made for places like this, with its echoing bird song and the dull buzz of insects and clear, open views. I pause, look around and feel the sun on my skin, and think again how much I will miss all of this when I am back in Manchester.

As ever, when I am in danger of feeling too sad about leaving, I remind myself that Manchester also has lots of beautiful open spaces and that I will be able to get takeaway Thai food delivered to my door, hail black cabs in the street and do my Christmas shopping at the Trafford Centre. A host of urban delights awaits me back home.

I knock, but don't wait for a reply – they already know I am here. It's not the kind of place where there is a lot of random passing traffic. The door is on the latch and I let myself in, shouting hello as I walk through to the main living room.

Predictably enough, the house is still decorated to the tastes of Bessy, Frank's late wife. Perhaps less predictably, her tastes seem to have run to classy dark colours, plain-painted walls and a distinct lack of clutter on the tasteful pieces of wooden furniture.

Cherie is perched on her tall chair, crutches propped up next to her. The pink tips of her hair are flowing over her shoulders, reminding me that I also have a giant neon streak curling its way down the side of my face. As I generally don't spend a lot of time in front of mirrors, I am often surprised when I see it there.

She gives me a little salute as I enter and matches it with a huge smile. I suspect she must have been bored here and feel bad that I've not visited her more – but there are only so many hours in the day and keeping the café ticking over has been the priority.

'I come bearing cake,' I say, laying the smaller box down on a side table. 'Shall I make us a cuppa?'

'Only if you want one,' she replies, pulling a face. 'Frank seems to make me tea every half an hour. I swear he sets that fancy phone of his with an alarm and comes running back here to get the kettle on. That'd be all well and good, apart from the fact that it makes me run to the loo just as often…'

'Ha!' I say, slouching down into a squishy armchair opposite her. 'I'd like to see you run right now!'

She is sport enough to laugh at that and reaches for one of the cakes. I wait until she takes a bite and see her face crease into pleasure. As ever, that makes me feel happy.

'Gorgeous,' she says, when she's finished chewing. 'Orange?'

'Yep,' I reply, grinning. 'I've had them on the breakfast menu for the last few days. I call them Morning Sunshine Muffins. Basic muffin recipe, but I use skewers to make holes through them when they're baked and pour over a glaze made of fresh orange juice, zest and sugar. Bit messy, but… well, yum.'

'All the best things in life are messy,' she replies, giving me a wink. I wink back and wonder if this will lead onto a rash of double entendres. Like I say, she must have been bored. She has probably been storing up all her risqué one-liners.

'I've brought you your mail,' I say, pulling a wedge of envelopes, cards and flyers out of my bag. She sets them on her lap and doesn't look overly keen on opening any of them. I often feel the same about my mail, as it is usually full of bills, but I know first-hand that although Cherie may have some worries in life, money is definitely not one of them.

Still, I've adopted the same avoidance tactic here, even though they won't be my bills. I've been getting Lizzie to pile them all together in a corner for me to pass on, without going through them once.

'I'm glad you came by, my love,' she says, idly flicking through the envelopes, as though looking for any that might be interesting. 'I've been wanting to see you about something anyway. I think it's time we had a little talk…'

There is something about the way she says this that instantly makes me feel nervous. Although she doesn't have kids of her own, she is an old hand at being a mother figure to what seems like an entire village.

I am immediately on my guard and have a scary list of things in my mind that I suspect she might be about to tell me off about.

It could be Matt – perhaps we've been rumbled and she's about to quiz me on how far it's gone. Maybe it's the fact that I let Lizzie launch the honesty-box system without asking. Perhaps she's been checking her bank balance and seen some mysterious debits on there she needs to query. Or… the absolute worst of all… Edie May or her fictional fiancé have been round here and dobbed me in it with regard to Brenda.

I clench my lips together and try to stop the nervous tap of my toes against the parquet flooring, and ignore the prickling sensation that is disco-dancing its way over my scalp. Oh God, I think. She's going to kill me – crutches or not, I'm sure she could still manage it.

'Okay,' I say, sounding much braver than I am feeling. Externally, I hope I look normal. Internally, I am bricking it.

'I was wondering…' she says, tucking stray hair behind her ear as though she, too, is bricking it – or maybe just pebbling it – 'if…'

She leans forward a little and I notice a slight wince of pain. Cherie is such a force of nature, it's easy to forget that she had major surgery very recently.

'If you'd like to stay,' she finishes, raising one eyebrow. She continues to flick through the mail on her lap, as though waiting for my brain to catch up with what she's just said.

'Stay?' I repeat, frowning in confusion. I glance at my watch. 'For a bit, yes – got to make a move soon, though, there will be ravening hordes of teenagers heading over to the Rockery in search of cake before long…'

'No,' she says, waving a hand to cut me off. 'I don't mean now. I mean in Budbury. At the café. Would you like to stay, permanently?'

'You mean, like, forever?'

'That's often what permanent means, my sweet. Look, I can see this has come as a surprise to you, Laura, but I've been considering it for a while. Even before *this* happened.'

She gestures at her injured hip and the crutches with utter contempt, before carrying on.

'You've fitted in from day one, haven't you? You and the kiddies. It's a special kind of place, this, and it's not for everyone... but I think it could be for you. I realised how right you were that day with Jean, the walking lady? The way you took care of her and settled her and made a real difference to her. She'll always remember you and the Comfort Food Café, for that small kindness, you know?'

I shake my head, not quite believing what I am hearing.

'No she won't, don't be daft! I'm sure she'll just go on her way in life and won't think about it again at all... and... Cherie, this is a bit mad, even for you! I know you're hurt now, but you're going to make a full recovery, you know that. And you've told me yourself that once the summer season's done, it quietens right down. You don't need me, you really don't.'

'It's not just a matter of need,' she replies, 'and it's not about my broken hip. Or maybe it is a little bit. Maybe the hip, and being forced to take some time out, and being here instead of in the flat on my own, has made me reconsider things a bit. Take stock, you know? Have a think about where I am in life and what I want from it.'

She gazes out of the front window as she speaks and I follow her eyes to see that Frank is out there. He is leaning into my car boot and I see he's putting a bowl of water in there for Jimbo, which I really should have thought of myself.

I may be a little befuddled by her offer, but I'm still with it enough to join the dots. Maybe Cherie has finally realised that there is more to her and Frank than banter and bacon butties. If so, I'll be happy for them – but it doesn't really change anything in my life.

'I'm going to retire,' she announces, firmly, turning her face back towards me. 'And I think you're the person to take over. I can pay you, and pay you well, and we'd find somewhere more permanent for you and the kids to live. They've settled in, you can't deny it. And you've made friends yourself. This could work, if you just give it a chance.'

'Making friends for the summer isn't real life, Cherie!' I say, with some zeal. I suppose, deep down, I have been pondering these subjects myself – wondering how much substance there is to my life here; how genuine Lizzie and Nate's friendships are; how serious this thing between me and Matt is, or could be…

'Course it is,' she replies, not to be dissuaded. 'And if you stay, the summer doesn't ever have to end. It'll just change colour and get a bit colder. Look, just tell me you'll think about it, all right?'

I shake my head and stand up. I feel unnerved and unsure and thoroughly discombobulated by this turn of events. I was sad about leaving, yes, but I was set on it. It seemed the only thing to do. Now Cherie was presenting me with options that I wasn't at all sure I even wanted.

Life, sometimes, is much easier when you don't have too many choices. Manchester is my reality – it is my parents and my sister and school and home and, most of all, my precious memories of David. It is my oxygen.

This? This has been wonderful. Life-changing. Utterly brilliant. But it simply isn't real.

'I've got to go,' I say, refusing to engage with the whole silly idea. 'I have to get pizzas in the oven. I'll see you soon, all right?'

I turn to leave, realising that I've been thrown completely off course and not managed to even sniff around the subject of how Cherie would feel about seeing her sister again. I daren't sit back down, though, because I know she'll only take that as encouragement.

'Laura!' she says, calling me back. 'At least take these, will you, before you make your mind up? Take these and then tell me this isn't real.'

She hands me a small stack of old-fashioned postcards, which she seems to have sorted from the pile of mail on her lap. I glance at them and see pictures of beaches and castles and stately homes and surfers, all from different spots in Devon and Cornwall. I turn one over and see immediately that it is from Jean.

They are all from Jean. All eight of them. Cherie was right. She had thought about us again and it had mattered and it had made a difference.

I shove the postcards roughly into my bag to read later, blink sudden tears from my eyes, and leave.

Chapter 31

'It's… lovely!' says my mother, wrapping a strand of my curly pink hair around her finger and staring at it with a smile as fake as Katie Price's boobs.

Like mothers throughout the ages – myself included – she has no sense of personal boundaries when it comes to her offspring. I count myself lucky that she's not whipped out the nail scissors she always carries in her handbag and snipped my pink streak off, before patting my head and saying 'there, that's better, isn't it, love?'

I resist the urge to slap her hand away, because that would be juvenile, and the kind of thing I would have done when I was fifteen. I am at least a tiny bit more mature these days and understand that she is at least trying.

I don't think for a minute that she actually thinks my radical new hairstyle is lovely. In all honesty, neither do I. It was a drunken accident, but I suspect that telling her that might actually make her worry about me even more, so I keep quiet. Perhaps she will just assume that it is a small act of mid-life crisis rebellion. Much like moving to Dorset for the summer.

My parents have arrived and I feel like my worlds are colliding. While I managed to keep them separate everything was fine. Now they are melding and I feel like I am stuck in some kind of science-fiction movie, where I might slip through a crack in the space-time continuum.

Not, I think, as I glance over at my dad, that I would mind that right now.

He is sitting at one of the window seats at the café, with Frank and Matt. Matt, the man who has come close to defiling his daughter on several occasions. Matt, who she is secretly planning to spend the night with as soon as they have left. Matt, who keeps giving me furtive glances over my father's shoulder and small smiles that I am sure are meant to reassure me.

The three men look absolutely fine together and I suspect that Frank is regaling them with tales of his brief but obviously memorable time at RAF Wilmslow. My dad worked as an engineer in Wilmslow for years and can talk endlessly about it as well. Matt, as far as I know, has never even been there, so it must be a really interesting conversation for him.

I'd go and rescue him, but I'm too busy trying to convince my mother that I am actually, honestly, well and truly, fine.

They arrived about an hour ago and came straight to the café as I'd suggested. I have brought the kids' bags with me and, as I expected, they arrived before lunch. My parents are also fans of the Early Start for long journeys – this may be where I have inherited it from – and Dad is immensely proud of making it all the way from Manchester in just under four hours.

Their plan is to take Lizzie and Nate to a holiday park in Weymouth for a night, then bring them back here before they drive through to Cornwall. They're spending a few days there and then heading back up North around the same time I am.

They assure me that Becca has been tasked with looking after my garden, which immediately makes me worry that I will go home to parched grass, withered bedding plants and shrivelled-up hanging baskets. Possibly some graffiti art on the patio as well.

I have kept both Lizzie and Nate close at hand, allowing them only as far as the beach, knowing that Mum and Dad were likely to get here earlier than they'd said. I have already texted them to effectively say 'get your arses up here now', and am hoping they arrive soon.

Now the lunchtime crowd has cleared enough for Willow and Sophie Wellkettle to cope without me, I have no choice but to interact with my mum.

I feel mean saying this, or even thinking it, but she doesn't make things easy. She has always been on the over-protective side and since David's death who can blame her? She watched me go through the mill emotionally, saw me through several crises, stepped in to take up the slack with the kids and the housework and did absolutely everything that a good mother would do in such a situation.

The only problem is that she doesn't seem to know how to stop. I understand that and as a parent, I sympathise. I'm sure I'd be just the same if it was Lizzie, heaven forbid – yet it's not that easy to take when you're on the receiving end. Logically, I get it, and I appreciate it. I know it's done through love. But part of me, if I'm honest, resents it. That probably makes me a horrible person, but it's the truth.

As soon as she arrives, I start to feel like I need to prove myself. Like I need to reassure her and show her that I am fine. That we are all fine and that she needn't worry. Sadly, the hair isn't doing much to help that – nor is the fact that the children are down on the bay rather than here with me, literally tied to my apron strings.

'Are you sure they're safe?' she asks, for the fifth time since she walked through the door.

'Yes, completely,' I reply, reminding myself to be patient. 'The sea is very shallow here. It's a very safe spot. Plus they have friends there with them and we can actually see them from the terrace. They'll be on their way up, there's no need to worry.'

She has already managed to quiz me about everybody's health; about whether I am sure I am coping with the extra burden of running the café; about Matt, Sam and every other male of mating age she has seen, and about Lizzie's friendship with Josh. Or, as she puts it, 'that sixteen-year-old'.

I realise that in her eyes, a sixteen-year-old boy is only interested in 'one thing', and that she is worried about her grand-daughter. And I must confess that over the course of our weeks here, I have had some concerns on that front myself.

While I am perhaps slightly more aware than my mother that in this day and age, boys and girls mix a lot more socially in a non-romantic way, I am also not stupid. Lizzie likes Josh and Lizzie is a pretty girl. So far, nothing much seems to have happened between them – and I have to trust my own daughter enough not to automatically assume the worst.

Josh, I tell her, is a nice boy. Which is true. Three days after Lizzie started her Honesty Box, I called into the café late to make some phone calls and I found him lurking outside. As soon as he saw me, he blushed all the way from his peach-fuzz moustache to his beanie cap.

Turned out he'd been coming here every evening, checking on the stock and making sure everyone had paid for what they'd taken. If there was any shortfall, he put it in the box from his own pocket, just so that Lizzie wouldn't be disappointed the next day. This had struck me as an almost unimaginably sweet thing to do, and it convinced me that I really didn't need to worry about him using and abusing her in any way.

I glance at my phone, looking for any kind of distress beacon from the kids, as it seems to be taking them a while to make it up from the beach. I suspect it is purely down to reluctance on their part. When they were little they used to love going to my parents' house, but since they've got that bit older, they've lost some enthusiasm.

Mum and Dad are lovely people, they really are. They're kind and pleasant and solid and reliable, and unfortunately for them, their favourite activities involve bingo, watching history documentaries on television, touring garden centres and eating cake in National Trust tea shops.

Personally, I can see the attraction of all these things, but Lizzie and Nate don't entirely agree. Weymouth is, by local standards, a throbbing metropolis. There's a fairground and amusements and a huge beach and live entertainment and bars and a Sea Life. It's like Sodom and Gomorrah compared to Budbury – but Lizzie is convinced that they'll only be allowed to walk along the prom and go bird-spotting.

I feel marginally guilty – I am, after all, planning a far more exciting evening for myself – but, well, not guilty enough to object to their trip. They're lucky they have both sets of grand-parents still around, even if one half is currently on a world cruise. And I, I remind myself, should be more grateful too – they're both in their early sixties, but as fit and healthy as they could possibly be.

Just as my mum starts to suggest we send out a search party, peeking over her glasses in that way she does when she's worried, Lizzie and Nate breeze through the café door. They are immediately engulfed in huge grandmotherly hugs that they endure valiantly, with a minimum of face-pulling.

Nate, bless him, only tugs away when she starts patting his rosy cheeks and kissing him. His rosy cheeks get even rosier, and I know that although he is still young enough to like a good cuddle in private, doing it in public dents his inner sense of teenybopper machismo.

My dad gets up and walks towards all, giving Lizzie a quick

hug but settling for a high-five with Nate. It always looks funny seeing older people doing high-fives, I think. My dad in particular always looks slightly uncomfortable with it, like it's some kind of Masonic handshake he's not quite mastered.

'Right!' I say, with perhaps slightly too much enthusiasm, 'is everyone fed and watered?'

I know they are, as I served Mum and Dad myself, and Lizzie and Nate brown-bagged it down at the beach. There is a chorus of yesses and the obligatory pause while Lizzie captures the moment for posterity on her phone. Honestly, if she doesn't take a snap of it, it's basically not happened – it's the modern-day equivalent of the tree falling in the woods.

I get their bags from round the back and force them both into another hug, even if Nate is still reeling from the last one. I find myself hanging on to them a little too tightly and feel an unexpected sting of tears behind my eyelids.

I suddenly feel sad and weepy and reluctant to let them go. Never mind Weymouth, I don't even want to let them out of my arms. I only release my death grip when Nate squirms so hard he accidentally elbows me in the gut, and even then I still hold on to his hand.

I have been looking forward to my night with Matt and now it is taking one step closer to becoming a reality I feel swamped with guilt – as though I am getting rid of my precious babies purely for a quick bonk. Obviously, that's not true – my parents were the ones who suggested this, not me. And hopefully it won't be a quick bonk, either.

I blink rapidly so the tears don't fall and try and put a brave face on it. I turn to my mum and she wraps her arms around me and squeezes me even harder than I squeezed Nate and Lizzie.

'I love you,' she whispers into my hair, 'you know that, don't you?'

I nod and hug her back and feel terrible for getting annoyed with her earlier. She's just a mum – and I'm her precious baby.

'Now,' we both say at precisely the same time, 'does anybody need a wee?'

Chapter 32

I am lying in the bath at Hyacinth, soaking up to my neck in lavender-infused bubble bath that I bought from the gift shop down by the beach.

I've done the clean-up, and tomorrow the café is closed, so for once I don't have to worry about getting up early, dragging the kids out of bed, or being careful I don't drink too much in case I'm over the limit the morning after.

In fact, I am free to get horrendously drunk, sleep in for most of the day and not worry about the children at all – or at least not worry about them now, as Mum has called to say they arrived safely.

Lizzie has also sent me a photo of them all standing by the sign for an RSPB Bird Reserve. The look on her face is absolutely priceless. 'Party on, princess!' I reply, adding a few jaunty emojis just for fun.

Now, after doing a bit of housework and sticking in a load of washing, I am rewarding myself with a long soak. I have the radio playing and the small window open so I can hear the birdsong from outside, and a paperback held aloft in my hands. It is an original 1980s copy of Jilly Cooper's *Rivals*, which I found on the bookshelves in the café, and it is still a racy good read.

I am very much enjoying getting reacquainted with Rupert Campbell-Black, and imagining what Matt might look like in jodhpurs. I have seen him in shorts and swimming trunks and tiny white towels, so his legs are not a mystery to me and I reckon he might look pretty good.

We have agreed that we will meet up later on, at about six, and possibly go out for dinner. Part of me simply wants to stay in and get on with the schedule, but part of me is very nervous and realises that having a drink first might help.

The trick, I think, will be hitting that sweet spot – the spot where you have had enough to drink to make you relax, but not so much that you start telling strangers they have beautiful eyes. I'm thinking that for me, that is probably at the three glasses of wine mark. Too much more and I might want to sing karaoke or wrestle a scarecrow or bring a traffic cone home, all of which would be fun but not exactly what I have in mind for this evening.

I notice that I am starting to wrinkle up like a prune and fold over the page in my book. I lay it down, unplug the bath and stand up. I have shown remarkable foresight and draped a towel over the mirror that is on the opposite wall. The last thing I need is to end up posing, looking at my naked body from various angles, sucking my tummy in and marvelling at the size of my arse. None of these things are confidence boosters.

All of this, of course, is very new to me. David and I were together from being children. Of course, I was nervous – we both were – once our relationship became more physical, but it was all part of the adventure. The next logical step for two people who loved each other so much – and two people who trusted each other so much.

I think that's what made it work so well. The trust. I know that Becca thinks I'm mad, only ever having slept with one man, but she doesn't get it. I suspect she thinks I have no idea about physical pleasures, and that because I've not experimented with other partners I couldn't possibly have been fulfilled.

In reality, our sex life was brilliant. We went through dips and hollows, like all couples, especially after the kids came into the picture, but we were as compatible in that department as we were in all the others.

I always fancied David and he always felt the same about me. I rarely felt bad about my body because I'd never had reason to. It was good enough for David and that was good enough for me.

So now, here, preparing to meet up with only the second man who is likely to see me naked (unless I blindfold him and pretend it's a kinky game), I really don't need to be confronted with my own flaws.

I shaved my legs and trimmed other relevant areas earlier in the shower and now I amble into the bedroom and lash on some fancy moisturising cream that I was bought for Christmas and never had the need to use.

Once I am smooth and buffed and fragrant, I snuggle under the duvet, my hair still wrapped up in a towel turban.

It is strange being here without the kids. Slightly too quiet, but also a tiny bit delicious – like I am indulging in a forbidden luxury, spending time completely on my own.

I roll over onto my side and look at the photo on my bedside cabinet. The one where we all look so happy. So together.

'Hello, you,' I say, smiling at David in his scuba-diving mask. Obviously, he doesn't reply – but this time I don't expect him to. There have been moments, admittedly low points for my mental health, where I have genuinely imagined that he would.

'I don't know what you'd think about all this,' I continue, safe in the knowledge that nobody can overhear me.

'Obviously, if you were still around, you'd be furious and probably go over to Black Rose and punch Matt's lights out. But if you were still around, my love, this wouldn't be happening, would it? I never looked at another man and don't think I ever would have done. Apart from Daniel Craig, of course, but you always said you were okay with that… anyway.

'You're not here. I wish you were, for all kinds of reasons, but you're not – and I think this is something I want to do. Need to do, maybe.

'Much as I love you, I can't live the rest of my life waiting to die, can I? And I don't think you'd want that, either. Remember that time we talked about it, after you got food poisoning in Italy and thought you were on your way out?

'We both said we'd want each other to find someone else – although I think I probably wasn't as gracious as you, because I wasn't going through a near-death experience at the time… what was it I said? I think, if I remember right, I said that I'd be okay with you meeting someone new, as long as she looked like Camilla Parker-Bowles. Bit mean, that.

'But… well. Here I am. The kids are doing great and I'm feeling better. I've no idea if you're sitting up there in heaven laughing at me right now or wishing me all the best, or screaming at me. Or if there's a heaven at all.

'I suppose if I knew that, I'd have more job offers than temporary café manager, wouldn't I? Or permanent, if Cherie had her way… well. Wherever you are, David, I love you. Nothing will ever change that. And if you are perched on a fluffy white cloud looking down at us all? I'd suggest it might be an idea to close your eyes for a bit…'

I place a kiss on two of my fingertips and reach out to place them on David's photo-face.

After a few more moments of chilling out, I get up and get my clothes on. I wear my strappy green sundress because it matches my eyes and because it's the only going-out frock I have with me, which narrows down the choice. I settle for flat sandals, as again, I don't have huge amounts of choice – my missing high-heel wedge was never recovered from the Field of Shame.

I have put on my best matching underwear and hope that it's not a set that Matt has previously seen spraying out of a busted bin bag or hanging from a car aerial. I dry my hair with some gunk so it is long and curly and wild rather than insane and frizzy and frightening, and apply a little make-up.

I look, I think, not at all bad. My tummy is tingling and my heart feels a bit fluttery, and I am both nervous and excited. I remind myself that I am a thirty-five-year-old mother-of-two and although my life has been different from most people's, I am not inexperienced, and I have no reason to doubt myself.

Matt, like David, has never shown me anything other than kindness and compliments and has certainly never given me cause to feel insecure about my looks. Or, in fact, anything at all. We have had fun together and enjoyed all of our illicit sneaking around probably a tiny bit too much for alleged grown-ups, and we are clearly very attracted to each other. This needn't be complicated. I have enough other things in my life that are complicated – I want this to be simple.

Part of me knows, as I skip down the stairs, that I am fooling myself. That I am in fact *over*-simplifying. That this is possibly, in fact, one of the most complicated situations I have ever had to navigate. That – most anxiety-making of all – I have absolutely no idea how I will feel afterwards.

That not-knowing part suddenly fills me with dread and fear. I am not used to this sensation. Grief, pain, loneliness – yes to all of them, with knobs on. But not knowing how I feel about a man I am intending to have sex with? This is completely and hideously uncharted territory.

I sit on the bottom step and quickly call Becca. She may be the younger sister, but right now she's probably the one with all the wisdom.

'I'm terrified,' I say, as soon as she answers. And I realise, as the words spill out, that this is true – despite my careful preparations and my one-sided chat with David, and my insistence on keeping everything between me and Matt as simple as I can, I am terrified.

'Of what?' she asks. I can hear traffic roaring behind her and guess that she is out in town. I can hear car horns honking and people shouting and music blaring and the background beep-beep-beep of the green man flashing. All of these once-familiar sounds now feel slightly alien to me.

'Everything. I'm terrified it'll be crap and I'll have forgotten what goes where. I'm terrified I'll be rubbish or freeze up, or burst into tears halfway through. I'm terrified I'll call him David in the heat of passion and totally freak him out.'

'None of those things are going to happen, and if they do, from what you've told me about Matt, he will be understanding. But Laura – it might also be brilliant.'

'I know,' I reply, blowing out a long, anxious breath, 'and I'm terrified of that most of all. What if you're right, Becs? What if this does all mean more to me than I'm letting myself think? What if you were right to warn me to be careful?'

'You know better than to listen to me!' she says, sounding exasperated. 'I'm usually drunk! And, seriously, I regret even saying anything – I know it gave your confidence a knock just when it needed a boost and I'm sorry. I was just being daft and cautious and over-protective, you know? A bit like—'

'Mum,' I supply, knowing exactly where that sentence was going.

'Yes, which has just made my pancreas shrivel up with horror. Look, you of all people deserve a little bit of fun. Have a glass of wine, chill out and see how it goes. And just because you sample a starter, don't feel obliged to go on to the main course – if it's not rocking your boat, for any reason at all, you call a halt to the proceedings and leave. Stop putting so much pressure on yourself, and on him. Don't forget he'll be nervous as well.'

She has a point. From what Matt has told me, he hasn't been with anybody else since Legs, either, and he knows my history. From his perspective that's a lot of responsibility – and the last thing he needs is me having a nervous breakdown. This is, I remind myself, supposed to be *fun* – not some awful task you have to complete on a Japanese game show.

'You're right,' I say, already feeling a tiny bit better. 'I knew you'd help, oh wise one.'

'Yeah, well, I am the Mrs Miyagi of Sex. Wax on, wax off, all right? You'll be fine. Now, I'm going to go – I have three sailor boys chained to the wall of my torture dungeon and I need to get back to them. But call me tomorrow, okay? Or tonight. Even if it's three in the morning – call me if you need me.'

'Okay. Love you.'

'Love you too – now scoot!'

I put the phone down, but stay on the step for a few more seconds.

She's right. Of course she is. I need to relax. Chill. Step out of the pressure cooker and let things take their natural course instead of trying to force something or predict the unpredictable.

I amble through to the kitchen and get a bottle of prosecco out of the fridge. It's been sitting in there for a couple of days and the spoon I shoved in the top of the bottle hasn't exactly kept it fizzing, but I pour myself a glass anyway.

I take a sip and it is icy cold and alcoholic and I immediately feel better. I even manage to laugh at myself a little for whipping up such a high-maintenance cocktail of panic and over-analysis.

I am, after all, going to be spending the evening with a drop-dead gorgeous man – one who resembles a young Han Solo, for goodness' sake! I should be celebrating, not thinking it to death.

Cheered by Becca's chat, my own thought processes, the image of Han Solo and possibly the prosecco, I glance at my watch and see it is almost six.

I grab Jimbo's lead from the back of the door and pick up our mutual overnight backpack – we have agreed to have our sleepover at Matt's, as it is bigger and kids don't live there and there isn't a photo of my dead husband by the bed (though I didn't mention that part as it seemed weird).

I have spare pants and my make-up bag and my toothbrush and some perfume, plus Jimbo's special low-fat dog food. He, I know, will be more than happy to spend the night at Matt's, though we'll have to be careful where he sticks his snout, as usual.

I walk towards his red tartan bed, which I'm planning to take with me and shake his lead over his head.

'Walkies!' I say, in a high-pitched crazy-lady voice. He's been more and more difficult to mobilise recently and I may need to hold a piece of bacon in front of his nose for the entire journey to Black Rose.

Typically, of course, there is no response.

'Come on lazybones! Time to go see Matt!' I add, kneeling down to hook the lead onto his collar.

As I do, I realise that he isn't moving. At all. His tail isn't thumping, even a tiny bit, and he isn't looking at me with one sleepy eyelid half-raised, like he usually does. He isn't snoring, or snuffling, or making any sounds at all.

He's not, I am forced to acknowledge, as I collapse back onto my bottom and sprawl on the wooden floorboards, even breathing.

Chapter 33

I wake up fully clothed, wrapped in a blanket, on top of Matt's bed. He is there with me, one arm thrown across me protectively, his breath warm on my neck.

For a second I feel fine. More than fine. I feel elated to be here in his arms, safe and secure and happy.

Then it all comes crashing down on me and I remember why my eyes feel glued together and my throat is dry and my hair is tangled and plastered messily to my face.

I remember that Jimbo is dead and David is dead, and the part of me that was starting to come alive again now feels crushed beneath the grief. That I am so miserable that I wish I was dead too.

Silently, the tears start to flow again, oozing out from between crusted lashes, pooling into an already damp patch on the burgundy pillowcase. I look up, instinctively, seeking the picture of David on the bedside table, before my sleep-deprived brain puts all the pieces together.

I am at Black Rose, with Matt. From the watery sunlight creeping in through the curtains, it is early morning. I have slept fitfully and restlessly and probably been an absolute nightmare to share a bed with.

I called Matt as soon as I realised what had happened with Jimbo and he arrived what felt like seconds later, running at full speed through the door, clutching the vet's equivalent of his medicine bag.

He knelt down beside him with his stethoscope and checked his heartbeat. He checked his breathing. He lifted his eyelids. And finally, sadly, reluctantly, he gave Jimbo's greying muzzle one last stroke and his velvety soft ears one last tickle.

He stood up to face me and gave me a sweet smile.

'I know,' I'd said, feeling my lips tremble and the tears begin to fall. 'I already know… it's just… he was still warm…'

'He's not been gone long,' replied Matt, reaching out to hold my hand, his eyes scanning my face, his fingers stroking mine. 'And it was peaceful. Looks like that old heart of his just couldn't keep going any more.'

I felt the tears sliding down my face and I slid with them – all the way to the floor. I held Jimbo's head on my lap and I kissed him and cuddled him and petted him and drenched him in tears. I told him what a good dog he was and how much we'd miss him, and how much I loved him.

I know he's just a dog, but in that moment I would have given literally anything for him to open his eyes, let out that snuffling noise that made him sound like a pig and lick my face.

Matt sat down on the floor beside me, his arm around my shoulders, and let me talk and weep and sob. I'm sure he'd seen it all before in his job, crazy owners refusing to let their pets go.

'I was upstairs,' I said, my voice trembling, words coming in bursts between sudden shaking breaths, 'getting ready for our date. I was upstairs, tarting myself up, while Jimbo was down here on his own. He shouldn't have been on his own… he was a good dog… he deserved so much more than that… I should have been with him…'

Matt lightly kissed the side of my head and turned my face around to rest on his chest. He was wearing what looked like a new shirt, fresh white cotton that he'd probably bought for our night out.

'In my professional opinion,' he said, stroking my hair back, 'he was asleep. You know he loved to sleep.'

'Yes,' I sniffle, 'it was one of his very favourite things.'

'It was. And he was very good at it. I think Jimbo had had a nice walk around the Rockery with you earlier – and I know he did, because I saw you go past – and then he came back here and probably got fed some nice food, and had a few sloppy gulps from his water bowl. I think he probably followed you around the kitchen for a while, hoping for a sausage, and I think he was perfectly happy.

'Then he went to his basket – his lovely, comfortable, warm basket – and curled up in a ball. The ball he's still in now. He went to sleep, Laura. That's all. He just went to sleep. He wasn't in pain, and he didn't suffer, and you didn't let him down. He knew you were just upstairs, and he was happy here, just like this.'

The grief and the guilt and the misery had piled up, making my heart hammer in my chest and my ears buzz and my fingers tingle. It was a pain so raw, so primal, that it felt like a panic attack. It used to happen all the time after David died, but had settled down into rarity. Until now. Until Jimbo.

I was still sobbing, almost hysterically, and had to fight to get words out between gulps of air.

'I should have given him a sausage! And I should have held the ladder! And I should have made him go to hospital, even when he said he was fine!'

Of course, poor Matt probably had no idea what I was raving on about – but he was intelligent enough and sensitive enough to put it together, to use that intuitive nature of his to understand that this pain, this emotional distress signal, was about more than the death of a very old Labrador.

He held me tighter, and simply let me cry. He muttered soothing words, and encouraged me to breathe, and lightly stroked my back, and eventually, when I had nothing left to pour out, he physically picked me up in his arms and carried me over to the sofa.

He sat down, taking me with him, scooped onto his lap like a child that needed comforting, and held me there, cuddled into him, my knees curled up and my head buried in his chest.

I don't know how long we stayed like that, but I do know that it wouldn't have mattered to Matt if it was hours or even days. He was there for me, my friend, my not-quite-lover, my ally in Dorset life.

He was there for me through every sniffle and every frantic, sucked-in breath and every smear of mascara on that new shirt of his.

And when the worst of it has subsided and I was able to breathe again, and my eyes were red and swollen and sore, he leaned down to gently kiss them both.

'I'm taking you back to Black Rose,' he said, in a tone that suggested there was no point in arguing, even if I was capable of it. 'You're spending the night with me.'

I opened my eyes as wide as I could, and felt suddenly scared again – surely he didn't think I could still…

'And no, of course I don't mean you're spending the night with me in that way,' he added, his lips tugging sideways in a sad smile. 'I understand. But I won't leave you, Laura, all right? You need to be with someone and I'm afraid I'm the best you've got right now.'

So he'd taken me back to his cottage and settled me down with a glass of whiskey and the TV on for background noise, and he'd taken Jimbo away. He'd carried him, basket and all, into his truck, and driven him to his surgery. I didn't want to ponder what happened next, or how I could tell the kids, or what we'd do with his poor, furry body.

All I could do was sip the whiskey and stare at the screen without seeing a thing, and fight off the sense of impending desolation as best as I could.

I didn't want to fight it – I wanted to give in to it. I wanted to lie down on the floor and let it float over me like a rolling black fog. I wanted it to take me and suffocate me and make all of the things that were hurting me go away.

I'd felt like this before, and I knew what would happen if I did let that black fog roll over me. I would lose myself and lose my will to live, and lose my ability to be of any use at all to my children.

It would be like the time that Becca came to stay, and much as I was suffering, I knew I couldn't allow myself to inflict that kind of pain on Lizzie and Nate and my sister and my parents ever again.

So I sipped the whiskey and I watched a reality TV show about allotments and I shivered inside the blanket that Matt had draped around my shoulders, and waited for him to get back.

When he did, he made me hot tea, also with whiskey in it, and convinced me to eat a few chocolate Hob Nobs. Normally, that wouldn't be much of a challenge, but just then it was the last thing I'd felt like doing.

'I'm sorry,' I'd said, as I watched him watching me. His hair was furrowed where he'd been running his hands through it, and his lovely white shirt was soggy with my tears and stained with my make-up, and the fatigue and concern was clouding the usually sparkling hazel of his eyes.

'This hasn't turned out quite the way we'd planned, has it? I'm so sorry…'

He'd frowned and sat next to me, and tucked the blanket closer around my shoulders.

'You have nothing to be sorry about,' he said, shaking his head. 'We're all fragile, aren't we? And we all need a little help sometimes, no matter how tough we seem on the surface. I'm sorry for a lot of things, Laura. I'm sorry for everything you've been through. I'm sorry about David, and Jimbo, and the fact that you've suffered so much.

'But I'm *not* sorry about being here for you, or about my shirt – I see you looking at it – or about the fact that we didn't finally get naked. I'm not sorry that you needed me, and I'm not sorry that I'm going to spend the rest of the night holding you in my arms, keeping you as warm and safe as I humanly can. And tomorrow… well, we'll get through tomorrow, all right? We'll get through it together.'

I squeezed his hand and yawned. I was exhausted and emotionally drained and could only feel grateful for his tenderness, and his blanket, and his seemingly never-ending supply of whiskey.

It's funny the paths life takes us on – five weeks ago Matt was the dishy stranger helping me unpack my roofbox on my first day in Dorset. The man Jimbo took an instant and inappropriate interest in.

Now I am sitting on his sofa and he is helping me to drive back the siren call of that rolling black fog – helping me hold on to the here and the now. Helping me to survive.

'I'm so tired,' I said. 'Would it be all right if we went up to bed?'

He'd led me up the stairs, and although I'd always expected the night to end with that, nothing was happening as I'd expected or hoped. Instead, he was sweet and respectful and handled me with such astonishing care. I fell on top of the duvet and he wrapped me up, and that's where I stayed.

Now, fully awake and wishing I wasn't, I try to extricate myself from his embrace. As soon as I move, his grip tightens and I hear him sigh my name, still half asleep.

I allow myself one more moment where I rest easy and glory in the feeling of lying next to him, being wrapped up in him, so close I can feel his heart thudding into my back. One more moment where I let myself think it's all still simple.

Then I get up, still wrapped in my blanket, and leave the room. The certainty of what I am feeling is adding to my pain, and my feet drag like they are made of lead. I need to escape. To run. To get away, from Black Rose and from Matt.

Because now, even without sleeping with him, I realise that Becca was right. That Matt does mean something to me. That he means way too much to me.

And I know that I am still far too fragile to risk giving so much of myself to someone else.

I simply wouldn't survive another loss.

Chapter 34

The weather is strange today; clear blue skies interrupted by stretches of scudding white cotton-bud clouds that seem to blow across the horizon so fast they look like they're on a time-lapse video.

It is warm, but with a strong breeze blowing up from the coast that is swirling my hair around my face and flinging Lizzie's ponytail up into the air.

We are gathered together in the Budbury Pet Cemetery, a place I never knew existed until this morning. It is in a beautiful, meandering walled garden behind the Community Centre and apparently predates that building by decades.

The weathered brick walls are covered in climbing ivy and the pathways that wind through the space are carpeted with pine needles and leaves from the trees. There are small grave markers and larger headstones and wooden crosses, and simple home-made tributes of framed photos and hand-drawn cartoons. They're probably the most touching of all, a child's vision of their beloved pet.

The earliest dates I can see go back to the 1920s and there seem to be mainly dogs and cats, but also a few tiny plots for rabbits, mice and birds. In one corner there is even a donkey called Petunia, who laid her head to rest here in 1958 after years of carrying children up and down the beach.

Although the main street of the village is not far away, you can only distantly hear the passing traffic and the sound of people walking by; the walls and the trees seem to insulate this place, keeping it shady, still and silent.

Lizzie and Nate had come home early this afternoon, after I called my mum to let her know what had happened. To be honest, I actually texted my mum to tell her what had happened and then ignored my phone when she called back.

I know that was a cowardly thing to do, but I just wasn't up to talking about it. I didn't want her to hear the weakness in my voice or to suspect how feeble I was feeling. Instead, I texted again saying I was busy but fine. Both were lies.

The kids, once they arrived back at Hyacinth, flew into my arms. Both of them at once. This is an absolute rarity and we huddled together in the living room, crying and snivelling, and trying to console each other.

My mum and dad stood back, holding each other's hands. My mum, in particular, looked tearful, and after I finished smothering the children I dashed over to hug her too.

'I'm so sorry, love,' she said, wiping my tears away and holding my hair back from my face. She looked at me so sorrowfully, but also with that familiar concern, searching for traces of the nervous breakdown she is right to suspect.

'I'm okay, Mum,' I said, giving her what I hope was a reassuring smile. 'I'm sad, and I'll really miss Jimbo, but I'm coping.'

And, I suppose, I am. As best as I can. I feel empty and hollow and like I am made of straw, as though an especially strong gust of wind would send me tumbling and flying down towards the bay, like a child's lost helium balloon.

But I need to at least appear as though I am all right. I need to get through today and get through Frank's party, get through my last few days in Dorset and head home. Once I'm home, I'll feel differently – I'll be able to forget all about this crazy summer, these crazy people and the crazy ride I've been on with Matt.

I'm not sure if what I am feeling for him is real or if it is just gratitude. Gratitude for his kindness, his gentleness, for the way he has coaxed me back to life like a frost-bitten seedling who needed some time in the sun. Or whether he is just my belated rebound man – the first person I've been attracted to since David's death.

It is probably, I think, watching him, one of those. It has to be, because I couldn't cope with anything more damaging.

Matt has already been here for a while with Edie May, who heads up the pet cemetery committee. He has dug a Jimbo-sized hole and he has wrapped him in his favourite red-and-black-tartan blanket. He has been in the 'cool room' at the vet's surgery – I really don't want to know what that is, so I don't ask.

The kids pat his blanket-wrapped head and between them Sam and Matt lower Jimbo down into his little grave. I don't even realise I am crying until Lizzie grabs my hand and looks at me with her own big, tearful green eyes. Nate is blinking it all back, trying to be the tough boy, until I place a hand on his shoulder to comfort him and it all breaks free.

They have both chosen small gifts to leave for Jimbo, which they step forward and add. Nate has brought a fluorescent-green tennis ball with the fluffy skin chewed and mangled so much it is barely recognisable as a spherical object. He really could chew when he put his mind to it, Jimbo. Lizzie adds in a small plastic box, the kind you get Chinese takeaway in, which contains two cooked sausages. His favourite.

There is a small crowd of us here, in the shady, square, walled cemetery and I am grateful for all of their support.

Cherie is there, leaning on her crutches, hair flying wild in the breeze; Frank next to her, holding his cap respectfully in his weather-worn hands. Sam and Matt are waiting for Lizzie and Nate to stand clear, Matt with a shovel at his feet. Ivy Wellkettle and Sophie are smiling sympathetically and the entire Scrumpy Jones family is there – Joanne, Joe and Josh. Joe is holding two carrier bags that clink when he moves, so I suspect he has brought me a sample of his cure-all cider.

Willow is there, staring sadly at the grave, dressed as usual like a space punk princess in her distressed leggings and clunky, silver spray-painted Doc Marten boots. Edie is next to her, their arms linked.

And on either side of me and the children stand my own mum and dad, with their neat haircuts and their sensible glasses and their matching expressions of worry. My dad has his arm around my shoulders and is squeezing me a bit too tight, and my mum is holding Nate's hand. Lizzie is squashed in the middle, her eye liner running. I see Josh looking at her with such concern, I want to go and kiss him myself.

'Well,' says Edie, gazing around at us all. 'We're here to say goodbye to Jimbo on this sad day and we're going to do it the traditional way. I think, Joe, you've brought the supplies?'

Joe nods and passes one carrier bag to his wife. Joanne pulls out a stack of plastic tumblers and Joe pops open a few bottles of his cider cave special and pours until each cup is half full. Josh plays his part by handing them out to everyone in turn.

There is a quiet and slightly awkward moment where we all stand there, holding our plastic glasses aloft, cider bubbles fizzing, not really knowing what to do.

'Here's to Jimbo,' says Matt, after a few moments. He holds his glass high and says, 'He was a bloody good dog.'

Somehow those simple words are exactly right. Jimbo was a

bloody good dog and even thinking it cracks open an unlikely smile. Once I remember what a good dog he was I feel slightly lighter.

When David died lots of well-meaning people told me to remember him as he was – to forget those images of him hooked up to the life-support machines and to instead focus on the good times.

After a while, I wanted to punch anybody who said that – because we just hadn't had enough good times for that to cheer me up. He was only thirty-three, for goodness' sake.

We'd had a wonderful marriage and two beautiful kids, but it was over too soon. It was hard to focus on the good times we'd had when I was facing a whole lifetime without him, knowing that there would be no more good times to celebrate. That he wouldn't be at Lizzie's wedding, or see our first grandchild, or do embarrassing country dancing to Cotton Eye Joe with me at my fortieth like we'd planned.

Remember the good times, they'd say. Go screw yourself, you know nothing about it, I'd silently reply, hiding my resentment with a smile – because I knew that they, like everyone else, did mean well.

With Jimbo, though, it actually does help. If I separate the pain of losing David from the pain of losing Jimbo and give that bloody good dog the send-off he deserves, it does help.

I have so many silly memories of him: as a puppy chewing up whole rolls of toilet paper and then hiding in the airing cupboard; the way he'd chase cats until one of them hissed at him, then he'd hide behind our legs; the time he got off his lead at a campsite in Scotland and threw himself right into the swimming pool, splash-landing in the middle of an aquarobics class.

He was funny and silly and greedy and loyal and lovely – he was a bloody good dog.

We all raise our glasses and join in, before taking swigs of Joe's cider. Or, in the case of my dad, a tiny sip as he is driving on to Cornwall this afternoon. They'd wanted to stay, but I'd done the acting job of my life and persuaded them that everything was fine.

As my Dorset friends all start to troop out of the pet cemetery – single file, as you have to go through a narrow wooden gate to reach the real world again – I am left with Lizzie and Nate, my parents and Matt, who is tactfully waiting until we leave before he fills in Jimbo's grave.

'Are you sure you'll be all right?' says my mum, staring into my eyes so intently she appears to be trying to read my mind. And, as she's my mother, I have a shaky moment where I wonder if she actually can.

'I'll be fine, honestly,' I reply, holding her hand and giving it a squeeze. 'And I've only got a few more days here anyway. I'll be home before you know it.'

My dad steps in and gives me a quick hug.

'Of course she's fine, Val,' he says to my mum, nodding towards the people single-filing through the gate, and at Matt, standing there pretending he can't hear every word.

'Can't you see she's in good hands?'

WEEK 6

In which I wave goodbye to the Comfort Food Café…

Chapter 35

Busy is good. Busy is useful. Busy is a distraction. Busy gives you a brilliant excuse to avoid things you want to avoid and concentrate instead on the things that allow your brain to stay inside your head, rather than causing it to dribble out of your ears.

So, I've been busy. Mostly very genuinely. Normal café life continued and the party-planning took on a life of its own. I found myself living with my mobile phone permanently attached to my body, often precariously perched between my jaw and my neck as I tried to talk and cook at the same time. How it didn't end up in a Mars Bar Milkshake, I don't know.

There is one big rule about Frank's annual birthday party – that nobody who is employed at the Comfort Food Café is allowed to work on the night. So, bizarrely, I find myself talking to the caterers and to the agencies who hire out the staff and to the people who are setting up the outside bar and providing the beer and the wine, and it is all exhausting.

Seriously, I think it would be easier to simply do all the catering myself than have to answer even one more question about how many paper plates we'll need and whether we want plastic champagne stems or not.

I've spoken to the band – The Honky Tonk Fossils from

Dorchester – and I've spoken to the PA people and I've spoken to the DJ and I've spoken to the fancy-dress-shop guy, who is delivering a load of fun country-and-western costumes for people to wear on the night, in case they foolishly forget their own.

I've spoken to all of my mystery guests and I've spoken to Cherie's sister Brenda, and I've spoken to my mum and dad, who are enjoying their time in Cornwall.

I've spoken to pretty much everybody, in depth, about everything – apart from Matt.

Poor Matt. I've avoided him like the plague for the last two days. I hope he hasn't noticed, or if he has, that he's assumed it's because I'm so busy. As I tell everyone within earshot how busy I am, all the time, he can't help but realise.

After Jimbo's burial, I have only been alone with him once, when I called round to Black Rose that night to thank him. To thank him for his kindness, for looking after me and for taking care of Jimbo as well. They were thanks that he thoroughly deserved and I'll never forget how much he has done for me.

But Jimbo's death and the aftermath, made me realise how fragile I still feel. Not all the time and not to the same desperate extent as I did a few years ago. I'm so much stronger – I'm able to function like a normal human being, hopefully be a good mum, run a busy café, plan a party and give every outward indication that I am absolutely one hundred per cent fine and dandy.

Inside, though, the picture is a little more fuzzy. I do feel strong, in some ways, but the way I reacted to Jimbo's passing and to waking up in Matt's arms have made me suspect that at least some of that strength still lives in a house built on sand.

Right now, throwing myself any deeper into a relationship with him would potentially test exactly how solid the foundations of my emotional stability are, and it's simply not something I'm willing to do.

I can't afford to take that risk – not only for my own sake, but for the sake of the people who rely on me and the people who love me.

I have no doubt at all that Matt would be honourable and behave with integrity in any relationship. He is also, which I can never quite persuade my libido to forget, drop-dead bloody gorgeous and an extremely talented kisser with exceptionally gifted hands.

But it is still a risk. If I let it go any further, if we effectively have a sexual hit and run before I disappear back to Manchester, I may well get hurt in ways that I'm not yet equipped to handle.

It all sounds so sensible and obvious when I explain it, when I think about it. But when I feel it instead, it is like a sore spot I can't stop prodding.

I will be thrilled to get Frank's party out of the way, for so many different reasons – not least of which being that I can leave the day after. The café will be closed, and when it reopens there will be very few tourists left as all the families, including mine, go home to get ready for the new school year.

My duty here will be done and I can leave Willow and Joanne to keep it going for the locals until Cherie is back. I can run home, tail between my legs, and focus on ironing school uniforms and finding lost trainers and washing stinky PE kits and packing pencil cases. I am looking forward to the mind-numbing mundanity of it all.

Right now, though, there are only a few hours to go until people start to arrive and things are hotting up. The catering firm has arranged trestle tables for the food and the bar staff are already here, dressed in their own cowboy hats and sporting water pistols in their jeans pockets. The water pistols will be used later for refilling shot glasses, apparently.

I think, for the thousandth time, that this could get very messy.

The band has done its sound check and they have all line-danced their way into the village for a few 'snifters' at the Horse and Jockey before the gig. Even messier.

Their stage, such as it is, is a raised wooden platform on the patio at the side of the café, where the barbecue is usually set up. We had planned for them to use the inside if it was raining, but so far the weather is as kind today as it has been for most of the summer.

We have had bales of hay, which are set up around the stage, brought over from Frank's farm, along with other country-and-western-style accessories that Cherie has insisted will look great – a giant wooden cart wheel that I am convinced will roll off down the cliffs with the tiniest of nudges, an old leather saddle that has been draped across one of the bales and one of those giant wooden totem poles you see in movies.

I have no idea whether Cherie has all of this random stuff in storage somewhere, or if she's been amusing herself ordering it while she recovers – all I know is it was delivered in a big white truck and had to be hauled up the hill by a team of sweating men in tracksuits.

The stage and the café itself are strung up with fairy lights, which I am sure will look magical once it's dark, and every one of the outdoor tables has its own candle in a glass lantern that will be lit up nearer the time. There is a hog roast already set up and later there will be platters of meats and cheeses and breads, bowls of salad, a hot plate with chilli and tacos, and chilled trays of desserts and puddings.

The smell of the hog roast, together with the thought of all the party food, makes my mouth water, and I am reminded that I've not actually eaten all day – busy, you see.

Willow is around somewhere and has warned me that I am very close to being in breach of the not-working-at-Frank's-party rules. Lizzie and Nate are inside, still a little subdued, still a little sad.

It would be arrogant and selfish of me to assume that I am the only one who felt Jimbo's passing so keenly. For most kids their age, losing a family pet would have been their first experience of death. Mine, sadly, are old hands at it – and this has definitely re-opened some half-healed wounds for all of us.

I glance inside and see them slouched at one of the tables, Lizzie looking at her phone and Nate gazing down at the bay, scruffy blonde head resting on his folded arms,. They're also sad, I know, at the thought of leaving this place. Of leaving the café, the Rockery and all their Dorset friends. Of saying goodbye to the beach, the village and the sheer amount of freedom they've had this summer.

We were all pretty quiet when we were packing our stuff up, ready to head off tomorrow. We've lost a lot – and we all had a little cry when we put Jimbo's lead and collar into the boot and noticed how much more space we have now there's not a fat Lab lying in it.

But we've also gained a lot – the kids seem to have all kinds of souvenirs from the beach: fossils, shells, old coins and shiny stones washed iridescent by the sea.

I seem to have gathered a collection of ugly nick-nacks from the gift shop, as well as my postcards from Jean, and the new set of colouring books that Edie May bought for me yesterday afternoon. Most of our clothes, bundled up in bags, are already stored in the roofbox – and this time I took a footstool home from the café so I wouldn't need to get Matt to pack it up for us.

It's going to take us all a while to readjust when we get back, and I'd be a fool if thought it was going to be easy. Lizzie, in particular, has really mellowed since we arrived here – her budding bitch has calmed, taking a more amusing diversion into sarcasm, and she just seems much more laid back and content. As a result, we've been getting on so much better and the respite from her diva tantrums has been terrific.

But like she blamed me when I dragged her away from her Manchester life, I have to be prepared for the fact that she might blame me for dragging her away from her Budbury life as well. It could be a rocky ride, at least until she gets back into her city-girl rhythms.

And Nate? Well, he'll miss his mates and the space to run and play, and he'll miss his Man Buddies too. Sam, Frank and Matt – their endless patience with playing football, teaching him guitar and taking him fossil-hunting, and introducing him to the business end of a dairy cow. They've been good for him, and good to him.

I realise that I am starting to veer towards the melancholy and snap back to attention and look at my clipboard. I always wanted to be the sort of person who had a clipboard – and now I've finally made it into the big time.

I have a list of what needs doing and who needs chasing, and a timeline that is already slightly wonky. There will come a point where I simply have to give up on the schedule and go with the flow – but that will be later, once the Special Guests are out of the way and I can either run screaming from Cherie's attempts to chop me up with a tomahawk – I am sure there is one here somewhere – or relax happily, knowing that I've done something special for them.

For now, though, I decide there is nothing on the Clipboard of Justice that can't wait a few more minutes.

I wander through to the café and sit with Nate and Lizzie. Nate looks up at me from his head-on-arms position and gives me a half-hearted smile. Lizzie barely looks up from her phone.

'Do you guys want some cake? I have some chocolate orange

sponge left,' I say, returning to my default comfort food setting.

'No thanks, Mum,' says Nate, turning his eyes back to the view of the bay.

'Cake doesn't solve everything,' says Lizzie, finally putting her phone down and leaning back in her chair. She looks at me through narrowed eyes and I am reminded of a snake about to pounce on a mouse.

'True enough, but it often helps,' I reply, keeping my tone mild. The last thing I want is a fight with her; I know she is only behaving like this because she is unhappy. 'Are you upset about something? If you are, then tell me, and I'll see if there's anything I can do to help.'

'You don't mean that,' she snaps, crossing her arms in front of her chest in a classic sulky-teen pose. 'That's just something patronising that parents say to make their kids feel respected.'

'No, that's not true,' I answer, biting down on a giggle – she is, of course right. Most of the time, that is what we do.

'I will try and help, Lizzie – but I can't if you don't tell me what's bothering you.'

'I don't want to go back to Manchester,' she says simply, meeting my eyes face-on, her expression one of pure challenge.

'But that's where we live, sweetheart – I know this has been lovely, but it's not our home.'

'Why couldn't it be, though?' she insists. 'They have schools here, too. I'm not stupid, I know it wouldn't always be like it's been this summer. I know there'll be homework and curfews and mean girls and stuff here as well. But we've been happy, haven't we? All of us. Much happier than we were in Manchester.'

'Yeah,' murmurs Nate, apparently too tired and fed up to even lift his head from the table. 'What she said.'

I intend to simply exhale, but the breath ends up puffing out of me like a bugle as I try and come up with a decent answer.

An answer that reflects the temporary nature of our time in Budbury and how we can't know what life here is really like.

An answer that reinforces the fact that Manchester is our home and always has been our home, and was also their Dad's home.

An answer that reminds them how much they would miss their grandparents and their Aunt Becca.

An answer that is honest and heartfelt and true, but completely bypasses my own personal need to get away from this place, from Matt and from the danger that I feel surrounded by.

Sadly, that answer is as elusive as a unicorn riding on the Loch Ness Monster's back. I manage one step up from the parental catch-all of 'just because', but not by much.

'I know it's been fab,' I say. 'But it was only a holiday, kids. For all kinds of reasons, we have to go home tomorrow.'

Chapter 36

I am a shaking, trembling, almost-hyperventilating bag of nerves by the time people start to arrive. As is tradition, apparently, Frank gets here later, once everyone is assembled, so he can make a grand entrance.

This sounds very unlike the Frank I know, who is more likely to make a wry comment than a grand entrance, and I suspect it is a tradition started by Cherie to make him feel special. As this is only the second time he's done this without his wife, I also suspect that the 'tradition' is also a very recent one.

I have asked Surfer Sam to go and fetch Cherie and Frank from the farm in his Jeep, to save Frank having to bother driving. In reality, it's because I also need to get rid of him for a little while as well.

Now, as we wait for them all to get here, I am able to at least pause and look around at the place and try and soak up some of the atmosphere of my last night at the Comfort Food Café.

The sun has slid down over the bay and splashed into the sea and the night sky is a deep, velvety blue, clear and star-studded. The fairy lights are on and sparkling, draped over the café and the stage and the fences that wind their way up from the bottom of the hill on the pathways. Each of the table lanterns are glimmering and flickering as well and it feels a little bit like we are in some magical fairy kingdom.

There are probably around a hundred people here, sitting at the tables, milling around, waiting by the hog roast, helping themselves to plates of food from the packed trestles.

Most of them are wearing at least some element of fancy dress – cowboy hats, Stetsons, Mexican sombreros I suspect they've salvaged from last year, Indian head dresses. Some have thrown themselves into it a bit more enthusiastically, with cowboy boots, chaps, lassoos and guns (hopefully fake) in holsters.

Willow is fabulously outfitted as a slutty saloon girl, with torn fishnets, a red-velvet bodiced dress and Victorian-style ankle boots. Edie has kept it more conservative and is wearing an old-fashioned bonnet, as though she's about to set off on a wagon-train journey. It looks especially amusing with her usual sensible cardigan and clunky walking shoes, and is way too big for her head.

Lizzie and Nate have grabbed some accessories from the fancy-dress rail, and are busy with their friends, shooting each other with water pistols and trying to knock each other's hats off.

I have had neither the time nor the inclination to make a lot of effort with my outfit. In fact, I was quite happy to simply wear boot-cut jeans and a pink gingham shirt and hope for the best. Willow, however, had other plans, and has 'styled' me into what she calls a 'spunky frontier gal'.

The pink gingham shirt has been unbuttoned enough to flash a bit of cleavage and untucked from my waist, the tails tied in a knot at the front. My hair has been parted down the middle and braided into giant plaits that hang down the side of my head. One of the plaits, of course, is bright pink.

She has drawn freckles on my cheeks with eyebrow pencil and also added glossy red lipstick. It has all been topped with a cowboy hat perched on my head at what I could optimistically call a 'jaunty' angle, as even with plaits my hair is stupidly big.

I secretly fear that I look like a chubby, middle-aged Daisy Duke after a night on the Jager Bombs, and refuse to look in a mirror.

The DJ has put on some twangy country-and-western tunes as background music, and the bar is doing a roaring trade, especially as it's free. The crowd is definitely eating and drinking, and well on its way to being merry as well.

Brenda, Cherie's sister, arrived about half an hour ago, escorted by her son Robbie, who I'd spoken to on the phone. Robbie is hugely tall, built like a bear and hovers over his mum like a protective parent.

I saw why when I looked at her and realised that she is not only physically on the frail side but terribly nervous. She is shorter than Cherie by a good few inches and far less robust in build, but she has the same round, crinkled face. Possibly a few more worry lines than her younger sister's laughter lines, but perhaps that's to be expected.

'Thank you so much for coming,' I said, holding her hand, scared to squeeze too tight. 'I know it's a long way and this must all feel very strange.'

'Och, it's like coming home. We grew up just over the county line in Devon, you know, but I've never been back until now... just too many memories, most of them sad. I never pictured her ending up back in this part of the world, though. I'm surprised at that. I thought she'd still be jollying her way round the globe or living in an artists' commune or some such thing... But I'm glad you invited me, anyway, dear, and I hope the poor love doesn't drop dead of a heart attack the minute she sees me.'

Her accent is a bewildering mix of West Country and Scottish and she gave me a little smile with that last comment to show that she was joking. Which is good, all things considered.

'I doubt it,' I replied. 'She has the constitution of a whole herd of oxen. Look, I know you don't know anybody here, and you've been on the road a long time. Would you like to come and sit inside the café for a while? Relax and have a drink, catch your breath?'

'Aye, I think that might be a good idea,' she says, and Robbie nods in agreement. 'I'm thinking that maybe it would be better if she came in and met me in private, too. It's been a lifetime apart and neither of us knows how we're going to react. Better to not do it in public, I reckon.'

She is, of course, right, and if I'm honest it's also taken one extra element of pressure away from me. I already have several people here I need to play hostess to, and some of them have come a very long way for this party.

I glance at my watch and see that it is past nine. Sam will be here any minute, with Cherie and Frank. I look around and get a visual pinpoint on everybody's location. I am trying to choreograph this, but it already feels out of control. I shrug and decide I've done as much as I can – now all I can do is say a little prayer.

Edie catches my eye, nodding her wobbly bonnet at me, and gives me a double thumbs-up. I grin back at her and wonder where Matt is. He disappeared off somewhere this morning and I haven't seen him since then.

Part of me is desperate to see him one last time and the other part – the weak, pathetic part – is hoping he has a sudden engagement elsewhere and I can slink off in the night and head back to Hyacinth.

We will be setting off early in the morning – as per family rules – so I am not drinking at all. Once this party is well and truly going with a swing, and once I've seen how all my plans turn out, I will be corralling the kids into the Picasso and heading back to the cottage. I am so physically drained I am hoping that I immediately fall into a deep sleep and don't lie awake all night torturing myself about things I can't control.

I am prevented from worrying any further by Scrumpy Joe's sudden yell of, 'They're here! Action stations!'

He has been on lookout duty, standing on one of the wooden tables, looking down towards the car park. He jumps back to the ground and runs over to tell the band.

The Honky Tonk Fossils have been warned about this and are all prepared to start a rousing live rendition of 'Happy Birthday'. I hear the twanging of their guitars as they get ready and have to laugh again at how brilliant they look.

I suspect they have an average age of about seventy-five and every single one of them has a bushy beard and long hair in a Willy Nelson style. Several of them have impressive beer bellies and they are all suited up in black shirts with mother-of-pearl buttons. Pure awesome.

I nip over to my table full of VIPs, who are all chattering away to each other in such a variety of accents that it sounds a bit like the United Nations over there, and warn them that our birthday boy is about to arrive.

I gaze back at the café, dimly lit inside, and see that Brenda and Robbie are at their window seat, so they'll be able to see what's going on as well.

I take a very deep breath and wait. And wait. And wait some more.

The wait turns out to be a little longer than anticipated because Cherie has refused to be wheelchaired all the way up to the café. This was probably completely predictable and totally in character.

When she finally appears at the top of the path, she is using her crutches, Frank by her side and Sam lurking behind with the now-discarded chair.

Cherie has completely outdone herself on the costume front

and is a magnificently dressed Lily Langtry in deep, plum-coloured taffeta. She has more cleavage on show than I do and a feathered head dress over perfectly coiffed, pinned-up, pink-tipped hair. The skirt of her dress is shimmering and swishing around her ankles as she painstakingly makes her way into the café garden.

By her side, one hand cautiously on the small of her back, is Frank, who looks just as amazing. He is in full Wyatt Earp garb, complete with a full-length black coat, hat and sheriff's badge. He – or possibly the woman next to him – has drawn on a twirling moustache with what looks like it might be eye liner and he even has an old-fashioned pocket watch on a gold chain dangling across his waistcoat.

The entire crowd bursts out into cheers and applause, and Frank gives a little mock bow and tips his hat, every inch the courteous Wild West lawman. Cherie manages a small curtsey and the band launch right in to their hilariously 'country' version of 'Happy Birthday'.

As the song goes on, people come up to the two of them, hugging them and shaking their hands and patting their backs and wishing Frank all the best.

It is quite a sight, this tall, lean eighty-year-old, in full fancy dress, standing amid the fairy lights and the candles and his friends, celebrating his birthday surrounded by love, laughter and very dodgy singing. It is a tribute to the man and I can only hope to have half as good a life as he's had.

Once 'Happy Birthday' is done, the band starts up on something equally twangy that may or may not be from the Kenny Rogers oeuvre, I'm not really sure. Country isn't my speciality. The small crowd that had gathered around Frank starts to disperse, heading back to their tables, or to get top-ups on the drinks or more food.

I walk towards him and give him a big hug of my own.

'Happy Birthday, you old devil,' I say, kissing him on the cheek.

'Careful now, lass,' he replies, in his mock-Northern accent, 'you'll make an old man blush, looking like that.'

'Ha!' I respond, poking him in the stomach and giving Cherie a little wink. 'It'd take more than me to make you blush, Frank. But… I do have a special birthday present for you.'

'Oh yes?' he says, blue eyes crinkling at the corners. 'What's that, then? What do you get for the man who has everything?'

'I get him this,' I say simply, beckoning for my guests to come forward.

Peter, Frank's son and Luke, his grandson, emerge from the darkness and walk towards us. I watch Frank's expressions as they approach and see the emotions flicker across his rugged old face: shock, surprise, doubt, disbelief, and finally – wonderfully – absolute joy.

He is taller than both of them and throws his arms around their shoulders, tugging them towards him and roaring with delight.

For a good couple of minutes, all three men disappear in a scrummage of hugging and backslapping. They whirl around a bit, a six-legged beast, and Frank's hat comes flying off in the huddle. I scoop it up and keep it safe for him.

Once they finally all calm down and Frank catches his breath enough to talk, they stand in a tight circle, all three of them looking exhilarated and slightly out of puff.

Frank reaches out and holds his son by both shoulders, giving him a little shake as he stares at his face, as though he can't quite believe what he's seeing.

'What are you bloody doing here, Peter?' he says. 'And why didn't you tell me you were coming?'

'Well, it wouldn't be much of a surprise if we told you, would it, Dad?' Peter replies, his voice yet another mash-up – West Country and Aussie this time. He's blonde, solidly built and looks very similar to the smiling teenager standing next to him.

'Besides, Luke here has been nagging me for ages to bring him to the farm again. He wants to be a vet and I reckon there's no better place to learn than here.'

I have kind of rehearsed this part with Peter during our phone conversations, late at night for me and early in the morning for him. His dad, he already knows, is a proud man – one who has deliberately avoided reaching out for help, even when he needed it, and has carefully hidden his pain and loneliness from his family.

He's fooled them all for a long time and the last thing Frank needs or wants is to think that anybody feels sorry for him.

Peter had been genuinely convinced that his father was too busy for them to visit and I didn't disabuse him of that idea – I simply explained that we were having a big party for this eightieth and that this would be a lovely surprise.

It was only after talking it through with Peter that the rest of the plan fell into place. Luke genuinely does want to train as a vet and had always planned to take a year off before his studies start. I've spoken to Matt and he's agreed to let him do some extended work experience at his surgery, assuming that Frank will be willing to let his grandson stay for a few months.

Looking at the besotted expression on his face, I'm guessing that won't be a problem – the end result being that Frank gets his family back for a while and also gets to feel like he's helping *them* out too. Okay, it wouldn't leave Machiavelli quaking in his boots, but hopefully it's just enough to stop Frank getting annoyed with me for interfering.

'A vet, is it?' he says, looking his grandson up and down with a grin on his face that can only be described as daft. 'You'll be needing a lot of education for that, lad, and you won't find all of it at university, either… the farm's the place for you, sure enough. How long can you both stay? Is Erin here with you?'

'She's stayed at home with her mum for the time being,' replies

Peter. 'But if it's all right with you for Luke to stay on for a while – I believe the local vet's said he can work with him if he likes – then I'm sure we can arrange for her to visit too. As long as they won't get in the way, Dad – I know you're busy on the farm and I wouldn't want them to be any trouble.'

'I'm not too bloody busy for that! Of course they can stay, long as they like – I'd welcome a bit of trouble! I haven't had enough of that recently!' says Frank, moving in to hug them both again. It's like he still can't believe they're there and has to keep touching them to reassure himself they're real.

This is the first time I've ever seen Frank lose his cool in any way at all and I am very much loving it. I gaze around, wondering where the 'local vet' in question is, but can't see him anywhere.

Still, I don't have much time to think about that, because just about then stage two of my party plan comes to fruition. I can tell that it has from the sheer amount of noise that suddenly erupts behind me.

Cherie raises her eyebrows at me in a question and I shake my head and smile, pointing to a table at the back of the garden.

The table where I've stashed all seven of Surfer Sam's sisters. They run in age from thirty-three to fifty-one, and I am not even going to try and begin to remember all their names – although I know there is a Theresa and a Siobhan and a Denise in the mix, at least.

They flew in to Exeter from Dublin earlier in the day and are possibly the noisiest people I have ever met in my entire life. In a good way. I'm also struck by how many of them are, and the fact that Sam's mum was basically producing babies for almost twenty years. No wonder she gave them all the odd Pot Noodle. I would too.

Sam has only now found them and has completely disappeared beneath a flurry of siblings, all of them screaming and yelling and laughing. It's only the fact that he's so much taller than them that allows me to still see his shaggy blonde head. His face is creased up in amusement and he is enthusiastically hugging them all back.

He may be ready for them all to leave again in a few days – once they've started nagging him and trying to persuade him to come home and marry a nice girl and settle down, which he says is their constant refrain. But right now, he looks thrilled – and I'm thrilled for him. He's a great bloke and he deserves a bit of fussing from the women in his life.

Cherie is standing next to me now, looking on at the family reunion in front of her and glancing back at the family reunion going on behind her.

'I assume this is all your doing?' she asks, her tone amused, her feathers bouncing around in the slight breeze that's blowing up from the bay.

'It is,' I say, nodding. 'And I'm afraid you paid for at least some of it. Peter and Luke got here themselves, but I did shell out for all the girls' flights from Dublin. I didn't think you'd mind...'

I look at her cautiously, knowing that however much she is enjoying watching other people's reunions, she might not feel quite the same in a few minutes, when I've forced her to endure her own.

'Of course not,' she says, leaning in to give me a one-armed hug. She needs the other to hold one of her crutches.

'You've done a brilliant job. I knew you would, but even I never imagined all of this; you've outdone yourself... the look on Frank's face when Peter and Luke walked towards him! Lordy, that was one of the most wonderful things I've ever seen... and the fact that Luke's staying, it'll mean so much to him... he's been lonely. We both know that. And you understand loneliness better than most, I think, Laura... so, well, thank you.

'Thank you for what you've done for Frank and Sam, and for

me. Thanks for keeping the café going, keeping Edie company and becoming such an important part of our little world. And please don't forget what I said – you are wanted here, my love. You're needed. You can always change your mind. You can always stay.'

Oh God, I think, as she finishes her speech. So genuine. So heartfelt. So… premature.

'You might not think that in a few minutes,' I say, which instantly and understandably confuses her.

'Why ever not?' she replies, frowning.

'Umm… well. It'd be easier to show you than tell you. Just promise me you'll stay calm and you won't have a heart attack, and you won't scalp me with a tomahawk.'

'I'm not planning on a heart attack, my sweet, but I'm not at all sure I like the sound of all this, so I'll reserve judgement on the second one for now.'

I bite my lip and head towards the café, gesturing for her to follow me. She does, although we make slow progress – partly because of her crutches and the uneven ground, and partly because people keep stopping her to ask how she is, say how lovely it is to see her and compliment her on her frock.

By the time we reach the doors, I think I am possibly about to be sick.

I open them and step inside. It is dimly lit in here, still in semi-darkness and I know that from the outside we are shadowy figures as I lead Cherie to the table, where the sister she's not seen for over fifty years, and the nephew she's never met at all, are sitting and waiting.

Brenda stands up as we approach, Robbie towering at her side, ready to leap into action if needed. I meet his eyes and we both share a nervous smile.

Brenda, of course, has the advantage. She knows exactly who she is, why she's here, and who is standing in front of her. She's had time to process the idea, prepare herself and plan what she wants to say and how she wants to react.

Cherie has had nothing of the sort and to start with she simply looks at the two people in front of her, bewildered. She looks at me, as if to ask what's going on, and then squints some more at Brenda, which makes me wonder if I should go and flick the main lights on so she can see her better.

And then, after a few more moments of silence, where Brenda simply smiles at her and waits for her brain to imagine the unimaginable, Cherie's mouth forms into a silent 'O' of surprise.

Her hands fly to her cheeks in shock and sudden tears begin to slide down her cheeks. It's going to ruin her make-up and for that alone I might deserve a good tomahawking.

'My Lord… is it you, Brenda?' she stutters, sobs wracking her body. 'Is it really you?'

'Aye, it is, you daft moo,' says her sister, shuffling forward to put her arms around Cherie.

Cherie is by far the taller and bigger of the two women, but there is something about the way Brenda holds her, stroking her back and pouring out comfort, that feels somehow stronger. Older. She's still the mature one even now, after all these years.

Seeing Frank and his family was emotional. Seeing Sam and his girls was sweet. Seeing this – seeing Cherie weep on her sister's shoulder, wobbling on her crutches, clutching Brenda to her as though she will never let her go? This destroys me.

I feel my own floodgates begin to open and scrunch my eyelids up tight and shake my head. This is not my drama. This is not my reunion or my rollercoaster, or my turn in the spotlight.

This is for Cherie and for Brenda, and nobody else.

'Oh, I'm so sorry…' I hear her saying. 'I can't tell you how sorry I've been, all these years… I was such a selfish little idiot and I've regretted it so much… please forgive me!'

She is speaking between sobs and sounds breathless with emotion.

Brenda pulls away and looks up at her big sister's face. She wipes the tears away and smiles at the feathers in her pink-tipped hair.

'There's nothing to forgive, Cheryl,' she says. 'We're too old and too ugly not to realise that there are more important things in this world than grudges from a lifetime ago. Now sit down, before you fall down.'

Cherie – for pretty much the first time since I've known her – does as she is told and sits down at the table. Brenda sits opposite her and the two touch fingers across the tablecloth.

They spend a while just looking at each other and I wonder how strange it must be. To have last seen your sister's face when you were in your twenties and not to see it again until now. To fast-forward from youth to maturity, bypassing all the shared experience and life events that got you there, instead skipping straight to the wrinkles and grey hairs and broken hips.

It must, I think, unable to imagine this happening with me and Becca, be unbelievably strange.

'So,' says Brenda. 'This is my son, Robbie.'

'It's lovely to finally meet you, Auntie Cheryl,' he says and I hear Cherie take yet another gulp of desperate air. She doesn't seem able to stop crying. I think I may have broken her, but in a good way – a way that will allow her to heal even better than new.

I turn and decide that it is safe to sneak away now. There is a lot of raw emotion in the room and a lot of catching up to do, I am sure, but nobody seems like they will be having a heart attack or going on a killing spree.

I will talk to Cherie again before I leave – and leave for good – but for now, my work is very much done. I leave them to it and silently walk back out into the party, closing the door behind me to give them their privacy.

Out here, it's a different world. The Honky Tonk Fossils are playing something loud and fast that involves fiddle-playing and a lot of stomping. One of them is standing in front of the hay bales, leading the crowd in a line dance. I see Sam and his sisters yee-hahing with the best of them. I see Scrumpy Joe busting some shockingly good moves.

I see Willow whooping it up with gusto. I see Lizzie and Nate and the other teenagers joining in at the back, where they can still look cool. I see Frank and Peter and Luke, all with pints of cider in front of them, talking, Frank's face still lit up with happiness.

I see Willow's mum, Lynnie, smiling at it all from her specially laid-out corner of the garden. I wanted her to be able to come and for Willow to be able to be here with her, so I have set up a small yoga area with mats over to one side. It seems to be Lynnie's natural inclination to go back to that time in her life, so we worked with it.

I suspect that later, when even more of the free bar has been drunk, she may get some customers – although I'm not sure how good they'll be at the balancing poses.

I see Edie May sitting on one of the tables, tapping her feet on the bench, and I see Scrumpy Joanne sitting with her, sipping a drink and looking vaguely unhappy to be surrounded by so many people. Her feet are still tapping, though, so the Fossils are doing something good.

And finally, as I lean back against the door of the café and swallow down the feelings that are threatening to choke me, I see Matt. And he's headed right towards me.

Chapter 37

I can't run and I can't hide. I can't even dash off and pretend I'm busy, as this party is very clearly already doing just fine without me.

All I can do is plaster a smile on my face and hope to get through this in one piece before I can run away and lick my wounds.

'Hey,' he says, simply, as he approaches. His eyes flicker, briefly, to my cleavage, and I am reminded that I am looking pretty slutty and that he is only human.

He's also, truth be told, looking awesome himself, in his usual snug-fitting Levis and a denim shirt that is stretched tight across broad shoulders, pearly buttons open deep enough for me to see a slither of muscular chest. He's wearing a cowboy hat and he is wearing it well. As, of course, you would expect from a young Harrison Ford.

'Hey,' I say back. 'How are you? I've not seen you all day.'

'Yeah, I was… busy. You know how it is.'

As I have been using the excuse of being 'busy' for some time now, I do know exactly how it is. I wonder if Matt is also using it as an excuse and he is as keen for me to leave as I am to go. If perhaps this thing has become too complicated for him to handle as well. For some reason, this hurts, even though it is also totally hypocritical.

'I do know how it is. Did you see Frank?' I reply.

'I did. It's pretty much the happiest I've ever seen him. He introduced me to Peter and Luke and they're going to call into the surgery next week some time. Once they've all slept off their hangovers.'

'I think there might be a lot of hangovers in Budbury tomorrow,' I say, looking around at the line-dancing, the packed bar and the amount of discarded plastic cups already spilling out of the bin bags that are tacked to each table.

'Not you, though, I take it? You seem decidedly... sober.'

I nod. Avoid looking directly into his eyes, not wanting to make this moment any more intimate than it needs to be.

'Early start tomorrow. Don't want to be doing it under the influence.'

'Right. What time are you thinking of leaving?'

'No later than six,' I reply. He nods and doesn't look shocked – he is probably the kind of sensible person who also sets off on journeys at stupid o'clock to avoid traffic as well.

'Okay. Makes sense. Look, we haven't seen much of each other recently, and I... well, I have something for you. It's in my van, down by the beach. Walk with me? One last time?'

I feel my eyes widen and my pulse rate speed up, and hastily take a long, deep breath to calm myself down. I don't really want to go for a walk with Matt. I don't want to say goodbye, I don't want to hold his hand and I don't want him to kiss me. Because any one of those things will be just too much.

I cast my eyes around, desperately looking for an excuse in human form. All I find are happy people having fun. Damn every last one of them.

'I know you're looking for a reason to say no,' he says, sounding half-annoyed and half-amused. 'And that's just plain rude. Now I'm going down to the van and I'd like you to come with me.'

I bite my lip and simply nod. I am being a bit of a prick, I know.

Together we take the longer route down to the bay, following the winding path that curves around the hill, rather than the steps. Even with the fairy lights I don't fancy the steps.

By the time we reach the bottom and the car park, the noise from the café is slightly less vivid. Still very much there, but muted by both the distance and the sound of the waves coming in to the bay.

I follow Matt to his truck and wonder what he is going to produce from it. The Picasso is pretty much full already, so I hope it is small and can potentially be squashed into the corner of a roofbox or crammed into the glove compartment.

Matt stops and turns to face me. His expression is serious and he looks over my shoulder a little, which I always know means he is nervous.

'You don't have to keep this present, I'd just like to stress – if you don't want it, and I completely understand if you don't, then I am happy to keep it myself,' he says, avoiding my eyes in the same way I did to him earlier. 'There is no pressure here, either way.'

'Okay,' I reply simply, feeling more twitchy by the second.

He nods and opens the boot, and I immediately realise that there is no way I am going to squash this particular gift into the corner of a roofbox, and I definitely won't be able to cram it into the glove compartment.

Looking up at me is a puppy. A black Labrador puppy, with eyes so big and so dark that liquid light seems to reflect from them. He makes a little yipping noise and tries to chew his way out of his crate.

A completely involuntary 'aaaah…' noise escapes my lips and I offer my fingers for him to nuzzle through the bars. He stands up and I see that he isn't a complete baby – he's definitely older than Jimbo was when we got him.

Matt opens up the crate and lifts the dog into his arms. I look at him there and wonder how I am supposed to resist this – a gorgeous man in a cowboy hat, cuddling a Labrador puppy. I mean, it's all obscenely cute.

'He's four months old and he's called Midge. He was part of a litter bred by some people I know over in Exeter. That's where I've been all day. He was on the small side when he was born and he never got picked when buyers came… so. He's yours now. Or mine. Or ours, even.'

I reach out and tickle the back of Midge's ears and they are as velvety soft as I expect. He leans his face into the palm of my hand and licks me. He is adorable.

He could be mine. He could be Matt's. Or he could be ours.

I try to process these words as Matt hooks up Midge to a lead and starts to walk towards the beach. I follow, on auto-pilot, catching up with him as he disappears into the darkness.

The tide has recently been in and as we walk I feel the sand solid and damp beneath my boots, and the occasional crunch of shells. The moonlight is shining across the water, coating every ripple with a shimmer of silver, and the cliffs are dark, shadowy outlines in the distance. The café, lit up and loud, is a beacon of activity in the otherwise sleepy bay.

Silently, we walk, both of us watching the ambling puppy as he tugs at his lead and strains, sniffs and pees on just about everything he comes across. This is a small beach – but a big wide world to a little dog.

After a few minutes, we reach the rocks and Matt sits down on one of the boulders. I stand and stare at him for a little while, then sit by his side. Midge jumps up and paws at my knees, so I lift him up to sit on my lap too. I never was any good at instilling discipline in dogs. Or children, now I come to think about it.

I absently stroke his ears, smooth the fur of his head and feel him sink quietly into a semi-doze. If he was a cat, he'd be purring.

I look out at the sea and the moonlight, and the sheer wondrousness of sitting at what feels like the edge of the world.

'You haven't said a word,' says Matt, finally breaking the silence. 'About Midge. About anything.'

'I'm not sure I have any words left, Matt,' I reply, sadly. 'I'm just all worded out. This… this is a lovely thing to do for me. Everything you've done for me has been lovely. You are lovely. But lovely isn't enough and I'm not sure about anything any more…'

I stop talking because I wasn't lying when I said I'd run out of words.

'None of us are sure, Laura,' he replies, when he realises I have finished.

'Anybody who claims they're sure about life is either lying or stupid. But I am sure about one thing – I don't want you to go. I don't want you to leave and I don't want Nate and Lizzie to leave either. I don't know what the future might hold for any of us, but I owe it to you and to myself to at least tell you that much.

'We have something here, don't we? I'm not saying it's for life or that it will ever be the same as what you shared with David, but it's… something. It's special. I feel it and I know you feel it too. So don't go. Stay here, with me. With Midge. And give us a chance.'

'But why?' I ask, sounding a little bit like a petulant child. 'We hardly know each other!'

'Really?' he replies, his tone gentle and steady – probably exactly the way you should deal with a petulant child.

'I don't think that's true. We may not have known each other long, but we know each other well. I never thought, after Marianne, that I'd ever feel this way about any woman again. And I was happy with that. I was in hibernation and that suited me. Then you came along and poked me wide awake, and here I am. Eyes wide open. A little bit scared, but willing to try.'

'That was her name, then?' I ask. 'Marianne? I don't even know what happened with you two.'

'I found her in bed with my best friend at our engagement party, to cut a long story brutally short. He was also my partner in the vets' practice, which is one of the many reasons I had to leave – I thought I might kill him if I stayed. They'd been seeing each other behind my back for months and when I found out I lost the two people closest to me in the whole world, both at the same time.'

'Plus your dog.'

'Yes,' he says, with a small laugh. 'Plus Nico. I know it's nothing like what you went through, but it… damaged me. In ways I never thought would heal. Until now. Until you.'

I turn his story over in my mind and my first instinct is sympathy, and regret, for everything he's suffered and any part I might play in his future suffering.

I can feel his big, warm body next to mine, his thigh pressed against my thigh, his bulk sheltering me from the breeze and I want to touch him. To lay my hand across his and comfort him. But I don't – because it wouldn't be right.

'Well, in some ways, Matt, I think it might be worse than what I went through… not as dramatic, not as permanent, but still awful. I mean, David never chose to hurt me. He didn't leave me, or betray me, or stop loving me – he was taken. It's different.

'And I'm sure you will heal – but not because of me. Honestly? I'm a disaster area and I can guarantee you don't want to take this on. It wouldn't be good for you, or for me, or for Midge… I can't do it, Matt. I can't make any kind of commitment to a puppy, never mind to you.'

'I'm not suggesting marriage, Laura! We can take it slowly. See what happens. We can—'

'No, Matt,' I say, interrupting him. 'We can't. I can't. I'm sorry, but no. Midge is beautiful and you are… well, you're amazing. But I can't. I'll be leaving in the morning.'

'Why?' he asks, simply, the pain raw in his voice even though I suspect he is fighting hard to hide it. 'Am I wrong? Have I misjudged all of this? Are you leaving because you don't have any feelings for me?'

I turn to face him and gently stroke the side of his face, tracing my fingers across his cheekbones, his jaw.

'Matt, I'm leaving because I have too many feelings for you. I'm falling in love with you and I'm just not ready.'

He leans in, kisses my fingertips as they pass his lips, then holds my hand in his.

'You can't choose when you fall in love, Laura, or who you fall in love with.'

I remove my hand from his and stand up. I give Midge one last cuddle and lay a kiss on his soft black head. I pass him back to Matt, who gently takes him into his arms.

'I know that. But I can choose to say no to it.'

I walk away and try to ignore the sound of a crying puppy as I leave.

Chapter 38

As soon as I get back up to the café, I am immediately hijacked by Lizzie.

'Where have you *been*?' she hisses. 'You've been gone for hours!'

I glance at my watch and reply as calmly as I can, 'I've been gone for less than twenty-five minutes, to be fair. What do you need me for?'

'We've got something for you.'

'What do you mean by "we", and what do you mean by "something"? It's a not a puppy, is it?'

She stares at me like I am absolutely insane, then obviously notices that I am not a hundred per cent coherent. Her expression softens and her talon-like grip on my arm eases enough to return blood flow.

'Erm, no. It's not a puppy. Just... go and see Cherie, will you? She's over there with her sister. Her *sister* – did you even know she had one? And Frank's son is here and his grandson, who is pretty cute, and Sam's seven thousand sisters... it's all pretty weird.

'There are all these new people here and everyone's kind of high, and... well. It's weird, is all I'm saying. Now don't go anywhere – I'm going to tell Cherie you're here. It'll take you too long to go to her, you look half dead.'

She bustles off and I can't help but smile at the way she sees the extra party guests as 'new' people, despite the fact that she only arrived here herself a few weeks ago. Her energy levels are soaring while mine are sinking.

I want nothing more, by this stage, than to pack the kids into the car and leave. I want to avoid Matt coming back up to the café, I want to avoid Cherie noticing that I am upset and I want to avoid any big, soppy goodbyes with all of my Budbury friends. I am going to miss them all so much, for so many different reasons.

I sit down at one of the tables and blow out the candle on my table, hoping that nobody will find me.

Off to the left, I see Lynnie and Edie May on the yoga mats, Lynnie showing her ninety-year-old client how to breathe properly as they lie flat next to each other. I have a sneaking suspicion that Edie has actually gone to sleep, which does at least make me laugh.

All hopes of anonymity and a quiet escape are smashed to tiny pieces when I hear Cherie's voice loud and clear over the microphone, which she has borrowed from one of the Honky Tonk Fossils.

'Laura!' she shouts, over the sound of the chattering crowd. 'Where are you, Laura?'

I know she won't stop and the only way to get off this cliff without her spotting me is make a jump for it. Even I am not that desperate.

I remind myself that I owe Cherie a lot and that no matter how I feel right now, Cherie was the person who gave me this chance when I needed it most. I can't blame her for the fact that I have ended up with a heart that is at least a bit bent out of shape, if not completely broken.

I drag myself wearily to my feet, practise a fake smile as I step into the light and walk towards her. I am embarrassed to hear the sound of applause and a few random cheers as I reach her, just in front of the stage. She is leaning back against a hay bale and her feather head dress is extremely wonky by this point in the evening.

'There you are! We were going to send out a search party,' she says, grinning at me. 'There are plenty of people here with lassos tonight and at least half a dozen sheriffs, so don't try and make a run for it, outlaw!'

I glance at the crowd and see that she is right. There are lots of toy guns being held in the air, hats being waved and ropes being swung around over people's heads. I hold up my hands in mock surrender and silently pray for all of this to be over with as soon as possible.

'Laura, we wanted to say thank you, all of us. You've made this summer special for everyone and we're all going to miss you. I know I speak for Frank and Sam as well as myself, and all of our families, when I say how grateful we are for this party and all the little surprises you organised for us. It means the absolute world to us all, it really does. So, this is a little gift from everyone – which we couldn't have managed without a lot of help from Lizzie. I know you're planning to set off early tomorrow…'

She pauses while the crowd does a comedy 'boo-hiss', like we were in a pantomime, and then continues, 'But this is for you to take home with you as a keepsake. We'll miss all of you – Lizzie and Nate just as much. The café won't be the same without you, Laura, and the beach won't be the same without Nate and I'm pretty sure Scrumpy Joe's Cider Cave will go bankrupt as soon as Lizzie stops promoting them…'

There is a ripple of laughter at that, but I see that Joe is, in fact, looking genuinely upset. My daughter, the marketing genius.

'Just remember,' says Cherie, handing me a wrapped package and an envelope, 'that you are welcome back here at any time. For as long as you like. There will always be a place for you here. Just say the word and we'll all be waiting.'

She passes me the microphone, which I look at in absolute horror. Public speaking isn't really my thing even at the best of times and this is one of the worst of times.

'Umm…' I mumble, feeling my skin flare up in embarrassment. 'Thank you, all of you. We've had a brilliant time and made some great friends, and… well. Thank you. We'll miss you all as well.'

I am on the verge of tears as I finish and hand the microphone back to Cherie. I look at her pleadingly, silently begging her to end this and she sees my desperation.

She nods, looks at me with concern and makes a move towards me. I know she will want to find out what is wrong, or comfort me, or try to fix what cannot be fixed.

I back away, knowing at least that I can outrun her, but am stopped by the arrival of Lizzie, brandishing her phone.

'I need a few more, to complete the set,' she says, waving the phone in the air and starting to direct us all into position.

'Mum, Nate, stand with Cherie…'

Numbly, I do as I am told, staring into the screen and hoping against hope that I manage to look anything other than glassy-eyed and mentally compromised. I have my photo done with Cherie, then Frank and then both of them. And then Sam, some of his sisters and Ivy and Sophie Wellkettle, who are both dressed as Annie Oakley type cow-girls with fake shotguns.

I am forced into a group with the Scrumpy J Jones collective and am smothered in kisses by Willow for our picture together.

Edie May comes the closest to cracking my less-than-calm-but-at-least-not-tearful exterior, when she wraps her skinny arms around my waist and tells me how much she'll miss me and how much her 'fiancé' will miss my strawberry cheesecakes.

Just when I am beginning to hope that it is all finally over, and that I can leave, Matt emerges from the top of the path and walks into the garden.

His face is serious and his eyes are subdued, and the minute he sees me, he looks over my shoulder. I desperately want to run to him, throw my arms around him and console him – I can't bear how miserable he looks. But it was me who made him look that miserable, which means that I don't get to be the person who tries to make him feel better as well.

The minute Lizzie lays eyes on him, of course, she press-gangs him into a photo, grabbing his arm and dragging him towards me. She is not quite old enough or sensitive enough yet to pick up on the tension in the look we exchange or the tentative way we stand next to each other, carefully not touching, for the picture.

Cherie, of course, misses none of it – and instantly frowns at me, her face alert and concerned.

'Right!' I say, as soon as the photo session is done. 'Time to go, kids!'

I grab my wrapped gift and the card, which I just know will contain rude comments from half the village, and head for the path. Lizzie and Nate are moaning and complaining and making outraged noises about how they haven't said their proper goodbyes, but they do at least follow.

I keep my pace brisk and my face forwards and I don't look back, not even once.

Chapter 39

It is six in the morning and the kids are sulking in the car. Nate has chosen to express his discontent by sitting next to Lizzie in the back rather than next to me in the front.

I have left a note for Cherie, along with the keys to Hyacinth House, on the kitchen table, and have made a flask full of coffee to take with me.

I couldn't sleep much last night, so spent several hours cleaning the cottage, returning books and DVDs to the Games Room and trying not to have a nervous breakdown.

The nervous breakdown avoidance wasn't massively helped by the fact that when I made my pilgrimage to the Games Room – at 3am, as you do – the lights were still on downstairs in Black Rose. I couldn't help put picture him in there, with Midge. Possibly drinking more of his whiskey. Possibly sticking pins into a curly-haired voodoo doll. Who knows?

I finally managed a couple of hours' kip on the sofa, passing out almost against my will, and waking up again about thirty minutes ago, still exhausted.

I staggered around the cottage on auto-pilot while I waited for the kids to drag themselves out of their comas and get dressed. I did that thing you do when you're leaving your holiday home and checked all the drawers and the bathroom cabinet and the kitchen cupboards.

The only trace we seemed to be leaving behind was a vast stash of carrier bags, which somehow seemed especially melancholy.

Now the kids are finally loaded in the car, the coffee is ready to go and I am taking one last look at the Rockery.

At the still-green lawn in the centre and the water feature covered in the lilac clematis, and at the lush hanging baskets. At the sign to the swimming pool, the path to the gnome-filled woods and all the cottages with their crazy names. At the fields beyond, the rolling hills that lead down to the village and the hazily blue sky that is already streaked with golden sunlight.

It feels like a million years since we first arrived here, Jimbo in the boot, knickers all over the place, everybody knackered. A million years.

The kids are slouched in their seats, both of them avoiding my gaze. They're tired, overwrought and unhappy, and all of it, as far as they can make out, is my fault. I am in for a fun journey.

I am about to get in and drive away when the door to Black Rose opens and Midge comes tumbling out. He is a scrap of bouncing black fur, running around in circles, peeing on the flower beds, the water feature and on his own paws.

He sees me and gambols over, and I am aware of the kids staring out of the window at him in wonder. Of course, I remind myself, they had no idea that Matt had offered me a puppy – and quite a lot more – and it must seem near-miraculous to them that a miniature Jimbo has suddenly appeared on the horizon.

It took me about twenty minutes to get them into the car and they are out again in less than twenty seconds. The irresistible power of the puppy.

I know, obviously, that Matt will come tumbling out of Black Rose as well as Midge and I try to prepare myself. This mainly involves swearing quietly and wishing we'd left five minutes earlier.

He emerges, hair tufted in all kinds of directions, wearing a white T-shirt and a pair of snug-fitting jersey boxers. I avert my eyes from those and instead look at his face. His face is tired and stretched into a huge yawn. He looks completely exhausted as he rubs at his eyes and blinks a couple of times before he even seems to notice us.

'Oh,' he says, following Midge over in our direction, looking on as the puppy rolls on his back and squiggles hysterically while the kids tickle his tummy. 'How are you? You look tired.'

'*I* look tired?' I say, managing a small smile. 'Have you looked in a mirror this morning?'

'Ah… no,' he replies, belatedly trying to smooth his hair down. 'I guess I am. Midge wasn't really in the mood for sleeping and neither was I. So I drank some whiskey and played the guitar, and Midge chewed up my socks and peed on my duvet.'

'Sounds like a fun night,' I say.

'I've had worse… look, are you going to be all right to drive? You don't look very… refreshed…'

'I'll be fine,' I reply. 'I'll just take some cocaine when we get to Bristol.'

'Kidding,' I add, just in case he isn't sure. He does look pretty whacked.

'I know,' he replies, a slight sideways grin finally gracing his face. I feel the tug again – the tug towards him. And again, I fight it.

'Right,' I say, not quite clapping my hands, but almost. 'Come on kids – time to set off.'

They reluctantly stop playing with Midge and stand up straight. Lizzie gets back in the car, shooting me daggers as she does and Nate lingers a moment. Looking young and uncertain, he holds out his hand for Matt to shake, like a very small man.

Matt shakes the extended hand and then pulls him in for a quick hug as well. Nate stays there for a second and I can't even look at his face in case I see tears. Matt ruffles his blonde hair and Nate finally gets into the car.

I turn to meet Matt's eyes and it almost breaks me.

'Be careful,' he says simply. 'And don't get too lost.'

He reaches out to touch my fingertips with his and I let him. Fingertips can't get me into too much trouble.

'We won't,' I reply. 'I'll set up the sat nav.'

'Sat nav?' he says, a faint but distinct note of contempt in his voice. 'I never use them. Sat nav's are for—'

'Slackers?' shout Lizzie and Nate through the open car window, as they have clearly been listening to every word.

He grins at them and leans down to pick up Midge. Always a wise move with a puppy when a moving car is involved.

'I was going to say cheats, but yours sounds better. Take care guys. I'll miss you… all of you.'

With that he turns around and strides back to Black Rose. Midge's small black face is lolling on his shoulder, watching me as I get into the car, close the door and drive us out of the Rockery.

Chapter 40

Nate has said only one thing to me since we set off.

That thing was: 'Matt's a nice bloke, Mum. You should give him a chance.'

As Nate is twelve, I refrain from launching into a debate with him about the validity of my romantic life choices and concentrate on the driving.

Lizzie has also said only one thing to me since we set off.

That thing was, 'I can't believe you left the puppy behind.'

I also can't believe I left the puppy behind, so I don't engage with her either. To be honest, I'm quite glad to let them sit in silence, to drink my coffee and to simply drive.

I feel simultaneously much stronger and much more messed up than I did on the drive down here from Manchester, which is an interesting cocktail.

I do know, though, that whatever it is, it is progress of sorts. Even feeling messed up about another man is a positive step – or at least I hope I will be able to look back on it like that at some point or another. Possibly in about twenty years.

We drive like this – in an uncompanionable silence – for perhaps two hours, before Lizzie announces that she needs a wee.

I tell her to hold it for a little while longer and then find a service station on the M5 Northbound. We traipse out of the car and I am momentarily thrown by the fact that I automatically go to the boot, to let Jimbo out as well.

It catches me unawares and I gulp back a moment of painfully raw grief as I snatch my hand back and follow the kids to go to the loo.

We stock up on some essentials and sit outside for a few moments, me with my coffee and them with orange juice and water. Neither Lizzie nor I are in the mood for food, but Nate, being a twelve-year-old boy, is tucking into a couple of hash browns.

It's another gorgeous summer's day and I'm sure that back in Budbury it's absolutely beautiful. I can close my eyes, picture the sun reflecting off the sea and feel the soft, warm sand of the bay between my bare toes. And if I was there, I'd be able to hear the sound of the waves, the chirruping of the skylarks and the buzzing of the bees around the lavender pots in the café garden.

Instead, I am inhaling second-hand diesel fumes, listening to the roar of trucks shooting by on the motorway and looking at a one-legged pigeon peck at a discarded sausage roll. Even this early, it's busy here and I'd felt jarred and harassed even making our way through the crowds to the toilets.

'Better get used to the noise, Mum,' says Lizzie, sarcastically. 'We'll be back in the city before you know it.'

We actually live in a relatively quiet cul-de-sac, but… well, she has a point. There's no getting away from it – Manchester is a lot different from Budbury. Not worse – just different. We'll all be suffering from a bit of culture shock for a few days, I'm sure.

Nate is quiet apart from his munching and I'm not sure if he's still annoyed with me, or just tired.

Lizzie, obviously frustrated by my lack of fighting spirit this morning, sighs and pulls out her phone. She has stopped taking pictures now and I can't say that I blame her. Service stations are not usually especially photogenic. She starts swiping through her album and I see that she is looking back through the shots she took last night at the party.

'Did you look at the rest?' she asks, her head bobbing back up as she speaks.

'What do you mean, the rest?' I reply.

She looks completely exasperated with me and lets out one of those 'give-me-strength' noises that parents usually make about teenagers, not the other way round.

'Well, these are the pictures from last night. If you're at all arsed, we can get them printed out and add them to the rest.'

'Okay. If you say so. I still have no idea what you're talking about, though.'

Nate looks at me as he chews then speaks around a half-swallowed mouthful.

'I don't think she's even seen it, Lizzie,' he says.

My daughter stares at me, horrified and shocked and possibly, I think, a little bit hurt? She grabs the car keys from the table and stomps off in such a temper I half expect to see a black cartoon rain cloud hovering over her head.

I think she is just going back to sulk in the car and shrug it off. I decide to finish my coffee in the not-that-fresh air, before imprisoning myself in solitary confinement in a metal box again for the next part of the journey.

Instead, I soon see her stomping all the way back again, face still angry, brandishing the gift that Cherie had presented to me last night.

The gift that I had left in the back of the car, untouched and unopened, and completely forgotten about.

To be fair, I'd had bigger things on my mind – but there was no point trying to explain that to Lizzie. Cherie said that she'd helped with my farewell gift, so she is understandably upset that I have discarded it.

She slams it down on the table so hard that my coffee cup quakes and declares, 'Go on. Open it.'

She has her hands on her hips, her voice is huffy and I am well and truly in the doghouse. I think at least some of her anger is justified, so I do as I am told. I open it.

As I tear off the pretty wrapping paper, bit by bit, I see a black, leather-bound photo album inside.

It is, I realise immediately, exactly the same kind of black, leather-bound photo album that David always used to store our holiday pictures in.

I glance at Lizzie in surprise and I lift the album up, turning it to one side. Sure enough, she's done the rest as well – I see a white sticker and written on it, in black marker, is BUDBURY – 2016.

Tears suddenly well up in my eyes and I look at her, and I love her so much, and I am so sad, and so grateful, and so overwhelmed, that I can't even try and stop them.

I feel them drip down my cheeks and I try to say how sorry I am for not looking at the present earlier, and how much this means to me.

She shakes her head and sits down next to me. The anger has drained out of her and her eyes are shining too. Nate is staring at the table top, so I suspect he is feeling less than manly right now as well.

'It's all right,' she says. 'Don't worry. I know I'm the best daughter ever, no need to embarrass us all.

'I just thought… well, it's what he used to do, isn't it? Dad? Every year. And now he's not here and we have to start making our own memories, don't we? At least I think we do. So… I thought this would be a start.'

I nod, still not capable of speaking, and stroke a stray lock of golden hair away from her forehead. I can see she is annoyed but tolerating it and it reminds me of the way I am with my mum as well.

'Just look at it,' she says, pointing at the album.

I open the first page and see that the pictures are ordered chronologically. They start with our journey and all the disasters that befell us. Poor Nate being sick. Us in a layby after getting lost. Jimbo curled up in the boot. A close-up of my Meatloaf's greatest hits CD.

I turn the pages and see the whole of our summer unfold before me. All of the pictures I've heard Becca talking about are here – it's a complete print-out of the infamous Instagram chronicles.

I see myself with a cupcake shoved in my mouth on that first night, I see Matt with a bra wrapped round his head and I see our first views of the Comfort Food Café and the beach.

I see beautiful shots of the bay, the cliffs and the countryside. Of the cider cave and Frank's farm, and of her friends, and of Josh, never without his beanie cap.

Of Nate playing football with Matt and Frank and Sam, and Nate in the playground, and Nate with the guitar, frowning in concentration as he plucks out a few chords.

There are pictures of Cherie, face smiling and eyes crinkling, wearing an apron and covered in flour. Willow, doing a cartwheel, pink hair flying.

Edie May, her face half in shade as she sips tea in the café garden. Sam, posing for the surfing shots we sent to Becca, blonde hair sparkling with water. Frank, leaning against the back of his Land Rover, toasting the camera with what looks like a pint of cider.

There are photos of our trip to Sidmouth, the woods in the Rockery and me doing yoga with Lynnie. And there are so many bittersweet shots of Jimbo. Mainly of Jimbo asleep, in multiple locations, but also one of him looking adoringly at his precious Bella Swan as she lies curled up in his basket.

Eventually she points out a familiar picture to me. The one I've seen before, on her phone – the one of me and Matt holding hands, laughing, down at the beach.

We look so happy, so carefree. So very, very relaxed. The pain of it sears through me, sudden and hot and raw.

'This,' says Lizzie, pointing at the picture. 'Is my favourite. This is the way you used to look, Mum, back when Dad was around. And this is one of the reasons we didn't want to leave.'

I cast a glance in Nate's direction and he just nods, looking glum and defeated. The fact that there was something going on between me and Matt clearly isn't news to him.

'I know you want to stay, love,' I say, placing my hand on top of hers. 'But it's... more complicated than that.'

'No,' she replies, shaking her head so her blonde ponytail wobbles, 'it's really not. It's just you making it complicated. I know you're probably worried and scared, and going through all kinds of what-if-he-dumps-me dramas in your mind. But you're not a kid, are you? I mean, I'm the kid here – you're a grown up. You're supposed to be able to make big decisions and take risks, and do what's best for us...'

'That's what I *am* doing!' I reply, frustrated at both my inability to explain myself and the fact that part of me wants to agree with her.

'The thing is, Mum,' chips in Nate, in his quieter, more reasonable voice, 'that we don't want to go back to the way things were. If we have to go back to Manchester, we'll cope. We'll miss the village, but it'll be all right – because it's not just about where we are. It's about the way we all feel. And we don't want to go back to the way... well, the way we all were, before we left.'

'He means the way *you* were,' adds Lizzie, as ever less tactful.

'What does that even mean? The way I was?' I ask, genuinely confused.

'Like a zombie mother,' she replies. 'Going through the motions. Looking after us. Doing the cooking, the cleaning and helping us with our homework. But doing it all like you were dead inside. We're not stupid, Mum, we knew you were miserable – we just thought that was the way it was going to be from now on. We didn't think anything would ever change, that you'd ever be your old self again...'

'And then you did change,' says Nate, firmly. 'We went to Budbury and you started working at the café and you made all your friends, and you met Matt and you started to be...*you* again. You stopped doing that thing where you stare off into space for, like, hours at a time, and we know you're thinking about Dad.

'And you stopped locking yourself in the toilets every time you needed to cry and thought you were hiding it from us. And you stopped going to sleep with Dad's old dressing gown.'

Lizzie is nodding furiously and I am looking at my children in something like wonder. I am so shocked, so sad, to hear everything that they are saying. I have put them through so much, been so selfish and have somehow managed to convince myself that I was doing all right.

I've written them off as 'just kids', when in reality they've been more perceptive than most of the adults in my life.

'I'm so sorry,' I say, reaching out to hold both their hands. 'I had no idea, I really didn't... God, I'm sorry... you shouldn't have had to go through all of that... it wasn't fair...'

'You couldn't help it,' replies Lizzie, matter-of-factly. 'We knew that and we didn't blame you. But what wouldn't be fair, now, is to go back to it. For the whole of this summer, it's been like having our old mum back – and we want to keep her, okay? We don't want to let her go.

'We want to go back to Budbury and start again, and see what happens... I know you're frightened. But if that was us, you'd tell us to be brave, wouldn't you?

'So this is us, telling you to be brave. Manchester without Dad isn't home any more. It's not like leaving our old house will make us forget him. Nothing will. But none of us are happy there and we were all happy in Dorset. Maybe we won't always be, I don't know. But we want to go back. Both of us.'

I look at Nate and he nods in agreement.

'What about you?' he asks, a note of hope creeping into his voice.

I gaze at both of my beautiful children and I love them so much it feels uncontainable.

'I think,' I say, closing the photo album shut with a little bang and standing to my feet. 'That it's time to go home.'

Chapter 41

We run up that hill, all three of us.

Admittedly, I am the slowest, but I still spring up those steps faster than I ever would have thought possible.

They wait for me at the top and we all hold hands once more, before we walk through the wrought-iron arch, with its sign of curved roses, and into the garden of the Comfort Food Café. Back home.

Everyone is there, clearing up the debris from the night before. Cherie is sitting at one of the tables, crutches propped next to her, directing the traffic. Edie May is next to her, her bright-orange VANS backpack at her feet, a paperback on her lap.

Frank, Peter and Luke are rolling away the hay bales and Willow is dumping all the leftover food into a recycling bag. The Scrumpy J Jones family is absent and I feel a beat of disappointment as Lizzie realises Josh isn't here.

Sam and his sisters are all present, though, laughing, joking and shoving each other as they patrol the garden with big black bin bags, collecting paper plates, plastic cups, cracked water pistols and crushed cowboy hats.

We run towards them and Nate yells, 'Hey! Everybody! We're back!'

My son is so excited he is almost visibly vibrating and even Lizzie has a very un-cool grin on her face as we wait to be noticed.

They all pause and turn towards us and there is an instant response of shouts, greetings and more laughter.

Frank abandons his hay bale and walks over to us, grabbing me up in a huge hug.

'About bloody time,' he says, eyes crinkling with happiness. 'Some people will do anything to get out of a bit of cleaning.'

I hug him in return and head towards Cherie.

'I knew you'd be back,' she says, simply, reaching out to squeeze my hands. 'Felt it in my old broken bones, I did. Knew I could rely on you, my love.'

'Well,' I reply, delighted to see her, but still casting my gaze around looking for someone else. 'You know that "reliable" is my middle name, don't you?'

'Ha!' she exclaims, 'I thought it might be… and by the way, he's in with the dogs. Go get him and put him out of his misery, for goodness' sake!'

I don't even bother to feign ignorance. I think we've all come too far for that. Instead, I lean down, and lay a big, soppy kiss on her cheek.

'Thank you,' I say. 'For everything.'

I leave Cherie behind and I dash over to the dog paddock. I open the gate and immediately see him over at the far end of the field with Midge.

He appears to be trying to teach the puppy to sit in return for a treat, but Midge is so excited about the food he can't stay still and his bottom is hovering in the air above the grass.

As soon as I shut the gate behind me, his ears prick and he turns around. He runs in my direction, tail whipping from side to side and I kneel down to scratch his ears. He licks my face and pees on the spot, so I am pretty sure that the puppy is pleased to see me at least.

I stand up and walk towards Matt. He is, predictably enough, not wearing a shirt again and his hair is flopping slightly over his forehead. His gaze is fixed a little to my left and I'm not so sure he feels quite as enthusiastic about seeing me as Midge does.

I can't blame him. He took a chance, he had the courage to take a gamble and I was a big, fat coward. A coward who hurt him.

'You've come back,' he says, stating the obvious and shoving his hands into the pockets of his shorts, almost as though he wants to keep them out of trouble.

'I have,' I reply, simply, closing the distance between us until we are only inches apart.

'Did you forget something?' he asks, finally looking down and meeting my eyes.

'Well,' I say, laying one hand on his side and pulling him closer. 'For a start, I forgot my puppy.'

I stroke his warm skin and mash my hips up against his a little, and wrap my arms around him so we're squashed up close together. I hold him tight and run my fingers over his lower back, and hook my fingers into the waistband of his shorts so he's completely trapped.

'Is that all?' he responds and I see him trying to fight the grin that is spreading across his face.

As he speaks, he reaches down and wraps his hands in the curls of my hair. I know this move of his. It is the preamble to turning my face up for a kiss, and it is one hundred per cent guaranteed to turn me into a puddle of mush.

'Funny you should ask, but no,' I say, smiling up at him, letting him know how happy I am to be there, puddling with him, in the sunshine on the hill, with a puppy dancing around our feet.

'I also forgot this,' I add and stretch up on my tippy-toes so that our lips can touch.

He kisses me for a long time, extremely thoroughly, and I enjoy every single moment of it.

'I'm sorry,' I say, when we eventually come up for air. 'For leaving. And for not being brave.'

He throws his arm around my shoulder and I feel so snug there, tucked into his side. Like it's exactly where I am supposed to be.

'It's all right,' he says, as we walk together back to the garden. 'I forgive you.'

He opens the paddock gate and Midge runs ahead of us, straight to a delighted Nate.

Our friends are all there, waiting for us, and I'm simply not sure it would be possible for them to look any happier.

Lizzie walks towards us and nods approvingly.

'Right,' she says, pulling her phone from her jeans pocket. 'Let's make a start on the next album…'

The End

Down Dorset Way…

I must admit that when I booked our first holiday in Dorset, I actually secretly wanted to go to Cornwall, one of my favourite places on earth.

But with three kids and two dogs in the car, and the prospect of a lengthy drive from Liverpool, it seemed like a good compromise – a similar vibe, but with less time swearing on the motorway.

We headed off to our cottages near the village of Maiden Newton half expecting it to be a poor man's Poldark country.

We couldn't have been more wrong. Instead, we found a rich and varied county full of rolling hills, stunning countryside and of course a world-renowned coastline. We found pretty villages and wonderful pubs and gorgeous food. We found welcoming people, friendly faces, and heaven on earth for both the children and the dogs.

This is the land of Thomas Hardy and Tess of the d'Urbervilles; it's Far from the Madding Crowd and it's the French Lieutenant's Woman and it's Broadchurch. It's absolutely bloody gorgeous, and I deny anybody looking down at Durdle Door in the morning not to fall in love with it.

We stay at Lancombe Country Cottages, a dog-friendly, family-friendly haven set between coast and country. Like Cherie's properties at the Rockery, they're wonderfully located – but unlike the Rockery, they are beautifully decorated inside as well!

Just a short drive away from there, you can find the resorts of Weymouth and Poole; Lyme Regis and West Bay, the Jurassic Coast and areas of outstanding natural beauty. Like Laura and her family, we never want to leave – but real life isn't fiction, so we always have to!

It's been wonderful creating a whole Dorset world for my characters to inhabit, and I hope you have enjoyed sharing their stories.

Sadly, the Comfort Food Café is entirely fictional – but the kind of beautiful view from its clifftop location are not. If you're tempted to go and see for yourself, my friends at Visit Dorset have provided us with their list of the area's Top Ten Views to Fall in Love With – and seeing is believing!

1) Gold Hill, Shaftesbury – this steep cobbled street is famous for its picturesque appearance; the view looking down from the top of the street has been described as "one of the most romantic sights in England" and was made famous in the 1970s Hovis advert.

2) Hengistbury Head – this headland south-east of Christchurch was an important trading port even from the Iron Age but is now a Nature Reserve; stand on top of the plateau and you will see views of Christchurch Harbour, Mudeford, Isle of Wight and Bournemouth beach

3) Hambledon Hill – standing on top of this prehistoric hillfort situated near Blandford Forum gives glorious views across the Blackmore Vale. Nearby Fontmell Down offers similarly spectacular views.

4) Ballard Down – One of Dorset's most attractive hills, Ballard Down offers fantastic views of the Dorset heaths, Poole Harbour and Old Harry Rocks.

5) Chesil Beach view near Abbotsbury – the coastal road from from Bridport to Abbotsbury (the B3157) offers wonderful views along the Jurassic Coast and just before you arrive in the picturesque village of Abbotsbury, Chesil Beach stretches before you with views to Portland.

6) Golden Cap –this is the highest point along the south coast of England and on a clear day, you can see to Dartmoor in Devon.

7) Hardy's Monument, Portesham – erected in 1844, a monument to Sir Thomas Masterman Hardy who captained Nelson's ship HMS Victory at the battle of Trafalgar and was born in Dorset; views across both heathland and the coast.

8) Swyre Head – the highest spot in the Purbeck hills near Swanage; the hill commands extensive views from the Isle of Wight to Portland.

10) Pilsdon Pen – Pilsdon Pen is an Iron Age Hillfort on the highest hill in Dorset and is only 30 metres short of a mountain! The hill offers sweeping views across the hedged landscape of the Marshwood Vale and is a perfect spot for a picnic.

You can find out more at www.visit-dorset.com, or connect with them via twitter @dorsettourism, www.facebook.com/VisitDorset, or www.instagram.com/visitdorsetofficial.

And now for the yummy bit…

The Comfort Food Café is entirely fictional – but I would love to go there! As well as the fab location and delicious food, I wanted to create a place where people felt safe and valued and content. A place where everybody knows your name, just like they used to in Cheers!

And while Cherie's café might be made up, the Hive Beach Café in Dorset is gorgeously real. It overlooks the beautiful beach at Burton Bradstock, one of the prettiest places on the Jurassic Coast, and has stunning views out across Lyme Bay.

Its location is idyllic, and so is its food. The café specialises in fresh fish and seafood, which is sourced locally using sustainable methods, and cooked simply and well. The café also has a reputation for friendly and welcoming service, and its creative team in the kitchen.

Now in their 25th year, they've produced two cookery books, and have also kindly agreed to share a few of their recipes here with us as well. These are taken from the Hive Beach Café Family Cookbook (£16.99, Bristlebird Books). If these tingle your taste-buds, you can find out more at http://www.hivebeachcafe.co.uk/, or follow them on twitter @HiveBeachCafe.

Fish & Saffron Stew
Serves 4

Though it will undoubtedly be the delicious chunks of monkfish and seabass, and all the juicy king prawns that'll take the plaudits in this dish, the real credit here goes to the icky bits – the fishbones and shells – that intensify over time create the wonderful flavours in the stock base. Not that your kids need to see them, of course. You'll strain them out long before any child has chance to turn up their nose and say 'yuck'. And they certainly won't argue with this deep, dense, warming stew when you place it – still sumptuously steaming – into the middle of the dinner table.

Ingredients
1 small monkfish
1 small seabass
500g king prawns
Handful mussels
1 bulb garlic, outer layers removed
1 carrot, roughly chopped
2 leeks, roughly chopped
1 fennel head
1 onion, roughly chopped
3–4 ripe tomatoes, quartered
Pinch saffron
1 sprig thyme
1 bay leaf
1 tsp fennel seeds
Handful coriander leaves, chopped

Fillet the monkfish and seabass, or alternatively, ask your fishmonger to do it for you. Make sure you reserve the fishbones.

Dice the monkfish and seabass meat into chunks, and set aside. Then peel the prawns – reserving the shells.

Wash the mussels in cold water and discard any that do not close when tapped.

To make a stock, place the fishbones and prawn shells in a large saucepan and gently heat it to release the flavours. Next, throw in the garlic, carrot, leeks, fennel, onion and mussels; then add the tomatoes, saffron, thyme, bay leaf and fennel seeds. Cook until softened and then cover with water.

Bring the stock up to a gentle simmer (without letting it boil) and cook for around 30 minutes. Once all the flavours have had time to intensify, strain the stock and return to the heat. Reduce by half.

Just before serving, add the diced monkfish and seabass to the stock and let it cook for a couple of minutes. Divide between 4 bowls and finish each with a sprinkle of coriander.

Seabass Fillet with Mango & Chilli Salsa

The seabass we serve at the Hive are line caught by local fishermen who lift them from the turbulent waters of The Race off Portland Bill and bring them to the Café within a couple of hours of them leaving the sea. But if you can't get seabass as quickly as this, then ask your fishmonger for the most recent catch. The firm texture and delicate flavour of the fish complements the sharp and fruity salsa in this recipe perfectly. We recommend serving it with a crisp green salad and sautéed new potatoes.

Ingredients:
2 ripe mangos, peeled and deseeded
1 red chilli, finely chopped

1 red onion, diced
Small bunch of chives, chopped
2 limes
Olive oil
4 wild seabass fillets

First prepare your salsa. Dice the flesh of the mango into small pieces and place into a bowl, then add the red chilli, chives, red onion, lime zest and juice. Season with sea salt and freshly ground pepper and set aside.

Preheat a non-stick frying pan. Oil and season the seabass fillets and place them skin side down into the pan. Don't turn until they're cooked two thirds through (when the flesh is beginning to change from a translucent colour to a more solid one). Then turn down the heat and let them cook through slowly.

Take 4 plates and place a seabass fillet on each one. Serve immediately with the mango and chilli salsa.

Pan-fried Scallops with Truffle Mash & Crispy Pancetta
Serves 4

Wholesome and hearty, with more than a hint of luxury provided by the dash of truffle oil in the mashed potato, this dish makes a fulsome family feast. The saltiness of the pancetta is the perfect contrast to the delicacy of the scallops. Enjoy.

Ingredients
4 large potatoes, peeled
8 slices pancetta
1 clove garlic, crushed
200g butter

Truffle oil
Double cream
Olive oil
16 scallops
½ lemon, juiced
Handful wild rocket

Boil the potatoes until soft then drain. Leave for a couple of minutes then mash until light and fluffy. Set aside in a warm place.

Preheat a hot grill.

Lay the pancetta slices out on a tray and grill until crisp. Set aside in a warm place.

Combine the garlic with 150g butter and set aside.

Preheat two heavy-bottomed frying pans – one of which needs to be very hot. Put the mashed potato into the cooler pan with a knob of butter, a drizzle of truffle oil and a splash of double cream. Keep stirring the mash until it's piping-hot, then turn the heat right down and season to taste.

Oil and season the scallops, then place them into the other hot frying pan. Arrange them in a clockwise direction, remembering your starting point. After around 90 seconds, turn the scallops over in the same order.

Add the garlic butter and the lemon juice to the scallops pan. Remove the pan from the heat as soon as the butter has melted.

Place the truffle mash in a large serving bowl, arrange the scallops on top and finish with wild rocket and the pancetta slices. Drizzle over the pan juices and serve immediately.

Lemon and Lime Ginger Lovely
Serves 8-10

This is an impressive, refreshing dessert that is super-quick to make. The sharpness of the citrus fruit offsets perfectly the rich combination of double cream and condensed milk. Crushed ginger biscuits make a delicious spicy-sweet base. Don't forget to get the kids involved in crushing them. Wrap them in a tea-towel and bash them with a rolling pin. They'll have never had so much fun in the kitchen.

Ingredients
250g ginger biscuits, crushed
115g melted butter
300ml double cream
170g condensed milk
3 lemons, juiced
2 limes, juiced

Combine the ginger biscuits with the melted butter in a bowl and mix. Spoon half of the biscuit mixture into serving glasses and set aside.

Whisk the double cream until it has the consistency of custard. Pour in the condensed milk and whisk again, slowly adding the lemon and lime juice until the mixture if thick and creamy.

Spoon the mixture into the serving glasses and scatter the remaining ginger biscuits over the top. Chill in the fridge for an hour or so until you are ready to serve.

Dorset Apple Cake
Serves 4

There is no definitive recipe for Dorset Apple Cake. It's one of those dishes that provokes fierce arguments between villages throughout the county, as everyone seems to believe that their way is the only way. The constant in all, of course, is wonderful local apples, baked with butter and sugar to produce a deliciously sticky cake that goes perfectly with Dorset clotted cream. Cut yours into generous slices before serving and make a big pot of tea to sit alongside it on the table.

Ingredients
285g softened butter, plus extra for greasing
6 Bramley apples, peeled, cored and chopped into 1cm pieces
1 lemon, juiced
345g caster sugar, plus extra for sprinkling
2 tsp cinnamon
4 large eggs
450g self-raising flour
Milk
2tbsp Demerara sugar

Preheat your oven to 180C/350F

Take a deep, 30cm cake tin and grease the inside with butter. Line with greaseproof paper and set aside.

Place the apple pieces in a bowl and toss with the lemon juice. Set aside.

Cream the butter, cinnamon and caster sugar together in a bowl with an electric whisk until pale and fluffy. Beat in the eggs, one at time, and whisk in a little of the flour after each egg to keep the mixture smooth. Pour in a little milk to thin it if the consistency becomes too thick.

Drain the apple pieces and stir them into the mixture.

Spoon the mixture into the prepared cake tin, gently level the top and sprinkle with the Demerara sugar.

Bake the cake in the oven for one hour or until it has risen and browned on the top (if the cake is getting too brown, you can cover it with a sheet of greaseproof paper after 45 minutes or so). The cake is cooked when you insert a skewer into the middle and it comes out clean.